D0537379

WITHDRAWN
FROM
STOCK

ALSO BY
DEREK LANDY

DEREK LANDY

THE **DEMON ROAD** TRILOGY

HarperCollins *Children's Books*

First published in hardback in Great Britain by HarperCollins *Children's Books* 2016
HarperCollins *Children's Books* is a division of
HarperCollinsPublishers Ltd
1 London Bridge Street, London SE1 9GF

Visit us on the web at www.harpercollins.co.uk

Derek Landy blogs under duress at www.dereklandy.blogspot.com

1

Copyright © Derek Landy 2016

Derek Landy asserts the moral right to be identified as the author of this work

HB ISBN: 978-00-0-815698-5
TPB ISBN: 978-00-0-815697-8

Typeset in Joanna MT Std by
Palimpsest Book Production Ltd, Falkirk, Stirlingshire

Printed and bound in Great Britain by
Clays Ltd, St Ives plc

Conditions of Sale
This book is sold subject to the condition that it shall not,
by way of trade or otherwise, be lent, re-sold, hired out or
otherwise circulated without the publisher's prior consent in
any form, binding or cover other than that in which it is published
and without a similar condition including this condition being
imposed on the subsequent purchaser. All rights reserved.

MIX
Paper from
responsible sources
FSC
www.fsc.org
FSC C007454

FSC™ is a non-profit international organisation established to promote
the responsible management of the world's forests. Products carrying the
FSC label are independently certified to assure consumers that they come
from forests that are managed to meet the social, economic and
ecological needs of present and future generations,
and other controlled sources.

Find out more about HarperCollins and the environment at
www.harpercollins.co.uk/green

This book is dedicated to all the horror icons who passed away while it was being written.

This is for Gunnar Hansen, and Angus Scrimm, and the mighty Wes Craven. Icons. Inspirations. Heroes.

And I'm left with nothing funny to say.

Sorry.

1

THEY WERE ALIVE WHEN SHE WALKED IN.

Fourteen people, including the short-order cook and the waitress with the badly dyed hair in this little rest stop just outside of Whitehorse in Yukon. Everyone looked tired, this time of night. They ate pie or drank coffee or read newspapers or sat in their booths, focusing on their phones. Nobody glanced up when Amber entered. Nobody talked. Music played, drifting through from the small kitchen. Something by Bon Jovi. It was safe in here. None of these people wanted to kill her. She was getting good at spotting the telltale signs.

She went straight to the restroom. It was chilly, and not very clean, but she didn't mind. She'd had to pee in worse places these past few days.

When she was done, she washed her hands. In the cracked mirror above the cracked sink, her hair was a mess and there were bags under her red-rimmed eyes. Her pale skin was blotchy. She looked like she needed a shower. She looked like a scared girl on the run.

Funny that.

Her belly rumbled and Amber turned off the faucet, wiped her hands on her jeans, and left the restroom.

They were all dead when she walked out.

She went instantly cold. All moisture left her mouth, her knees weakened, and every nerve ending jingled and jangled and screamed at her to run. But she couldn't run. Her legs wouldn't obey. She could barely stay standing.

Some of them had been attacked where they sat – others while they tried to escape. Bludgeoned to death, every one of them. A woman in a brown cardigan was slumped over her table, blood leaking from the mess in the back of her head. A trucker in a plaid shirt had half his face caved in. The waitress had been dragged across the counter. Blood dripped from the dented gash in her temple, forming a growing pool on the floor beneath her. Amber couldn't see the cook, but knew he was lying on the floor of the kitchen. She could see his blood on the wall.

Fourteen people when she'd walked in. Fourteen corpses. But now there was a fifteenth person. He was sitting in the booth next to the door, his back to her, wearing a baseball cap and a grey, faded boiler suit. He was singing along to the radio. 'Every Rose Has Its Thorn' by Poison.

The booth moved closer to her. Closer still. No, it wasn't the booth that was moving – it was Amber. She frowned, looked down at her feet as they took another step. Apparently, they were on their way out of the door, and they were taking the rest of her with them. She was okay with that. She didn't want to stay here, anyway, not with all those corpses. She just had to pass this guy and then she could run out into the quiet street, shout for Milo, and he'd come roaring up in the Charger and they could get the hell out of there. Easy. No fuss, no muss.

The man in the boiler suit had a claw hammer on the table in front of him. It was bloodstained. There was a chunk of scalp hanging off it.

"How you doing?" he asked.

Amber froze.

He didn't have a nice voice. It was curiously strained, like he'd spent most of his life shouting.

She kept her eyes on the door and took another step. And another.

"Amber, isn't it?"

She stopped.

"Yeah," the man said. "It's you. I expected something else, to be honest. All the things you've done, I expected someone a little more..." he licked his lips, "...impressive."

She looked at him. She had to. Her gaze moved slowly, and reluctantly, from the door to the booth. First she looked at the claw hammer, then at the remains of the pie he'd been eating. Then at his rough, worn hands, and the blood-splattered sleeves of his boiler suit. He was thin. Wiry. He had a narrow face and a pointed chin and a nasty smile. No hair. His cap had a faded logo Amber couldn't make out. Her eyes finally settled on his and she had the strangest feeling of vertigo.

"You're the one killed the Shining Demon's representative, right?" the man asked. He had an accent. Southern. Georgia, maybe. "Made him go splat? I like your style. I'd been searching for the best way to kill that prick for years, but you got there first."

"What do you want?" Amber asked.

"It ain't what I want, little girl. It's what you can give me." He slid slowly out of the booth. He wasn't tall, he had maybe two inches on Amber, but she took a step back nonetheless. "You're my ticket," he said.

"To what?"

He breathed in, and spread his arms. "All this." His right arm dipped, and he picked up the claw hammer.

"Why did you kill these people?"

He gave her one of those nasty smiles. "No one told me I wasn't supposed to. Besides, it's been way too long since I got to kill new folks. Do you know what it's like, little girl, do you have *any idea* what it's like to be trapped in a middle-of-nowhere town where the biggest challenge is to find someone worthy to stalk? Jesus H. Christ, what is it with the young people of today? I'm old-fashioned and I make no apology for it. I like to stalk and kill teenagers. I like a challenge, you know what I mean? Teenagers are fit and strong and they're surrounded by family and friends... but do you know what makes them so perfect to stalk? They run to parents, they run to cops, they tell them a bad man is trying to kill them, but no one takes them seriously. The look on their faces when they realise they're alone – that they are truly *alone* – after a lifetime of being told they'll be supported no matter what... Well. It's just heaven, is what it is. But these days, trying to find one who can put up a decent fight is an impossible task. Worthy teenagers are a dying breed, and that is a sad state of affairs."

That smile of his broadened. "So what about you, Amber? You gonna put up a fight? You've got that look about you. It's in the eyes. Man, isn't this just typical? I find a teenager who may actually be able to mount a challenge and I'm not allowed to kill her."

Amber frowned. "You're not allowed?"

"Nope. No killing the girl, those are my orders. I'm just here to bring you back."

"You're working for Astaroth."

"On a first-name basis with the Shining Demon, are you? Must be nice. But yes, I am guilty as charged, as I said at my trial. Now you've managed to stay ahead of the Hounds, which is a feat that few have accomplished for this long, but now the professional is here to take care of business and to stop all this silliness."

"I have money," said Amber. "I can pay you to walk away."

The man laughed. "Money? I don't have any use for it. Besides, you can't match what he's offering."

"Try me."

"Freedom, little girl. See, I made a mistake when I made my deal with the Devil. A lot of us do. We get fixated on the people who caught us. All I wanted was to get my revenge on that Podunk little town – but when I was done? I couldn't leave. I didn't exist beyond its borders. The Shining Demon will, ah, broaden my remit. I'll be able to travel. Kill people in new places. And this is just a taster of that. Look at me – Elias Mauk – killing in Canada. I'm gonna take my show on the road."

"I... I read about you."

"I'm flattered."

"You're dead."

"That too."

"You were executed."

"Fried," he said, whipping off his cap. A thick band of still-sizzling flesh wrapped around his head where the electricity had been focused. Amber could smell the burning skin from where she stood.

Mauk put his cap back on, and grinned. "They said I murdered twenty-two people. It was more like forty, but that was back when I was alive. Ever since the chair, my body count has grown. And after this? It's gonna skyrocket."

He took a step forward and she took a step back, holding up her hands.

"I don't want to fight you," she said.

"Oh, Amber, don't you dare disappoint me now. Killing a room full of people is distressingly easy for someone like me. You gotta put up *some* resistance, at least."

"You're not the first serial killer I've faced," Amber said. "You're not even the first returned-from-the-grave serial killer I've faced. I killed Dacre Shanks."

"Shanks ain't got nothing on me."

"Not anymore he doesn't," she said. "He came after me and I killed him. Now he's dead and it's the kind of dead that you don't come back from. I'll kill you, too."

"I am liking this confidence," said Mauk. "You're definitely making the butterflies flutter, I'm not gonna lie to you. But Shanks was nothing. Take his precious little key away from him, and what did he have to offer? Tell me if this is true – when you found him, was he stuck inside one of his own dollhouses? I've heard he was stuck inside one of his own dollhouses. That's funny. How'd you kill him? You step on him? Hell, you're heavy enough."

"Oh, I wasn't like this when I killed him," said Amber.

"No?"

"No," she said, and she shifted.

Her bones lengthened and realigned and she grew taller. Her excess weight spread throughout her body and she became slimmer. Her brown hair turned black and her flushed skin turned red and two ebony horns blossomed from her forehead and curled back.

"There you are," breathed Mauk. "Oh, you are magnificent."

Amber didn't bother agreeing as she grabbed him. She knew she was magnificent. He swung the hammer, but she ripped it out of his hand and tossed it aside. She picked him up, her newly formed muscles not even straining with the effort, and hurled him across a table. She caught a glimpse of her reflection as she stalked after him, and her sudden beauty was almost enough to make her pause. She still wasn't used to it. A slight reconfiguration of her features was all it took to turn her from ugly human to mesmerising demon.

Ugly. There was a word she'd never used about herself before. Plenty of others had, in their crueller moments, but never her. She didn't stop to wonder what it meant, as she watched Mauk take a steak knife from a dead patron, and it didn't bother her. Precious little did when she was a demon.

Incredibly, Mauk was smiling as he came forward. Her skin tightened and black scales formed, and the knife skimmed across her armour without drawing blood. He tried stabbing at her again, but she was much too fast. She gripped his wrist and twisted. The knife fell and she hit him twice and he wobbled, and she took hold of the back of his head and sent him sprawling across the floor.

"Told you you should have walked away," she said, and her fingers grew to claws.

Mauk groaned, turned over, and looked at her. He was still smiling. She didn't like that. She was used to people dismissing her when she was herself, when she was ordinary old human

Amber, but not when she was like this. When she was like this, she demanded *respect*.

"Oh, I'm sorry," said Mauk, "you think you're winning this little exchange? There's a lot more to beating me than hitting me a coupla times." He got to his feet. "See, when I kill, I like to... play. And my playmates, well... they just do whatever I tell 'em. Ain't that right, my friends?"

The corpses stirred, and all the dead people in the rest stop slid out of their booths and stood, and Amber heard some distant part of herself scream.

2

ALL HEADS TURNED and dead eyes opened. Amber backed off as the patrons came at her, their faces blank and splattered with their own blood.

"Stay back," Amber warned, shoving the waitress. "Don't touch me. Don't you dare—"

They grabbed her and she cursed, struggled. She didn't want to hit them, didn't want to hurt them, but they were dead, they were already dead, and it was too late for them so she started slashing with her claws, punching, headbutting, and they kept coming, and now her arms were pinned and one of them had her by the throat and they pushed her back, this solid mass of corpses working as one, and they forced her into a booth and started crawling on top of her until she could barely breathe.

"Get them off me!" she screamed. "Get them off!"

Through the tangle of limbs, she watched as Mauk put the claw hammer on the table. Then he stepped back, taking a small pouch from inside his boiler suit. He dipped his fingers in, drew out a handful of black powder, and crouched. Amber lost sight of him, but she knew what he was doing. He was making a circle.

"We're gonna be taking a trip," he said.

"I swear to God, I'll kill you."

He stuck his head up into her line of sight. "Hey, you be nice to me and I'll be nice to you. The Shining Demon only told me to bring you to him alive. Now there's *alive*, and there's *barely alive* — I don't much care which one it ends up being." Then he ducked down again.

She listened to the soft hiss of the powder. There were six or seven people lying on top of her, but they were still. They didn't even breathe. Her eyes settled on the claw hammer. She tried to reach for it.

Mauk stood, put the pouch back into his boiler suit, and slid into the seat opposite. He pulled the hammer a little closer to him.

"Your parents were after you, ain't that right?" he asked. "Yeah, I heard all about your folks and their friends. They actually wanted to eat you? That's messed up — and I should know. But you evaded them — you, a sixteen-year-old kid, evaded a bunch of demons a hundred and something years old. Not only that, you killed the representative, smushed that overrated pile of crap Shanks, and you've managed to stay ahead of the Hounds of Hell."

He whistled in admiration. "I mean, they'd have caught you eventually. It's what they do. Astaroth sets the Hounds on you, they don't give up till you're caught, and there ain't nothing you can do about it. You don't fight the Hounds. You can't beat 'em. Never heard of anyone managing that. You can't hide from 'em, neither. They got your scent. But look at you. You're still running. That says something about you, little demon. Says you are not to be underestimated. Under different circumstances, I would have been honoured to have stalked and killed you."

He put a pair of handcuffs on the table. "But, seeing as how

I'm gonna be delivering you to the Shining Demon, I gotta take precautions."

The corpses moved on top of Amber, and they stretched out her right arm, pinning it to the tabletop.

"You'll be wearing these," said Mauk. "I don't like to do it. I was in chains when they caught me and I didn't much like it, and putting shackles on such a beautiful beast as yourself seems to me a crime of some magnitude. But I ain't gonna underestimate you." He opened the cuffs, then laid them to one side. "And with that in mind I gotta think about those claws of yours. No telling what manner of mischief you could get up to with those things. So we're gonna have to do something about them, too."

He picked up the hammer as the corpses flattened her hand fully against the table.

Amber started to panic. "What are you doing? What are you going to do? Tell them to let go of me. Tell them!"

Mauk's free hand pinned her thumb. She turned it into a claw, tried to slash at him, but he laughed, and raised the hammer.

"Don't," she said. "Please don't. I swear I—"

"This little piggy," said Mauk, and brought the hammer down.

Pain rocketed through her and Amber screamed, tried to kick and flail, but the weight of all those bodies on top of her made that impossible. Tears came to her eyes, rolled down her cheeks. The pain was so immense that she almost didn't feel him singling out her next finger.

"No!" she cried. "Please!"

He didn't bother saying anything this time. With a happy smile on his face, he smashed the bones in that finger, too.

"You bastard!" Amber howled. She was sobbing. She was actually sobbing. "You bastard, I'll kill you, I'll kill you, I'll rip your—"

The third finger was smashed and Amber lost her words to the screams that were being ripped from her throat. The fourth followed. Then the fifth. Finally, the corpses released their hold on her. She tried to retract her arm, tried to clutch it close to her, but to do so it'd have had to pass through the tangle of corpses. She held it in mid-air while she cried and struggled to breathe.

Then the corpses moved again. They had her left hand in their grip.

"No!" she screamed, trying to keep it underneath her, jammed between her chest and the cheap upholstery. But now they were turning her, turning her on to her back, and as her left arm was being pulled out of the tangle her right arm was being pulled in, and her broken fingers jolted and sent fresh waves of pain straight into her thoughts, blinding them, freezing them, slicing through them and leaving them in tatters. When the wave crested and her thoughts became her own once more, her face was pressed tight into someone's torso, and she could feel the surface of the table beneath her left palm and Mauk's grip on her thumb, and she squeezed her eyes shut.

The hammer found its target and she gasped.

It found its next target. And the next one. And now she was screaming once more, but it didn't change anything, because she only had two fingers that weren't broken and Mauk quickly reduced that to one. Amber fought the urge to puke. If she puked, she'd choke on her own vomit.

"And this little piggy went wee, wee, wee, all the way home," said Mauk, and smashed her little finger.

While she screamed, the corpses climbed off her. One by one, the weight lessened, and she could turn her head now, and breathe in lungfuls of air to help her cry. Someone – Mauk, probably – had her hands in his. His skin was rough. Calloused. She barely felt the handcuffs slide around her wrists. The last corpse climbed off her and she sat up.

"There," Mauk said. "That wasn't so bad, now was it?"

She ran her forearm over her eyes – that movement alone was enough to bring fresh tears – then blinked at him as he sat there, smiling.

"I didn't wanna have to do that," he said. "But I'm a cautious fellow. I see that you have sharp teeth, too. Let's do each other a favour, okay? You try not to bite me, and I won't smash each and every one of those pearly whites. I'd hate to have to ruin your beautiful smile. It is beautiful, ain't it? I bet it is. Smile for me. Go on. Just a little smile."

Her demon side wanted to snarl and snap and sneer, but her human side, the ugly, ordinary, weak side, just wanted to be spared any more pain.

She raised the corners of her mouth in a twitching, pathetic smile.

"I knew it," said Mauk. "I've often wondered how much better-looking I'd be if Astaroth had made me a demon, instead of bestowing upon me the gifts I'd asked for. I'd be taller for a start, huh?" He chuckled, then slid out of the booth. "Come on now, girlie. The Shining Demon don't like to wait."

It took a few moments, but Amber got out of the booth, stood on shaky legs. The circle of black powder Mauk had made was just big enough for the two of them to stand in.

"Careful not to scuff the edges," said Mauk.

She wanted to turn, run, but the corpses were watching her. She couldn't fight, not with the handcuffs on and not when the slightest touch would bring her to her knees.

Mauk held out his hand. "Come on, Amber. Time to give this Devil his due."

Amber took her first step, and headlights swooped against the window as a black 1970 Dodge Charger pulled up right beside the front door.

"Dammit," said Mauk, ducking slightly.

The waitress clamped her hand over Amber's mouth, muffling her cry of pain as she was dragged backwards. The other corpses went back to their seats while Mauk stood at the counter with his cap pulled low, pretending to read the menu.

The diner door opened, and Milo walked in.

Tall, clad in blue jeans and cowboy boots and a dark shirt with some grey in his hair and some grey in his stubble, he was usually good-looking enough to make people sit up and take notice. But not tonight. The corpses sat, slumped, heads down.

Mauk walked up behind him. "Excuse me, sir?"

Milo turned as Mauk started to swing the hammer. It was halfway to its target when Mauk's whole body froze and his eyes widened.

They stood there, both men, looking at each other.

Milo always kept his gun holstered on his belt, under his shirt. He drew and fired in the time it took Mauk to blink. At point-blank range, Mauk went straight down.

But then the corpses started to stand up again. Amber tried shouting, tried to tell Milo they were already dead, but the waitress's corpse tightened its grip. Milo backed away from the lumbering dead, keeping his finger off the trigger.

20

Amber opened her mouth wide and bit down on the waitress's dead hand. Her fangs cut through bone as easily as flesh, and she spat out fingers as the corpses dived on Milo. They wrestled the gun from his hand and held him while Elias Mauk got back to his feet. He hadn't lost that expression of surprise.

"You?" he said. "You're her travelling companion?"

Milo stopped struggling, and watched as the incredulity spread across Mauk's face.

"I heard you'd died," the killer said. "I heard you'd finally lain down and accepted your miserable fate. What the hell are you doing here? What the hell are you doing with *her*? Answer me, goddammit!"

Mauk whacked the hammer into Milo's head.

"Milo!" Amber shouted, doing her best to tear free. The waitress pushed her up against the counter, jamming her chest into the corner while her broken fingers jarred against the underside, and Amber whimpered and went still.

"What's that?" Mauk said, frowning. "Milo? That's what you're calling yourself these days?" He shrugged. "As good a name as any, I guess."

The corpses held Milo upright. Blood ran from his hairline, following the contour of his cheekbone to his clenched jaw. His eyes were bright, unclouded by concussion, and they were focused entirely on Elias Mauk, who now had one foot in the circle of powder he'd made.

Amber's eyes flickered to the pack of cigarettes on the countertop, and the silver Zippo lighter beside it. She pushed back against the waitress, just enough to bring her hands up. The corpse responded by shoving back even harder, but Amber had already picked up the Zippo between her palms and brought it to her mouth. Her lips closed round the lid and pulled it open.

"You got old," Mauk said to Milo. "Got some grey in that hair. See, you should've done what I done — you should've died first. That way, you don't age — you get to stay young and beautiful forever. Like me." He laughed.

Amber tilted the Zippo, pressed the wheel against the countertop, remembered all the stories she'd ever heard about how these lighters were supposed to start first time, every time, and then she shot her arms out straight. The grooved wheel dragged and sparked and the lighter lit.

She set it carefully down on the counter.

"I'm not gonna say it's good to see you," said Mauk. "Obviously, it ain't. But it is good that you're here. The instructions were: *delivering the demon girl's travelling companion is optional.* As in I don't have to include you in the package if I don't feel like it. So I can kill you right here and right now. I can bash your brains in. How's that make you feel, you taciturn son of a bitch? That gonna get a reaction outta you? Or how about this? I can take my time, break every bone in your body before putting you outta your misery, or you could beg for mercy and get it over with, lickety-split. So what's it gonna be? You gonna let me kill you slowly, or you gonna beg your old friend Elias for a quick death?"

"Well," Milo said at last, "this is awkward."

"What is?"

"I actually have no idea who you are."

Mauk laughed. "Bullshit."

"I'm serious," said Milo. "Should I remember you? I feel like I should, but..."

"Okay, I'm confused," Mauk responded. "Are you lying to delay the inevitable, or are you just determined to be an asshole about this?"

Milo shrugged, which only pissed Mauk off even more.

With the hammer raised and ready for a swing, Mauk said, "You wanna try remembering me, or should I just get to cracking open your skull? All the same to me, buddy boy. All of a sudden, my curiosity over how you found yourself on that side of the line has faded to the square root of *nothing*."

"Have you always talked so much?" Milo asked. "I think I'd have remembered someone who talks so much."

Mauk's lip curled. "I'm gonna enjoy this."

Amber gritted her teeth, then twisted and rammed a shoulder into the dead waitress. The jolt to her hands made her cry out, but she used that pain to stomp on the corpse's knee. The waitress toppled away from Amber.

"Somebody grab her!" yelled Mauk, but Amber was already closing her hands around the lighter, feeling the flames lick her palms, and as the corpses reached for her she dropped, sending the Zippo spinning across the floor.

It met the circle and the powder went up in blue flames, and before Mauk had even looked down the circle was complete.

"Oh goddamn—" was all he had time to say before he vanished.

Free of his influence, the dead bodies crumpled to the floor. Milo stood, scuffing the circle with his boot, and the flames went out.

He hurried over to Amber and helped her stand. He stared at her bloody, twisted fingers.

"Jesus," he whispered.

She sagged against him and he held her weight. "I don't feel well," she mumbled.

"I'll get you to a doctor," he said. "But first you're going to have to change back."

"No. No, it'll hurt too much."

"We don't have a choice. I'm sorry."

"I'll heal. I'll heal by myself."

"Your fingers need to be reset. If we leave them, they'll heal wrong. We need a doctor to do it right. I'm sorry. You have to do this."

She tried arguing, but no words would come. Milo was right. She knew he was.

She reverted. The transformation itself, the shortening of all the bones in her body, both broken and intact, made her cry out.

But now the true pain came at her. No longer blocked by her demon form, it rushed at her all at once and burst behind her eyes. Her vision swam and the world tilted, but instead of falling to the ground she was lifted off her feet. The last thing she was aware of was Milo carrying her to the door, and then she blacked out.

3

WHEN THE NIGHT FINALLY slouched its way across the horizon, Virgil was there to greet it grudgingly, his old bones shivering in the chill. There was a time, long ago, when he would have looked forward to the night, back when he could spend it sleeping soundly. There was a time, even longer ago, when he could have spent his nights doing other stuff, too – drinking and carousing and getting into trouble.

These days, the only trouble he got into was when his thoughts got mixed up in his head, and the only sleep that came to him was light, irritated and sparse.

How many times had he made the trip to the bathroom the previous night? Five? Six? Pretty soon he'd need to keep a bedpan close by, just to make sure he didn't embarrass himself. Either that or just bite the damn bullet and check into one of those retirement homes, places with *Lodge* or *Manor* or *Tranquil* in their names. *God's Waiting Room* would be more apt.

Even though they were headed into summer, he turned up the heat on the thermostat. There was cold, he'd found out, and then there was *Alaska* cold. He didn't like being cold. Never had. He was a California kid, born and raised in the sun. And here he was, living out his winter years in goddamn Alaska. Was it smart? No, but then neither were the decisions that had brought him here.

His house was a shrine to the life he'd once led. His awards, all five of them, took up two shelves in the display cabinet. The movies he'd been in – cheap things, mostly, aside from *Inferno at 30,000 Feet* – were documented in the framed posters on the walls, but it was his TV work for which he'd won the greatest acclaim. A cult hit before anyone knew what a cult hit was, *When Strikes the Shroud* had brought werewolves and vampires and terrible gypsy curses into the living rooms of America for three wonderful seasons in the early 1970's and, in the centre of it all, had been Virgil Abernathy, playing the eponymous Shroud, the masked, besuited, two-fisted seeker of truth in a world mired in nightmare.

Three glorious years. Talk of a movie. And then tastes changed and attention spans wandered and the Shroud was at last felled – not by killer or crazy or creature, but by ratings. Or rather the lack of them.

Not that he was bitter. Not that he allowed thoughts of what might have been to intrude upon his daily life. Not that he allowed himself to dream of yesterday instead of facing up to his mistakes of today, which were legion. No, none of that for Virgil Abernathy, once a hero to boys of every age and a seducer of women. No, to Virgil Abernathy there was only today. There was only the cold emptiness of today in a town that had never particularly wanted him, in a life that was growing ever more tired of him.

"Maudlin nonsense," he muttered to his cold, quiet house.

And what had they replaced him with, he wondered (and

not for the first time)? A quick perusal of the TV channels answered that little question. Reality television and twenty-four-hour news. Game shows and competitions where all your dreams came true if the people at home liked you enough to vote. Rich people doing ugly things. Poor people doing stupid things. And the shows? The scripted shows? Populated by actors with sharp cheekbones who did nothing but smoulder or grimace in equal measure. Where was the art? Where was the substance? He flicked over to a commercial for a pill whose never-ending list of possible side effects included death, then turned off the TV.

His doctor had told him, for the sake of his heart, not to cause himself any unnecessary agitation. But then his doctor was an idiot.

Virgil turned off the lights. Time for bed. Another day over with. Another one under his belt. He was building up quite a collection. Had more days than he could count. He wasn't quite sure what he would do with them, once he'd collected them all. Maybe he'd set them free. Maybe he'd go to Edison's Shard, the rocky outcrop overlooking the disused quarry in the hills behind his house, and throw the days to the wind, watch them flutter and fly and disappear. Or maybe he'd just stuff them in a jar and bury them in the backyard. Either one would suffice. No one would be using them again.

He was headed for his bedroom, but stopped, as he always did, by the window in the living room, and peered through the curtains. He glowered at the house beside his, with its porch lights that blazed with the force of a thousand suns every time a damn grizzly wandered into the backyard. How many times had he complained to that damn fool Snyder? In his younger days, there was no one who would dare say no to him, not when Virgil's ice-blue eyes started to narrow. But that was then, and things had changed. Robert Snyder was a man in his forties, singularly unimpressive and a convicted felon to boot, and yet he felt confident enough to smirk away Virgil's complaints. A boor of a man.

Virgil could see him right now, watching TV. Kimmel or Fallon or one of those. They were all the same to Virgil. Monologuers, the lot of them. Snyder sat in his undershirt with a beer in his hand. He looked warm. Virgil despised him.

He was just about to let the curtain fall back when movement caught his eye. There was someone else in the house.

Snyder had been married, but they'd split three years ago and she'd moved across town, back in with her mother. What was her name? It didn't matter. What mattered was that, since Snyder's wife had left him, Virgil had never seen anyone else in that house. No women, no friends, no one. No one but Snyder. And now this... this *shape*.

He was tall, whoever it was. Thin, too. He moved past the windows quickly but without urgency, from dark room to bright room to dark room. Virgil lost track of him and frowned slightly, wondering why he was still watching. Who cared if Robert Snyder had made a new friend? Virgil certainly didn't.

Snyder drained the last of his beer and stood, scratched his expansive belly, and walked into the kitchen. He stood at the sink, looking at his reflection in the window, unable to see Virgil in his darkened house directly across from him. He washed out the empty beer bottle. Recycling. Well, he wasn't all bad.

The visitor, whoever he was, came into the kitchen. He was pale, his skin a funny colour, and his mouth was wide. Very, very wide. He walked up behind Snyder and grabbed him.

And then snapped Snyder's neck.

Virgil's heart lurched in his chest and he ducked down. He didn't know why he ducked down, he just did. Ducking down seemed like the thing to do. But now that he had, he was finding it hard to straighten up again. He half waddled to the bookcase, moving away from the window. His legs were burning, the treacherous things. When he was in the clear, he straightened up slowly, groaning as his hip popped and his back creaked.

Moving a little easier now, he sneaked to the window once more and peeked out. He couldn't see Snyder or the figure. Either the killer had dragged him away or else he'd just let him drop out of sight.

Virgil thought about how crappy a neighbour Snyder had been. He had been rude and disrespectful and had threatened Virgil with physical harm on more than one occasion – and, while Virgil had held serious doubts about Snyder's ability to follow through on those threats, there was no getting away from the fact that Snyder had been a young man in his forties and Virgil was an old man in his eighties with a bad heart. That was not, by anyone's standards, a fair fight.

But Snyder was not a young man in his forties anymore. He was a body now. A corpse. He was remains. Whatever hopes and dreams he'd ever harboured were gone, evaporated into the ether the moment that figure had laid his hands on him. Virgil felt some sympathy for the guy, but it was the shallow type of sympathy that was easily forgotten and quickly put away.

Movement caught his attention. The figure was walking towards the back door.

Virgil hurried to his own kitchen, banging his leg off a chair in the dark. Cursing all the way to the window over the sink, he peered into Snyder's overgrown backyard as the figure slipped out into the night. He seemed smaller now, under the moonlight. He had dark hair. That was odd. In the kitchen, Virgil could have sworn he'd been bald. He wasn't nearly so pale, either, and he wore slacks and a vest over a short-sleeved shirt. The killer glanced his way and two thoughts spiked in Virgil's head.

The first was, *He's seen me, he's seen me, he knows I'm here*, a thought that faded when the killer's gaze moved on without stopping, taking in a full sweep of his surroundings.

The second thought was, *I know that guy. I know that guy, but it's impossible. It can't be him. The guy I'm thinking of is eighty years old and living in Arkansas.*

He watched the killer jump the back fence and disappear, then stayed where he was for twenty minutes before he allowed himself to relax. Slowly, his heart stopped beating a tango. The thought occurred to him that it might be a good idea to call the cops. He took his phone from his pocket. The screen lit up, way too bright in this dark house, and he did his best to remember how to work it.

Headlights swept past the window. Virgil moved quickly back to peer out, just in time to see a police cruiser stop in Snyder's driveway. Relief washed over him. The lights weren't flashing, but he didn't mind that, not when he saw Chief Novak step out. Novak was a good cop – strict as hell, but smart and fair. He was with another officer, a big guy – Virgil thought his name might have been Woodbury – and as they walked up to Snyder's front door he debated whether or not to tell them what he'd seen.

The front door must have been unlocked because the two cops walked right in. Virgil saw them cross the living room, heading into the kitchen, until they were standing where he had last seen Snyder. They looked down and talked to each other. They didn't seem surprised. They didn't even seem perturbed. They both bent down and when they straightened up they were carrying Snyder's body between them.

"Oh, goddamn you," Virgil whispered, watching them take the corpse out of the house and dump it in the trunk of the cruiser. Woodbury went back to shut the front door, then rejoined Novak and they drove off.

Virgil stood there in his dark house.

"Well, hellfire," he said.

4

It was a brand-new dream, this time.

Amber was back home, in Orlando, and it was hot and muggy and the a/c wasn't working, but the heat wasn't affecting her like it usually did. Her brow was cool as she sat at the table and told her parents about her day at school. She hadn't been bullied and she hadn't been called in to Principal Cobb's office, so today had been a good day.

Her parents listened, nodded, smiled with affection, and offered advice and encouragement. Betty set the table while Bill fussed with the oven. He opened the oven door and the heat spilled out and circulated with the already warm air. Dream-Amber started to sweat.

The dream did that fast-forward thing that dreams do, and now they were eating, and talking, and chatting. Bill and Betty remained cool. Amber's sweat poured down her face and splashed on to her plate, but she was starving, so she finished her food and asked for a second helping. Her parents laughed and Bill took her plate and stood, carving knife in hand. He cut a large slice from the roast, and Amber noticed for the first time that the roast was Imelda, laid out on a large silver tray on the table, garnished and basted and smelling divine.

Bill handed Amber back her plate and she dove in, chewing on the tender meat while blood mixed with the sweat on her chin. It was glorious. Imelda's skin crackled in her mouth.

Then she realised it was a dream and she woke up.

The first thing she registered was the cold. The second was the happy purr of the Charger as it gently rocked her in her seat. And the third, as she opened her eyes, was the pain in her hands. She lifted them off her lap, wincing but not screaming, which was an improvement. She could only see the tips of her fingers above the thick bandages – they were purple, swollen and sore.

"How you feeling?" Milo asked, keeping his eyes on the dark road ahead.

"Like all my fingers have been smashed," she replied.

"Not all of them," he said. "The doctor said your left thumb is badly bruised, but not actually broken."

"And there I was feeling sorry for myself," she mumbled. She looked down at herself. "Did I puke? I don't remember puking."

"You did," said Milo.

"Damn." She noticed he was wearing a different shirt. "Did I puke on you?"

"You did."

"Sorry."

"She gave me pills for you. You can take another in a little over an hour."

Which left just enough time for the pain to build nicely. Amber straightened up, careful to keep her hands steady. "That guy... he said Astaroth knows where we're headed."

Milo nodded. "Figured as much."

"Did you recognise him?"

Milo shook his head. "You catch his name?"

Amber hesitated. "Elias Mauk," she said.

"I've heard of him," said Milo, "and I got the impression we'd been friends once."

"Friends? He wanted to kill you."

"We must have had a falling-out. Hell, for all I know, maybe we were partners. Serial killers in cahoots."

"His face didn't spark any memories?" she asked. "His voice?"

"Nothing," said Milo. "My life is still as blank as it's been for the last twelve years."

"He, uh, he seemed to know that Milo isn't your real name."

"Yeah." They got to a dark and empty crossroads, and the Charger creaked pleasantly as they turned right. "I wonder what it is."

The phone in her jacket rang. Amber held up her bandaged hands.

"Oh yeah," Milo said. She twisted slightly and he reached into her pocket, took the phone out, and thumbed the answer button. He set it to loudspeaker.

"Uh, hello?" said the voice on the other end. "That Amber?"

"I'm here," she said.

"Oh, Amber, hi. This is Jeremy?"

"Hi, Jeremy."

"The guy you gave that hundred bucks to?"

"I know who you are, Jeremy."

"Right," Jeremy said, "yeah, sorry. Anyway, you wanted to know if a group of bikers turned up?"

Her mood turned cold and plummeted. "Yes, we did."

"Well, they just passed through town," Jeremy said. "Not more than two minutes ago. Five of them. Long hair, leather jackets, beards, the works. Rode straight through without stopping. Didn't look left or right, just kept looking ahead."

"Thanks, Jeremy," said Amber. "Don't spend that money all at once."

Milo hung up and slipped the phone back in her pocket. She looked at him.

"How far back is Jeremy?"

"Twenty hours," said Milo. "Maybe twenty-two." He glanced at her. "We knew we couldn't shake them."

"I know," she said. "But still... It'd be nice if something went our way for once, that's all."

"Astaroth can send whoever he likes," said Milo. "The fact is, the Hounds are at least twenty hours behind us and we are ten hours away from Desolation Hill. No one's going to stop us."

"You need to sleep."

"I will. We're on a straight blast into Alaska. Once we sneak across the border, I'll take a few hours' rest. When we get where we're going, I'll sleep a full night."

"That's providing everything we've heard about Desolation Hill is true."

"You think Buxton was lying?"

"No," said Amber. "But just because Gregory hid there for a few weeks doesn't mean we can."

"We don't have a wide variety of options available to us," said Milo. "He thinks we'll be undetectable to the Shining Demon and the Hounds once we're inside the town limits, and I trust him to know what he's talking about. That'll at least give us time to get our breath back and formulate some kind of plan."

"Because our plans always work out so well for us."

He didn't respond to that. She didn't expect him to.

They drove on in comfortable and familiar silence. The knob for the radio remained, as ever, untouched. Even if she'd wanted to turn it, her bandaged hands would have made that impossible. Besides, she'd grown out of her fear of quiet moments. She didn't need music to fill the silences anymore.

She took a few more pills and the rising pain faded to a manageable throb as she looked out at the endless parade of trees. She wondered what kind they were. It was hard to tell in the dark, but she thought they were spruce, although she was no expert.

"What kind of trees are those?" she asked Milo.

"Green," he said, and that's how the conversation ended.

They passed sleeping houses and sleeping cars and an impressive array of parked pickups with slide-in campers that reared up and over like one dog humping another. It got ridiculously cold in the car and Amber wrapped herself awkwardly in a blanket. The stars tonight were astonishing.

"See the stars?" she asked Milo.

"Bright," he grunted.

She nodded. Yup. They were indeed bright.

She slept, then, and didn't dream, and when she opened her eyes the Charger was slowing and there were lights flashing lazily ahead of them.

She sat up straight, the blanket covering her hands. "Cops?"

"State trooper," said Milo. His face was pale, his features tight. They were already in Alaska, which meant he'd been driving too long. The Charger had started whispering to him.

Amber saw the trooper, in his jacket and a wide-brimmed

hat, holding up one hand. The Charger stopped beside him and Milo wound down the window.

"Hey there, folks," the trooper said, leaning in and smiling. "This is a heck of a nice vehicle you've got here. Don't see many of these old muscle cars round these parts, let me tell you. What is she, a '69?"

"'70," said Milo.

"1970," said the trooper, and whistled appreciatively. "Gee whiz, you've kept her in a good condition."

"Thanks," Milo said.

"Sure thing!" He bent lower, and smiled in at Amber. "Hey there, little lady."

He had light stubble on his chin and his shirt didn't fit right. The top button wouldn't close round his thick neck. There was blood on his tie.

That was all Milo needed. He'd been behind the wheel for nine or ten hours without much of a break and certainly no sleep, and this was all it took to make him snap. He shifted, growing horns, his skin and hair now the deepest, most impossible black, and, when he snarled, the same red that spilled from his eyes spilled from his mouth. He grabbed the trooper's tie and yanked hard as he hit the gas. The Charger lurched forward, picking up speed, dragging the hollering trooper along with it. They passed the patrol car and Amber glimpsed a bare leg sticking out of the grass behind it.

The man in the trooper uniform gurgled and cursed and clung to the side of the Charger as they hurtled uphill. His right hand disappeared for a moment, then came back, holding a pistol that he quickly dropped when they went over a bump.

They got to the top of the hill and evened out, and Milo

released his hold and the road snatched the man from the window. Milo braked, testing Amber's seat belt and jarring her hands.

He put the car in neutral and got out.

Amber stayed where she was, the Charger's low rumble helping to calm her beating heart. The sky was beginning to brighten. Cold, startlingly fresh air filled the Charger.

There was a sharp wail of pain that was abruptly cut off.

She angled the rear-view to watch Milo drag the body into the bushes. Once that was done, she knew, he'd go back down the hill, stuff the real trooper's corpse in the trunk of the patrol car and park it somewhere out of sight.

Then she'd insist that he get some sleep. They were in Alaska now, with maybe five hours of driving ahead of them, and the Hounds were still twenty or so hours behind. For the first time since all this began, Amber allowed herself to wonder if this was maybe the first step towards everything being suddenly okay.

5

It took longer than expected to find Desolation Hill.

They finally got to it a little before midday. This troubled Milo. Amber could see it in his face, and she didn't have to ask why. They should have turned on to its streets without even thinking about it, such was the power of the Demon Road, or the Dark Highway, or the blackroads, or whatever name you used to describe the phenomenon of horror seeking horror. Such things were intertwined. Fate guided travellers on the blackroads, steering them to people and places that had been similarly touched by darkness. Sheer coincidence alone should have led Milo and Amber right on to the town's main street.

Instead, they took several wrong turns and passed the turn-off without even noticing it. Once they'd found their way on to it, the road took them on a winding line between snow-topped hills until they came to a sturdy old sign that said

You Are Now Entering Desolation Hill

Just before the sign, a narrow track led off to their right, and directly beyond it the main road continued straight for a while before veering off and getting lost behind overgrown bushes and tall trees.

Milo pulled the Charger over to the side of the road.

"Why are we stopping?" Amber asked. "We're here. We actually made it. What's the problem?"

"We don't know what's waiting for us," said Milo.

"Sure we do," she said. "I've read you the town history. It's short and boring. It's a small town with a creepy name where nothing exciting ever happens."

"That the internet knows about."

"The internet knows all," she said. "It's the one place we'll be safe from the Shining Demon."

"But why?"

"Is that important?" she asked. "I mean, obviously it's important, yeah, but is it important now? Is it important right now, at the side of the road? All we need to know is that we'll be safe in there."

"Buxton only lasted a week."

"He said it was a weird place. That's fine with me. I can handle weird. Milo, we can sort this out later. We can ask questions and get answers. But I'm tired. You're tired. We need a good night of sleep. We need to stop running."

He sighed, and rubbed his eyes. "Yeah. Yeah, I guess you're right."

"Damn right I'm right."

"Okay then, we go in, we don't attract any attention. We speak only when spoken to. We fade into the background, understood?"

"I'll try."

"Try?"

"It's a small town in the middle of nowhere. Newcomers are going to be noticed. That's kind of inevitable."

"Yeah, maybe, but we do our best to keep a low profile."

"Agreed."

Milo paused for a moment longer, then put the Charger in gear. "Okay then."

They pulled out on to the road and passed the town sign and the Charger bolted forward suddenly and Amber yelled as she shifted, pain flaring in her hands, the shock of the change nearly blinding her to the fact that Milo, too, had turned into his demon-self. He jammed his foot on the brake and the Charger slid to a halt, growling in protest.

Cradling her hands to her chest, Amber met Milo's burning red eyes. They were narrowed. He looked behind them, then in front, then stuck his head out of the window and looked up. Expecting an attack. Expecting something.

They waited. The Charger waited. But nothing came.

Milo's skin lightened and the burning red left his eyes and mouth, and his curved horns retreated into his hairline.

"What the hell?" said Amber.

Milo examined his hands. "I don't know. I can still feel—"

He shifted again without warning, into that black-skinned, horned demon, and he snarled in irritation and immediately reverted to his normal self.

"That was weird," he muttered, then looked at her. "You're going to have to change back."

"But it hurts."

"You have to change, and then you'll have to fight against the impulse to shift again. It's strong. It's very strong."

"For Christ's sake..."

She gritted her teeth and reverted, and fresh pain sprang from her fingers and blinded her to her own thoughts and there was another flash of pain and she was a demon again.

"I can't do it," she gasped. "I can't."

"Revert," said Milo. "And hold."

"Give me a minute."

"Now, Amber."

"I'll try again in a minute, you dick!"

"Now," Milo snarled, his eyes starting to glow red, and Amber snarled back and reverted and this time she held it, despite the pain, and she focused on staying a normal, clumsy, ugly human...

And when the pain retracted far enough she took a deep, deep breath.

"Well done," Milo said, settling back into his seat.

"This is horrible," said Amber. Every inch of her wanted to shift. Her nerve endings jumped. Her skin was electric. The human form she inhabited was all wrong. "I feel like I need to pee," she said. "I don't need to pee, but you know that feeling? When you're about to burst and you know that all you have to do is relax and it'll suddenly feel so much better? It's like that, times a thousand."

Milo looked at her for a while. "Right," he said at last. "Not the analogy I'd have used, but fair enough."

"What's wrong with us?"

Milo didn't answer. He just got out of the car. Amber turned in her seat, watched him walk to the sign. He passed it and turned, a curious look on his face. He took a big step back to the Charger and shifted.

He stepped to the other side of the sign and reverted.

Scowling, he walked back to the car, shifting as he did so. By the time he got behind the wheel, he'd reverted again.

"This town is a curiosity," he said.

"You think whatever shielded Buxton from the Shining Demon is the same thing that's making us shift?"

"It's likely the reason, yeah. Pity he didn't mention this to us before he flew off."

"I don't like this," said Amber. "I don't like this feeling."

"How're the hands?"

"They hurt. Like, a huge amount."

"We'll get to that motel you found on the map," said Milo. "You'll be able to shift behind closed doors, and you'll heal faster as a demon. A day or two, tops."

He was probably right. The swelling had already gone down and her fingers were returning to their normal colour. Being a demon had its advantages.

"Sorry for calling you a dick," she said.

"That's okay. Sorry I snarled."

"Guess we're a little ruder than we'd like to be when we're horned up."

Milo looked at her.

"I should probably use a different word for that," she said.

"Probably," he agreed, and they started moving again. The town was affecting the Charger, too – its rumble was deeper, and somehow even more menacing, than usual.

Amber had examined the map online a dozen times before now, and as they drove she did her best to match it with her surroundings. They passed a used-car lot (TODD'S NEARLY NEW CARS! BEST PRICES!) hemmed in by a chain-link fence. The cars stood in their rows like prisoners in an exercise yard, their gleaming potential bridled by circumstances beyond their control.

Beyond the lot was a gas station, complete with small convenience store, and then they were in the town proper. Main Street was the widest street the place had, and the longest, and it boasted a church and a healthy array of businesses. The Hill Hardware Store was next to Lucy's Laundromat, which stood opposite Doctor Maynard's office, which in turn stood next to Reinhold's Pharmacy. Moraga Discount Store was the massive building on the east side of the square, a slightly raised public meeting place in the exact centre of Main Street that the road itself circled. The west side was taken up by the grander Desolation Hill Municipal Building, which had eighteen steps leading up to its doors and pillars on either side, marred only by the scaffolding that scaled it from ground to peak like the skeleton of a building that had been left there to die. There was nothing on the square itself except what looked like an old wooden mailbox on a post that had been set into the concrete.

The Charger drew some curious looks as it passed. Amber was used to that – it was certainly an impressive car. But today she thought the attention they were getting was different, somehow. Not hostile, exactly, just... wary.

Milo turned off Main Street, passed a bar named Sally's, and kept going through a residential neighbourhood. The town itself continued up into the hills, into all those trees and all that snow, but they took a narrow blacktop without a yellow line up to a tall building that looked like it should have been perched on the edge of a cliff somewhere. The Dowall Motel was the only place to stay in the area, not counting a few bed and breakfasts, and the sign said there were vacancies.

They parked outside and got out. It was the beginning of May and there was a startlingly blue sky and yet Amber's breath still crystallised in the air. She doubted it was much above forty. On Main Street there had been no snow, but up here, elevated slightly, it was still packed tightly at the sides of the road.

Amber had spent her whole life feeling miserable in the heat, so she wasn't about to start complaining about the cold. Even so, the temperature was making her hands throb with a renewed vigour, and she hurried into the motel while Milo carried in their bags.

Inside, it was warmer. The wooden floorboards creaked under her weight. A moose head hung over the front desk, its terrific antlers rising to the high ceiling. A man came out of the back room. He looked young, in his thirties, but his side-parted hair had already gone grey and he held himself so stiffly that a sudden draught might possibly have snapped him in half.

He saw them and looked confused. Amber smiled, and led Milo to the desk. The man wore a little badge that identified him as Kenneth.

"Hi, Kenneth," said Amber.

Kenneth didn't answer. He had a mole under his right eye.

"We'd like a couple of rooms, please."

Kenneth looked at them for quite a long time before speaking.

"I wasn't expecting visitors," he said.

This struck Amber as a somewhat strange thing to say.

"This is a motel, isn't it?" Milo asked.

"Indeed it is," said Kenneth.

"And you rent out rooms to visitors, don't you?"

"Indeed we do," said Kenneth.

"So do you have any spare rooms to rent out to us?"

"Indeed I have," said Kenneth. "I just wasn't expecting you, that's all."

Silence threatened to descend.

"Should we have called ahead?" Amber asked.

Kenneth blinked at her. "We don't take reservations over the phone."

"Online?"

"We don't have a website," he said. "My mother never approved of the internet. She said the internet was a filthy place for perverts and degenerates who only want to watch pornography."

"It also has cats," said Amber.

"We don't allow animals," Kenneth said quickly. "My sister is allergic to animal hair. If you have cats, you can't stay here."

"We don't have cats," Milo said. "We don't have any animals. Is there anyone else staying here right now?"

"No."

"Then could we please have two rooms?"

Kenneth hesitated.

"I'm a little puzzled," said Amber. "You don't take bookings online or over the phone, and obviously you don't like it when people turn up unannounced... so how does anyone actually stay here?"

"The motel is not very busy," Kenneth said.

"I'm not surprised."

"I can let you stay," Kenneth decided, "but only until Wednesday. On Wednesday you must leave. We are fully booked up for Wednesday."

Amber frowned. "How?"

"I'm sorry?" said Kenneth.

"How has anyone been able to book for Wednesday, since

you don't take reservations over the phone and you don't have a website?"

"A long-standing arrangement," said Kenneth. "You must be gone by ten o'clock on Wednesday morning."

"I guess we could stay at a bed and breakfast," said Milo.

"You misunderstand," Kenneth said. "You must leave our town. On Wednesday we have our festival."

"I like festivals," said Amber.

"It is a private festival," Kenneth said. "For invited townsfolk only. You must leave by ten in the morning."

At no stage did Amber think Kenneth was joking, and yet she waited for the punchline all the same. When it didn't come, Milo spoke up.

"Sure," he said. "That's fine."

Kenneth hesitated. "Maybe you shouldn't stay," he said.

"Of course we should," Amber assured him. "We'll be gone by the time the festival starts — it's all good. We totally understand. Today, tomorrow, Monday and Tuesday and then we move on. You got it. How long does the festival last?"

"One night."

"Then how about we come back on Thursday?"

"Thursday and Friday are for clean-up."

"Then Saturday," Amber said, smiling. "If we leave and come back for the weekend, would that be okay?"

"Yes."

"Excellent. We'll do that. So put us down for four nights now, and then Saturday. If we like it here, we might even stay longer."

Kenneth nodded. "Very well. Welcome to the Dowall Motel. This is a family business."

Amber gave another smile. "Well, okay then."

Kenneth showed Amber to her room, and Milo dropped off her bag and followed Kenneth to his. Amber shut her door. The room was old-fashioned but clean, and smelled of fresh air and green trees. It had a fireplace that wasn't to be lit and a good-sized bed. It had a bathroom with a bathtub and a window that looked out over the town. It was a good room. A fine room.

Amber stood at the window. From here, she could almost see the road they had come in on, the one with the sign. That would be the road the Hounds would use. They were anywhere between ten and fifteen hours away, but it took Amber a long time to stop watching for their arrival.

6

VIRGIL FOUND THE NUMBER scrawled in an address book that had slipped down the back of a file cabinet. He tried to ignore the other names – seeing them brought pangs of recognition and regret – but despite himself he glanced through them. Here was Erik Estrada's number. Good kid, that Erik. Burt Reynolds. Lynda Carter. Ah, Lynda Carter. Robert Culp. Farrah Fawcett's number was here. He'd never managed to get with Farrah because of his (strained) friendship with Lee Majors – but he'd wanted to. Oh my, how he'd wanted to.

Then he found the number he was looking for, and he took out his ridiculous phone and eventually figured out how to make a call.

It was answered by a woman who told him the person he was looking for no longer lived there. She went off for a few minutes, eventually coming back with another number. He called that, and it was answered by a man who gave him the number of a retirement home. Virgil rang the home, gave them the name, and waited.

"Yeah?"

The voice on the other end sounded old, frail and ill-tempered.

"Javier?" said Virgil.

"Yeah?"

"It's Virgil. Virgil Abernathy."

There was a silence, and then,

"Why?"

"Why what?"

"Why? Why're you calling? Why the hell're you calling me? It's been forty years and now you're calling me and I want to know why, goddammit. If you're calling to apologise, you're about forty years too damn late."

Virgil frowned. "Why would I be apologising?"

"You're the one calling me!" Javier shouted. "You're the one calling and now you have the, the, the *nerve* to ask *why* you're calling? I'm the one asking why! I ask, you answer!"

"Javier, I really think we're getting our wires crossed here..."

"Dementia, is it?" Javier said. "You know that you owe me an apology, but you can't remember why, is that it? Y'know something? I'm glad. I'm glad your mind is leaving you. Couldn't happen to a nicer fella."

"My mind is fine, Javier, but to be honest you're starting to irritate me here."

Javier hooted down the phone. "Oh, is that right? Oh, *is that right?*"

"I just called to check on you," said Virgil. "I've been thinking about the old days a lot and I saw someone last night who could have been your double from back then, someone who I would have *sworn* was you if I hadn't known what age you were. I'm calling to ask if you have a son or a grandson and if they're anywhere close to Desolation Hill."

"I don't know where that is," said Javier, "but it sounds like just the place you deserve to be."

"Do you have anyone in your family that looks just like you did forty years ago, or not?"

"No!" Javier yelled. "I don't have *any* children, you dirty, lying, treacherous sonofabitch! I never had children and I never got married! The only woman in the world I ever loved looked at me like I was a joke and it was all your fault!"

"What are you talking about?"

"I'm talking about Darleen!"

Virgil frowned. "Who?"

"Darleen! Darleen Hickman!"

"I don't know who that is."

"The wardrobe lady on set," Javier said, anger biting at his words. "I fell in love with her and you knew it. There was a future there. A possibility. But you couldn't let that happen, could you? You couldn't stand the thought of any pretty girl being with anyone but you, the *star of the show*."

"What is it you think I did, Javier?"

"You know damn well what you did. You gave me that nickname."

"What nickname?"

"Don't make me say it."

"I don't know what it is we're talking about."

There was another silence, and then, "The Goat-molester."

Virgil's laugh was as loud as it was unexpected, and he immediately felt bad. "Oh right, yeah. That. Uh... and that damaged your relationship with the wardrobe lady?"

"*Darleen*," said Javier. "And of course it did. Everyone was laughing at me behind my back. Nobody took me seriously from that moment on. She had feelings for me – real, actual feelings – but how could she look at me in the same way once she'd lost all respect for me?"

"I'm... I'm really sorry, Javier. I'd forgotten all about that."

"I hadn't," said Javier bitterly. "That ruined my life, Abernathy. Ruined it. And it's all your fault."

"I'm sorry," said Virgil. "I am genuinely sorry, Javier, I really am. I had no idea it would cause you such hardship. The only thing I can say is that it wasn't done with any degree of maliciousness. It wasn't personal."

"It felt personal."

"And I regret that. I do. Please accept my apology."

"You know what?" Javier said. "I don't. I've been waiting forty years for you to say sorry, and now that you have, it means nothing to me. You were a sonofabitch then and you're a sonofabitch now. I hope you do get dementia. I hope you get dementia and you die a slow, horrible death."

"Right," said Virgil. "Well, in my defence—"

"Your defence can go to hell."

"In my defence," Virgil persisted, "and taking all things into account, with the benefit of hindsight and whatnot, I don't know... maybe you shouldn't have molested that goat."

Javier hung up.

7

SOMEONE KNOCKED ON HER door and Amber woke immediately and went to spring out of bed. As she was moving, she realised two things. The first was that she had shifted during the night and was now in full demon mode. The second was that she was about to put her full weight on to her left hand, and there was nothing she could do to stop it.

The pain hit her like an electric shock. She pulled her hands into her chest, rolled off the bed, and landed on her feet in a crouch, gritting her teeth to keep from crying out.

That knock again. It was calm. Unhurried. No urgency to it.

Amber waited for the worst of the pain to pass, then straightened, and moved slowly to the door. "Who is it?" she called.

"Me," said Milo.

"Anyone else with you?"

"No."

She gripped the key between her palms and turned it, and the lock clicked and she stepped back as Milo opened the door.

He saw the look on her face and frowned. "Hurting?"

"A little. I'll take the painkillers."

"You shift when you were sleeping?"

"Yeah. You?"

He nodded. He was clean-shaven and his eyes were calm – the benefits of a good night's rest. "I'm going to head out to the edge of town," he said, "keep watch for the Hounds."

"Let me get dressed."

"No need. I'm just going to be sitting there. You take a look around, see what's what. If we *can* hide out here, it'd be nice to know what the town has to offer."

Amber frowned. "You mean… we're going to be apart? During the daytime?"

"Is that okay with you?"

"Sure. It's just… I haven't been alone in the daytime for… a while."

"You'll adjust."

"What do I do?"

"Whatever you want. Go for a walk. Have some breakfast. Relax. It'll come back to you. Oh, and…" He pointed to her face.

"What?"

"You can't go out horned up."

"Oh yeah. Sure."

He nodded, and walked off, and Amber closed the door behind him and locked it again. Then she looked around and wondered what the hell she was going to do.

She swallowed some painkillers and brushed her teeth and peed, and as she was peeing she looked at the tub and tried to remember the last time she'd had a real bath. She filled the tub and added in all kinds of crazy liquids until the bubbles nearly spilled out on to the floor. Then she took off her clothes and climbed in, one long red leg at a time. Bracing her bandaged palms on the tub's edge, she lowered herself into the water, gasping, until her ass touched the bottom. She laughed, then, and sank further, until the hot water was up to her chin.

"Oh, this is nice," she muttered to the room.

She closed her eyes, breathing in the steam, letting it clear her head of any residual sleepiness. It had been so long since she'd been able to relax, to think of anything other than the chase. Even now, there was a part of her that was still on edge – but it was a small part, and she could have easily drowned it out if she'd been so inclined.

But of course she didn't. Just because Gregory Buxton had vanished from the Hounds' radar when he was in this town didn't mean she would, too. And even if she did, so what? The Hounds would still be able to ride on in here and search. They didn't need supernatural powers to find her – they just needed eyes.

So she kept that edge, the part of herself that remained wary, and she let it bite at her thoughts and burrow into her head. That edge had helped keep her alive after Imelda had died. After Glen. After her parents.

She wondered about them, where they were, what they were doing. How they were doing. She felt a curious mix of satisfaction that she'd fouled up her parents' plans, that she'd forced them to go on the run with Grant and Kirsty Van der Valk, that Astaroth was almost as pissed with them as he was with her... but also concern. That part puzzled Amber. She didn't care about them. They had bred her to be killed and eaten, just like they had her brother and sister whom she had never known. She was not concerned for their well-being.

She was definitely, definitely not. She was almost sure of that.

Thoughts of her parents irritated her, but there was only one other person she could think about that would banish them to the back of her mind, and that was Glen. She only thought about him when she was in demon form. Her heart was harder when she was like this, better able to cope with what had happened to him. With who he was now. What he'd turned into.

She'd been aware of him following her. Some nights she'd look in the side mirror and glimpse something moving behind them. Some nights, when the Charger was quiet, she could hear him above her, his clothes fluttering in the wind.

Why he was following her, she didn't know. She'd been told that most breeds of vampire were pack animals — they stuck close to the one who'd turned them. But the vampire that had killed Glen had vanished, and his undead family back in Cascade Falls were in disarray — certainly the patriarch was no longer around to guide them. Amber had seen to that personally.

That might be it, of course. Glen could be following her to kill her, to exact revenge for Varga's death. She doubted it, though. Revenge didn't seem to be Glen's style, soulless monster or not. No, what was infinitely more likely was that Glen's preoccupation with Amber — especially in her current form — had stayed with him even after his death. Maybe it was the one thing he was clinging on to. Maybe he had designs on a coffin built for two.

Amber closed her eyes and held her breath, and submerged so that only her knees and her hands and her horns were above the water line. Down here, in the muted world of the bathtub, she opened her eyes again and looked at herself. She couldn't blame Glen for his preoccupations, of course. Was she not as magnificent as everyone said? Was her figure not astonishing? Were her features not flawless?

She loved being this way. She loved being tall and red and horned and beautiful. She loved being sexy. She'd never been sexy, not as an ordinary human. Sexiness was for other girls, not for her. Never for her.

She broke the surface of the water, and smiled.

Until now.

After her bath, Amber went for a walk. The people seemed friendly enough, even if she did catch them staring at her from time to time. On three occasions she actually glanced at her bandaged hands to make sure she wasn't in demon mode, then she put it down to the fact that visitors were probably a rarity around here.

It was a pretty town, surrounded as it was by trees and snow-covered mountains and looking up into a huge blazingly blue sky. It had a smell to it, too – fresh and open and healthy. Invigorating, even. Amber fully acknowledged all of this. Further, she had no trouble admitting that it was downright lovely to see every store open for business – that being quite a change after spending the last few weeks driving through small towns teetering on the edge of survival.

Watching the people file into church, she figured that there was absolutely nothing about Desolation Hill that she found disagreeable, and yet something had got its hooks into her and was pulling her down.

Deciding that breakfast might improve her mood, she stepped into Fast Danny's, the only one of the three cafe/diner joints on Main Street open on a Sunday morning. There were a few patrons sitting at tables, all of whom examined Amber when she walked in. She ignored them, chose a table in the corner, and sat, started reading through the menu.

The waitress came over, a woman in her forties who looked like she'd had a busy morning. Her nametag identified her as Brenda.

"Just passing through?" Brenda asked, which struck Amber as an odd thing to greet someone with. At the Firebird, Amber had always greeted customers with a smile. There was no smile on show here.

"Kinda," said Amber.

"Oh yeah?" Brenda said, but not in a conversational way.

Amber had a soft spot for people waiting tables. She knew what a crappy job it could be. That being said, Brenda's attitude was not going to be earning her any tips.

"I'm staying for a few days," Amber said. "At the motel."

"The Dowall Motel?"

"Is there another one?"

Brenda didn't bother to answer that. "Were you told about the festival?"

"Yeah. But we weren't told what kind of festival it is."

"It's a local one," said Brenda. "Townsfolk only."

Amber decided that she didn't like Brenda's dismissive tone. She didn't like being dismissed. Her skin itched. All she had to do was relax and she'd shift, and then she'd be taken seriously. Then she'd be respected.

"That was mentioned," she said quietly.

Brenda nodded, apparently satisfied. "Okay then, what can I get you?"

And, all of a sudden, Brenda was in full waitress mode and Amber was left with all that hostility and nowhere to put it. "Uh..."

Brenda looked at her, eyebrows raised, waiting.

Amber felt the hostility drain from her. "The Danny's Breakfast, please."

"Will do," said Brenda. "Eggs sunny side up or scrambled?"

"Scrambled."

"Coffee or juice?"

Had she really been about to jump up and rip the waitress's face off, just because of her tone of voice? She felt amazingly stupid right now.

"Juice," she said. "Thank you. Oh, and..." Amber held up her hands. "I had an accident."

"So I see."

She gave Brenda a weak smile. "Would it be possible to have my breakfast, like, cut into smaller pieces?"

"You want it all chopped up?"

"Yes, please. Well, besides the egg. Because that'll be scrambled."

"Okay," Brenda said dubiously. "Might cost you a little more, though."

Amber frowned. "To cut it up?"

"It's an unusual requirement."

"But it'll only take ten seconds."

The waitress shrugged. "We'll see if the cook is comfortable doing it. Will that be all?"

Amber hesitated. "Yes."

Brenda nodded, and moved away as an old man came in.

"Hey there, Brenda," he said.

Brenda smiled for the first time. "Good morning, Mr Tomlinson. How are you?"

"I'm doing good, thanks," said Tomlinson. "And you?"

"Doing fine," said Brenda. "Nice weather we're having."

"It is. It is nice weather."

"Is it the usual, Mr Tomlinson?"

"Sorry?"

"The usual?"

"Oh yes, the usual. Ham on rye with mustard."

"With the crusts cut off."

"Just go ahead and cut them crusts off, you betcha."

"You got it."

The moment Brenda turned away from him to deliver the order, her smile was gone, and Amber watched as Tomlinson's own smile slowly faded. He stood there, staring into space. Amber's mom had once said something about friends and fake smiles, but that was Amber's mom, so Amber banished the memory from her mind.

A woman came in behind Tomlinson and the smile suddenly reappeared as he turned.

"Morning, Jackie," he said.

"Morning, Brett," Jackie said. "Good weather for fishing."

"It is."

"Getting your usual?"

"Yes, I am. Ham on rye with mustard, with the crusts cut off. Hey, how's little Everett doing?"

"He's doing fine," said Jackie. "He had a bad cough that went on for a few days. I thought it might be a chest infection, but it cleared up on its own."

"I heard that," Tomlinson said, nodding. "I heard he had a cough."

Brenda arrived back, handed Tomlinson a brown paper bag. "Here you go, Mr Tomlinson. Your usual."

"Much obliged, Brenda," Tomlinson said, handing over the

60

exact change. He tipped his hat to them both. "You have a good day now, ladies."

They smiled at him and he walked out, and then they turned those smiles on each other.

"How you doing today, Jackie?" Brenda asked. "How's that boy of yours?"

"He's good," Jackie said. "He had a cough, but it cleared up. You all set for Book Club tonight?"

"I am," Brenda said. "What did you think of it?"

"A little racier than what I'm used to," Jackie said. "Did you like it?"

"I thought it was fine. Racy, like you said."

"Maybe too racy?"

"Probably too racy. What can I get for you?"

"Just a coffee, thanks. In one of those cardboard cups."

"To go?"

"To go, yes. With cream and sugar."

Brenda smiled as she busied herself at the coffee machine. "No fancy lattes or espressos for you."

"No, thank you!" Jackie said, and both women laughed.

Amber didn't know what the hell they had to laugh about, but she kept her mouth shut.

For the next few minutes, she sat there and watched the patrons and staff of Fast Danny's interact with one another. They were unfailingly polite and bizarrely cheerful, and they walked around with bright smiles at the ready – smiles that vanished the moment they thought no one was watching them. But Amber was.

When her breakfast was ready, Brenda returned to her table, set the plate down. Along with her scrambled eggs, she had bacon, sausages and hash browns – all fully intact.

"Um," said Amber, but Brenda was already walking away.

Amber looked back at her food, then tried to pick up her knife and fork. When she failed laughably at this, she did her best to catch Brenda's eye, but Brenda was doing an admirable job of ignoring her. Exasperated, Amber looked around, accidentally making eye contact with an old man sitting alone. He wasn't as old as Brett Tomlinson, but he was catching up fast. He gave her a little smile, glanced at her hands, and folded his newspaper. He stood and walked over.

"You need any help with that?" he asked.

Amber's first instinct was to thank him for his offer and decline − but that wouldn't get her food cut up.

"Thank you," she said. "Yes, please."

He nodded, hitched his pants and sat, then took her knife and fork and cut up the food.

"Thanks very much," said Amber.

"No problem," he said. "I'm Benjamin."

"Amber."

"What happened to your hands, Amber, if it's not too personal a question?"

"I, uh, I caught them in a car door."

He raised his eyebrows. "Say you did?"

She nodded. "Yep. Broke almost all my fingers."

"Caught both hands in a car door?" Benjamin asked. "What on earth were you doing?"

"Well, uh, I'm not actually sure. It was something stupid."

"I'd wager," said Benjamin, but in a nice way, and Amber laughed. "Was it that black car you came in? Oh, don't look so surprised. We're a small town in the middle of nowhere in

Alaska — newcomers set tongues a-wagging, and distinctive cars more so."

"I see," she said. "But no, it was another car. I'm just clumsy, I guess, and pretty useless until my fingers mend, so my uncle decided to take me on a road trip while I wait."

"Always wanted to go on a road trip," Benjamin said, a little wistfully, "but never had anywhere to go to. Where you headed?"

She shrugged. "It's not the destination that matters — it's the journey."

Benjamin chuckled. "That what your uncle says?"

"My uncle doesn't say an awful lot. What's it like here, by the way? I'm assuming it's a nicer town than the name suggests."

"You'd think," said Benjamin. He finished cutting the food and placed the knife and fork on the edge of the plate for Amber. "The people are pleasant, you can leave your door unlocked, and three hundred sixty-four days out of the year it's as peaceful as peaceful can be. But the days are long and getting longer, and, if you want my advice, I wouldn't stay here."

Amber sipped her juice. "No?"

He glanced around, making sure no one could overhear. "This is not a nice place to visit, Amber. I have no doubt you're going to be made to feel very unwelcome in the next day or so. You might even warrant a visit from the Police Chief himself."

"Seriously? We haven't done anything."

"That doesn't matter. Chief Novak is notorious for running transients out of town on the slightest of whims."

"We're not transients. We're staying at the motel."

"Novak'll still see you as a transient — as will the rest of the fine folk of Desolation Hill."

She leaned closer. "Benjamin, what's this festival they're all talking about?"

He smiled sadly, and shook his head. "I'm sorry. There are some things I'm not comfortable discussing in public. You have a good day now."

"Oh God, I'm sorry, I didn't mean to offend you."

He stood. "You didn't, young lady. Not at all. You have a good day now, you hear?"

He walked back to his table, picked up his newspaper, and left. Amber sat there until the rumblings in her belly became too loud to ignore, and she awkwardly picked up her fork and started spearing her food. She was halfway through her breakfast when her phone lit up by her elbow, and a message from Milo came through.

They're here.

8

THE ROAD THAT EVENTUALLY became Main Street was the road they had taken into town, but it veered and meandered on its way there, and it was quicker to just cut through the trees. The instant she moved out of sight, Amber let the change happen, and she shifted and gritted her teeth against the pain in her hands. A few seconds was all it took for the throbbing to fade, though, and then she was feeling a whole lot better about a whole bunch of things – the town, the cold... even the Hounds' arrival.

How tough could they really be, anyway?

She hurried, though. She didn't like the idea of Milo facing them alone. Together they'd have a chance. Together they might even win. The idea made Amber smile. The Shining Demon could send whoever he wanted after her. She liked the thought of sending them right back again.

Her human side tried whispering in her ear – something about overconfidence. Amber ignored it. She knew what she'd heard. She knew the Hounds were pretty much unstoppable. She knew, technically, that she and Milo would barely be able to stand up to one of them, let alone five. These things didn't matter. What mattered was how she was feeling right now, like she could take on an army of Astaroth's lackeys and tear them all apart.

As she ran, she started to hear motorcycles. No shouts, though. No gunshots. No sounds of fighting. She left the trees, stepped on to the overgrown grass that lined the road, where she could see exactly where she was going and there was no danger of her passing the town boundary. She glimpsed the Charger, parked in among a clump of bushes, and looked around for Milo.

Amber got low and crept forward. She could see the Desolation Hill sign now, and the track that ran off to her left. A biker came roaring up that track and she went instantly cold and all her assurances abandoned her. He slowed to a stop and was joined a moment later by another one. The first Hound had a beard and the second one didn't. The first was in denim and the second in leather. They both wore sunglasses. The first one's bike was gleaming chrome. The other one's was black. Neither of them spoke.

She couldn't take them on. Not the Hounds. With or without Milo. They were the Hounds of Hell and they were unstoppable and they were pitiless.

She heard another engine coming from behind and flattened herself in the grass as a car approached. It passed her, and the bikers parted so it could get by. She watched the driver of the car peer at the Hounds. The Hounds never even glanced at him.

"Curious bastards," Milo said from beside her, and she nearly screamed.

He was still in human mode. Amber didn't know how he could stand the itching.

"Were you there the whole time?" she whispered.

He nodded. "It's called hiding. You should try it."

"I hid just then, didn't I?"

"That was lucky. Red skin isn't the best camouflage in grass."

"Whatever." She looked back to the Hounds. "What the hell are they doing?"

"Not much," said Milo. "Every now and then, they... here, look."

Amber looked. One of the Hounds got off his bike and walked forward a few steps until he was standing right beside the sign. He sniffed the air.

"Can he smell us?" Amber whispered.

Milo didn't answer for a moment. Then he said, "I don't think they can get in."

Amber frowned. "Get in where?"

"Here."

Her frown deepened. "What do you...? Wait – you mean they can't get into the town? Why not? There's nothing..." She stopped, watching the Hound. "Uh, Milo, are we being chased by mimes?"

The Hound had put his hand out, but it seemed to meet resistance in mid-air, like there was a sheet of glass directly in front of him.

"That's the town line," Milo said softly. "Whatever's in here, whatever made us shift, is keeping them out. Looks like it's also screwed up their radar. This close, they should have already zeroed in on your position, but they're not even looking this way."

"Are you sure?" Amber asked. "How can you be sure?"

"Good point," Milo said, and he shifted into his demon-self and stood up.

"What the hell are you *doing?*" She tried grabbing his hand to pull him back down, but he was already stepping out on to the road.

The Hounds observed him as he approached. Amber stayed where she was.

To a chorus of revving bikes, Milo walked right up to the Hound and stood before him. When the Hound didn't do anything, Milo hit him. The punch whipped the Hound's head back, and it was enough to provoke him into making a move. But when his hands tried to close around Milo's throat, they bounced off whatever invisible barrier separated them.

Amber stood up. She could see the other Hounds now. Dressed in denim or leather, bearded or not, they all wore sunglasses and all rode different kinds of bikes. She saw a Harley, and that was the only one she recognised. None of them had any expression on their face. Aside from the sunglasses, that was the one thing they all shared.

The others turned off their bikes, and the sudden silence rushed in to fill the vacuum. They got off and approached, but remained on their side of the town line. Amber felt their eyes on her as she joined Milo. He reverted to normal.

"This is interesting," she said, unease running down her spine. "You think it runs around the whole town?"

"We'd better hope so," said Milo.

Amber stood up a little straighter and addressed the Hounds. "My name is Amber Lamont. You know that already, right? The Shining Demon sent you after me because, in exchange for his help, I promised to bring him a man named Gregory Buxton. When I took his help but didn't bring him Buxton, he called you. But Gregory Buxton is a good man – more or less. He's done some bad things, some very bad things, but he's a good man now, and I couldn't do it, I just couldn't deliver him to the Shining Demon. You don't have to deliver *me*, either. I haven't done anything to hurt you, and you can't get in here, anyway, so you could get on your bikes and ride away and tell the Shining Demon you couldn't find me. I'm sixteen years old – I don't deserve any of what's happening to me."

The Hounds didn't move. The Hounds didn't answer.

"Nothing?" Amber said after a moment. "You're not going to respond? You've got nothing to say? You've been chasing us since New York and you have absolutely nothing to say to me now that we're face to face?"

The Hounds looked at her.

"Come on," Milo said softly, his hand on her shoulder. He turned Amber round and they started walking to the Charger. "There's nothing more you can do. You put your case forward, now it's up to them. You did it calmly and you didn't antagonise anyone. I'm actually quite impressed with how you handled that."

"Yeah," Amber said. Then she swung round, walked back to the Hounds. "You know what?" she said. "You're a bunch of jerks. Standing there all silent. You think you're intimidating? You don't intimidate me. Everyone is *sooooo* scared of you – but we stayed ahead of you without a problem. The only reason you're this close to us is because we stopped and waited for you to catch up. And you *still* can't get me. So screw you, dickbrains. Go have sex with your motorcycles, and when you're finished with that go tell your boss that he can kiss my fine red ass."

She tried to give them the finger, but ended up waving her

bandaged hand at them instead. Hissing, she spun on her heel and marched back to Milo.

"Yep," Milo muttered. "Handled that very well."

She reverted, painfully, and they drove back into town without doing a whole lot of speaking. They parked in the motel lot beside a police cruiser and were heading inside when a uniformed man walked out, met them halfway.

"Mr Sebastian," he said. "Miss Lamont, good afternoon. Welcome to Desolation Hill."

He was in his forties, with dark hair and heavy-lidded eyes. He had a long, lined face, not entirely unattractive. His badge was gleaming on his black uniform beneath his open jacket, and his gun was holstered.

"Thank you," said Milo.

"My name is Trevor Novak. I'm the Chief of Police here."

"It's a very nice town," said Amber.

"It can be," said Novak. "Although it has a habit of attracting the wrong kind of visitor."

"Is that so?" said Milo.

"Regrettably. Especially at this time of year." Novak looked at them both before continuing. "You have been told, I understand, about our festival. Naturally, you're curious. I appreciate curiosity – it's what has me here talking to you, after all. And, while I'm not about to satisfy that curiosity, hopefully I can explain our attitude to you. We're a quiet town, or at least we want to be, and we value our traditions. This festival just happens to be our most cherished, most valued tradition."

"What does it celebrate?" Milo asked.

"Our history," said Novak. "Our culture. Our heritage. And our success. Many other towns, a lot like ours, dried up and were blown away after the gold rush. But Desolation Hill remained standing. Even more towns dried up and were blown away during the various recessions and depressions... but Desolation Hill has stayed strong. I put this down to the people. We have the single lowest crime rate, per capita, in America."

Milo nodded. "Certainly something to be proud of."

"It is, Mr Sebastian, yes. And I *am* proud."

"We're not planning on committing any crimes, if that's what you're worried about," Amber said, offering up a smile.

"I'm not suggesting you were," said Novak, not offering one in return. "I only wish to impress upon you the need to obey our rules. The festival is for townsfolk only. When you check out of the Dowall Motel on Wednesday morning, you will receive a police escort to the edge of town."

"Uh..."

"It's nothing personal," Novak said. "I trust you won't be offended."

"Not offended," said Milo. "But a police escort does seem a little extreme."

"We take our rules very seriously. I'm sure you have questions, I'm sure you have many, but please understand that to ask these questions of the townsfolk could lead to a certain degree of irritation. We have traditions we would prefer to keep private, and questions we would prefer not to answer. I'm sure you and your... niece appreciate this desire."

Milo took a moment. "Sure," he said.

"I can, of course, see the family resemblance immediately," said Novak. "Some of my officers, I'm afraid to say, are not so attentive to detail. They may have questions for you."

"I'm sure there's no need to bother them," Milo said.

Novak nodded. "That's what I was thinking. We like to mind our own business here. I trust you will do the same."

"Naturally," said Milo.

"Of course," said Amber.

Novak adjusted his gun belt, and nodded to them. "Very nice to meet you, and welcome to Desolation Hill."

"Thanks," said Milo.

Novak walked to his car, went to get in, but paused. "One of my officers alerted me to some bikers on the edge of town," he said. "They have anything to do with you?"

"No, sir."

"Well, okay then. Have a nice day." He nodded again, got in his car, and they watched him drive away.

"So what do you think of the place?" Milo asked.

"I haven't decided," said Amber. "People here are weird. They're downright rude to me and they're overly polite with each other. That Novak guy is a little creepy, and I don't have a clue what this festival is about, but already it's annoying the crap out of me. Plus, every second that goes by I just want to shift. It's actually uncomfortable to stay normal."

"It's worth it, though," said Milo.

"Yeah," she said, a little grudgingly. "I really like this whole barrier thing they've got going on. What are we going to do on Wednesday? We can't leave town — the Hounds will be on us the moment we try."

"I thought they didn't intimidate you."

"Are you nuts? Of course they do. I just said that because they were freaking me out."

"We're not leaving," said Milo. "We can't be escorted out, either — that'd be like delivering ourselves straight to them.

We'll check out early, find an out-of-the-way place to park that's still within the town limits, and camp out till Saturday. We keep our heads down, ignore anything to do with their festival, and we'll be fine."

"And in the meantime," said Amber, "we find out who put up that barrier. It's got to be someone like us, right? Someone hiding from a demon?"

"Maybe."

"If we can talk to whoever's behind it, maybe we can make a barrier of our own. You'd be able to do something like that, wouldn't you?"

Milo frowned. "Me? I know nothing about this kind of thing."

"Well, yeah, but you know the basics."

"What basics, Amber? I know the lore. I know some of the traditions. I don't know how to do anything. Buxton knows, not me, and he's too busy setting up a new life for himself to come up here and give us advice."

"Well... maybe we won't need him. Maybe whoever put up the barrier will show us what we have to do."

"I guess it's possible."

She gave him a disapproving frown. "You don't sound convinced."

"I hate to break it to you, Amber, but neither do you."

9

Austin Cooke ran.

He ran from his house on Brookfield Road all the way past the school, past the corner store that was always closed on Sundays, and up towards the fire station, where they kept the single engine that had never, in Austin's memory, been used for any fire-based emergencies. The volunteer fire fighters brought it out every once in a while and parked it at the top of Beacon Way, the only pedestrian street in Desolation Hill, and they held pancake breakfasts for fund-raising and such, but they'd never had to put out any actual fires – at least not to Austin's knowledge.

Once the picture of the smiling Dalmatian on the fire-station door came into view, Austin veered left, taking the narrow alley behind the church. His feet splashed in puddles. His sneakers, brand new for his twelfth birthday, got wet and dirty and he didn't care.

With his breath coming in huge, whooping gulps and a stitch in his side sliding in like a serrated knife, Austin burst from the alley on to the sidewalk on Main Street and turned right, dodging an old lady and sprinting for the square. A beat-up old van trundled by. Up ahead he could hear laughter. A lot of laughter.

Three of them – Cole Blancard, Marco Mabb and Jamie Hillock. Mabb was the biggest and Hillock had the nastiest laugh, but Cole Blancard was the worst. Cole dealt out his punishments with a seriousness that set him apart from the others. Where their faces would twist with sadistic amusement, his would go strangely blank, like he was an impartial observer to whatever degrading activity he was spearheading. His eyes frightened Austin most of all, though. They were dull eyes. Intelligent, in their way, but dull. Cole had a shark's eyes.

Austin waited for a car to pass, then ran across the street, on to the square. They heard him coming, and turned. Hillock laughed and punched Mabb in the arm and Mabb laughed and returned the favour. Cole didn't laugh. He only smiled, his tongue caught between his teeth. He had a large handful of paper slips.

Austin staggered to a halt. He didn't dare get any closer. He'd run all this way to stop them, even though he knew there was nothing he could do once he got here.

The ballot box was old and wooden. It had a slot an inch wide. Cole Blancard turned away from Austin and stuffed all those paper slips through that slot, and Austin felt a new and unfamiliar terror rising within him. Panic scratched at his thoughts with sharp fingers and squeezed his heart with cold hands. Mabb and Hillock took fistfuls of paper slips from their pockets, gave them over, and Cole jammed them in, too.

A few slips fell and the breeze played with them, brought them all the way to the scaffolding outside the Municipal Building. The three older boys didn't seem to mind. When they were done, they walked towards Austin, forcing him to move out of their way. Mabb and Hillock sniggered as they passed, but Cole stopped so close that Austin could see every detail of the purple birthmark that stretched from Cole's collar to his jaw.

"Counting, counting, one, two, three," Cole said, and rammed his shoulder into Austin's.

Austin stood there while they walked off, their laughter turning the afternoon ugly. One of those slips scuttled across the ground and Austin stepped on it, pinned it in place.

He reached down, picked it up, turned it over and read his own name.

10

THE VAN WAS OLD and rattled and rolled, coughed and spluttered like it was about to give up and lie down and play dead, but of course it defied expectations, like it always did, and it got them to Desolation Hill with its oil-leaking mechanical heart still beating. That was close to a 4,000-mile journey. Kelly had to admit she was impressed. She thought they'd have to abandon the charming heap of junk somewhere around Wyoming, and pool what little money they had to buy something equally cheap but far less charming to take them the rest of the way.

"I think you owe someone an apology," Warrick said smugly.

Kelly sighed. "Sorry, van," she said. "Next time I'll have more faith in your awesome ability to keep going. There were times, it is true, when I doubted this ability. Uphill, especially. Even, to be honest, sometimes downhill. You have proven me wrong."

"Now swear everlasting allegiance."

"I'm not doing that."

"Ronnie," Warrick called, "she won't swear everlasting allegiance to the van."

"Kelly," said Ronnie from behind the wheel, "you promised."

"I promised when I didn't think the van would make it,"

said Kelly. "Promises don't count when you don't think you'll ever have to keep them."

"I'm not sure that's technically correct," said Linda, still curled up in her sleeping bag.

"Hush, you," said Kelly. "You're still asleep."

"Big Brain agrees with me," said Warrick. "You tell her, Linda!"

"Two," Kelly commanded, "sit on Linda's head, there's a good boy."

Two just gazed at her, his tongue hanging out, and wagged his tail happily.

"Swear allegiance to the almighty van," said Warrick.

"Not gonna happen."

"Then swear allegiance to this troll," he said, pulling an orange-haired little troll doll from his pocket and thrusting it towards her. "Look, he's got the same colour hair as you."

She frowned. "My hair is red. That's orange."

"It's all the same."

"It's really not."

"Swear. Allegiance. To our Troll Overlord."

"Warrick, I swear to God, stop waving that thing in my face."

He kept doing it and she sighed again, and crawled over the seat in front to sit beside Ronnie. "Pretty town," she said.

Ronnie opened his mouth to reply, but hesitated.

She grinned. "You were going to say it, weren't you?"

"No, I wasn't."

"You so were," came Linda's muffled voice. Then, "Two, get off me."

Kelly grinned wider. "You were going to say appearances can be deceiving, weren't you?"

"Nope," said Ronnie, shaking his head. "I was going to say something completely different. I was going to say, 'Yes, Kelly, it does look like a nice town.'"

"But...?"

"Nothing. No buts. That was the end of that sentence."

"Warrick," said Kelly, "what do you think? Do you think Ronnie is fibbing?"

"I'm not talking to you because you have refused to swear allegiance to either my van or my troll doll," said Warrick, "but, on a totally separate note, I think our Fearless Leader is totally telling fibs and he was, in fact, about to utter those immortal words."

"You're all delusional," said Ronnie. "Now someone please tell me where I'm supposed to go in the whitest town I've ever been to. Seriously, there is such a thing as being *too* Caucasian."

"Take this left coming up," Linda said.

"She's a witch!" cried Warrick.

"It's GPS."

"Not a witch, then," Warrick said. "False alarm, everybody. Linda is not a witch, she just has an internet connection. You know who *was* a witch, though?"

"Stefanianna North was not a witch," Kelly said.

"You didn't see her!" Warrick responded. "You don't know!"

"Neither do you. You were unconscious the whole time."

Warrick sniffed. "It wasn't my fault I was drugged."

"You weren't drugged," said Ronnie, "you were high. And that *was* your fault because it was your own weed you were smoking."

"Aha," said Warrick, leaning forward, "but why was I smoking it?"

"To get high."

"No," Warrick said triumphantly. "Well, yes, but also because of the socio-economic turmoil this world has been going through since before I was even born. My mother had anxiety issues when I was still in the *womb*, man. That affects a dude, forces him to seek out alternative methods of coping later in life."

"So that's what you were doing?" Kelly asked. "You were coping?"

"I was trying to," Warrick said. "And that's when Stefanianna came to kill me. I don't remember much—"

"Because you were high."

"—but I do remember her saying something like, 'First I'll kill you, then I'll kill your friends.' And I was all, like, hey, don't you touch my friends, because I'm very protective of you guys, you know?"

Kelly nodded. "We bask in your protection."

"But then Two woke up," said Warrick, "and, as we all know, witches are terrified of dogs, especially pit bulls."

"That's not a thing," said Linda.

"Well, maybe not particularly pit bulls, but we all know that witches are terrified of dogs, right?"

"That's not a thing, either," said Linda.

Warrick frowned. "So what are witches terrified of?"

"Fire," said Ronnie.

"But then why did she run away? The moment she saw Two she screamed and ran."

"That's because Stefanianna is terrified of dogs," Kelly said.

"Yes!" said Warrick. "Exactly! See?"

"But that doesn't mean she's a witch."

"Why doesn't it?"

"Because why would it?"

Warrick frowned again. "I don't... I don't see what you're saying here."

"Take a right, Ronnie," Linda said. "Should be a hill up ahead."

Ronnie took the right. "I see it. That where we're going?"

"Yep." Linda sat up. Her dark hair was a mess.

"How was your nap?" Kelly asked.

"Terrible," Linda answered. "I feel like a hamster in a ball that's been kicked down a hill for three hours. And Two kept farting."

Two whined in protest.

"That wasn't Two," Warrick said meekly.

"Oh, you're so gross," Linda said, crawling forward. She left the cushioned rear of the van and joined Warrick on the long seat behind Kelly.

They got to the top of the hill and Kelly read the sign.

"The Dowall Motel," she said, and frowned up at the building. "You know, for a pretty town, this is a creepy motel."

"They better allow pets," Warrick said.

"I don't care," said Linda. "All I want is a real bed tonight. I'm sick of sleeping in the van."

"Swear allegiance," Warrick whispered.

They parked, and got out, and Kelly immediately reached back in to grab her jacket. Two hopped out as well, started to hump a small tree, but Warrick shook his head.

"Sorry, buddy, you're gonna have to stay in the van until we find out if they allow pets."

"He doesn't understand you, Warrick," said Linda, rubbing her arms against the cold.

"Well, no, but he understands basic English, though."

Linda looked at the dog. "Two. Stop having sex with the tree. Sit. Sit. Two, sit." She raised her eyes to Warrick. "He's not sitting."

"You know he doesn't like to be told what to do. It's conversational English he responds to, not orders. We're not living in Nazi Germany, Linda, okay? We have something here in America that I like to call freedom. Freedom to choose, freedom to worship, freedom to congregate in groups of like-minded individuals, freedom of the press and free speech and freedom to do other stuff... Land of the free, home of the brave. That's where we live, that's how we live, and that's why Two won't sit when you order him to sit."

"Fine," said Linda. "Then you tell him to do something."

"I'm not gonna tell," said Warrick. "I'm gonna ask." He cleared his throat, and looked down at Two. "Hey, buddy," he said, "mind leaving the tree alone and waiting in the van for a minute?"

Two barked, and jumped into the van.

Linda picked up her bag and slung it over her shoulder. "Coincidence."

"Two's a smart puppy dog."

"Of course he jumped into the van. It's freezing out here."

"Come on, Linda," Warrick said, shutting the van door. "Swear allegiance to the doggy."

Kelly walked on ahead, into the motel, where the first thing that registered was a moose head on the wall behind the front desk.

The woman at the desk looked up. She was tall, skinny, with a mole beneath her right eye and a blouse buttoned all the way up to her throat. Dear God, she was wearing a brooch.

Kelly smiled. "Hi."

The woman, whose nametag identified her as Belinda, frowned back at her. The others walked in, and Belinda's eyes widened and she stepped back.

"You," she said in a surprisingly husky voice. "We do not allow your kind in here."

Ronnie and Linda froze.

"Me?" said Ronnie, a black man.

"Or me?" said Linda, a Chinese girl.

"Him," said Belinda, pointing a trembling finger at Warrick.

"Me?" Warrick said. "What'd I do?"

"You're a... you're a *beatnik*," Belinda said, the word exploding out of her mouth like a chunk of meat after a Heimlich.

"I am not!" said Warrick.

"We do not allow beatniks in this motel!"

"I'm not a beatnik! Stop calling me a beatnik!"

"Excuse me," Kelly said, still smiling as she neared the desk, "but what seems to be the issue with beatniks?"

"My mother never approved," Belinda said, practically livid with disgust. "She said never shall a beatnik sleep under this roof, and I say a beatnik never shall!"

Kelly nodded. "That's very understandable. Beatniks are terrible people. Although Warrick isn't actually a beatnik."

"My mother said they will come in various guises."

"Uh-huh. Yes, but the thing is Warrick isn't one of them."

"I hate jazz music," said Warrick.

"He does," said Kelly. "He hates jazz music."

"He's got a beatnik beard, though," said Belinda.

Warrick frowned. "My soul patch? I just don't like shaving under my lip. My skin is sensitive, man."

"I assure you," Ronnie said, giving Belinda a smile, "my friend isn't a beatnik. He just shaves like one. He listens to regular music and I don't think I've ever heard him talk about bettering his inner self."

"I leave my inner self alone and it leaves me alone," said Warrick. "We're happier that way."

Belinda hesitated.

"The moment he starts wearing berets and playing the bongos," Kelly said, "we'll kick him out ourselves."

"Very well," Belinda said dubiously. "In which case, welcome to the Dowall Motel. This is a family business. How may I help you?"

"We don't have any reservations," said Ronnie, "but we were wondering if you had any rooms available? Two twin rooms, ideally. We don't mind bunking up."

"How long will you be staying?"

"We're not sure," said Ronnie. "A week, maybe?"

Belinda shook her head. "Sorry, no. Out of the question."

"I'm, uh, not sure I understand..."

"There is a town festival," Belinda said, "for townsfolk only. You can stay until Wednesday morning, but will then have to leave."

"We can do that," said Linda. "What does the festival celebrate?"

"The town."

Linda smiled and nodded. "And it is surely a town worth celebrating."

"A question, if you please," said Warrick, squeezing between them. Belinda recoiled slightly. "This motel. Is it pet friendly?"

"I'm sorry?"

"Is it friendly to pets? For instance, my dog. Is it friendly to my dog?"

Belinda looked horrified. "Are you asking if your dog is allowed inside the hotel?"

"That is what I'm asking, yes."

"No."

"Is that a 'No, my dog is allowed,' or a 'No, my dog isn't allowed'?"

"No pets are allowed on the premises," said Belinda. "My brother is extremely allergic. Having an animal under this roof could kill him."

"What if I told you he was house-trained?"

"Absolutely not."

"What if I told you he would not try to have sex with any potted plants you may possess, or any of your favourite stuffed animals? Still no? Then I will be forced to sleep with him in our van. Is that what you want? Me sleeping in a van? This isn't California, let me remind you. This is Alaska. It gets cold here. You're really okay with me spending the night in a van, freezing to death while my oversexed dog humps my head?"

"Animals are not allowed."

"What if we sneak him in without you noticing?"

"We're not going to do that," Ronnie said quickly.

Warrick nodded, and did the air quotes thing. "Yeah, we're 'not'."

"We're actually not," said Linda. "If Warrick won't go anywhere without that dog, he can sleep in the van and take the consequences. The rest of us would like beds, please – until Wednesday."

"When you will depart," said Belinda.

"When we will depart," echoed Linda.

They were shown to their rooms and Kelly dumped her bag on her bed and went to the bathroom while Linda showered quickly. Then they switched, and got changed, and met the guys outside.

They drove through town, familiarising themselves with the layout before focusing on the quieter streets. They followed the few small scrawls of graffiti like it was a trail of breadcrumbs, losing it sometimes and having to double back to pick up the trail again. It took them the rest of the afternoon, but finally the trail led them all the way to a park, at the bottom of the hill that led to the motel.

"Well, that was a waste of time," said Kelly.

They got out, went walking. Kelly zipped up her jacket while Two ran in excited circles. On the east side of the park there was a small building that housed the public restrooms. Facing the park, it was a pristine example of a public utility that was kept up to snuff. But the interesting stuff was all across the back in layers of names and promises and oaths and declarations.

Kelly was a quick study, but even so her ability to decipher the messages hidden in graffiti could only take her so far. Ronnie was better at it, and Linda was better still, but Warrick was the master. He was the one who'd told them all about it, after all. Graffiti was the cave painting of the modern world, he'd told Kelly after she'd taken her first trip in the van.

That had been her recruitment, she supposed. Once she was part of the group, one of the gang, he felt comfortable telling her his secrets. A town's history, its true history, he said, could be found in the scrawls and crude pictures hidden from the prying eyes of the disapproving authorities, those to whom whitewashing a wall was the same as whitewashing a mind. They could paint over the truth as many times as they wanted, but the truth could always be scrawled anew.

Kelly found declarations of love and accusations of infidelity, she found boasts of conquests, of prowess and of physical exploits, and she found pictures of genitalia that were suspect in their accuracy.

"Look at this," said Linda, pointing to a drawing of a thin man with a wide, smiling mouth, too big for his head. There was an artistry to it, some genuine talent, but there was something else – something about that smile that unnerved Kelly. Linda took a picture of it with her phone.

"Got something else," Ronnie said. "A name – Donnie Welker. Says here the Narrow Man got him in 2003."

Linda hurried over, documenting the message.

They found five more references to the Narrow Man, and then Warrick said, "Found it."

They crowded round him. On the wall, almost at the corner and faded, yet isolated from the other scrawls, almost as if nobody dared paint over it, was a short rhyme.

> The Narrow Man, the Narrow Man,
> He'll sniff you out, you know he can.
> Counting, counting, one, two, three,
> Your name he'll call, his face you'll see.
> Tap at your window, tap at your door,
> You can hide no longer, run no more.
> The Narrow Man, the Narrow Man,
> He'll drag you to hell, fast as he can.

"He's here, all right," said Ronnie.

"Look at this," said Kelly, waving to a group of kids hanging out in the trees behind them. "We have an audience."

Two bounded over. A few of the kids backed away, but most of them made a fuss over the dumb dog as he licked their hands and rolled on to his back so they'd scratch his belly.

Kelly and the others walked over.

"Hi there," she said. The kids regarded her warily. "Could you do us a favour? Me and my friends were wondering what that Narrow Man thing is all about. We've heard of him, we're kind of geeks for this sort of crap, but we've never seen anything so concentrated as this."

Some of the kids, the ones who were wary of the dog, glanced at each other and walked away.

One of the other kids who stayed gave a shrug. "So what's the favour?"

"Actually, less of a favour, more of a... job, really." Kelly took out a crumpled ten-dollar bill. "What can you tell us about him?"

"He's a story," said the kid.

"What kind of story?" Ronnie asked.

"Creepy bedtime story."

"He's the boogeyman," said a girl.

"Yeah, that's it," the boy said. "The boogeyman. Comes out and snatches away naughty boys and girls."

"What about the rhyme?" asked Linda.

"Just something we used to say. Something fun."

Warrick took a treat from his pocket, tossed it to Two. "He ever snatch away anyone you know?"

"Are you stupid or something?" the boy asked. "He's a story. He's not real."

Warrick jerked his thumb over his shoulder. "I think whoever drew that picture thought he was real."

"My cousin drew that," said a smaller kid at the back, "and you don't know what you're talking about. It's a nursery rhyme. Just something kids used to say."

"What about the *counting, counting, one, two, three* thing?" Ronnie asked. "What's that mean?"

The kids looked at each other uneasily, until Ronnie produced another ten.

The first kid tracked it like a heat-seeker. "Everyone in town votes," he said. "If you misbehave, parents and teachers and whatever will write your name on a piece of paper and put it into the box in the square. They do it to scare the younger kids into doing what they're told."

Kelly frowned. "And what are they voting for?"

Not to be outdone, the girl spoke up. "The Narrow Man comes for whoever gets the most votes. Or he's supposed to, anyway. But everyone knows the votes are never counted."

"That's pretty messed up," said Warrick.

"It's a crock of shit," the girl said, shrugging. "Like everything else people do here."

"What's the festival that's happening on Wednesday?" Kelly asked.

The kids clammed up. Warrick sighed, and gave each of them a ten.

"We don't talk about it," said the first kid.

"So what is it?"

"We don't talk about it."

"But... dude, I gave you another ten."

"So?"

They turned to go.

"Wait," said Ronnie. "What's your cousin's name, the one who drew the picture? Maybe we can talk to him."

"Doubt it," said the small kid, "but whatever. Give me a twenty, stop your dog from humping my leg, and I'll tell you."

11

AMBER SPENT MONDAY MORNING in Fast Danny's. Brenda served her breakfast, then juice, then coffee, and then two hot chocolates, and Amber sat at her corner table with her earphones plugged into the iPad, using the cafe's Wi-Fi to watch all of the In The Dark Places episodes she'd missed while on the run.

She'd hesitated before pressing play on the first one. Her life in the last five weeks had become stranger and much more fantastical than anything she'd ever seen on a TV screen. She'd witnessed true horror. She'd been subjected to true violence. She herself had killed. She herself had eaten human flesh. She had interacted with beings who existed beyond death, who traded in souls and powers beyond imagining, and she was pretty sure she was being stalked by a vampire. What effect could a dumb TV show have on her now?

As it turned out, an astonishing one.

Watching Dark Places was like going home – but instead of the home she'd always known, that cold place of silence and secrets, it was her other home, the home she had made for herself inside the world of the stories she loved. She knew everything about the actors, knew their birth dates and their pets' names, but as each episode began the actors vanished and their characters appeared, and Amber forgot about the horrors biting at her heels and lost herself in the stories unfolding before her. She interacted with Brenda when she had to, ignored the curious looks of the people who frequented the cafe, and sipped her hot chocolate. The only part of her, the only part, that she did not relax was the part that was keeping her body from shifting into its demon form. That remained vigilant.

When she'd finished watching the final episode of the season – it had ended on a cliffhanger, of course it had ended on a cliffhanger – she took out the earbuds and sat back, absorbing the drama. The cafe was almost full by now, with people eyeing her table covetously.

Brenda saw that she had emerged from the screen, and came over. "Can I get you the cheque?"

Amber thought for a moment. "No, thanks," she said. "But I'll take a look at your lunch menu."

Brenda made a big deal out of sighing, and headed off to fetch a menu. Amber grinned to herself.

She checked her phone, saw no message from Milo, and logged on to the Dark Places forum. Her bandaged hands made typing difficult, but not impossible.

The Dark Princess said...
I have returned...

RetroGamer! said...
Hi Proncess
*princess

Sith0Dude said...
hey

RetroGamer! said...
Damn typos.

Elven Queen said...
Princess!! We missed u!
Thoughts on finale?

Sith0Dude said...
Hey Elven Queen

The Dark Princess said...
Just saw it. WOW.
Though kinda knew they wouldn't let Gideon die off
so easily.

Elven Queen said...
Yeah, saw that twist coming from 3 episodes ago!

Sith0Dude said...
why is everyone ignoring me?

RetroGamer! said...
Was talking to BAC 10 minutes ago

Balthazar's-Arm-Candy said...
There's my girl!

The Dark Princess said...
BAC!
The world is a brighter place once more!

Balthazar's-Arm-Candy said...
How've u been doing? Things been sorted since last time we chatted? *fingers crossed*

The Dark Princess said...
Not really, but I'm bravely fighting my way through it!

Sith0Dude said...
ur all ignoring me

Balthazar's-Arm-Candy said...
Made up your mind about the con yet? Full cast PLUS Annalith's gonna be there.
Wish I could go.

Elven Queen said...
Not ignoring you, Sith0Dude.

The Dark Princess said...
Haven't really been thinking about it, but don't think it'll be possible. Things are still screwy

RetroGamer! said...
Everything ok, Princess?

The Dark Princess said...
I'm fine. Life's just weird at the moment and not looking like it'll ever go back to normal.

Elven Queen said...
Normal is boring.

Balthazar's-Arm-Candy said...
You back in Florida yet?

The Dark Princess said...
Furthest thing from it. Alaska! LOL

Sith0Dude said...
the north pole?

The Dark Princess said...
Alaska isn't the north pole.
Is it?

RetroGamer! said...
No.

Balthazar's-Arm-Candy said...
Penguins live in the south pole, polar bears live in the north pole. That's the rule.
Look out your window, Princess. What do u see?

The Dark Princess said...
Cars and people. No polar bears or penguins.

Sith0Dude said...
if you can't see penguins u must be on north pole. penguins would be everywhere on south cuz of no natural predators.

The Dark Princess said...
I don't think that's right, Sith0Dude.

Sith0Dude said...
No LAND based predators I meant. But they are prey to a range of top predators in the oceans.
Some penguins can swim up to 22 mph.
They get rid of saltwater they've swallowed by sneezing.

Elven Queen said...
Are you googling penguin facts, Sith0Dude?

Sith0Dude said...
no. just like penguins

Balthazar's-Arm-Candy said...
How's Wi-Fi in Alaska, Princess?

The Dark Princess said...
Better than expected! In a cafe right now and just streamed 4 eps without a problem. Say 1 thing for those polar bears, they know their Wi-Fi!

Sith0Dude said...

Most people think penguins mate for life, but Emperor Penguins usually take a mate for one year at a time

Elven Queen said...

Shut up about penguins Sith0Dude.

The Dark Princess said...

Gotta go guys. RL has just walked in.

Balthazar's-Arm-Candy said...

When will u be on next?

The Dark Princess said...

Hard to say, got a lot going on. Laters!

Milo sat at the table and Amber logged off the messageboard.

"The Hounds still where they're supposed to be?" she asked.

"They are. I followed one of them when he rode around the outskirts. Every so often, he'd test the barrier. Looks like it surrounds the whole town. We would appear to be safe, but I'm heading back out this afternoon, just to make sure. What have you been doing?"

Amber couldn't help it. She smiled. "Just chatting with my friends."

"And how are they?"

"Good. Still reeling from the final episode of *Dark Places*. It was brilliant. I'd tell you about it, but I don't want to spoil anything."

"I'm never going to watch that show," Milo said, beckoning Brenda over.

"You should," said Amber. "It's better than those westerns you like."

Milo grunted, then gave one of his smiles to Brenda that the waitress clearly appreciated. "Hey there," he said. "Could I have a coffee, if it's not too much trouble? Black, no sugar."

"Regular old coffee," said Brenda, "you got it. Anything else?"

"Nothing I can think of right now, thank you."

Brenda nodded, practically curtsied, and hurried away.

"Doesn't that get annoying?" Amber asked.

"Doesn't what get annoying?" Milo said.

"That," said Amber. "Women falling over themselves whenever you smile at them."

"Excuse me?"

"Oh, come on. You do that smiley thing and they go weak at the knees every time."

"That 'smiley thing' is me smiling."

"Yeah, but it's not, though, is it? You give them the extra big grin to get them blushing."

"Hate to disappoint you, Amber, but my smile is the same size regardless of who I'm talking to."

"So you're telling me that if Brenda was a dude, you'd give him the same smile?"

"Why wouldn't I?"

"Because you're flirting. Just admit it."

"I admit no such thing because I'm not flirting. You'll know when I'm flirting with someone because it'll be really obvious and really bad."

"You flirted with that lady back in Cascade Falls."

"Veronica."

"And did you or did you not get laid because of it?"

"What I did or did not do is none of your business, but that wasn't flirting. That was talking. I'm okay at talking, when I'm in a talkative mood, and sometimes talking leads to other things."

"Some people would call that flirting."

"I call it being friendly."

The woman at the next table got up to leave, but dropped her purse. Milo picked it up, handed it back to her. She smiled and he winked and she giggled.

As she walked away, Amber stared at Milo. "You winked at her."

Milo frowned. "What? No, I didn't."

"You so did! You actually winked at her!"

"Did I?"

"I can't believe you just did that."

"Yeah, whatever," Milo said. "What about you?"

"What *about* me?"

"What's your flirting technique like?"

"I don't have one," she said.

"Sure you do."

Amber shook her head. "It is literally non-existent, and I use literally both in the literal and figurative senses."

"You just need practice," Milo said. "Find someone you'd like to flirt with and strike up a conversation."

"Like who?" she said, laughing.

"I don't know," Milo answered, looking around. He nodded to a young guy across the cafe. "How about him?"

Amber smiled. "I don't think so."

"Coward."

"He's just not my type."

"What is your type?"

She shrugged. "Not him."

Brenda came over with Milo's coffee.

"Thanks very much," he said. Brenda smiled and blushed and hurried to another table before she melted.

Milo took a sip, and didn't meet Amber's gaze.

"Shut up," he said.

12

WHAT HE HAD, and let there be no mistaking this, was a bona-fide mystery on his hands.

A *murder* mystery, to be exact. How many of those fell into the lap of someone like him every day? A murder mystery with police collusion. He knew what they called that, of course. They called it *conspiracy*.

Were all the cops in on it? He had no way of knowing. Novak and Woodbury, certainly, and maybe that other one, Officer Duncan. The one that never smiled. He doubted Lucy Thornton was involved – she always struck him as an honest sort of cop. And if Thornton was honest maybe her pal Ortmann was, too. But again he couldn't be sure. They could *all* be part of this.

His heart was beating faster all of a sudden. This probably wasn't a good thing, but for once Virgil didn't mind. He was taking his pills and that's all anyone could be expected to do in his position. He had a mystery to solve, after all.

Sure, his paranoia had been getting to him. Every creak in his house was a footstep. Every passing car was a police cruiser, come to silence him. He wasn't getting much sleep. He wasn't eating much. But so what? He had important things to be doing, for God's sake. For the seventh time that day, he checked the windows and doors, made sure they were locked.

He watched an old man in a blue jacket shuffle along the sidewalk, reading from a scrap of paper and then looking up and around. Lost and confused, the same way Virgil spent most of his days. Not anymore, though. He realised, with a smile, that purpose had crept into his life when he wasn't looking. What an odd sensation that was.

He set about making himself a sandwich. He had to keep his strength up, even if he wasn't hungry. He laid out his ingredients, but hadn't even buttered the bread when there was a knock on the door. His good mood soured. That would be Mrs Galloway. Every year she knocked on his door, gave him that condescending smile, and enquired as to his well-being before asking about his plans for Hell Night with all the grace and subtlety of a... a...

Goddammit, he couldn't even think of a suitable insult.

Walking to the front door, he did his best to stifle his anger. It wasn't easy. She wouldn't even call it Hell Night. She called it "the festival" around him, as if he'd never heard the actual name in all of his years here. Condescending busybody that she was. He reached the door, calmed down, put a neutral expression on his face, and then opened it.

The old man in the blue jacket stood there. For a moment, Virgil didn't know who it was. He was probably around Virgil's own age. Hispanic. Shrunken. Then it came to him.

"Goat-molester?"

Javier Santorum snarled. When he did so, his false teeth clacked in his mouth. He drew back his spindly arm, his liver-spotted hand clenching into a liver-spotted fist. As a younger man, he'd telegraphed every punch in every fight scene they'd ever had (those in which he hadn't been replaced with a stuntman) and it seemed his real-life technique wasn't much better. He swung his fist in a wide, unsteady arc that Virgil could easily have dodged, back in the old days. But now, even though he saw it coming, he was still too slow to avoid it.

Javier's fist bounced painfully off his cheek.

"Ow," said Virgil.

"Yeah," said Javier triumphantly. "How'd you like them—"

Javier had been a stage magician before he'd become an actor – *Javier Santorum, Circus Magician and Escape Artist!* – but Virgil had been a boxer, and those instincts never leave you. His left jab had slowed considerably over the years, but it still had that snap to it, and he still landed it with unerring precision, right on the point of Javier's chin. Javier's eyes crossed and his legs gave out, and he sat down faster than he'd probably managed for quite some time, and then flattened out on Virgil's front porch.

"Oh goddammit," said Virgil.

For a moment, he wondered if he'd killed him, but the rise and fall of Javier's pigeon chest assured him that no, the idiot was still alive. He couldn't leave him out on the porch, though. It wasn't so much that the neighbours might wonder what was going on, but that Javier might get carried off by a bear or something on its way past. What an undignified way to go.

So Virgil prepared himself and, moving slowly, took a good grip on each of Javier's matchstick ankles. Straightening up even slower than he'd bent down, he got himself in a good position, and pulled. Dragging Javier into the house was easier than he'd expected. The man seemed to consist of nothing more than dried kindling and leathered skin. His head bounced off the doorsill and Virgil grinned.

When he was inside, Virgil closed the door and went to fetch a glass of water. He stood over Javier, then, about to upend it over the other man's face, when his mischievous streak lit up. He poured half of the water on to Javier's crotch, and the rest he dumped on Javier's face.

Javier spluttered, coughed, turned his head away and wiped his eyes. "What the hell... what the hell're you *doing?*"

Virgil put the glass on the hall table. "Reviving you," he said. "You looked dead."

"That's how I always look, you sonofabitch. You hit me!"

"You hit me first."

"You deserved it!"

"Sorry I called you Goat-molester," Virgil said. "It was the first thing that came into my head, honestly."

"I don't need your damn apology!"

"Then why are you here?"

"I came here to kick your ass!"

"You might want to do that from a standing position."

"Screw you! I'll get up in my own time!"

"Right. Sure. You wet yourself, by the way."

"Oh, for Christ's sake..."

Javier struggled into a sitting position, then wiped at his crotch with dismay.

"Need some help?" Virgil asked.

"Not from the likes of you!"

Virgil shrugged.

Javier rubbed his chin. "You sucker-punched me."

"No, I hit you back."

"Yeah, when I wasn't expecting it. I might have concussion. If my brain swells tonight, you're to blame. Everyone will know you killed me."

"Not if I leave you out for the bears."

"There are bears?" Javier said quickly, looking around like he expected one to come ambling through from the bathroom.

"This is Alaska," said Virgil. "We have everything here. Javier, are you sure you don't want any help getting off the floor? You're a long way down, and it's a long way up."

"I can do it myself," said Javier. "Look at you, talking like an old man. You probably need those handles in the tub, don't you?"

"Yeah," said Virgil. "I also have a seat in the shower."

"Ha! Like an old man!"

"Says the guy who can't get up off my floor."

"I'm waiting for my second wind!"

"What are you doing here, Javier? Why'd they even let you out?"

"Let me out?" said Javier. "It's a retirement village, not a goddamn prison camp! I leave when I want to leave! If I want to catch a plane, I catch a plane! Don't you be treating me like I'm an old man. I ain't dead yet!" Moving slowly, and carefully, Javier turned over on to his hands and knees.

Virgil watched him. "Did you travel across the country just so you could hit me?"

"Don't flatter yourself," Javier wheezed, crawling to the wall. "Hitting you was a bonus. Hitting you made the trip sweeter."

"So why are you here?"

"The mystery," Javier grunted. Using the wall to steady himself, he started getting to his feet. Virgil stared at him. He knew about the murder? How the hell did he know about the murder?

"My doppelgänger," Javier continued. "Want to... see him for myself. See if he... really is my double." Finally, Javier was standing again. "Oh, thank Christ," he muttered.

"Someone looks a little like you and you immediately get on a plane?"

Javier glared. "You said he looked *exactly* like me. That's what you said."

"I know what I said, but you couldn't have known that I wasn't exaggerating. You took my word on something like that? Why?"

"Because I want to see him, goddammit. Is that so hard to understand? If I have a double who looks just like me from years ago, I want to meet him. *Comprende?*"

"You can't meet him."

"The hell I can't! Where'd you see him? Just tell me where you saw him and I'll do the rest."

"He was in my neighbour's house..."

"Well, okay!"

"...killing my neighbour."

Javier paused. "What's that you say?"

"You heard."

"My doppelgänger killed your neighbour? That's what you're saying?"

"That's what I'm saying."

"Well... why?"

"I don't know."

"What do the cops say about it?"

"That's complicated."

"In what way?"

"They're in on it."

"In on what?"

"The murder."

Javier frowned. "You're going to have to start at the beginning."

"I was here. I looked into my neighbour's house as your doppelgänger killed him. He snuck out, and before I could call them, the police turned up. The Chief of Police, actually. They took the body out in the middle of the night and covered up the whole thing."

"Say it ain't so."

"I wish I could."

"What kind of pills are you on, Abernathy?"

"Heart medication."

"No pills that would make you hallucinate or imagine things or go crazy?"

"No crazy pills, no."

"Cos it sounds like you're on crazy pills."

"I know how it sounds."

"And you're saying my double, my doppelgänger, is a killer? And you don't know his name?"

Virgil hesitated.

"You do!" said Javier, eyes widening. "You do know his name!"

"I showed an old picture of you I got off the internet to the lady who delivers the mail, asked if she recognised this person. She said his name was Oscar Moreno."

"My picture's on the internet? Am I one of those internet stars I been hearing about?"

"No. As far as I can see, internet stars are cats and dogs and animals who do funny things."

"Like Mr Ed?"

"I don't think you're quite getting it, but that's okay."

"And where does this Moreno guy live?"

"Across town," said Virgil. "I looked him up in the phone book."

"Just like you used to do on the show."

"I guess."

"Is that what this is?" Javier asked. "Are you falling into some delusion where you can no longer separate reality from fiction? Do you think we're in an episode of the show right now?"

"If we were, you'd be Ernesto Insidio, evil mastermind, and I'd have to punch you again."

Javier let a slow smile creep on to his face. "I think you might be nuts."

"I really don't care."

"I actually think you might be losing your marbles. Do you know your own name? Tell me, are you Virgil Abernathy, washed-up television actor, or the Shroud, crime-fighting hero?"

Virgil looked at him, and shrugged. "I can't be both?"

13

Amber's hands were getting better. They were still stiff, still discoloured, but the throb had reduced to almost nothing, and she could actually move her fingers now. She tested them on the walk from Main Street to the Dowall Motel, wriggling them a little in their bandages. The iPad was in the bag on her back and it bounced with every step she took. She was walking fast. After a day spent in her human form, she was ready to crawl out of her own skin.

She passed a park where little kids played on jungle gyms and swing sets while their parents looked on. The afternoon had turned to early evening, but it was still bright, still way too bright, and it was cold and getting colder, and they were all wrapped up in thick coats. Amber barely felt it. She started up the hill, keeping her eyes on the motel at the top. She envisioned herself walking into her room and stripping off her clothes and shifting, and had to bite her lip to keep from moaning.

A car pulled up alongside her, its window down.

"Hello there!" the driver said brightly.

Amber frowned at him and kept walking.

He was fat and balding, unexceptional, but his smile was intense in its friendliness. "I was wondering if you could tell me where Daggett Road is...?"

"I'm not from around here," Amber said.

"What was that?" the driver asked, keeping pace.

"I'm not from around here," she repeated, louder.

He shook his head. "Sorry, still can't hear you." He pulled in ahead of her and Amber stopped walking. He got out, holding a map. He wore a bowling shirt that did nothing to hide his bulk.

"I'm not from around here," Amber told him again.

"I'm just looking for Daggett Road," he explained, coming closer.

"I can't help you," said Amber. "I don't live here, I'm not from here."

"But look," the man said, holding out the map. "I know where it is, I just don't know where I am."

Amber started to back up. "I can't help you."

"I won't take up much of your time," said the man. "I'm just trying to get to Daggett Road."

"Please stay back."

"Why?" the man asked, a wounded expression on his face. "I'm not gonna hurt you. I'm just asking for directions. Are you scared? Why are you scared? I'm just asking for directions."

"And I told you I can't help you."

"But you haven't even tried."

"I'm not from the area."

"I just want to find Daggett Road. Can you show me where we are on this map?"

"I don't know where we are."

"Of course you do," the man said, and chuckled.

"Sir, I don't know the name of the road we're on, I don't know how to find it on a map, and I don't know where Daggett Road is. There's a bunch of people down in the playground you could ask."

"What playground?"

"You just passed it."

"Yeah?" he said, and looked around. "Didn't notice it. Maybe you could help me find the playground on the map?"

He stepped towards her and she held up a hand. "Stop."

"Stop?"

"Stop where you are."

He laughed. "This is America, young lady. Land of the free. You can't tell me what to do. If I want to walk, I walk."

He took another step, and another, matching her backwards steps.

She snarled. "Sir, if you take one more goddamn step, you're going to regret it."

"Yeah?" said the man, and then he showed her the gun he was holding under the map. "Somehow, I don't think so."

Amber's eyes widened. The gun was an automatic, and it had a silencer on the muzzle.

"Don't do it," the man said. "Don't change. Moment I see horns, I'm putting a bullet between them."

She didn't need to ask him why he was here.

"Where is he?" the man said. "The Ghost. Where is he?"

"Who?"

"The Ghost of the Highway," the man snapped. "I know he's here with you, so where *exactly* is he?"

She thought about lying, but couldn't come up with a way

111

to exploit a lie, so she decided on the truth. "He's keeping an eye on the Hounds," she said. "You know about the Hounds, don't you?"

"Yeah, I know about the Hounds. But where is he?"

"I don't know," she said. "He drives around a little. Checks the perimeter."

He aimed for her head. *"Where is he?"*

Amber swallowed. "Over that way." She jerked her head to show him.

"Then we're going in the opposite direction," the man said. He motioned to the car. "In you get. Go on. No, the driver's side."

"What?"

"You're gonna drive us right up to those Hounds, and I'm gonna sit beside you and keep this gun pointed straight at your gut."

"I can't drive." She held up her hands. "I can't grip the wheel."

"What?" He shook his head. He looked furious. "What the hell did you do?"

"I didn't do anything," Amber replied. "It was a guy like you, someone who wanted to take me back to the Shining Demon. He did this."

"Shit." The man stared at her. He started chewing his lip. "Shit. Well, I can't drive. I gotta keep the gun on you."

"Don't know what you want me to do about it."

"Shut up," he said. "Shut up and let me... Okay, right, Plan B. We walk outta here."

"Walk out of town? That's *miles*."

"You think I'm happy about it? Walk ahead of me. We stay away from anyone we see, you understand? If you try to be sneaky and alert someone to what's going on, I kill them, you dig? Get going."

They got to the park and cut across it, staying out of sight of the kids and their parents. Every minute or so the man would issue another instruction to steer clear of houses or roads or people walking their dogs. They got to an old walking track and stayed on it for a while.

"So who are you?" Amber asked.

"I don't recall saying anything about small talk."

"This isn't small talk," she said. "I think I deserve to know the name of the man who's going to deliver me to the Hounds."

She heard the smirk in his voice. "Yeah, maybe. Name's Phil Daggett – though most people know me as the Yukon Strangler."

"Serial killer?"

"There is not a name for what I am."

"You a friend of Elias Mauk, then?"

"He's never had the privilege of meeting me. But he will. When this is over and I get the power I want, they'll all wanna meet me."

She glanced over her shoulder at him. His face was red and his breathing was laboured. He wasn't used to this much exercise. Neither was she, for that matter. She didn't want to imagine what her own face looked like.

"You're still alive," she said.

"Eyes front."

Amber looked ahead as she walked. "You're still alive," she repeated. "Most of the killers who sign up with the Shining Demon wait until they're dead to... Wait. You *haven't* signed up with him, have you?"

"No more talking."

She stopped suddenly, and turned.

Daggett pulled up, confused. "What do you think you're doing?"

"You haven't made a deal with him, have you?" she asked. "So why are you here?"

"Get moving."

"Not until you answer my questions."

"I will kill you right now if you do not start walking."

"The Shining Demon wants me alive," she countered. "So come on – what's in it for you?"

He hesitated. "If I hand you over, I get my deal."

"You tried to make a deal before this," she said, "but you weren't interesting enough, were you?"

"Watch your mouth."

"Explain it to me, Phil, or I'm not moving."

"Goddamn you, you little bitch...! You march when I goddamn say you march!"

"Explain."

Fury danced in his eyes. "I tried to make a deal," he said. "So what? I tried and it didn't work. It doesn't work for everyone. I understood. I didn't let it stop me. I kept going out, I killed more women – whores and sluts and filthy, filthy creatures, the lot of them – because I knew, I *knew* that if I could just prove myself worthy of his interest, all my dreams would come true. Then the night before last my bedroom was filled with this light, with this incredible light... I figured it was a sign. I figured he was calling me. I did the whole circle thing... and it worked, and I was in his castle."

"And he offered you a deal if you could come in here and drag me out."

"I jumped in my car immediately. I didn't think I'd be the first to find you, but hey." He shrugged, and smiled. "I guess it's my lucky day."

Amber frowned. "The first?"

Daggett laughed. "You didn't think I was the only one, did you? Everyone who's ever tried to contact him and failed, he summoned. They're all on their way here. Serial killers of all kinds are closing in on this town as we speak."

The guy who'd disguised himself as a state trooper. Just another psycho who'd had her in his crosshairs. Now it made sense.

"Since I've been here I've met others," Daggett continued. "Two of them even wanted to join forces with me, can you believe that? What, they gonna start a union next? Ridiculous. You can never trust a serial killer, not even if you are one. That's what I told them, but off they went. I'd have shot them both in the back, but there were too many witnesses – and that just proves my point even more! Serial killers cannot be trusted! Do you get it now? There's so many of us that it's over for you. You never stood a chance."

"But why you?" she asked. "Why not send more like Elias Mauk? They have powers. You're just a guy."

"Because we're the new breed," said Daggett. "Mauk belongs with Shanks and Utt and that guy in Iowa – relegated to the history books. Me and my brothers and sisters, we're the new generation of nightmares."

"New generation of assholes, you mean."

He raised the gun. "Move."

"You're not going to kill me."

He switched his aim to her leg. "I don't have to kill you."

"Do you know how far we are from the edge of town? You going to carry me all that way, are you? I know I'm not one to talk, I'm carrying around some extra baggage, but you? You're already close to dropping dead from exhaustion."

"Shut the hell up."

"You're not fit, Phil. You're not going to be able to carry me."

"No," said Daggett, "but I can shoot you in the leg, beat you into a coma, then go back and get my car. What do you think now, smartmouth? You gonna start walking now?"

Amber resumed walking.

"Yeah," said Daggett. "That's what I figured."

He kept pace behind her.

After another hour, walking with a gun pointed at her didn't seem like that big of a deal. She got flashes of panic when she heard him stumble, or trip over something, and the more they walked, the more he stumbled, but he didn't fall and the gun didn't accidentally go off.

They approached a carnival site, the rides and attractions covered with tarps and the grass growing wild and long. Sunlight glinted off a mirrored door. In the height of the summer, it probably looked a lot more impressive than it did right now.

They kept going. Her feet were hurting. She couldn't remember the last time she'd walked this much. Her skin itched. She wanted to shift and spin and tear his head off. Instead, as 10pm passed by and the sun went down, she kept walking. In this crazy twilight, it was still more than bright enough to see.

"How far?" Daggett said eventually.

"Dunno," she answered.

"I thought you knew where we were going."

She glanced back. "You pointed me in this direction – you said walk."

"You're in front," said Daggett. "That means you're leading the way. Jesus Christ, we could've been walking in circles, you stupid bitch."

She stopped and turned.

"Goddammit," he said, "stop doing that. Keep walking."

"Not unless you stop with the name-calling."

He stared at her. "What?"

"Stop calling me that."

"Are you... are you serious?"

"I don't like it. From the very start you've been, like, totally misogynistic. You may have a problem with women, fine, whatever – but I don't need to hear about it."

"I'm holding a gun on you."

"And that's bad enough without listening to your hatred."

"Are you shittin' me right now?"

"I'm not shitting you, no. Are you going to quit it with the misogyny?"

He scowled. "What's... what's misogyny mean?"

"It's the hatred of women."

"And if I quit hating women, will you keep walking?"

"Yes."

"Then okay, I'll stop being... whatever it's called."

"Misogynistic," Amber said, and started walking again.

"How do you know we're not walking in circles?" he asked from behind.

"I don't," she said. "You're the one with the map."

"It's a map of Vancouver."

"I have no way of knowing where we are, Phil, all right? No idea."

"Call me the Yukon Strangler."

"I have no idea where we are, Yukon Strangler."

They walked on in silence for a few moments.

"Just call me Phil," Daggett muttered.

Night had fallen – real night, with darkness and everything – by the time they heard the motorcycles. By this stage, they were surrounded by trees that appeared as solid blacks in a darkening haze. Yellow headlights came at them in shifting strips.

"There," said Daggett, giving her a shove. "Hurry. Go faster."

Amber picked up the pace. Puffing now, he hurried after her, barging through a last tangle of branches and leaves. He caught up with her just as she reached the Charger.

Daggett froze. "Hey," he said. "This is—"

Milo appeared behind him, gun pressed to the side of Daggett's sweaty head. "Drop it."

Daggett froze. Then, slowly, he held out his arm, and dropped the gun.

Milo pushed him up against the car, started to frisk him.

Daggett glared at Amber. "You tricked me."

She ignored him, and spoke instead to Milo. "His name's Phil Daggett. He wasn't interesting enough for the Shining Demon to make a deal with, but he'll get what he wants if he hands me over. He says he's not the only one who's been offered this."

Finished with the search and finding nothing, Milo stepped back and considered their options.

"We could put him in the trunk," Amber suggested.

"I don't like small spaces," Daggett said immediately.

"No point," said Milo. "The car would kill him slow, and we wouldn't be able to use the trunk for a week or two. Better to just kill him now, get it over with. He wouldn't hesitate to kill you."

"But I did hesitate," said Daggett. "Please, Mr Ghost, if you let me go, you'll never see me again."

"Don't call me that," said Milo.

"Sorry," said Daggett. "But I'm a big fan. A huge fan. I thought you were a legend, a myth, until a few days ago. When I was told you were with her, I... I have to admit, I cried with happiness. I'm just a huge, huge admirer of your work."

Milo grunted, holstered his gun, and picked up Daggett's. He examined it, inspected the silencer, shrugged and threw it in the back seat.

"Are you gonna let me go?" Daggett asked.

"No," said Milo. "You'd just come back in, try your luck again." He looked at Amber. "I know you don't want to hear this, but—"

"We should kill him," said Amber.

Milo stopped talking.

"It's safer, isn't it?" she asked. "We've got nowhere to keep him, we can't release him... Killing him is the smart thing to do."

"Please don't kill me," said Daggett.

"He's murdered people," she said. "He's the Yukon Strangler. We'd be doing the world a favour. It's his own fault, too. He came after me, so I'm not going to feel too bad about it."

"It's not my fault," said Daggett. "I had a terrible home life."

"I don't want to kill him," Amber said, "obviously I don't. I'd prefer if we didn't have to. But we do. It's the only practical..."

Her voice faded as she became aware of the man standing in the shadows behind Milo.

"I knew you people would be trouble," said Chief Novak. He had his hand on the butt of his holstered gun. "Turn slowly, Mr Sebastian," he said. "Keep your hands in full view, if you please."

Milo did as he was told, until the two men were looking at each other.

"I hope you're not thinking of pulling that gun," the Chief said. "I don't like your chances, to be honest with you. Unless you're some kind of quick-draw artist, I mean. Are you? You look like you might be. Me, I'm quick, but I wouldn't call myself an artist. Always, at the back of my mind, there's a little voice that reminds me that no matter how fast you are," and here he drew, his gun clearing the holster faster than Amber could register it happening, "there's always someone faster. Would you agree?"

Milo kept his hands well away from his own gun. "Always someone."

Novak nodded. "Yes, there is. Reach across with your other hand now, if you please. Take the holster off. Throw it in the car."

"Sure thing, Chief," Milo said slowly, and did as Novak said.

"That's what I want to hear," Novak said. "'Sure thing, Chief.' That's exactly what you should be saying to me. What about you, Miss Lamont? Want to accompany me to the station?"

Amber didn't see any other choice. "Sure thing, Chief," she said.

14

THE BAR WAS CALLED SALLY'S, and when they walked in they were greeted by two guys who could not dance.

There was no dance floor, but they had two girls up with them. The girls danced without enthusiasm, and the guys sang along to the music and jerked their bodies in search of a rhythm that remained amusingly elusive. Kelly didn't think they minded, though. They were way too drunk.

The bar was loud, but it was a weekday, and there weren't a whole lot of people there. Wait, was it a weekday? Kelly frowned. She really didn't know.

"Ooh, a redhead," said the guy propping up the near end of the bar. "I do like redheads." He was in his early twenties, good-looking. She didn't know how many beers he'd had, but it was probably too many. "Is it true what they say about them," he continued, "about how fiery they are? I heard redheads are animals in the sack. Are you an animal in the sack?"

He grinned. She looked at him, chewed her lip, and said, "You wouldn't happen to know a Ricky, would you?"

He slapped his own chest. "That'd be me."

"Yeah, I kinda knew it would be."

He leered. "What can I do for you, baby?"

"My friends and I were hoping to talk to you for a while," she said, "if you're not too busy. We'll buy you a drink."

"You don't look old enough to be buying drinks, miss," said the bartender, looking up. "I'm gonna have to card you."

She smiled politely. "I'm not drinking, and I'm not buying, but my friend Warrick here is *way* over twenty-one."

"And I demand a beer!" Warrick said, pounding his fist on the bar.

"Do not hit my countertop," said the bartender.

"Then I request a beer, please," Warrick said quietly, and stroked the bar. "Whatever Ricky here is drinking."

"I don't want a beer from you," said Ricky, "I want a beer from Red, here. What you wanna talk to me about, beautiful? If you like, we could go somewhere a little more private. I would gladly sing like a bird for you."

"Not interested in singing, Ricky. Just talking."

Ricky shrugged, and the two dancers came over. They had somehow lost their dancing partners. The first guy was huge. "Party-Monster!" he roared.

"Oh yeah," said Ricky, "introductions. Red, this is the Party-Monster. He likes to stir things up, go a little wild, and generally party like a madman. And that's Dave."

"Hello," said Dave.

"Hi, Dave," said Ronnie. "Hi, Party-Monster. We won't take up much of your time, Ricky, but if you'd be willing to talk to us, that'd be great."

Ricky peered at him. "Did it get dark in here all of a sudden?"

Dave and the Party-Monster burst out laughing.

Ronnie smiled, and nodded. "It's because of my skin, right?"

The laughter stopped. Ricky paled. "What?"

"The joke," said Ronnie. "It's because I'm black, isn't it?"

"I don't know what you're talking about," Ricky said. "I was just asking about the... the lights... they... I was just..."

"It's okay," said Ronnie. "It's fine. We all have our prejudices."

"I'm not prejud—" He frowned, tried again. "Prejudiced."

"You can make jokes about whatever you want to," said Ronnie. "It's a free country, isn't it?"

"Yes."

"We just want to talk to you, Ricky. That's all. Will you talk to us?"

"Uh... why?"

"Because you might be able to help us with something," said Linda.

The Party-Monster stared at her. "Your boobs are huge."

"They are big, yes. Do you have anything to add to that?"

The Party-Monster shook his head dumbly.

Linda nodded. "I didn't think so. Ricky, we want to know about the Narrow Man."

There was a scene in *An American Werewolf in London* where the two American guys walked into a Yorkshire pub, and all the talking stopped and everyone turned and stared at them. Kelly had just seen that movie a few months ago, after it was referenced on *In The Dark Places*. She was reminded of it now.

"I'm gonna call the police," said the bartender. "You come in here, disturbing the peace..."

He pulled out a phone and Ronnie smiled, leaned over, and snatched it out of his hand. "No cops," he said.

The bartender's eyes bulged with anger, and all of a sudden he was taking a baseball bat from behind the bar and he was swinging it and just as quickly Ronnie had snatched that from his hands, too.

"We just want to talk," Ronnie said calmly.

"Get them!" Dave yelled.

Ronnie dropped the bat and then dropped Dave as the Party-Monster made a grab for Linda. She flipped him over her hip and when he slammed to the ground she twisted his arm until he cried out. Ricky swung a beer bottle at Kelly's head, but she just stepped forward and slammed her forehead into his face.

Ricky staggered back against the bar, blood pumping from his nose.

Nobody else in the bar moved.

"Okay then," said Ronnie. He took hold of Ricky's arm and led him out of the bar. Linda released Party-Monster and followed, and Warrick went next, Two at his heels.

"Hey," said the bartender weakly, "no dogs allowed."

"Sorry about that," Kelly said, and handed the bartender back his baseball bat before following the others outside. She found them in the alley behind the bar. Ricky was standing with his back to a dumpster, both hands over his nose.

"You broke it!" he said when he saw her.

"Ricky, focus," Ronnie said, snapping his fingers. "Tell us about the Narrow Man."

"I don't know anything about that."

Ronnie flicked his hand against Ricky's, and Ricky howled. "My nose! Be careful!"

"Tell us."

Ricky took a moment for the pain to subside. "I don't know anything," he said, but with less aggression this time.

"Then how about we tell you what we know," said Linda.

"For a start, we know he's real. We know he kills kids. Have you seen him?"

"I haven't seen anyone. I got nothing to say to you. You're in so much trouble, you have *no idea*."

"Where can we find him?" Kelly asked.

Ricky laughed despite the blood. "You don't, you stupid bitch. He finds you. And you better pray he doesn't. You better pray I don't."

"You?" said Kelly. "I don't know how to break this to you, Ricky, but you're not a very scary guy."

"Not yet," he responded. "But I will be. You don't wanna be around for that."

"I don't even want to be around for *this*, but here I am. Make this easy on yourself, okay? We're not leaving you alone until we know where to find the Narrow Man. Where did you see him?"

He shook his head. "I didn't."

Ronnie sighed, and kicked Ricky's legs out from under him. Ricky slammed down on to his ass and cried out, and Linda stepped on his left hand while Ronnie pinned his right arm.

"Right on the tail bone, huh?" Ronnie asked. "Man, that hurts. Everyone knows how much that hurts. That is some exquisite pain you're going through."

"Let me go!" Ricky howled.

"Warrick," said Ronnie.

Warrick brought Two forward. "Hi, Ricky," he said. "This is my dog. If you don't tell us what we want to know, I'm going to take my hand off his collar."

Ricky shrank back. "He'll kill me."

"Hmm? Oh no. I mean, yeah, he would if I told him to, but he's not going to attack you, Ricky. He's going to seduce you."

"Wh-what?"

"He's going to hump your face, dude."

"No way."

"I'm serious. Look at him. Look at his big silly smile. Look at the way his tongue is hanging out. Two is ready for some lovin'."

"Get it away from me, you freak."

Warrick released his grip, Two bounded happily forward, and Ricky thrashed.

"Okay, okay! I'll tell you!"

Warrick took hold of Two's collar, pulled him back a little.

"You're responsible for the mural on the wall, aren't you?" said Linda. "You've got some serious artistic chops there, Ricky. Whatever happened to that?"

Still glaring at Two, Ricky said, "I grew up."

"Debatable. But the way you drew him... it was like you'd seen him with your own eyes. Is that what happened?"

"Why?" Ricky asked. "Why are you asking all this? Do you have any idea what you're getting into?"

"Why don't you tell us?" said Kelly.

Ricky sneered. "And ruin the surprise? No way."

"Tell us about the time you saw him."

"I didn't know what I saw, all right? I was thirteen. I was stupid. I was a kid. You know how stupid kids are. *Duh, I'm a kid!*"

"That's a great impression of a kid," said Kelly.

"And I was half asleep, for Christ's sake. I woke up in the middle of the night and..."

"And what?"

"It was a dream," said Ricky.

"What did you see?"

"I dreamed that I saw him standing over my brother's bed."

"The Narrow Man?" Ronnie pressed. "The figure you painted on the wall?"

"Yeah," said Ricky, "him. Only it wasn't him, I found out afterwards. It was someone else. A drifter. He came in and took my brother, and I was half asleep and I thought it was a monster."

Kelly frowned. "He took your brother?"

"It was a homeless guy, a vagrant, passing through town. We get a lot of those here. He snuck in through the window I'd left unlocked."

"Was he found?" Linda asked. "Your brother?"

Ricky shook his head.

"What about the vagrant?"

"Chief Novak caught him a week later," Ricky said. "He was burning bloodstained clothes, up in the hills. He confessed, told him he'd take him to where he'd buried the body, but then he ran at the Chief and the Chief had to put him down. Had to put him right down."

"But the person you saw taking your brother," said Kelly, "it *wasn't* a homeless guy, was it?"

"I was dreaming that," said Ricky. "You understand? It wasn't the goddamn Narrow Man. It was a frickin' homeless guy. The Narrow Man is a kids' story. I was a kid, I didn't know what I was seeing – that's how my mind interpreted it. All of this was explained to me later."

"Why did he go after your brother?" Warrick asked.

"How the hell should I know? He was sick in the head. Probably saw us out playing and made his choice. World is full of perverts."

"What about the voting?"

Ricky glared.

"Did your brother get many votes that year?"

Ricky straightened up. "You don't know anything. You act like you do, but you don't. The Narrow Man isn't real. A homeless guy killed my brother because I left the window unlocked. That's all it is. That little ballot box? It's to keep kids in line. That's all. And you know what? It works."

Kelly looked at Linda, saw her slight shrug.

"Thanks very much, Ricky," Kelly said. "I've really enjoyed our talk. In answer to your earlier question, I am dynamite in the sack, but unfortunately you'll never experience that for yourself."

"Wouldn't want to," Ricky said immediately.

She smiled, and Warrick led the way across the road to the van. As Ricky struggled to his feet, Ronnie turned back.

"Hey, Ricky? What's this town festival we've been hearing about?"

Now it was Ricky's turn to smile, and when he did he gave them all a good look at his bloody teeth. "You'll find out," he said. "Stick around and you'll find out."

He laughed, then turned and ran into the shadows. They heard him slip and crash into something and howl in pain.

"Have a good night," Kelly called, and climbed into the van. "What a nice guy," she said.

15

THE DESOLATION HILL POLICE DEPARTMENT occupied the back of the Municipal Building, which stretched from Main Street to its little brother, Market Street. Unlike the side facing the square, the rear of the building didn't have any steps or pillars to proclaim its majesty, but it did have a parking lot and a wheelchair ramp.

The cruiser swung into the lot. One other cruiser and three civilian vehicles were already parked here, but the Chief had his own space, clearly marked. They stopped and Novak picked his hat off the passenger seat and got out. He opened Amber's door and nodded. Her hands were cuffed behind her back, so she adjusted her position, got one foot out and stood, nearly overbalanced. Novak steadied her with a hand on her shoulder. Milo came next, sliding sideways, ducking his head and then standing beside her.

"You now," Novak said to Daggett.

"Can't you come round and open this one?" Daggett asked.

"I shined these shoes this morning," Novak said. "The less walking I do, the longer they'll stay shiny."

Daggett muttered something under his breath, then started sliding awkwardly across the seat. He got one leg out, tried to shift his bulk, and looked up. "Little help?"

"Out," said Novak. "Now."

"Could I have some help?" Daggett said loudly. "I have glandular problems and I would appreciate some assistance, officer."

"I'm not an officer," said Novak. "I'm the Chief."

Daggett glared, then took a deep breath and heaved himself out of the cruiser. His foot caught and he fell to his knees, then sprawled on to his belly. "I'm hurt! I'm hurt! I'm gonna sue! You haven't even charged me with anything! I've committed no crime and now I've injured myself!"

"Up," said Novak.

"I'm gonna sue!"

"So sue standing up," said Novak.

He reached down, took hold of Daggett's left ear, and twisted. Daggett howled, his legs kicking, and Novak pulled him slowly to his feet before letting go.

"You saw that!" Daggett shouted to Amber and Milo. "You both saw him assault me! I have witnesses!"

"Pretty sure your witnesses were fixing to kill you before I showed up," said Novak. "I doubt they care about your civil rights." He swept a hand towards the ramp leading up to the double doors with a police badge on the glass. Amber led the way, then Milo, and Novak followed Daggett, who kept complaining even though no one was listening.

The doors slid open and Amber stepped into a gleaming police station, all bright and clean and tidy. There was a civilian behind the desk with an ID badge around her neck, talking quietly into a headset. When Novak came in, she relaxed, nodded to him, and did something behind the desk that resulted in a door to their right beeping as it opened.

At Novak's gesture, Amber walked to the door, and passed

from gleaming and sleek to concrete and grey. There was another door just beyond and she waited at it while Novak moved up beside her. He took a card from his pocket and passed it over a sensor and the door clicked and he pushed it open.

There were two jail cells with barred walls and barred doors on each side of the room they walked into. All were empty. Amber walked into the first cell on the left. Milo walked into the second. Novak put Daggett in the cell opposite. He had them all back up to the bars and he took off their cuffs, then walked out.

"You haven't charged me with anything!" Daggett shouted after him. "You haven't charged me!"

The door shut with a click.

Amber looked at her cell. The bunk had a thin pillow and a thin blanket. The sink had a small bar of soap. The toilet, at least, had a seat, but no curtain or anything to protect her privacy.

"Hey," said Daggett. "Hey, girlie. This is all your fault, I hope you realise that. If you hadn't tricked me, we wouldn't be in this mess."

"You wanted to give me to the Hounds," she said. "I think I prefer being here, to be honest."

Daggett shook his head, a look of disgust on his face.

Milo watched him, and said, "The Yukon Strangler, eh?"

Daggett grabbed the bars and pressed his face between them. "You keep that quiet!" he said. "You say one word about that and I'll start telling tales of my own. Maybe a little something about the Ghost of the Highway, see if that gets Deputy Dawg's interest."

Milo gave him a smile. "I doubt it would. Those murders are fifteen years and three thousand miles away. But a self-confessed strangler from just over the border..."

"I never confessed to nothing," Daggett said.

"You confessed to me," said Amber. "You said you'd strangled lots of women – although you didn't call them women, did you? You had lots of names for them, but not women."

Daggett sneered. "Is that what this is? You're still upset because of the name-calling?"

"I'm more upset about the actual murders."

"Unless you want your name on that list, you little bitch, you shut the hell up."

Milo sat on his bunk, leaned back against the wall. "I would not call her that if I were you," he said. "You know about her, right? You know why Astaroth wants her?"

"I know enough," said Daggett.

"So you know what I could do to you," Amber said.

"You'd have to find me first."

"I've found you, Phil. You're right there."

Daggett swallowed. "I'm gonna get out. They haven't charged me with anything. I'll get out and I'll wait for you and you'll never see me coming."

"Bet I'll smell you," said Amber.

The door clicked, and Chief Novak came back in, carrying a fold-up chair. Daggett retreated from the bars, his bravado punctured for the moment. Amber had no doubt he'd be back to full bullshitting flow after a few minutes of sulking, so she turned all her attention to Novak.

The Chief placed the chair in front of Amber's cell and sat and crossed his legs. He folded his hands on his thigh. His uniform pants were crisp – the crease like a thin blade. His shirt was immaculate, his badge perfectly straight. His tie hung like it was weighted.

His heavy-lidded eyes were unexceptional. They were neither dull nor bright. Forgettable eyes.

He sat there and looked at Amber and then at Milo and didn't say anything. Milo looked back at him, in no hurry to break the silence, either. Amber felt like she was the only one whose nerves were acting up. She knew it was a ploy — the first to fill an awkward silence loses the game — but she also knew that the longer she stayed quiet, the guiltier she seemed.

"We don't know that man," she said, her eyes flicking to Daggett. "He drove up beside me and he had a gun. I didn't know what to do."

Novak nodded, and said, "Why don't you tell me what you are?"

"I'm sorry?"

Novak kept his eyes on her, but didn't repeat the question. The way he used silence was like a weapon that both slid past her defences and battered them down.

"I'm just me," she said. "I'm scared and I don't know what's going on. Please."

"Your bottom lip trembles," Novak said, "like you're about to cry. Are you a delicate flower?"

"I'm fine."

"Are you in pain? Your hands are bandaged."

"I'm just scared," she said. "I was attacked today and now I'm in a jail cell."

He nodded, then looked at Milo, before turning his head to look at Daggett. "How about you, Mr Daggett? How do you fit into all of this?"

"I'm gonna sue you."

"So you have said. Do you have a licence for that gun you were carrying, by the way? I know Mr Sebastian has a licence for his, but do you?"

"Gun's not mine," said Daggett. "It's his. I was returning it."

"Is that so?"

"Yes. And if he says it's not he's lying."

"And was it you who added the sound suppressor? Because, without a signed BATFE form, such a modification is illegal in this country."

"It was, uh, it was like that when he gave it to me."

"I see," said Novak. "And why are you here, Mr Daggett?"

"You arrested me without charge."

"Why are you in *Alaska*, Mr Daggett, not why are you in this cell? More to the point, why are you in Desolation Hill?"

"It's a free country."

"But it's not *your* free country, now is it? You're Canadian. Will I find a record of you crossing the border, I wonder? I'll have to check on that. And if you smuggled that gun through with you, you could be facing some serious charges."

"I told you, it's not my gun."

"Who sent you, Mr Daggett?"

"No one sent me. I'm here of my own—"

Novak stood. "I must warn you. I am interested in what Mr Sebastian and Miss Lamont have to say. You do not interest me. Either you make your answers interesting, or I have no use for you."

"You don't scare me."

"And yet I do," said Novak. "Your words fail to impress. For a criminal, you're not a very good liar." He turned back to Amber. "We can only conceal our true natures for so long before the cracks begin to show. With each new crack, more is revealed of what lies beneath. I know what this town does to people, Amber. I know what it does to people out there, I know what it does to people like me, and I know what it does to people like you."

134

Amber didn't say anything.

"It's taking all of your focus to stay in this form," Novak continued. "So relax. Stop straining. Let your true nature reveal itself. Think of how good it would feel, to let go. To let it happen. Think of the relief."

Amber started with, "I don't know what you're..." and then her words faded away. He knew.

Novak smiled at Amber. "There is another way it will reveal itself," he said, and drew his gun and shot Daggett in the chest.

The shock passed through Amber quicker than electricity and she shifted even as she jumped back, her horns growing before Daggett's body hit the floor of his cell.

"There," said Novak. "Isn't that better?"

She stared at him as he holstered his gun.

"I could tell you were uneasy," Novak said. "Demons like you always are. Most of them wear their discomfort on their faces, but there are always a few who hide it better than others." He looked at Milo now. "Mr Sebastian, it's almost as if you're ashamed of your dark side. Won't you join Amber, in all of her glory?"

Milo said nothing. He hadn't moved from where he was sitting.

Novak shrugged. "Tomorrow I'll be taking you to meet the mayor. He has some questions he wants to put to you personally. For now, though, I'm going to have to bid you goodnight. I'll have one of my people remove the carcass, don't you worry, and you'll get supper in half an hour or so. We don't starve our prisoners, not in Desolation Hill." He smiled for the first time. "We're not monsters."

16

THE BALLOT BOX STOOD in the square like a miniature, badly designed lighthouse in a sea of concrete. But the very fact that it stood alone, that there was nothing else to distract from it, gave it a surprisingly unsettling aura at night-time. Kelly didn't know quite how to put her feelings into words. Warrick did, though.

"That is one creepy piece of wood," he said, peering out through the windshield.

Kelly didn't like the way the road split to encompass the square, because it really didn't seem like it was the square that was being prioritised here, but rather the ballot box at its centre. Suddenly the town didn't feel quite so pretty. Suddenly it felt like there was something rotten at its core.

There was no one else on Main Street. It was a cold night, and the well-behaved people of Desolation Hill were all at home in bed. Well, most of them. Maybe even all of them – apart from one boy.

He was small, maybe eleven or twelve, but he carried a big baseball bat, and he was walking towards the ballot box like he was fixing to do some serious harm.

"We may be in for some vandalism," Kelly murmured. "Should we—?"

Ronnie was out of the van before she'd finished that sentence. She hopped out, too, and Linda and Warrick and Two followed, Two pleased to be out in the open air once again. By the time they'd jogged across to the ballot box, Ronnie was already talking to the kid.

"Guys," he said, "this is Austin Cooke. Austin, we've heard about the box. About what happens when you get the most votes. Is that why you were going to smash it?"

"Cole Blancard stuffed it with my name," Austin said. His voice cracked. His eyes were wide with panic, but he was forcing himself to remain calm. Kelly liked him immediately. "Just cos he picked me out of everyone in my grade. I don't even know why."

"You take it seriously, then," Linda said. "Everyone else we've spoken to says it's harmless, just used to keep kids in line."

"Yeah? Bet they've never had a hundred pieces of paper with their name on shoved into it. They wouldn't be saying it's harmless then."

"You believe the Narrow Man is real?"

Austin hesitated.

"We're not going to laugh," said Ronnie. "We've encountered weirder things than this."

Austin nodded. "Yeah. I think he's real."

"Have you told your parents how worried you are?" Kelly asked. "Maybe they'll take you out of town."

"They won't. It's Hell Night on Wednesday. They won't take me anywhere."

Warrick frowned. "Hell Night? That's the name of your festival?"

Austin nodded. "Messed up, huh?"

"What happens on Hell Night?"

"Don't know. It's loud, though. And it's nuts. The next few days, everyone's replacing broken windows and cleaning the streets and walking around with bruised faces and broken arms... People die. Did you know that? My uncle died at a Hell Night two years ago. Other folks, too."

"How?"

Again, Austin shrugged. "I'm a kid. I don't get to see. I just get put down in the panic room."

Kelly frowned. "You have a panic room?"

"Every house in town has one," said Austin. "That's where we sleep while Hell Night's going on. We can't even leave our houses the next day, sometimes the next two days. That's when they clean up."

"Are all kids put in panic rooms?" asked Ronnie.

"Everyone who isn't an adult, yeah."

"And you've never asked your older friends what goes on that hurts so many people?"

"I have," said Austin. "We all have. But it's always the same. Like, last year, the Herrera twins had just turned eighteen, so they were gonna be out on Hell Night for the first time, and then they were gonna tell us all about it. But when we went looking for them after it was all over they'd barely speak to us. Few days later, they just said we wouldn't understand, and walked off. There was a huge group of us and we all used to hang out together, but after that night... it stopped."

"And your parents...?"

Austin's lip curled briefly. "My parents spend all year looking forward to Hell Night."

138

"But kids go missing here," said Linda. "We've seen the numbers. Crime is practically non-existent, but unexplained deaths and disappearances are through the roof. Surely someone in this town is concerned about that?"

"As long as they get their Hell Night," said Austin, "I don't think they give a shit what else happens."

Ronnie looked at the ballot box. "You think you have the most votes in that thing?"

"Thanks to Cole Blancard."

"Austin, we're going to help you."

"How?"

"We're going to stop the Narrow Man."

The boy frowned. "Why?"

"Because that is what we do."

"But how? You don't know anything about him."

"We know how he picks his victims. The people cast their votes and he tallies the entries."

"So... what are you gonna do?"

"You had the right idea, old chum," said Warrick, adopting an English accent as he passed the cricket bat he'd been holding to Ronnie. "We're going to smash that silly old voting box, what-ho?"

As if to mark the target, Two approached the ballot box, took an exploratory sniff, then started humping it.

"And that's just the start," said Kelly, taking off her jacket despite the cold. She held out her hand. "May I?"

Austin hesitated a moment, looking at the tattoo sleeves on her arms, then gave her his baseball bat.

"Everyone move back," said Ronnie. "We are about to engage in distinctly criminal behaviour."

Warrick dragged Two away from his latest conquest as Kelly gave Linda her jacket, and, as the others moved into the warmth of the van, she approached the box by Ronnie's side. She took a few practice swings with her bat and looked around.

"The coast appears to be clear," she said. "But I guess appearances can be... can be... How's that end?"

He grinned at her. "You're not going to make me say it, you know."

"Sure I am. It's your most favourite thing in the world to say, and it's only a matter of time before it passes from your lips."

"I admire the dedication, if nothing else."

They pounded the box. It took quite a beating, it had to be said, but it was no match for sports equipment swung with malice. The stand splintered and Ronnie caught the box with a sweet upswing, and the whole thing was busted open.

At that moment, lights lit up behind them and Kelly turned, gritting her teeth as the lone yelp of a siren sounded. "Goddammit," she said.

"Goddammit," Ronnie echoed, but quieter. Much quieter.

Kelly turned back, expecting to see the square covered in little white scraps of paper caught in the night's gentle breeze.

Ronnie prodded the remains of the box with the cricket bat, but it was a lost cause. There were no scraps of paper. The box had been emptied long before they'd stepped out of their van.

"Put your goddamn hands in the goddamn air," said one of the cops as he approached. Kelly dropped the bat, and did what she was told.

17

AMBER WOKE, FULLY AWARE of where she was without having to open her eyes. The cell was dark, but not cold. She turned over, the thin blanket slipping from her shoulders as her horns scraped the wall. She jerked her head back, annoyed. It wasn't easy to sleep with horns. She turned again, growing increasingly frustrated with the blanket, and finally she opened her eyes.

Someone was standing over her.

She roared and kicked out, shock turning instantly to fear-fuelled aggression. The black shape melted into the gloom of the cell as she jumped from the cot, and then she was flinging the blanket ahead of her. It settled on to someone, a person-shaped thing in the darkness, and Amber dived at it. Her hands grew claws and she ignored the pain as she tore through the blanket, but there was nothing beneath, and she was suddenly on her knees, snarling, her skin tightening as black scales spread outwards from the nape of her neck.

"Amber?" Milo said from the cell next to her.

She didn't answer. There was still someone in here with her. She couldn't make him out, but she could feel him. Then her eyes moved to the corner of the cell like they were iron filings drawn to a magnet, and she saw him, his shape, standing there. She locked on to his outline and got up, not blinking, not letting him melt away for a second time. With some part of her aware of how animalistic she sounded, she closed in. The figure didn't move. When she was close enough, she lunged, grabbed clothing, forced him backwards to the bars. Then he was gone, nothing but smoke, and her arms passed between the bars and her horns smacked off them and the smoke became a person again, this time standing outside the cell, Amber's fists still bunched in his shirt.

Glen looked at her with empty eyes, and Amber felt the aggression leave her like some invisible sluice gate had been opened. Her scales retracted.

"Amber," Milo said. "Get away from him."

Too late did she realise her arms were still extended through the bars. Glen's cold hands encircled her wrists before she could pull them back in. His grip was strong. Too strong to break.

"Let go of me," Amber said, keeping her voice calm.

Glen's blank expression didn't change, and he didn't answer.

"What are you after, Glen?" Milo asked. He was standing by the door of his cell. "We've got nothing to offer you. Do you understand that? We don't know what you want and we don't know why you've been following Amber. You should go back to Cascade Falls. You should stay with your own kind."

There was no indication that Milo's words even registered.

"I'm sorry," Amber whispered. "I should have been there to save you and I wasn't. I'm truly sorry about that. Can we help you? Is there something we can do to help you?"

The thing with the cold hands wore Glen's face like it was its own, but behind it there was a vast emptiness as unknowable as it was chilling. How much of the real Glen remained, Amber couldn't guess. The eyes were dull, the features slack. There was not a flicker of interest, not even when he parted her arms. The backs of her elbows came to rest against the bars, and still Glen slowly pushed. Amber gritted her teeth, squirmed, tried to pull herself free, tried to turn her wrists, but Glen's strength was immense. He was going to break her arms. He was going to snap her elbows. Black scales rose to the surface of her skin, but there was nothing they could do to prevent what was about to happen.

Her fingers turned to claws once again, and her claws scraped deep, bloodless furrows through his hands, but he didn't once flinch. His expression didn't change. He wasn't even doing her the courtesy of looking angry.

The overhead lights flickered suddenly to life, casting their harsh glare over Glen's pale skin, his sunken cheekbones, his dead eyes. The sight of him in the light was as shocking to Amber as the sight of him in the dark. Elsewhere, a heavy door was unlocked with a click. She heard voices, getting closer.

Glen released her and immediately Amber pulled her arms in, curling them into her chest to ease the pain. Glen took one step back and turned to smoke, and the smoke whirled and fled upwards to the air vent. Not one wisp was left when the new prisoners were escorted in.

Amber remembered herself just in time, and reverted a heartbeat before they came into view.

The guy was in his early twenties. Square-jawed and good-looking, African-American with a tight haircut, he was placed in the cell opposite Milo's by the same cop who had come in to remove Daggett's body. The cop was big, with a few extra pounds that threatened the integrity of his uniform, but looked strong. Healthy.

The girl was a striking redhead with sharp cheekbones and tattoos on her bare arms. She looked nineteen or twenty, and she was slim, her chest small, but those arms were toned, like she spent a good portion of her spare time lifting weights or punching bags. From the way she carried herself, Amber figured it was probably the latter. She looked like a fighter, albeit a relaxed, friendly one, as she walked into the cell opposite. The cop who locked the door was a woman in her thirties, her blonde hair pulled back into a severe bun.

Amber glanced at Milo, but he was already returning to his bunk.

"Do we get a phone call?" the guy asked.

"It's late," the female cop replied. "Everyone's asleep. The Chief'll talk to you in the morning."

The cops walked out, and the guy sat down, but the redhead stayed standing. She smiled at Amber.

"Howdy," she said.

"Hi," Amber responded.

"Nice town."

"It isn't ours. What are, um, what are you in for?"

The redhead laughed. "Aw, man, I wanted to say that. How many times in your life do you get the chance to say something like that?"

"Judging by how unlucky we've been with the law lately," said her friend, "you'll probably get another chance to say it before too long."

The redhead moved to the bars, put her hands through, resting her elbows on the horizontal slat. "We're here because we were involved in an activity that could have been misconstrued as destruction of public property," she explained. "What about you?"

"I'm not really sure," said Amber. "I think we just annoyed the wrong people."

The redhead glanced at Milo, then back to Amber. "You two together?"

"He's my uncle," Amber said, a little too quickly.

"Hey," said the redhead, "I'm not judging. My name's Kelly. My friend here is Ronnie."

"I'm Amber. This is Milo."

"Very pleased to meet you both," said Kelly. She had a beautiful smile. "How long you been in town?"

"A few days," Amber replied. "Just passing through."

"Yeah?" said Kelly. "You just stumbled across the place? That's funny. We actually intended to come here, and we had the maps and we had the GPS, but we must have driven around this part of the state for two, three hours before we found the road that led us here. It's almost as if the town doesn't want to be found. But you two just stumbled across it, huh?"

Amber hesitated. "Yep."

"Well, isn't that something?" Kelly said, in a tone that teased.

"What, um, what brought you here, then?" Amber asked.

The lights went out and they were plunged into darkness.

"Ooooh," said Kelly. "Cosy."

Amber shifted at once, relaxing into it. Her eyes were sharper like this, and she could pick out Kelly's outline in the gloom. She backed up to her bunk and sat so that her own silhouette wouldn't give her away.

"Sorry?" Kelly said from the darkness. "What was your question?"

"What brings you here?" Amber asked.

"Business, of a sort," said Kelly. "We'd heard about Desolation Hill for years, or at least heard whispers about it, so we could hardly pass up the opportunity to come here and see it for ourselves. Kind of an odd town, don't you think?"

"Yes, I do," said Amber. "I'm not the biggest fan of its police force, though."

"Me neither. I find they tend to arrest the wrong people."

"I've found that, too."

"Where you from, Amber?"

"Florida."

"Wow. You're a long way from Disney World. I'm from California myself. Venice Beach. You ever been?"

"Can't say that I have. Are you enjoying the cold?"

Kelly laughed. "No," she said. "I was born for the sun, honestly. Alaska is beautiful, and I appreciate beautiful things, but I'm a girl who needs a lot of heat, you know what I'm saying?"

"And yet here you are," said Amber.

"Here we are..."

"You have any more friends?" Amber asked.

Kelly's tone changed slightly. "That's a peculiar question."

"Is it? Oh, I'm sorry." Amber ran her tongue over her sharp teeth. "It's just that I met someone this afternoon who wasn't very nice to me. I was wondering if you knew him. Phil Daggett?"

"Not a friend of ours," said Kelly. "What did he do that wasn't so nice?"

Amber shrugged to the darkness. "He had some pretty demeaning things to say about women."

"Well, there you go," said Kelly. "I wouldn't hang out with anyone like that. I only hang out with cool people. You a cool person, Amber?"

Amber bared her fangs. "Sometimes."

"You sound like a cool person. I can tell. I'm very in tune with coolness."

"I saw your tattoos."

"I have more," said Kelly. "I'll show them to you later, if you like. You have any?"

"No," said Amber. "My parents never approved."

"Squares."

Amber's smile widened. "Yeah. Squares. Do your parents approve of yours?"

"Don't have any," Kelly said. "Parents, that is. They died when I was a kid."

"I'm sorry," said Amber, when really she meant I'm jealous.

"It's cool," Kelly said. "What are your folks like? Apart from square."

Amber thought about this. After a while, she said, "They're perfect."

"Yeah?"

"Yeah. I hate them."

Kelly laughed because she thought it was a joke. Amber didn't laugh because she didn't know if that was actually the truth.

"Might I suggest we all stop sharing private information and go to sleep?" Milo said from his bunk.

"What's wrong?" said Kelly, amused. "You don't trust me with your personal details?"

"Not at all," said Milo. "But in a modern, high-tech facility such as this one, I wouldn't be surprised to learn that every word spoken in these cells was recorded and listened to by the fine law enforcement officers who keep this town safe from the likes of us."

"Huh," said Kelly. "I guess you have a point. What do you think, Ronnie? Think these walls have ears? Ronnie?" Amber watched Kelly's shape move to the bars separating her from her friend. "Oh, for God's sake, he's asleep already."

"That's my cue," said Milo, and turned over in his bunk.

Amber watched Kelly stand there and sigh. She muttered something to herself and went to her bunk. The moment she sat, her outline was swallowed by the gloom, and Amber listened to her take off her boots and lie down.

"Goodnight," Kelly said.

No one answered except Amber. "Night."

18

THE SUN WAS PALE and weak and it was a cold morning. They had the heater on in Virgil's Sienna as they sat there, staking out Oscar Moreno's house and trying to look inconspicuous.

"Are we doing it right?" Javier asked.

"Of course we're doing it right," said Virgil. "This is the only way to do it."

"We could be hiding."

"This is hiding."

Javier made a show of looking around at the residential street they were parked on. "I don't feel very hidden."

"We're hiding in plain sight."

"Or just hiding in sight, really. We should be in a different car, at least."

"This is the only car I have."

"It's a minivan," Javier said. "It can fit eight. How many people were you expecting to carry when you bought it? We are two old men sitting in a car designed for eight with the engine running. I think we stand out."

"We do not. And we need the engine running to get the heater going."

"We don't even know if he's home. Should we knock?"

"That doesn't sound very stealthy."

"But at least we'd know."

Movement caught Virgil's eye. A heavyset woman, walking their way. She hadn't seen them yet. "Oh hell."

Javier stiffened. "What? Did he see us? Where is he?"

"Not him," said Virgil. "Her. Duck down. Quickly!"

He tried to squirm lower, but his seat belt was on and his hips were old. Beside him, Javier wriggled in place, then tried leaning forward and sideways a little. It wasn't working, and their movements had attracted her attention so Virgil straightened up.

"Act cool," he said.

"I am cool," Javier replied, wheezing from all the effort.

Virgil lowered the window.

"Mr Abernathy!" said Martha Galloway. "Good morning! I was just about to call by your place and check up on you!"

Virgil gave her a tight smile. "How good of you. It's really not necessary, though."

"Nonsense, nonsense!" she said, waving her hand. "Checking up on the elderly in the community is a privilege, not a burden. Oh! And you have a friend!" She leaned in to smile at Javier. "And what's your name?"

Javier did nothing but scowl at her.

"Mrs Galloway, this is Javier," said Virgil. "He's a friend from back west."

"Well, it is a pleasure to meet you, Javier!" said Mrs Galloway, sticking in her arm in a bid to shake his hand. Virgil pressed himself back into the seat to avoid contact with her blouse. The smell of wildflowers and fruit filled his nostrils.

Javier, meanwhile, was glaring at the proffered hand, and keeping his own appendages to himself.

"I get it, I get it," Mrs Galloway said, retracting her arm and chuckling. "I'm the same way! I carry hand cleanser in my purse, wherever I go. Never know what kind of germs you might be picking up, am I right? Heaven knows, a common cold could kill someone of your age."

Javier opened his mouth to snap off what would no doubt be a hurtful retort, but Virgil got there first.

"Javier's thinking of investing in some property in the area," he said. "We were driving around and this house leaped out as something he might be interested in buying."

Mrs Galloway frowned slightly. "This house? Is it for sale?"

"Well, no, but for the right price it could be."

"I doubt it. Mr Moreno owns the hardware store, on Appletree Street? I doubt he'd want to move."

"Well, maybe we'll ask him," said Virgil. "Though we'd appreciate it if you kept this between ourselves."

"Oh, of course," said Mrs Galloway, putting on her serious face. It vanished a moment later, replaced by a smile. "So what are your plans for Wednesday, Mr Abernathy?"

"Going to stay with my daughter," Virgil said.

"Oh, that's wonderful! And can I just say that I really admire your determination to remain independent when so many other elderly people just choose to wilt and die in old folks' homes. You are a hero to me, Mr Abernathy, you truly are. I hope that when I am your age, if I'm lucky enough to reach it, I am capable of showing the same moral fortitude as you. I'm fed up to the back teeth of lazy people who live in old folks' homes and do nothing but drain our great country's resources and leech from the system."

"I live in a retirement home," said Javier.

"How wonderful for you!" Mrs Galloway trilled. "And do they treat you nicely there?"

"Nicer than out here, you miserable hag."

Mrs Galloway's face went slack, and Virgil winced at her apologetically and raised the window.

"I don't like being patronised," said Javier. "You have to deal with that kind of crap often?"

"Sometimes," said Virgil.

"Naw, I couldn't handle that," said Javier. "At least everyone in the retirement home knows the score."

"Is she still standing there?"

"Yep. Standing right beside your window."

"Christ's sake..."

"She's no longer looking in, though."

"Well, that's something."

"She's walking away."

Virgil watched her. A part of him wanted to reprimand Javier for the rudeness, but then he figured he didn't care.

"Hey," said Javier in a hushed voice, his eyes widening.

Oscar Moreno came out of his house, wearing a sweater vest and offering a big smile to a passing neighbour.

Javier stared at him. "It's me. Holy shit, it's me. You seeing this? That is me."

"Told you," said Virgil.

They watched him get in his car.

"But that doesn't just look like me," Javier said, "it is me. That's me travelling in from the past!"

"I know. Duck down."

They tried ducking but, much like the first time, all they could manage was to lean sideways slightly.

"Quick!" said Javier. "Follow him!"

"Why? It's Tuesday morning. He's probably just going to work."

"Oh yeah."

They waited until he was gone, and sat up.

"Jesus," said Javier. "Now what? I mean... okay, I believe you, he's my exact double. But now what do we do?"

"I have no idea," said Virgil.

"You don't know? You're the one talking about murder mysteries and conspiracies and solving this crime and all that stuff... and you don't know what to do?"

"This is new to me," Virgil said defensively. "It's taking some time to adjust to all of this going on. But I'm getting there."

"How many cops are on the force? Surely they can't all be in on it."

"But how would we know which ones are and which ones aren't? No, no – the authorities can't help us. We have to keep an eye on them. Watch them. They're in on this, so they could lead us to the next clue."

"Next clue? What? What was the first clue? What are you talking about?"

"I'm just asking myself a question, Javier. A question we should both be asking." Virgil paused dramatically. "What would the Shroud do?"

Javier closed his eyes. "Oh, *Madre de Dios*, you're going to get us both killed."

19

AMBER WAS BACK IN that rest stop in Whitehorse, and she was pinned by a mountain of corpses while Elias Mauk used his hammer to break her fingers. Only this time all the corpses on top of her were Imelda, and it wasn't Mauk with the hammer, it was Amber herself as a red-skinned, horned demon.

A song played. 'Magic Moments' by Perry Como. It had been used in the *Dark Places* finale, albeit ironically. Now it played in her dream, like a thin, scratchy record.

Her demon-self smiled as she brought the hammer down, and ugly old Amber screamed beneath the mountain of Imeldas. She tried to pull her hand back, but Glen was suddenly there, grabbing her wrist and holding it down. He didn't say anything. He may have been moving, but he was as dead as Imelda.

The hammer came down one last time and Amber was allowed to pull her hand back. Screaming, she watched her fingers as they twisted and snapped like they were still being pummelled by an invisible hammer. Then the corpses were gone and she was sitting up in the booth, and the demon was gone and now *she* was the demon, and her parents sat opposite.

Her father opened his mouth to speak, but all that came out

was 'Magic Moments'. He chuckled at something and Amber's mother rolled her eyes good-naturedly and opened her mouth to respond. More Perry Como.

They picked up their knives and forks and Amber did the same, but her strong red hands were bandaged and weak, and she dropped her knife and it fell to the floor. The waitress came over. She was dressed like Brenda from Fast Danny's, but was actually Kirsty. She looked tired and bored and worn down, with not a trace of her usual glamour. She set down a large tray covered with a silver dish. Her husband, Grant, stood at the door to the kitchen, wearing a chef's hat. He looked proud. There was blood on his chin. Kirsty uncovered the meal – Amber's ugly old head on a plate of lettuce and cold cuts.

Amber's parents started eating immediately. Amber hesitated, then dug her fork into the cheek and pulled away a chunk of meat dripping with blood. She popped it into her mouth and chewed. She tried to ask Kirsty for some salt, but all that came out was that damn song. Then she woke.

She lay where she was for a while, the song still playing behind her thoughts. She heard Ronnie ask Kelly how she'd slept, and Kelly said it was better than the damn van.

Amber reverted to normal, then pushed herself up on one elbow, making sure to hide the rips her claws had made in the blanket.

"Good morning," Kelly called over. "We've been told the Chief of Police himself is on his way to see us. We might be getting out."

"Freedom at last," Ronnie said, groaning as he stood. He stretched, arched his back. "Now begins the gradual assimilation back into society."

"Ronnie uses big words," said Kelly.

Amber smiled at them, then swung her legs out of bed and laced up her sneakers. Her fingers were practically back to normal. Milo was already awake, and sitting with his back against the wall like there was nowhere else he'd rather be.

The door clicked and Amber stood. She shivered, and noticed Kelly hugging her bare arms to keep warm. She had an intricate tattoo sleeve all the way down to her left wrist. The sleeve on her right was a work in progress.

Chief Novak walked in, uniform as crisp as ever and his shoes as polished. Accompanied by a younger officer, he ignored Amber and Milo and focused instead on Kelly and Ronnie.

"Good day to you," he said.

"Hi," said Kelly.

"I'd welcome you to our town, but I believe my officers have already done that."

"Yes, sir," said Kelly. "That nice lady officer. Lucy, her name is?"

"I believe you are referring to Officer Thornton."

"That's right," said Kelly. "Officer Thornton. She welcomed us as she was putting on the handcuffs."

Novak nodded. "When you were arrested for the destruction of public property."

"We'd prefer not to say anything about that," Ronnie said, "until we speak to a lawyer."

"Understandable," said Novak. "But I don't think we need to go that far, do you? In Desolation Hill we frown upon the frivolous waste of taxpayers' money."

"Does that mean we're not being charged?" Kelly asked.

"It could," said Novak. "But there'd be conditions."

Ronnie glanced at Kelly. "Such as?"

"You'd have to pay for the box you wrecked to be replaced. I'd say for materials and time, it'll come to forty dollars."

"We can pay that."

"That's good to hear," said Novak. "Second condition is that you leave town. Today. That one's non-negotiable, I'm afraid. If you can't agree to it, you'll be brought up on charges."

"No, no," said Ronnie, "there's no need for that. We'll leave."

Novak nodded. "Gone by midnight, then. In that case, Officer Ortmann here will sign you out. You can pay the fine at the desk."

"Thank you for being so understanding, Chief," Ronnie said as Ortmann unlocked the cells. They were led out, and Kelly waved at Amber as she went.

When they were gone, Novak turned to Amber and Milo. "The mayor is busy for most of the day," he said. "He'll see you when he's done."

Amber shifted. "You know about us," she said, "about demons. We're not here to cause any trouble, I swear. Those bikers on the edge of town, they're the ones you have to worry about. They've been chasing us—"

Novak walked for the door.

"Hey," said Amber. "Hey! We're not your enemy here!"

Novak didn't even glance back. "Anyone who's not us," he said, "is our enemy."

An officer named Duncan brought them their breakfast, and Amber recognised Fast Danny's bacon. Fragments of her dream came back to her, like eating part of her own face, but it didn't put her off her food. All this fresh air was giving her an appetite.

They sat in silence for most of the morning – apart from asking the other to turn round while each of them used the toilet – and Amber started wishing that Kelly and Ronnie had stuck around. Even if she'd had to revert in their presence, it would have been worth it.

"I wish you were better at conversating with," she said, taking the bandages from her hands.

Milo cracked one eye open from where he lay. "I'm sorry?"

"Talking," said Amber. "I wish you were better at talking."

He waited a few moments before responding. "Where's this coming from?"

"We've been sitting here for three hours and you haven't said one thing."

"We've driven for days without speaking."

"That's different," she said. She flexed her fingers. "That's in the car. You could just listen to the engine and that'd be enough. You can look out the window and... I don't know. Think, or whatever. In here it's different. Silence means something in here."

"What does it mean?"

"I don't know. Like we have nothing to say to each other."

He sat up. "I see," he said.

"Yeah, well..."

"There something in particular you want to talk about? Idle conversation is hard to come by when you're in a situation like ours."

"It doesn't have to be idle. It can be... I don't know. It can still be something. We can talk about something meaningful, can't we? I've been having bad dreams." She didn't mean to say that. It just slipped out. "About my parents. And Imelda. Nightmares."

"Hardly surprising," Milo said.

"I'd just like to talk to someone about them."

He frowned. "And you think I should be that person?"

"You are literally the only friend I have."

"You've got online friends."

"They don't know about any of this stuff, are you nuts?"

"Okay. You want to talk," said Milo, "we'll talk."

She sighed. "Never mind."

"Tell me about the nightmares."

"I just did."

He looked puzzled, and actually scratched his head. "I'm sorry, Amber, I'm really not getting what it is you want here."

"Never mind, okay? It's fine."

He stood up, walked to the bars, and looked at her. "Then do you want to talk about last night? About Glen?"

She didn't answer.

"Do you know why he's still coming after you? Did he say anything?"

"Nothing," Amber said. "Not a word."

"Do you think he wants to hurt you?"

"No. I mean, maybe, because of what he is... but no, I don't think so."

The door clicked and opened, and Officer Lucy Thornton came in with two styrofoam containers stacked in her hands. Amber thought about reverting, then decided to stay as she was.

"Chow time," Lucy announced, passing them their lunch. She didn't blink at Amber's appearance.

"You know about demons," Amber said.

Lucy cracked a smile. "We're hard to find, but they do find us."

"We're not here to cause trouble," said Milo. "There's

something about this town, though – it stops certain types of people from entering. Do you know how?"

"I'm paid to do my job," said Lucy. "And right now that means giving our prisoners their lunch."

"We're not the bad guys," said Amber.

"Maybe," Lucy replied. "Maybe not. But here in Desolation Hill we have a zero-tolerance policy as far as strange demons and other supernatural phenomena go. If we see it and we don't like it, we get rid of it."

"It's not only demons you have to worry about," Amber said, pressing her face to the bars as Lucy walked off. "The guy we were arrested with, he was a serial killer. There's more on their way. We can help you."

Lucy opened the heavy door, but turned before she stepped out. "We deal with serial killers all the time," she said. "We deal with demons and murderers and even vampires every once in a while. We are, as far as I know, the only police force in the world that deals with these kind of things on a regular basis, and we're very good at our jobs. You two really did pick the last place on Earth that a demon would ever want to end up. Seriously."

Then she was gone.

20

KELLY AND LINDA HAD lunch in the small dining room in the motel. Their waiter, Kenneth, was also their cook, and he was also on duty at the front desk. He wasn't a very good waiter, and wasn't a very good cook, but Kelly wanted to believe he was wonderful at checking people in.

"Still thinking of going vegan, are you?" Linda asked as she watched Kelly pick at her food.

"Meat's never held sway over me, you know that," Kelly replied. "But how do I exist in a world without scrambled eggs? How do I do that?"

"Unhappily, I'd imagine."

"Yes," said Kelly, jabbing at the air with her fork. "Unhappily indeed. I'm gonna need support, you know. I'm gonna need someone there to make sure I'm sticking to vegan principles of... whatever the hell vegan principles are."

"Warrick would be good at that."

"Warrick thinks a vegan is an alien on *Star Trek*."

"Ronnie then," said Linda.

"Ronnie's way too practical. Most of what we eat is junk food by necessity. He'd only tell me to eat what's available.

Picky eaters are hungry eaters. He actually said that to me once."

"You'll have to tell him eventually," said Linda. Then her eyes narrowed. "Oh, you're sneaky."

Kelly smiled. "Speaking of which..."

"Oh, you are a sneaky one."

"...when are you going to tell him that you're leaving the gang?"

"That was way too sneaky. You've got issues if you can be that sneaky to a friend. To your best friend, of all people."

Kelly shrugged. "I'm just untrustworthy, what can I say?"

Kenneth came in and walked up to their table. "Can I get you anything else?" he asked.

"No, thank you," said Kelly, giving him a big smile.

His eyes flicked to the tattoos that peeked out from beneath her jacket sleeve, and he sniffed and walked back the way he'd come.

"What a nice man," Kelly said, then raised her eyebrows at Linda. "You haven't answered my question, by the way."

"I don't know," said Linda. "I guess I'll tell him... soon. But what time is the right time? I mean, look at us. Look at where we are and what we're dealing with. We actually crossed the country to be here and to do this. That's not right. It's not normal. Sane people run from bad situations, not to them."

"No one ever said we were sane."

"This is true," said Linda, "but with me, I think it's been a temporary insanity. I think I'm coming around to the idea of normal again. You know, after everything. After the Sol Foundation. After Boston."

Kelly's smile faded. "Yeah."

"I'll tell the other two when we're done here," Linda said.

162

"The moment we get back on the road, no matter how this turns out. I just can't do it anymore. You think I'm a coward?"

"No way," Kelly said immediately.

"You think they will?"

"Not a chance. It's gonna suck though, being the only girl in the van."

"I'm sure you'll pick up someone else to replace me. That's how we work, right? We pick up strays along the way. What about the girl you were talking about, the one in jail? Think she's mixed up in all this craziness?"

"I got the distinct impression. But her friend's a little on the surly side. We'll have to keep an eye out for them. We don't know yet if they're allies or enemies."

"You're so cynical," said Linda. "When I first met you, you weren't nearly this cynical."

"When you first met me, I was covered in blood and going into shock," said Kelly. "People change." Her phone buzzed and she looked at it. "Oh shit."

Linda's face slackened. "What?"

"The kid, Austin Cooke," said Kelly. "He's gone missing."

There was a cruiser parked outside the Cooke house on Brookfield Road. A few neighbours milled around on the lawn, looking concerned and chatting quietly. A reporter from the *Chronicle* newspaper was in there now, having walked very quickly past the van parked on the other side of the street. Kelly had flicked through the latest issue of the *Chronicle* and had not been impressed with either the stories or the spelling.

The side door opened and Ronnie climbed in, then shut the door behind him.

"The cops are saying he ran away," he said, rubbing his hands together to get some warmth. Two went over immediately, and Ronnie warmed his hands on the dog's fur instead.

"What are his parents saying?" Kelly asked.

"Nothing much, from what I've heard. They said goodnight to him and this morning he was gone. Mrs Cooke is distraught. Mr Cooke is shaken. That's the full extent of what I've been able to pick up."

The door opened again and Warrick climbed in. "It is chilly out there, man," he said, tossing a sealed bag containing one of Austin's T-shirts to Linda before stealing Ronnie's source of heat.

"Hey," Ronnie said to Two. Two looked back at him with those big brown eyes as if to apologise, and then Warrick picked him up and rolled back on the cushions with the dog in his arms.

"Was it difficult?" Linda asked, putting the T-shirt in the strongbox.

"Naw," said Warrick. "Lot of folks around, leaving a lot of doors open. Got to the laundry basket and back again without anyone even seeing me. Weird bunch of people, though."

"In what way?"

"Dunno." Warrick endured a few seconds of face-licking before sitting up. "I'm not sure I'm buying their concern. It all seems like an act." He looked at Ronnie. "You get that impression?"

"I did, actually. To be honest, I'm not even buying his parents' act. They're upset, sure, but... I don't know. I think it was more for show than anything else."

"Austin *could* have run away," said Linda. "He was scared

enough. If he didn't think his folks were going to take him out of town, maybe he went by himself."

"Maybe," said Ronnie.

"But not after he met us," Kelly said. "Right? Now he has a group of people on his side."

"A group of *strangers* on his side."

"Better strangers who care than family who don't. If he was going to run away, he would have told you last night when you were dropping him off. He would have asked us to drive him away from here."

"We should have done that, anyway," said Warrick. "We should have driven him out of here the moment we thought he was in danger."

"We didn't know," said Ronnie.

"We suspected," said Warrick. "And when was the last time we were wrong about something like this?"

They went quiet.

"The Narrow Man has him," said Warrick.

"Okay," said Ronnie. "Fine. Let's all agree that the Narrow Man has Austin. The fact is, we don't know what that means. He could still be alive. Raymond Carchi kept his victims imprisoned for a *week* before he killed them. We need to operate on the basis that Austin is alive, and we will believe that until we're presented with evidence to the contrary. Linda, what's our next move?"

"Find the Narrow Man."

"Kelly, how do we do that?"

"Talk to people. Check for witnesses."

"We have a plan," said Ronnie. "But there is one thing we should all keep in mind. When Ricky's brother was taken, the police blamed a vagrant. That vagrant was shot and killed on sight. We can't trust the cops. They're either covering their own asses, or they're covering up for the Narrow Man. Whichever it is, they are not our friends."

"So keep a low profile," said Warrick, nodding. "You got it, Fearless Leader..." His voice trailed off.

"What?" Linda asked. "Warrick, what is it?"

Warrick pointed at two old men standing on the sidewalk, watching the Cooke house. "That guy look familiar to anyone?"

"Which one?" asked Kelly. "Actually, no, it doesn't matter – neither of them do. Why? You recognise one of them?"

"One or both," Warrick said, frowning. "I think we should talk to them."

They got out and tried not to look intimidating as they approached the old men. Two bounded over to them happily.

The one in the blue coat smiled down at him. "Hello there," the old man said. "Who's a good doggy? Huh? Who's a good doggy?"

"You sound like an idiot," said the other old man.

"Excuse me, gentlemen?"

The old men turned, and Kelly gave them a smile.

"Hi," she said. "I was wondering if you could help us with something. My name's Kelly. That's Ronnie and Linda and that's Warrick. The dog there is Two. He likes you."

"He's a good judge of character," said the man in the blue coat. "It's why he's not making a fuss of my miserable friend here."

Kelly laughed. "Could I ask your names?"

"Sure you could," said the old man in blue. "I'm Javier, this is Virgil."

"You kids aren't from around here, are you?" Virgil asked.

"No, sir, we're not."

"Do you know the missing boy?" Ronnie asked.

"Nope," said Virgil. "As far as I'm aware, never even laid eyes on him."

"The police are saying he ran away."

Virgil nodded. "That's what they're saying, all right."

"We don't think he did," said Linda.

"Well now, that is interesting," said Virgil. "Javier, you hear that, you deaf old bastard?"

"I heard," said Javier, "and I'm not deaf."

"Have you shared this idea of yours with the authorities?" Virgil asked.

"Not yet," Ronnie said.

Virgil nodded. "You're smarter than you look."

"The police are covering it up, aren't they?"

"I don't know. Maybe. But this wouldn't be the first crime they've covered up."

Ronnie frowned. "What else are they covering up, Virgil?"

"We can't talk here," the old man said. "Too many eyes, too many ears. Come back to my house. I'll make tea."

They followed Virgil's car to a quiet street on the edge of town with a big garage and a neatly kept garden out front. It was a short trip, made longer by how slowly Virgil drove.

"I love old people," said Kelly.

"You're weird," said Warrick.

"They remind me of how my grandparents used to be. All wrinkly and decrepit."

"Charming," said Linda.

They got out of the van, joined Javier at the front door as Virgil let them all inside. Two went straight through to the living room, jumped up on the couch and went to sleep. The living room was normal. The rest of the house was not.

Posters of old movies lined the walls, props and costumes were displayed in glass cases, and old screenplays were packed on to every bookshelf.

"I *knew* I recognised you!" Warrick cried. "You're Virgil Abernathy! I used to watch your reruns all the time! I am such a huge fan! I wrote you a letter once and you sent me back an autographed picture! Warrick Wyman! You remember me?"

"I, uh, I think so," said Virgil. "Maybe, yes. Warrick, good to finally meet you." He smiled to the others. "Oh, I had a show, back in the seventies."

"Not just *any* show," said Warrick, "you had the *best* show. *When Strikes the Shroud* was the king of shows. This was even before *The Night Stalker*, wasn't it?"

Virgil nodded, allowing a little pride to creep into his voice. "We started a year before *Kolchak* and ended the year after. In our final season, we were moved to the Friday night slot and that was a death sentence, so when we were cancelled nobody gave a damn. But there was a time when the show was pretty hot stuff. Come on into the kitchen."

He led them in, and put a kettle on the stove.

"What the hell are you doing here, man?" Warrick asked.

"My daughter lives a few towns over," Virgil said, taking down a half-dozen mugs. "Came here to be closer to her and her kids."

Javier cleared his throat. "I, uh, I was on the show, too."

Warrick slapped his own forehead. "Oh my God! Javier Santorum! Dude, you were, like, the best villain ever!"

"Well," said Javier, chuckling, "I don't know if I'd go that far, but I was a pretty good bad guy."

"You had such a great voice," said Warrick. "What was that thing you always said? 'Fear is a choice no one makes, but—'"

"Fear is a choice no man makes, but all men must endure," Javier corrected.

"That's it!" Warrick cried. "That's the one! This is amazing! This is wonderful! So did you fall in love on set, or what?"

Javier's smile became puzzled. "Sorry?"

Virgil frowned. "Uh, Warrick, we're not... an *item*."

"You're not?"

"I'm just helping Virgil solve the mystery," Javier explained.

"What mystery is that?" Ronnie asked.

"You first," said Virgil. "What brings you to town?"

"A kid is in trouble."

"Who, this Cooke kid?" said Virgil. "But you're not from here, so what do you care? It's hardly any of your business."

"Well," said Warrick, "that's the problem, isn't it? It's never anyone's business, not if they can help it. So, while everyone looks the other way and makes excuses and ignores what's going on right in front of them, innocent people are dying."

"Again I ask, why are you taking an interest?"

"It's what we do," said Ronnie. "We help people."

Virgil nodded, and smiled. "Good. That's good."

"Tell us about this mystery *you're* working on."

"Not just a mystery," said Virgil. "A *murder* mystery. My neighbour got killed a few nights ago. I saw it happen. The killer's a guy called Oscar Moreno, owns the hardware store on Appletree Street."

Linda frowned. "It, uh, it's not much of a mystery if you already know who the killer is."

"Ah, but there's the rub. It wasn't Oscar Moreno who killed him. Well, it was, but he was also someone else. Taller. Thinner. Weird skin and a big mouth."

Linda took out her phone, brought up the picture she'd taken of the Narrow Man drawing. "He look anything like this?"

Virgil put on his spectacles, and peered at the phone. "Yep," he said. "That's him. Well, roughly."

"Let me see," said Javier, shuffling in. "Who is he?"

"He's called the Narrow Man," Linda said. "Pretty much an urban myth until now."

"It was no myth that killed my neighbour," Virgil said. "It was a shapeshifter." He held up a hand. "Now, before you dismiss me as a nutcase, hear me out. I have a computer, and Javier knows how to use it."

"I took a course," Javier explained.

"Last night," said Virgil, "we were doing some research. It was that... that Narrow Man guy that did the killing, but as he was leaving the house he turned into Oscar Moreno."

"Wearing my face," said Javier. "An exact copy of my face."

"That's right," said Virgil. "He changed his looks, his height, his weight... I think that's all they can do, though."

"That's what the website said," Javier nodded.

"Yeah," said Virgil. "Shapeshifters can change their appearance, but only in a limited kind of way. I'm not talking about him turning into a panther or anything like that. This isn't *Manimal*."

Kelly frowned. "What's *Manimal*?"

"It's a show I was due to guest on that got cancelled before we filmed my episode," Virgil explained as he made tea. "It was supposed to be the start of my comeback, but that's fine, that's the way it goes sometimes."

"Why did he kill your neighbour?" Linda asked.

Virgil shrugged. "Robert Snyder was a thief. That's not just my opinion: he'd been to jail for it. He probably stole something from Moreno, that's what I think."

"Or tried to," said Linda, "and saw something he wasn't supposed to."

Virgil shrugged. "Maybe, yes."

"Does he know you know?" Kelly asked.

"I don't think I'd be alive today if he did."

"I wouldn't be so sure," she said. "Why did he pick Javier's face? Sounds like he wanted you to see."

"He had no way of knowing I'd be looking out my window at that particular moment."

"I don't know, Virgil..."

"If he knows, he knows – so what? Nothing I can do about it. I'm not going to hide away in the town bunker. That's not how I'm going to go out."

"What do you know about Oscar Moreno?" Ronnie asked.

"Not a whole lot. I've passed his hardware store a thousand times, never been in. He lives on the other side of town, on Chester Road. We do have something in common, though – neither of us is from Desolation Hill originally. He married a widow after her husband died, moved into a house with a couple of kids and has pretty much been a stand-up guy about it all. Nobody we've spoken to had a single bad word to say about him."

Ronnie nodded. "We've seen that before. Depraved killer

establishes himself as a pillar of the community. It's a common trait."

Javier scowled. "You kids need a new line of work if these are the people you're mixing with."

"Every so often, we find someone worth the effort. Austin Cooke, for instance. We're pretty sure the Narrow Man has him."

Both Virgil and Javier froze.

"What... what'll he do with him?" asked Javier.

Ronnie hesitated. "Eventually, he'll kill him. We think. A kid goes missing around this time every year and they're never seen again."

"That's true," said Virgil. "Jesus, that's all him? That's all the work of one guy? I thought... I believed what the cops said. Accidents. Running away. All that crap. I believed them."

"You couldn't have known," said Kelly.

"You said 'eventually, he'll kill him'," Javier said. "What did you mean by 'eventually'?"

"I mean we have no reason to believe that Austin is already dead," said Ronnie. "In fact, we're working on the basis that he's alive."

"So this is a rescue mission you're on."

"Yeah. Pretty much. And it's been made a whole lot easier now that we know where to find the Narrow Man."

"So what're you going to do?" Virgil asked. "Storm the place, all guns blazing?"

"That's rarely the smart move," said Ronnie. "Austin's safety is our first priority. If we can find out where he is and get him out without causing a fuss, that's our best option. Once he's safe, we can go back for Oscar Moreno. Would you guys have any idea where Moreno would keep Austin?"

"None, sorry," said Virgil. "Although I doubt he'd take him home, not with his family there. He has the hardware store, of course. I always use the one on Main Street. It's bigger. Every time I pass his store, it looks dead."

"So if he needed somewhere to hide a kid..."

Virgil shrugged. "Maybe. I don't know. But what if you go snooping around and he finds you? If he is a shapeshifter like I think he is, he's going to be more than a handful. From what we've read, shapeshifters are pretty hard to kill."

"We'll find a way," said Ronnie. "We always do."

"Sometimes," said Warrick, nodding.

21

THEY ATE THEIR MEALS, and a civilian came to take away the remains. He didn't seem intimidated by Amber's horns any more than Lucy had been, but unlike her he didn't stop to chat.

Another three hours rolled slowly by, and they were well into the fourth when Lucy returned with Ortmann. They cuffed Amber and Milo and took them outside, into an SUV with three rows of seats and tinted windows. They were seated in the middle row. Lucy climbed in behind the wheel and Ortmann sat in the back, and they waited a few minutes until Chief Novak climbed in beside Lucy. Then they drove off for the mayor's residence.

It was set away from the town proper, and occupied a generous expanse of woodland and meadow to the north, where a large river curled down from the hills and brought with it melting snow and ice. The house itself was a grand old colonial, wood-framed and broad and two storeys tall. They were met on the front steps by a man with a badly burned face, wearing a transparent plastic mask over his scars.

"Novak," the burned man said in greeting. His eyes moved to Milo and then Amber, examining her horns without comment. When he was satisfied, he grunted and turned, led the way into the house through an ornately carved door. Novak followed immediately after, and then Amber and Milo. The other two cops were right behind them.

They passed a grand central staircase that swept up like angel wings to the second floor, then the burned man brought them through a set of double doors, into a drawing room with huge windows that looked out on to the sunset and the river that sliced through the hills. An old man stood by the window, his hands clasped behind his back. He had probably been waiting for them in this exact pose. He was, quite obviously, a dick.

The old man turned. He may have been tall once, but age had shrunk him. His white hair was sparse on top and unkempt around the ears, but the rest of him was neat and orderly. His suit was three-piece and he had a folded handkerchief in his top pocket. He wore small glasses.

"Mayor Jesper," said Novak, walking up to him. Jesper did the politician's handshake – shaking with one hand while grasping the elbow with the other.

"Chief," said Jesper. "Good of you to come. Officer Thornton, Officer Ortmann, nice to see you again."

"Mr Mayor," Lucy said, while Ortmann nodded respectfully.

Novak stood aside, allowing Jesper a clear view of Amber and Milo.

"And these are our visitors," the mayor said. "Mr Sebastian, you are a demon also, are you not?"

Milo didn't say anything, and Jesper chuckled. "I'll take that as a yes. So what do you say we dispense with the usual bullshit and skip straight to the question-and-answer section, eh? What did he offer you?"

Amber frowned. "What did *who* offer us?"

Jesper shook his head. "No, no, we are dispensing with all that, didn't you hear? No ducking of the questions will be permitted."

"I'm not ducking," said Amber. "Who are you talking about?"

"This will go better for you if you cooperate," Novak said.

"I'm trying to," said Amber. "Listen to me – no one offered us anything. You seem to think we're here for some specific reason, when really we're just running as fast as we can from those men on the motorcycles."

"The Hounds of Hell," said Jesper.

He knew of them. Of course he did. "Yes," said Amber.

"You're running from them, you say? Are you sure you're not *working with* them?"

She frowned. "What? No. Christ, no. Why would we be? I don't understand any of this. What do you think we're here for?"

"I know what you're here for," said Jesper. "You're here to kill me."

She stared at him. The only response that occurred to her was, "No, we're not."

"What did he offer you? Eh? What do you get if you kill me?"

"Seriously," Amber said, "we're not here to kill you. We hadn't even *heard* of you until a few hours ago. We were told this town might be a safe place to hide from the Hounds. That's the only reason we came."

"You're responsible for the barrier," said Milo.

Jesper looked at him, and said nothing.

"It keeps the Hounds out," Milo continued. "The Shining

Demon, too, I'm guessing. You're hiding from him, the same as we are."

"Is that right?" Amber asked the old man. "Well, that's great! It means we can work together!"

"I don't need your help to keep them out," said Jesper.

"But... but we're on the same side!"

The burned man chuckled beneath his mask.

"I doubt that," said Jesper. "The barrier keeps Astaroth and his representatives at bay, but he can still send through his little demons and killers to try to cut my throat."

"He didn't send us. I swear."

Jesper peered at her. "What were the terms of your deal with him, to get like this?"

"I didn't get this way because of a deal," she said. "My parents, they bargained, but I was born this way."

"Hmph. Interesting. Then what did you do to make him angry enough to send the Hounds?"

"I... I cheated him."

A smile twitched at Jesper's mouth. "I see."

"We're not your enemy. We can be allies if you'd just let us."

Jesper turned, walked back to the window, his hands once again behind his back. "Why? What do you propose? In what way can you possibly bring any advantage to me? You have drawn the Hounds back to Desolation Hill. You have focused Astaroth's gaze upon me again after all this time. We are not, and can never be, allies. Your presence here is unwelcome."

"But... but nowhere else is safe."

"Desolation Hill isn't safe. Not for you."

"So what are you going to do?" Amber asked. "Hand us over to the Hounds? You'd be sending us to our death."

Jesper shook his head. "What they do with you is not my concern."

"Bullshit," said Amber. "Handing us over is the same as killing us."

"I don't involve myself in such matters," Jesper said. "I leave that to Chief Novak and his fine police force."

"Your Chief of Police has already murdered a man!" Amber said. "He shot him right in front of us!"

"Philip Daggett was a serial killer," Novak said, sounding bored.

Jesper waved his hand. "I don't involve myself in such matters," he repeated. "My police take care of the unfortunate necessities. I focus on keeping this town running."

"What did you do?" Milo asked, his voice quiet.

Jesper turned to him.

"You know why the Shining Demon is coming after us," Milo continued, "but why is he coming after you? What did you do?"

"You really want to know, Mr Sebastian? Then answer my question. Are you a demon also?"

Milo didn't say anything. But after a moment he shifted, and Jesper hurried closer, eyes wide.

"My, my... You're not one of his, are you? Astaroth's demons are red and beautiful, but you... You are night itself, and wonderful. Demoriel, am I right"

Milo didn't respond. Steam rose from his red eyes.

Jesper nodded, more to himself than anyone else. "Definitely the work of Demoriel. You have a car, yes?"

"We have it impounded," said Novak. "Haven't even gone through it yet."

"I'd be careful when you do," said Jesper. "Demoriel tends to make deals with people with horses or carriages or, these days, cars. These animals or vehicles are linked to his demons. I'd say Mr Sebastian's car could certainly harbour a nasty surprise or two. The truly interesting thing is, I have read that Demoriel is very particular in choosing those to whom he grants power. What was it about you, Mr Sebastian, that he was drawn to?"

"That's not what you asked," said Amber. "You asked if he was a demon. He answered. Now it's your turn."

Jesper dragged his eyes away from Milo – reluctantly – and gazed at Amber for a few moments before chuckling again. "Very well, very well. I am a man of my word, after all. Officers, would you mind leaving us?"

Lucy and Ortmann hid their surprise well, and nodded and left. When they were gone, when it was just Amber and Milo standing there with Jesper and Novak and the burned man, Jesper continued.

"This land was not always American, did you know that? When I was born here, it was controlled by Russia. That was nearly three hundred years ago."

Amber refused to be impressed by his age.

"Back then, things were tough," Jesper said. "I'm sure you can imagine if you try hard enough. I was born into poverty and I spent my life clawing my way out of it. And, just when my fortunes were beginning to turn, I realised I had become an old man. My life was hardship and bitterness and it was almost over."

"So you made a deal with the Shining Demon to prolong your life," Amber interrupted, "and something went wrong along the way."

Jesper smiled. "You don't know nearly as much as you think you do, young lady. But yes, that was one of my goals. And so, a little over two hundred years ago, I summoned the Shining Demons."

Amber frowned. "Plural?"

Jesper nodded. "Brothers, from what I was told. Astaroth and Naberius. They appeared before me and we negotiated. They agreed to provide me with power and success and one hundred more years of life, and they named their price."

"Which was?"

"An offering."

"A soul?"

For the first time, discomfort flickered across Jesper's face.

"It's usually a soul," Amber pressed. "That's what I'm told, anyway. How many were they asking?"

Jesper looked away. "One a year until the contract expired."

Milo reverted. "So who decided it should be the souls of children, Mr Mayor?"

There was some part of Amber that was aware of how horrible that was, and yet it failed to rouse her anger. She didn't mind. With her horns on, she was enjoying the look on Jesper's face too much to bother with feeling outraged.

"I'm assuming it was a practical necessity," Milo continued. "A man of your age couldn't be expected to target people who might be able to fight back. Let's face it, kids are easier to kill."

"Is that true?" Amber asked. "You agreed to murder one child every year for a hundred years? Wow. That takes commitment, Mr Mayor. Your depravity is impressive."

"Do not mock me," Jesper responded.

"Hey, listen, from one monster to another, good going."

Novak was suddenly at her side, cracking his gun into her skull. The world tilted and Amber fell to one knee.

"I'm not a monster!" Jesper shouted down at her. "I was scared! I didn't want to die and I was scared, so yes, I agreed to it. But I'm not that person anymore."

"If you say so," Amber said, glaring at Novak. She looked back at Jesper. "But if the contract was for a hundred years, and that was two hundred years ago, what happened?"

Jesper calmed himself before answering. "Naberius returned to me five years before my contract expired – alone this time. He offered to extend the deal to twice its length if I would help him trap his brother."

"Family back-stabbing," Amber said, getting to her feet. She could relate.

"He instructed me to build a cell in the caves beneath the town, and in the middle of that cell I was to carve a circle inscribed with ancient symbols. Then I was to collapse all tunnels that led to it. He provided the keys that would form a bridge of sorts between the cell door and any other door."

"I've seen one of those," said Amber. "A brass key, right? Dacre Shanks used one."

"Perhaps," Jesper said. "Naberius made three such keys. I only know for certain where one of them is, the one that had been given to me. I constructed the cell. He constructed the keys. All we had to do was fool Astaroth into stepping into the circle, which would trap him for eternity."

"But Astaroth found out," said Milo.

"Yes," Jesper said ruefully. "He appeared, told me he had known all along, and then explained the new plan. When the day came, he played along until the final moment, when he pushed his brother into the circle instead."

Amber smiled. "This is all so treacherous. I love it."

"Once Naberius was trapped," Jesper said, "Astaroth chained him and left him to spend eternity underground. As for me, I began thinking of the day when Astaroth would come to claim my soul. So I stopped delivering the offerings to him, and instead delivered them straight to Naberius. I siphoned off his power and used it to construct the barrier around this town."

"You're using Naberius as a battery," said Milo.

"It's the only thing that will keep Astaroth at bay."

"So the offerings," Milo said, "the kids you're killing, they're being used to keep up Naberius's strength?"

"I'm not killing them," Jesper said quickly. "I couldn't keep doing it, so I passed on the key to someone who could. I just... I don't concern myself with that side of things anymore."

Amber look at Novak. "Is that your job, then? Killing the kids?"

"We keep the peace," he answered. "That's not our department."

"Is it you?" Amber asked, now looking at the burned man. "Do you kill them?"

"It is no one in this room," said Jesper.

Amber frowned. "So who does it? Is it someone you hire? Is it a freelancer? Are you seriously saying you've outsourced your blood sacrifice?" She laughed. "This is crazy! I love this goddamn town! It's all so messed up!"

"Do not mock us!" Jesper yelled in his quavering voice. "Do not mock the sacrifices made by our young people!"

"That you're killing, asshole."

Novak jammed his gun into Amber's neck.

"Change back," he said.

"Screw you."

"Your smart mouth is getting you in trouble," Novak said. "It's going to get you killed right here and right now. Do yourself a favour and change back."

Amber glared defiantly at Jesper, but when she looked at Milo he was nodding to her calmly. She gritted her teeth, and reverted.

There was no more pain from her healed fingers, but the headache kicked in immediately and she could feel the bruise from where Novak had struck her even as he tightened the cuffs. If she shifted now, she'd probably break her own wrists, so she stayed as she was. She'd had enough of broken hands for the time being.

"For the good of the town, the sacrifices must continue," Jesper replied. He was much calmer now. "This is regrettable. What is also regrettable is your presence here, as it endangers the lives and well-being of the people of Desolation Hill. As a conciliatory gesture, I'm afraid we must give Astaroth what he wants, and hope that he'll be satisfied with that."

"You're going to hand us over?" Milo asked.

"For the good of the town, I must. Chief Novak?"

Novak levelled his gun at them. "Walk," he said.

22

IT WAS SOMEWHERE AROUND ELEVEN, and they drove back the way they'd come, then veered off, took a bumpy trail that someone had worn down through sheer stubbornness, until they got to the spot right on the edge of town where a police cruiser was parked, headlights on, facing the five Hounds.

"If you do this, Astaroth will kill us," Milo said.

Novak ignored him.

"Please," Amber said, leaning forward, "at least let us have a fighting chance. Take the handcuffs off."

"Sit back," Lucy warned.

"Chief Novak, please."

"Sit back!" Lucy snapped.

Amber sat back. The handcuffs bit into her wrists.

The SUV stopped beside the cruiser. A cop was waiting for them, the guy they'd seen the previous night. They sat in silence for a moment, just long enough for Amber to start hoping that Novak would change his mind.

"Let's get it done," Novak said, and the car doors opened. Officer Duncan pulled Amber out into the cold night air. She didn't struggle as she was walked towards the Hounds. There was no point.

Beyond the invisible barrier, the Hounds waited. They made no move. They didn't say anything. They just stood there, with their beards and their stubble, wearing their sunglasses even now, as the gloom rushed in. Silently waiting. Expectant.

Duncan's grip was solid. Amber could have shaken it off if she broke her wrists and shifted, but all it'd take would be the slightest of pushes and she'd be stumbling into the arms of the Hounds. Novak was beside her. Beside him, Milo, held by both Ortmann and Lucy.

Novak looked at each of the Hounds and they looked back. Ten seconds dragged by. Fifteen.

Novak chuckled drily, and shook his head. "Oh, this is unfortunate," he said at last, to the Hound right in front of him. "I would have handed them over, I really would have. If only you weren't so smug about it."

The Hounds, with their expressionless faces, didn't react as Novak turned to Lucy. "Put them back in the car," he said. "Release them somewhere else along the boundary. Your choice."

"Sir?"

"There is no reason I can see why we should make it so easy for Astaroth's pets." Novak returned his attention to the Hound. "You're going to have to sing for your supper, dog."

Suddenly Amber was being pulled backwards to the SUV. Duncan opened the door, practically threw her in, as Milo was shoved in from the other side. Lucy jumped in behind the wheel, Ortmann beside her, and she gunned the engine and they kicked up pebbles and dirt as they turned. Amber looked back as the Hounds got on their bikes and prepared to give chase.

"You could let us out at our car," Milo said. "Let us lead them away from here."

Lucy didn't reply. Keeping a firm grip on the steering wheel, she took them through the outskirts of Desolation Hill at a blistering pace that snapped branches and almost tore the axle off the SUV. The headlights sweeping round the town's perimeter could now only be glimpsed in the distance.

They found a small road and swerved on to it, jamming Amber hard against Milo. They straightened up and Amber was sent the other way, and cracked her head off the window. Lucy killed the SUV's headlights and put her foot down, and trees blurred against the darkening sky.

Then Lucy braked, and Amber cursed as she almost slid off her seat entirely. Next thing she knew the door was open and Ortmann was dragging her out.

"Go," he said. "Run."

She broke from his grip, looked around, tried to get her bearings. Lucy took her by the arm, led her to Milo. She pointed at a tree stump ahead of them.

"That's where the boundary lies," she said. "Better start running."

Milo turned to her. "Give us the keys. Let us drive out of here."

"You run," said Lucy.

"Give us a fighting chance, for Christ's sake."

"You run," said Lucy, taking a rifle from the SUV. "We see you trying to double back, we'll shoot you in the legs."

They could hear it now. A motorcycle.

"You're killing us," said Amber.

Lucy turned to Ortmann. "Drive to the edge of Mill Farm," she said, "headlights on full. Give a blast of the siren if you have to. Get the Hounds to follow you."

"On it," Ortmann said. He got in the SUV, flicked on the lights, and peeled out of there, and Lucy took a small key from her pocket and pressed it into Amber's hands.

"Go," she said. "Now."

Milo started running, and Amber followed. The moment she passed the tree stump the instinctive urge to shift drained from her body. They sprinted for the trees ahead, barely making it before a Hound roared by, following the SUV.

Amber watched him go, then turned back to Milo. He was already moving on, and she quickly lost him in the gloom.

"Milo!" she whispered, and started after him. "Milo, slow down!"

Milo stopped, and while he waited for her to get a little closer he hunkered down and passed the handcuff chain under his feet so that his hands were in front of him. Before she'd reached him, he started moving again.

"She gave me the key," Amber said. "Hold on a second."

"We're beyond the barrier," he said without looking back. "That means they can sense you again. The cop driving off won't fool that Hound for long."

And, just to prove him right, they heard the Hound coming back.

And then more bikes, coming in from ahead. Lights cut through the trees.

"Crap," Amber whispered.

They speeded up.

One of the bikes was close. Very close. The ground was becoming one big blanket of dark and Amber nearly tripped half a dozen times on roots or logs or vines or rocks, but she kept going, and kept going *faster*, and the bike was getting even closer, but its light was off and it was hard, it was *impossible*, to tell where it was, as there was sound all around them now, and then she stumbled on to a road in time to see a bike slam into Milo and flip him into the air.

"Milo!" she yelled, and the Hound braked and swung round 180 degrees in a sudden cloud of smoke, the headlight snapping on, and Amber ducked back before she was seen.

Milo rolled to a stop, and the Hound rode back to him slowly.

Amber watched Milo prop himself up on to his elbows and try to get his knees under him. The Hound passed, then stopped, leaned his bike on its kickstand and got off. He had a chain in his hands, a heavy one, and he twirled it. Milo got to one knee and the Hound lashed the chain against the side of his head.

Another Hound roared up, and Amber shrank back as the headlight searched the darkness around her. When it was safe, she looked again. The Hound with the chain had attached it to Milo's handcuffs while the other one circled them, then rode off. The Hound with the chain attached the other end to the back of his bike, and got on.

"No," Amber whispered.

The bike revved and shot forward, and the chain went taut and jerked Milo after it.

Amber couldn't help it. She leaped from cover and screamed, but Milo was already gone, dragged away into the darkness.

She stood there, her thoughts a horrified jumble. The bike's tail lights disappeared round the bend. The road looped. If she was lucky...

She broke left, running into the trees, her shoes slipping on the incline. She could have cleared this little hill with no trouble as a demon, but she wasn't going to let her own natural weakness stop her. Not this time.

She got to the top, met the road again as the first Hound passed. Gasping for breath, she crouched in the dark and waited. To do what? What the hell did she think she was going to do? If she shifted, she'd break her damn wrists, and then what good would she be to Milo?

The key was tiny in her freezing, slippery hands. She managed to get a good grip and tapped it against the cuffs, searching for the keyhole.

"Come on," she snarled to herself. "Come on, you useless piece of..."

The second Hound was approaching now, at speed. Amber could see Milo behind it, swinging wide on the chain. The road had ripped his shirt, and torn his boots and pants and underwear clean off. He was a bloody mess beneath it.

The key sank into the keyhole and hope flared in her chest. The Hound passed where she was crouching, dragging Milo with him.

Amber held her hands close together so as not to jar the key loose, and crossed the road and started up the next incline. Her legs were burning, screaming at her, but she kept going, kept climbing, aware of the other bikes now, roaring up from all directions. They could sense her close by, but if they had the ability to pinpoint her exact position she doubted she'd be able to keep out of sight like this.

They moved up and round the bend, joining the two in front. The incline levelled out and Amber sagged, took three deep breaths and shook out her legs, and ran through the dark from tree to tree.

The Hounds had left the road and had congregated in a clearing in the woodland. She stayed out of the glare of their headlights, her clumsy footsteps masked by the engines. They were off their bikes now. One of them took a bolt cutter from his pack. The others came forward, all holding chains. They knelt by Milo, obscuring him from Amber's view.

She refocused on the key. Tried turning it, but it jammed. Sweat stung her eyes. She looked back up as four of the Hounds walked to their idling bikes, and heeled up the kickstands. Their tail lights bathed Milo in red. He was naked, with great strips torn from his skin. Around each wrist and ankle, there was a chain. The Hounds attached those chains to their bikes.

All the strength left Amber's body.

The bikes moved slowly, inch by inch, in four different directions, until the chains went taut. Slowly, Milo was lifted off the ground. He opened his mouth, but his cry was drowned out by the revving motorcycles.

The fifth Hound, the one on the Harley, circled the lot of them, lazily waiting for Amber to surrender herself. The revving got louder. They knew she was there. They knew she was watching. The implication was clear.

Give up, or they'd tear Milo apart.

23

Sobbing, Amber retreated from the light. Her fingers trembling, she twisted the key again, then risked taking another grip and repeating the movement.

This time, it worked.

The cuff around her left wrist sprang free, and she gasped, and quickly rid herself of the handcuffs altogether. Then she shifted, and, as her skin turned red and her horns grew, her tears went away, and in place of her desperation came raw anger.

Her hands becoming claws, she jumped for the nearest tree and started climbing. She found a thick branch and crawled quickly along it. It bent with her weight so she leaped for another, swinging up into the next. She climbed some more, the night alive with the sound of the engines below her. She balanced on a branch, looked down, her teeth bared. To try to free Milo without first taking out the Hounds was a sure-fire way of getting him killed. Similarly, to attack any of the four Hounds that had him chained would also result in him being pulled apart. Which left one option, and one target.

She waited until he was about to pass directly beneath her, and she dropped.

She landed beside the Hound on the Harley, hands crashing down on to his shoulders. She yanked him off, dragged him backwards while his bike toppled, then grabbed his head, her claws raking into his face.

"Let Milo go!" she roared. "Take those chains off and let him go or I'll kill your buddy!"

The revving quieted. The Hounds looked at her.

She had a sudden, horrible thought that maybe she'd already killed the Hound in her grip, that she'd lost her only bargaining chip. But, although the Hound wasn't struggling, he was still staying upright under his own steam.

"Let Milo go!" Amber screamed.

Moments passed.

As one, the revving died. The four Hounds backed up a little, allowing the chains to slacken enough to lower Milo to the ground.

"Take the chains off," Amber commanded. The Hounds got off their bikes, but didn't move. "Do it or I'll break his neck."

The Hound in her grasp tried to straighten up, but she tightened her hold and put her lips to his ear.

"You try anything and I swear to God I will kill you without a second—"

The Hound spun on his heel, snapping his own neck while his hands closed on her upper arms. Amber cried out, let go, barely aware that the Hound's body was powering her backwards even as his head was still pointing the other way. Then the head spun with another violent crack, and the Hound righted himself and slammed her against a tree. She glimpsed her reflection in his sunglasses and then chips of wood sprayed her face as a gunshot rang out. The Hound looked around in time to catch a bullet in the forehead. He went down and Amber scrambled away.

More gunshots. Amber couldn't see where they were coming from. One of the Hounds ignored the bullet that hit him square in the chest. He couldn't ignore the next one, though, the one that caught him in the head. He tumbled backwards, bringing his bike down with him.

The shooter's aim was improving. Two headshots in a row left only one Hound standing. Amber ran, crouched over, to Milo. Before she'd even unwrapped the first chain, the Hound started towards her. Amber watched him come, waiting and hoping for the next shot. She wasn't disappointed. The bullet hit the Hound in the forehead and his knees buckled and he collapsed.

Amber freed Milo's legs. Then his arms. She got her hands underneath him and scooped him up, grunting only a little. She stood, turned, Milo in her arms, and flinched at another gunshot. But the shooter wasn't aiming at her. The first Hound had got to his feet and another bullet put him down again. The Hound closest to her was stirring now. They all were. Shooting these assholes in the head obviously wasn't enough.

Amber ran, carrying Milo.

Another two gunshots gave her a head start, and then they stopped. Whoever the shooter was, they had done their part, and Amber and Milo were on their own again.

She heard an engine, watched an old farm truck trundle by. She sprinted after it until she was right in its non-existent slipstream, and jumped, landing in a crouch to steady herself. She moved forward, laid Milo down, was about to pull the tarp over them both when the night was lit up with swooping headlights.

She heard herself snarl as two Hounds broke away from the pack and closed in, side by side. One of them reached over to the other bike, his hands closing around the throttle, taking control of the machine. The other Hound stood up on the seat with all the urgency of a lazy man stretching. Both bikes closed in on the farm truck, and the Hound stepped from the seat to the headlight, and then took a long stride on to the truck bed. He stood straight, the bump and sway of the road not bothering him in the slightest, while the two bikes slowed behind him. Amber didn't have a choice.

She launched herself at him. They tumbled off and hit the road, went rolling, her clothes ripping, but her black scales protecting her. As long as she proved herself worthy of all their attention, Milo might have a chance to get to safety. That was her plan.

They both got to their feet and she sprang at him, but the Hound ducked under her, grabbed her as she passed, and slammed her down on to the asphalt. She hit her chin and bit her tongue.

So much for her goddamn plan.

She tried to get up and a boot slammed down between her shoulder blades like a sledgehammer.

Amber lay there, gasping, dimly aware of the sound of a chain scraping against the ground. Then she was hauled up, and that chain was being wrapped around her neck, and her eyes snapped open and she started to struggle and a fist came in and her thoughts bounced away from her in a flash of white.

She fell to her hands and knees. An engine revved. Her neck was cold. Why was her neck cold? Oh yeah.

The chain.

The bike took off at speed and the chain went tight and Amber was pulled off her hands and knees.

24

THE ROAD WAS ANGRY and rough and blurred beneath her as she was dragged along its surface. Her scales rose instantly on her elbows and thighs and on her belly. She grabbed the chain with both hands, tried to stop it from choking her, tried to stop it from pulling her head off. The bike picked up speed. Her sneakers and socks were already gone. She heard her shirt rip. The road snagged at her pants.

She pulled herself forward, then brought her legs in and around until she was sliding along on her ass. The seat of her pants tore away. Her scales scraped. They covered her feet as well, and she put her heels down as she pulled herself, hand over hand, closer to the bike. When she had enough slack, she held on with one hand while the other unwrapped the chain from around her neck. Then she raised herself up, straightening her legs like she was on waterskis.

Despite herself, she grinned.

She risked a glance over her shoulder, made sure the other Hounds weren't following, and then hurled the chain upwards. It wrapped around a branch and Amber let go, went tumbling into the undergrowth a heartbeat before the chain snapped tight. She expected the bike to be jerked up on to its front wheel. She expected the Hound to be thrown. What she didn't expect was the thick, heavy branch to snap off like a matchstick and skip and jump down the road after him.

He slowed, then swooped back round.

"Balls," said Amber, and plunged into the trees.

She caught sight of the farm truck's lights and started on an intercept course. Behind her, around her, motorcycles revved and roared. She tripped, went flying, scrambled up and ran on, on to the road again. She glimpsed the truck disappearing round the next bend and hurtled into the treeline, always going downwards, letting gravity lend her speed. She crashed into trees and branches and fell again, tripped again, sprawled again, but she was up, always up, and now she could see that the truck was driving towards a building. A farm.

She burst from the trees as a motorcycle charged up the trail next to her. The Hound snatched the air close to her shoulder. Amber ducked and skidded on wet grass, went tumbling down an incline. Even as she tumbled, she was aware of the bike crashing, but that brought no sense of triumph – there was a black shape now sprinting down the incline after her.

Amber levelled out and rolled and launched herself up. Get to the farmhouse. Get inside. Find a weapon. The Hound was right behind her. She left the grass and ran on dirt. His footsteps were heavy but quick. Too quick. He was gaining. He was about to catch her.

The Hound snagged the back of her jacket and Amber jumped, letting her momentum take her forward even as she twisted. In mid-air she went to slash him across the face, but her body buzzed and she realised she was passing through the barrier, into the town. The Hound hit empty space, his entire body slamming into a wall of nothing, his sunglasses smashing, and he staggered back even as she hit the ground.

Amber rolled to her knees. Sucking in lungfuls of air, she grinned, and stood, safe behind the invisible wall, and gave him the finger.

The Hound straightened. His eyes burned with the same orange glow that radiated from the Shining Demon. Her grin faltered. The Hound pulled another pair of sunglasses from his jacket, and put them on. Amber backed away, then turned and hurried to the farmhouse.

She sank into the shadows, came round the corner, and saw an old man standing at the back of the truck, pulling the tarp off Milo. Milo hadn't shifted when he'd passed through the barrier. She dreaded to think what that might say about his strength, but she knew it wasn't good.

She reverted and zipped up her jacket. Her shirt was torn. Her pants were torn, too, especially around her ass, but there wasn't a whole lot she could do about that.

The old man, though. Amber recognised him. He was the old guy who'd cut up her breakfast. His name. His name. He'd told her his name and she'd forgotten it. What was his damn—

"Benjamin?" she said, and he turned, eyes wide. She held up her hands as she emerged from the darkness. "Benjamin, we talked a few days ago. At Fast Danny's. My name's Amber. That's Milo."

For a long while, Benjamin didn't say anything. Then he shook his head. "I don't think I should be involved in this."

"I'm not involving you," Amber told him quickly. "We just had to get away. You saw those bikers, right?"

"None of my business."

"Benjamin, my friend is badly hurt. Look at him. He's dying."

"I should call the police," he said, and started towards the farmhouse. Amber darted into his path.

"No!" she said, and Benjamin froze. She tried smiling. "I'm sorry, I didn't mean to... The cops, they know about this. They forced us out. In here, in town, those bikers can't touch us, but out there..."

"You should leave," said Benjamin.

"I need your help."

"I can't. I'm sorry, I can't."

"Drive us into town. Benjamin, please. Novak has probably taken our car somewhere. Everything I need to save Milo's life is in that car. Just drive us to it. I'll take care of the rest."

"Can't do that."

"Yes, you can."

"If the Chief found out—"

"He won't. I swear he won't. You're not going to get in trouble for this, Benjamin, I promise you. We haven't done anything wrong. We haven't hurt anyone or broken any laws."

"You must have," Benjamin said, squaring his shoulders. He walked past her, to the house. "Novak has his reasons."

Amber glanced at Milo, then hurried after the old man. "The mayor told him to do it. He's got it wrong. He thinks we're a danger to him, but we're not."

Benjamin's front door wasn't locked. He opened it and went inside, tried to close it, but Amber jammed her foot in. "Please leave me alone," he said.

Amber could have shifted, thrown the door open, but she didn't. "This is not a normal town, Benjamin. You must see that."

They locked eyes through the gap. A long moment passed. Then Benjamin sighed and stepped back, and invited her in.

The kitchen was warm, heated by embers that still stirred in the fireplace. There was an old sofa and a TV, a big table and two chairs, one of them piled high with laundry. A plate and mug near the sink. Boots by the door. This was the home of a bachelor or a widower. Judging by the once colourful, now faded curtains, Amber guessed a widower.

"None of this is my concern," Benjamin said softly, his eyes on the floor.

"Excuse me?"

His gaze flicked upwards briefly. "None of this has anything to do with me or any of the other folks here. We leave all that business to Mayor Jesper and Chief Novak. They can take care of it."

"What business? What do they take care of?"

"That stuff," Benjamin said irritably. "The weird stuff."

"Like what?"

"I don't know." He rubbed the back of his head. "I mean, this town's always been this way. I was born here and it's all I've ever known. Yeah, unusual things happen here, but—"

"This is a little beyond unusual," Amber interrupted. "Do you know anything of what goes on? What really goes on? Novak's a *murderer*."

"No," Benjamin said. "No, I refuse to believe that. Does he have to make tough calls? Yes. But he keeps the town safe and that's no easy thing."

"Who is he keeping it safe from? What are you hiding, Benjamin?"

"I'm sorry now, miss, but—"

"Amber. My name's Amber."

"Amber, I'm sorry, but I can't help you. If the Chief is after you, then you're a criminal, and that's all there is to it."

"No," Amber said, and shifted, "it's not."

His eyes widened at the transformation and he took a step back.

Amber watched him. "That usually gets a little more of a reaction," she said.

Benjamin pointed a shaking finger at the door. "Leave. I want you to leave immediately."

"Why aren't you freaking out, Benjamin?" Amber said, moving closer. "Why aren't you screaming right now? You're used to this, aren't you? You're used to freaks like me."

Benjamin backed up till he was standing against the wall. "This is my house and I demand—"

She lunged, pinning him where he stood and snapping her teeth an inch from his throat. He whimpered. Slowly, she raised herself to her full height and looked down at him. "Tell me what's going on, Benjamin."

"I don't... I don't know where to..."

"Where to start? Start by telling me about this festival of yours."

He swallowed. "They call it Hell Night."

"They?"

"They. We. Folk here. We call it Hell Night. Happens same time every year."

She stepped away, giving him some room. "What does?"

"The town," Benjamin said, "it... it changes. I mean, we know it's cursed. We're not stupid. You can feel it, sometimes. Something in the air. Something bad. It gets in your hair, your clothes, gets in your skin. Fills your head with bad thoughts. People would leave, I think, if other things weren't so good. Businesses are doing well, always have. The ground is fertile. Animals are healthy. Those bad thoughts are the price we pay for everything else being so good."

"What kind of bad thoughts?"

Benjamin reached out for the free chair, and collapsed into it like all his strength had left him. "They're always there, the bad feelings. Sometimes they're strong and sometimes they're not. You can never forget that they're there, but if you're lucky you can almost ignore them. On the run-up to Hell Night they almost fade away entirely... But on Hell Night itself they come back. That's when they're at their strongest."

"You said the town changes," Amber said. "How?"

"Streets get longer," Benjamin said, eyes glistening. "Houses get narrower. Sidewalks crack, like there's been an earthquake or something. And the people... the people change, too."

"In what way?"

"They change like you change," said Benjamin.

"They're demons?" Amber said, frowning. "For one night a year, they're demons? All of them?"

"Everyone over eighteen," said Benjamin. "Everyone below that age is locked away in the panic rooms. Near every home in this town has one. The kids can't get out and the adults can't get in."

"And... and what happens then?"

Benjamin smiled, but there was no humour in it. "The people in this town... they attack each other. The whole year, they've been saving up their badness for Hell Night, and when that night comes, they let it all out. They do... they do terrible things to one another. Terrible, shameful things. In the morning, everything's back to normal and most everyone's healed up. Most. Not all. We lose about five people a year to this, people who've been hurt too bad or just outright killed in the streets."

"Jesus."

"You know the funny thing? No one talks about it. No one mentions it. Your neighbour might have tried to gut you during Hell Night, but next morning both of you are pretending everything is sunshine and daisies. Resentment builds up. That adds to the bad thoughts."

"You said everyone over the age of eighteen changes," said Amber. "Do you?"

"I'm over eighteen, aren't I?"

"Do you know why? Why this is all happening? Was it ever explained to you?"

"No," said Benjamin. "And I never bothered to ask. I know it's got something to do with the mayor. That's obvious. One of our little pastimes here is doing what the mayor says but not... but not actually talking about him. You talk about him and sooner or later you're going to have to admit to one another that he's always been here. Things are easier to ignore when you don't talk about them."

"And what about the kids, Benjamin? What about the missing kids?"

"What? What are you talking about?"

"You've never wondered how Hell Night is powered? Or have you decided you just don't want to know?"

Benjamin didn't answer.

"You have a chance to do good here," Amber said. "Whatever sins you've committed in the past, whatever you've ignored or allowed to happen, I don't give a crap about any of it right now. My friend is dying on the back of your truck and I need to get him to his car. The cops, I think the cops have probably taken it."

"It'll be in the impound lot," Benjamin said. "On Maple."

"Can you drive us?"

"I don't... I don't usually involve myself in these things."

"I know. I know that. I wish there were some other way. But I need your help. Please, Benjamin. I'm begging you."

The old man rubbed his forehead. His hand was shaking. He cleared his throat, nodded, and stood. "I can drive you," he said.

"Thank you," said Amber. "Thank you. You're a good man. You're a good, kind—"

"I am *not* a good man," Benjamin said sharply. "All I want is to be left alone. I've gone my whole life without making a fuss, and I'm not about to start now. I'll give you a ride into town, but after that, please... please leave me alone."

25

OSCAR MORENO'S HARDWARE STORE was open late on a Tuesday night.

Kelly sat in the warm van with the others while Two snored and farted on the cushions, and they watched a steady stream of customers walk in with cash and walk out with hammers and nails and drills and sheets of plywood. All around town it was happening – stores and businesses being shuttered and boarded up, houses being reinforced. It was like they were preparing for a storm. Or a riot. Or maybe a little of both.

Finally, a little after midnight, Moreno himself emerged. The gang stared at the younger – the much younger – version of Javier Santorum as he locked up.

"This is freaky," said Warrick. "He looks just like Insidio did in the show. Or Javier, even. His hair's different, but... wow. Flashbacks."

"We could take him now," said Kelly. "The four of us would be enough, wouldn't we?"

"We've never gone up against a shapeshifter before," Linda said, not taking her eyes off Moreno. "I've never even heard of anyone who has."

"But against all of us...?"

Ronnie shook his head. "We don't go in unprepared. Ever. That gets us killed. Besides, we're not here for him. We're here for Austin."

Moreno climbed into his car — a nice, sensible Prius — and drove off. They waited a minute or two to make sure he didn't come back to pick up something he'd forgotten, then Kelly, Linda and Ronnie got out of the van. Warrick stayed with Two for the moment. Out of all of them, Two was integral to what they were about to do — their very own sniffer dog.

They stayed behind the van while three cars passed, then remained hidden as a woman walked by on the opposite side of the road. When the street emptied, they hurried across, but before they'd reached the far sidewalk a truck turned a corner and snatched them in its headlights. It immediately altered course, veering towards them.

"We can't be in trouble already," said Linda. "We haven't broken any laws today."

The truck pulled up right beside them and a girl jumped out from the passenger side. The girl from the jail. The driver — an old man — kept the engine running.

"Amber," said Kelly.

"You've got to help me," Amber said. Her clothes were in tatters. "If you're really not after us, then I need your help. Please."

Ronnie frowned. "Why would we be after you?"

"Because other people are," said Amber. "I need to know if I can trust you."

Ronnie hesitated, and Linda remained quiet, but Kelly spoke up. "You can trust us," she said. "What's wrong?"

Amber moved to the rear of the van, and pulled the tarp back.

"Jesus," said Linda.

Kelly and Ronnie lent Amber a hand and they lifted her friend off the truck. Milo, that was his name. He was ruined. A bloody mess. The moment they were clear of the truck, the driver put his foot down and got the hell out of there.

Kelly stepped back, her shirt smeared with blood. "What happened to him?"

"Bikers," said Amber. "They chained him, dragged him behind them."

"We saw bikers on our way into town," Kelly said, like that contributed to the conversation in any meaningful way.

"Listen," said Ronnie, "we have some basic medical training, but this... we can't handle something like this. We need to get him to a hospital. The nearest is maybe sixty miles away."

Amber shook her head. "We can't leave town."

"He won't survive unless we—"

"If he leaves this town, they'll kill him," Amber said. "If you can bandage him up, please do that. All I have to do is get him to his car. I'm pretty sure it's at the impound lot."

"What good'll that do?" Linda asked.

"It's just what we need to do. Please."

Ronnie hesitated for the briefest of moments. "Let's put him in the van."

Warrick got out, tied the dog to a fire hydrant, and helped them carry Milo across the street and into the van. When he was settled, Linda threw a blanket over him, then they closed the door and looked at Amber.

"I really think a hospital is the way to go here," Linda said.

"His car," Amber said. "We just need his car."

"You're the boss..."

"Thank you," Amber said. "All of you, thank you for doing this. I'm sorry I can't go into more detail, but..."

"You've got secrets," said Kelly. "Who doesn't?"

"Yeah, man," said Warrick, "we don't take this shit personally, we really don't. We've been on the Dark Highway long enough to learn to respect other people's privacy."

Amber looked up, eyes widening slightly.

"I had a feeling you'd recognise the term. You have that look about you. The bikers – they're part of whatever it is you're into?"

Amber nodded. "We've been running from them for weeks."

"What did you do to piss them off?" Ronnie asked.

"I'm... I'm sorry, I am, but I don't know if I should tell you. I don't know you and it might... It's dangerous."

"Danger's our middle name," said Warrick.

Kelly rolled her eyes, then smiled at Amber. "Warrick may be overly dramatic, but he's not wrong. This is what we do. We travel the Dark Highway and we fight the forces of darkness."

Amber frowned at her. "Why?"

"Because if we don't, who will?"

"I don't know," said Amber. "Whoever the darkness is threatening, I guess. So you actually drive around looking for trouble?"

"We each have our reasons," said Kelly. "What has you on the Highway?"

Amber hesitated. "My parents."

Warrick shook his head glumly. "They kick you out?"

"They're trying to kill me."

"That was my next guess."

"Or they were," said Amber. "Don't know if they still are. Last I saw of them they were running from the same thing I am."

"Which is?" Linda asked.

Amber gave a grim smile. "I think it's best if you don't know the details."

"Fair enough. Can I ask, though — why are you safe here? Why don't those bikers just come in after you?"

"Honestly? A big invisible wall keeps them out."

"Cool," said Warrick.

"And why are you here?" Amber asked.

"Children are going missing," said Ronnie. "One a year. Heard anything about that?"

"I guess I have," said Amber. "It's a long story, and I don't know if I understand it fully yet, but the mayor here, a guy called Jesper... You know about making deals with Demons?"

"We've had some experience with people who have," Linda said.

"Well, Jesper made a deal with the Shining Demon, Astaroth, two hundred years ago. The price he's paying is one child's soul every year."

Ronnie narrowed his eyes. "You know about this and Jesper's still walking around?"

Amber glared back. "When he told us, we were handcuffed. Then the bikers got us. We didn't have time to fight the good fight."

"No one's accusing anyone of anything," Kelly said, giving a glare of her own to Ronnie. "There's a kid who's just gone missing. For all we know, he might still be alive. His name's Austin Cooke. Did Jesper mention where he might be being kept?"

"I doubt he knows," Amber said. "He's absolved himself of all responsibility when it comes to that stuff. He outsources."

"Seriously?" Warrick said. "This is somewhere beyond cold." He went off to untie Two.

"Jesper didn't mention who he's hired?" Linda asked. "Did he talk about the Narrow Man?"

"He didn't really offer up any details, sorry."

"Maybe he'll offer some up to us," Ronnie said.

"Maybe," said Amber. "If you can get to him. Which I doubt. Those cops of his are killers. I saw the Chief shoot a man in cold blood. Yeah, the guy was a serial killer, but still. It wouldn't take much to convince them you're more trouble than you're worth."

"Do you have any idea what Hell Night is?" Linda asked.

"Oh yeah," Amber said grimly. "It's happened one night a year for the last hundred years. Tomorrow night this town goes nuts. All the kids get put into their own little panic rooms, and all the adults turn into demons."

Linda's face went slack. "*All* of them?"

"Everyone over the age of eighteen."

Warrick came back with Two, but as soon as the dog got within sniffing distance of Amber he stopped, his hackles raised, and started growling.

Amber backed off. "Whoa. Wow. Easy, boy."

Kelly and the others said nothing.

"Sorry," Amber said, keeping her eyes on Two. "Dogs usually love me."

"You sure about that?" asked Warrick. "Two here is a very talented doggy. He can track people, he can sniff out certain substances, and he can smell a demon a mile off."

Amber's face went slack.

Kelly frowned. "You a demon, *too*, Amber?"

"Uh..."

"Time to be honest with us. Your friend is bleeding to death in the back of our van. Are you a demon?"

Amber sagged. "Sort of."

"Two, quiet, please," said Warrick, and Two growled a little more, then sat and scratched himself. Warrick looked at Amber. "How can you be sort-of a demon? That's like being sort-of a Twinkie. You either *are* a delightful and nutritious snack or you're not. Which one are you?"

"I... I guess I'm the Twinkie," said Amber.

"What deal did you make?" Linda asked.

"I didn't," Amber said. "My parents did, and they had me, and I inherited."

Linda clicked her fingers. "That's why they were trying to kill you! They want to eat you!" Then she blushed. "Sorry. I've read about this kind of thing. Didn't mean to get so excited, though."

"No problem."

"So now you're on the run," Warrick said wistfully. "Travelling the Dark Highway, a lone wolf. With your friend, who is another wolf. Two lone wolves. Two wolves, really. Not really alone. Two wolves in a car. Travelling. One of them naked and bloody. The other with her ass hanging out."

"Oh God," said Amber, one hand going to the seat of her pants. "Oh my God, my ass is hanging out."

Kelly punched Warrick's shoulder. "Be nice."

Warrick rubbed his shoulder, physically hurt but emotionally wounded. "I was just saying her jeans have really taken a pounding. I didn't mean anything by it, Amber. Honest."

"It's okay," Amber said, blushing.

"So, uh... can we see?"

Amber looked at him. "Can you see my ass?"

"Oh! No! Sorry, that's not what I... no! I meant can we see you... change?"

"You don't have to," said Kelly quickly.

"You totally don't have to," Warrick agreed. "Only, I like to draw. I've been working on a comic strip, like, about our adventures? Inspired by our adventures, anyway. I've taken some liberties."

"A lot of liberties," said Linda.

"A few mild exaggerations," Warrick said.

"The character based on Warrick himself hooks up with a new girl in every story," said Kelly. "He also has more muscles and brains than the real Warrick, doesn't run from every fight like the real Warrick, is—"

"Nothing's been published yet," Warrick interrupted, "but I'm hopeful. If it doesn't work out, I'll do it all as a web comic. That's the plan. But my point is, I'm a very visual person. I mean, I'd just love to... What colour are you, for a start?"

"Red," said Amber.

"Red," said Warrick. "The classic red. You don't find very many reds around. You'd think you would, but they're mostly different shades of grey. Do you have, uh... y'know... do you have... uh...?" He touched his forehead.

"Horns?" Amber prompted.

"Yes," Warrick said meekly. "Do you have horns?"

"Yes," she said. "Do you want me to show you?"

He stared at her, and bit his lip. "Could you?" he asked softly. "If it wouldn't be too much trouble, I mean?"

"Sure," said Amber. "Will your dog mind?"

"Two will be fine once he sees how cool we are with you."

"Okay then," said Amber. She looked around, made sure no one was walking by, and then her skin turned red and she grew taller and stronger and her horns curled over her head.

Warrick's mouth dropped open. "Golly."

"You're beautiful," said Linda.

Ronnie didn't say anything. He just stared at her, up and down.

Only Kelly moved. She walked right up to Amber, stood toe to toe with her. They were of equal height now, if the horns weren't taken into account. Kelly raised her hand. Traced her fingertip along Amber's cheek, down to her chin, let it drop.

"You know what?" Kelly said. "I think I prefer you the other way."

Amber blinked at her.

Then she reverted, and Kelly looked down at her, and smiled. "There's my cutie," she said, just as a police cruiser turned on to the street.

"Shit," said Kelly, and grabbed Amber's hand and bolted into the shadows. Lights flashed and a siren yelped and she glanced back, saw her friends hightail it in different directions. She wasn't worried about them. They could all take care of themselves.

She ran with Amber until they came to a narrow, curving street, then they hopped a wall and waited, catching their breath.

"What if the cops search the van?" Amber asked, still panting. "If they find Milo, they might kill him."

"Ronnie won't let that happen," Kelly assured her. "The van is technically Warrick's, but Ronnie takes care of it and he is very protective."

"Then we need to get Milo's car," said Amber. She took out her phone, brought up a map. "The impound lot is three blocks away."

"What is so special about this car?"

"I just need it, that's all. I could do it myself, but..."

Kelly smiled. "Are you kidding? You are an *intrigue*. I'm not letting you out of my sight."

"Thanks," said Amber, and started walking.

"Besides," Kelly said, eyes flicking down, "your ass is hanging out."

Amber spun, hands behind her, and Kelly laughed and jogged to catch up. They walked side by side until they came to an old movie theatre, the kind with one or two screens that hadn't yet been taken over and refitted as a multiplex. A showing must just have ended, because a trickle of people was emerging into the night.

"That's more people on one street than I've seen since we arrived," Kelly whispered.

They circumnavigated the theatre, diving into shadows again further up. Kelly glanced back, but there was no one behind them. They walked on and she glanced back again, frowning.

"You okay?" Amber asked.

"Not really," said Kelly. "I don't think we're alone..."

"At least someone's paying attention," said a woman from in front, and Kelly glimpsed an outline, the shape of horns, and then reflected light shifted over red skin and she saw the most beautiful woman she'd ever seen standing there, fangs gleaming wickedly.

"Hello, sweetie," said the demon.

"Mom," was all Amber had time to say.

26

BETTY LAMONT PUNCHED HER daughter so hard that Amber wasn't even aware she'd hit the ground until after she'd stopped rolling.

She heard a muffled cry of pain, looked up in time to see Kelly being hurled into the wall and collapsing.

"We've never been apart for as long as this," Betty said, strolling after Amber. "There was that week you spent at camp when you were, what, eleven? But nothing like this."

Amber forced herself to her feet and shifted, holding out her hands to keep Betty at bay until she'd had time to recover.

Betty batted down her arms and grabbed her throat. "You're a mess. Are you aware that the seat of your pants is missing? I don't know what you've been getting up to, but I hope it's been fun."

And then Amber's feet left the ground and the world spun as her mother hurled her, head over heels, against a dumpster. Amber's spine hit the corner and she cried out as she crumpled.

"Your father and I have been having a great time," said Betty. "Grant and Kirsty, too, of course. First of all, we couldn't go home. I mean, that's to be expected, right? If your daughter sabotages the offering you're supposed to provide, you probably want to avoid places where the Shining Demon could easily find you."

Betty lashed a kick into her side that took all the breath from Amber's lungs despite the black scales that had formed.

"But it's not like we don't have friends, am I right? Acquaintances we've made along the way. And it's not like these friends would abandon us in our hour of need. Oh no, not them. They would take any opportunity to hold our fate in their hands. To lord it over us. So we've been scurrying from place to place, like rats. And it's all thanks to you."

Amber tried getting up. Betty's knee shot into her chin and she sprawled backwards. Betty paused.

"What *was* that camp you went to? Eager Beavers, or something like that? Between you and me, Amber, that week you were gone was absolute heaven. You have no idea how stifling you were, you really don't. We would have sent you to all kinds of camps after that if only you hadn't been such a baby. *Wah, wah, the other kids are horrible. Wah, wah, the other kids hate me.* Well, they weren't the only ones, sweetheart."

Betty took another step and Amber tried to kick her leg from under her, but Betty saw it coming and stomped hard on Amber's ankle.

"And now here we are in Alaska," Betty continued, grinding her heel down. "*Alaska.* I like the sun, Amber. You know that. I like the heat. I had no intention, ever, of venturing this far north. Yet here I am, in the cold, because of you."

Betty stepped off her ankle and Amber scrambled up, limping and unsteady.

"Mom, wait—"

"Mom?" Betty laughed. "You're really going to mom me, after

everything you've done? After everything you said to us in New York?"

"I didn't say anything—"

"You said 'screw you' to your father," Betty interrupted. "Disrespecting one of us is disrespecting both of us. That's what marriage means, Amber."

"What does family mean, then?" Amber fired back. "Do you have any cosy definitions for that? How about infanticide?"

"Actually, it would be filicide," Betty corrected. "Infanticide is when a parent kills an infant child. Honestly, just saying those words fills me with such regret. If only we'd killed you in your crib, it would have saved us so much trouble."

"Jesus Christ. How can you be so... evil?"

"You are such a hypocrite," her mother said, her eyes clear and bright as she advanced.

Amber stumbled back. "What? What are you talking about?"

"You went to the rallies, Amber. You signed the petitions, chanted the chants, showed your support for a woman's right to choose. You're pro-choice, aren't you?"

Amber frowned. "So are you."

"Of course I am," Betty said. "I'm all for terminating unwanted pregnancies."

"I'm not a pregnancy."

"You're still developing, though, into the person you one day hope to become."

"Is that how you've been justifying this to yourself?"

"I don't have to justify anything, Amber. We made you. You belong to us. We have every right to eat you."

"Yeah? Take a bite."

"The time for that has passed, as you well know."

"Then why are you here? The Hounds aren't chasing you, they're chasing me. Why aren't you hiding under a rock somewhere?"

"Because we are Lamonts," said her father from behind her. An involuntary groan escaped Amber's lips. "We do not hide for long," Bill continued, walking up to join them. "We do not cower. We're always looking for the next opportunity."

Amber looked at her parents, and she just *knew*. "You're working with the Hounds."

Betty fixed her hair, then traced her fingers over her horns. "The Shining Demon reached out to us. Who were we to say no to Astaroth, Duke of Hell?"

"What'd he offer you? A new deal?"

"The absolution of old debts," said Bill.

"Providing you hand me over."

He shrugged. "Naturally."

Amber's hands were still sticky with Milo's blood. If she allowed herself to be taken away, he was a dead man. "How about something more?"

"No bargaining," said Bill. "You've got nothing to offer us that we'd be interested in."

"How about power? Would you be interested in power?"

Bill's smile revealed his fangs. "What do you know about power, Amber?"

"The Shining Demon has a brother, did you know that? Naberius. He tried to betray Astaroth, but Astaroth turned the tables, and now Naberius is in chains. Didn't you even ask why this town makes you shift, or how they've constructed the barrier?"

Betty frowned. "The brother's power is being tapped."

Amber nodded. "Naberius, yes. I can take you to him."

"Revert. I can't tell if you're lying when you look like this."

Amber hesitated, then reverted. She moaned as the pain swept in, but resisted the urge to curl into a ball.

"You've seen him?" Betty asked. "This Naberius?"

"No," Amber said, her voice quieter. She hated how meek she was, wearing her ugly old face. "But I know where he is and I know how to get there."

"Tell us."

She shook her head. "I'll show you."

"Tell us or we'll kill your little friend," Betty said.

Amber glanced at Kelly's unconscious form. "He's in an underground cell," she said, "but you need a special key to get in. I have one — I took it from Dacre Shanks."

"Hand it over."

"It's in Milo's car," said Amber. "In the impound lot. I'll take you to it, I'll give you the key, and you let us go. When you release Naberius, I'm sure he'll grant you whatever you ask."

"Don't presume to speak for other people," said Betty. She looked at her husband. "She's right, though. We'd have his eternal gratitude. A Demon on our side."

"And another one wanting us dead," Bill replied. "Astaroth has just given us a second chance — if we do this, he'll pour his every resource into finding and punishing us."

"He will," Betty said. "But isn't this just the kind of thing we'd do?"

Bill looked at her, and surprised Amber by bursting out laughing.

"Indeed it is, my love," he said. "Indeed it is."

27

HER PARENTS REVERTED WHILE they waited for the Van der Valks to join them on Maple Street. Unlike Amber, their transformation did not rob them of their confidence or cruelty, and it only made them marginally less beautiful. They chatted to each other like they were the only people in the world. Amber was used to it.

Grant and Kirsty pulled up beside them, across the road from the impound lot. Amber, with Kelly's dead weight dragging on the arm slung round her neck, watched them get out of the car, but they barely glanced at her.

"Why are you standing around?" Grant asked Bill. "Do you really like the cold weather that much? We've got a life of freedom ahead of us. Dump her in the trunk and let's get to it."

"We're not handing her over," said Bill.

"What are you talking about?" Kirsty asked. "Why not?"

"There's another Shining Demon, Naberius, trapped underground. Amber here is about to get us the key to release him."

"And then what?"

"Then… anything. Everything. The possibilities are endless."

"You want to make a deal with this new Shining Demon? While the old Shining Demon is looking on? Astaroth will kill us all."

"One of our demands will be that Naberius protect us from Astaroth's anger."

"His anger?" Grant said. "His *anger*? Is that what you're calling it? You face someone's anger if you cut them off in traffic. This is something more. This is biblical. We're talking fury. We're talking *wrath*. You want to betray Astaroth for, what, a better deal with a Demon we don't even know? We don't need a better deal. Astaroth will wipe the slate clean the moment we give Amber to the Hounds. No more debt. Do you understand what that means? One day, once we're satisfied with the power we've accumulated, we could have children that we didn't have to kill."

Bill looked at his friend like he was something he'd stepped in. "Satisfied? When we're *satisfied*? We're never going to be *satisfied*, Grant. We're always going to want more."

"Grant and I want to start a real family," Kirsty said.

Betty stared at them. "When did you decide this?" she asked, stepping forward. "In the last few days?"

"Last few weeks, actually."

"And were you planning on discussing it with us? We have no idea what will happen to our power levels if we let children live."

"And yet, for this key, you're going to let your daughter walk away alive, aren't you?"

"It's a one-time thing," Betty said. "And it's worth the risk."

"But if it in any way diminishes us in the future, we're going to hunt her down," said Bill, and glanced at Amber. "This could just be a stay of execution. She knows that."

"So you get to have a child grow up and we don't?" Grant said. "You think we're just going to accept that?"

"This isn't about what's fair," Bill responded. "This is about what's in front of us. You think Amber is the kid we would have chosen to keep? It's just the way it's happened, that's all."

"This is bullshit, Bill."

"Which is why we're going to vote on it. You know which way Betty and I are voting. What about you? We were scared of Astaroth. When he offered us this chance, we gratefully accepted. Out of fear. I don't know about you, but that rankled us. He held all the power and we were just so eager to please him. Is that us? Is that you, Grant? Is that you, Kirsty? Have we got this far by being grateful to people more powerful than us? Or have we defied the odds, time and again, to forge our own path through the last hundred years? If any part of you, any part, thinks that this is worth the risk, that the gains may vastly outweigh the losses, then vote with us."

The Van der Valks glanced at each other.

"How do you know Naberius will even agree to our terms?" Kirsty asked.

"Of course he will," said Bill. "But if he doesn't, we'll leave him there, and hand over Amber as planned."

"No," said Amber. "You let us go when I give you the key, that was the deal."

"Circumstances have changed," said Bill. "Roll with it or get rolled over. Grant? Kirsty? Are you onboard?"

The Van der Valks looked at each other. Something passed between them, some flicker of expression.

"We are," said Grant eventually, but the reluctance was unmistakable in his tone.

"Excellent. Apparently, the key we want is in Mr Sebastian's delightful car, and the car is in this impound lot."

"I'll take care of it," said Kirsty, and crossed the road. She disappeared into the small outbuilding beside the fence. Amber glimpsed someone in there, a civilian. She heard a raised voice and breaking glass.

A minute later, the gate started to trundle open, and Kirsty emerged, the Charger's key in her blood-splattered hand.

"We should kill her now," said Grant, his eyes on Amber.

She was ready for this. "How do you know I'm telling the truth?" she asked. "How do you know the key really is where I say it is?"

"Our daughter is too smart for you, Grant," Betty chuckled.

Grant said nothing in response, but he didn't look happy. Kelly gave Amber's arm a squeeze, but apart from that she showed no signs of consciousness. Amber didn't respond to the squeeze, and continued to huff and struggle as they crossed the street.

The lot had three vehicles in it. There was a tow truck parked beside the gate, a rusted heap of crap slowly dissolving in the corner, and the Charger in the middle. It sat in its space like a big cat on its haunches, ready to spring. They stopped before they got too close, and Kirsty held the key out to Bill. He raised an eyebrow.

"If you think I'm going near that thing, you can forget it," Kirsty said.

"Good point," he murmured. "Amber, be a good girl and go fetch the magic key, would you?"

Instantly, Amber thought of Phil Daggett's gun, the one with the silencer, that Milo had dropped into the back seat. It was probably still there. The gun would even the odds. The gun could solve her problems.

"I've a better idea," said Betty, like she knew just what Amber was thinking. She yanked Kelly from Amber's arms and Kelly cried out. "We'll send this one instead." She grabbed a handful of Kelly's hair, and twisted. "Go to the car, whatever-your-name-is. In the glove box – Amber, the key's in the glove box, isn't it? – in the glove box you'll find a key. If that glove box doesn't grow teeth and bite your hand off, bring the key back to us and I promise we'll let you walk away. Do you think you can manage all that?"

Kelly had her jaw clenched. "Sure."

Betty smiled beautifully. "Good. Off you go."

Betty released her. Kirsty tossed Kelly the car key and Kelly started for the Charger.

"What the hell is going on here?"

Amber was the first to turn, the first to see Officer Thornton – Lucy – standing there, a look of alarm on her face and her hand on the butt of her gun.

Bill raised his hands slowly, and smiled. "Good evening, Officer," he said. "We were wondering—"

"Shut up," Lucy said, scanning their faces. She saw Amber and her frown deepened. "Oh goddammit."

Betty stepped towards her, hands open and palms up. "We just came to bring our daughter home, Officer," she said.

"Stop walking," Lucy said. "I mean it, lady, stop walking this instant."

Betty stopped. "Of course, Officer. Whatever you say."

"I'd like to make a complaint, actually," Grant said. "These people stole my car."

"That's a lie," said Bill.

"The hell it is!" Grant responded. "You drove all the way up here in a stolen car and I want him arrested, Officer!"

Grant stepped away from Bill, glaring at him, backing up towards the gate.

"Sir," Lucy said, "I'm going to have to ask you to stop moving."

"Arrest him!"

"Stop moving!"

Grant turned, puzzlement on his face. "I'm not the one who did anything wrong!"

"Sir, go back to where you were—"

As she spoke, Lucy drew her gun, and that was the signal. Amber's parents and the Van der Valks shifted even as Betty slapped the gun out of Lucy's hand. Grant lunged, grabbed her, and threw her. She hit the edge of the tow truck and spun away from it, sprawled on to the ground.

"Surprise," Kirsty said, closing in with her teeth bared.

"Yeah," said Lucy, standing, "surprise." And then she shifted.

28

OFFICER LUCY THORNTON GREW taller, broader, and strangely angular, the lines of her bones pressing out against her skin – that skin now a deep dirty green, and rough, like sandpaper. Her uniform struggled to contain her. Her hands were talons and, while she had no horns, her mouth was twisted into a permanent grin.

She was on Kirsty before Kirsty even knew what was happening, slamming those heavy knuckles into her face. Grant charged and Lucy hurled Kirsty at his legs. He tripped, sprawled, and Lucy kicked him under the chin. Then Bill was there, taking her off her feet. They fell, grunting and cursing and rolling into the shadows.

Amber shifted without even realising. She saw her mom go for Lucy's gun and she ran, dived, closed her hand around the barrel.

"Let it go," Betty snarled, doing her best to pull it away.

She elbowed Amber in the face and Amber growled and twisted, and Betty tumbled over her and now they were rolling as well. Amber's black scales rose in response, as did her mother's. The gun went off and Amber jerked away and ripped it from her mother's grip. It went spinning under the tow truck. Betty grabbed Amber's horns and slammed her head into the ground, then scrambled up and went after the weapon.

Amber rolled on to her back, her vision blurring. She heard an engine trying to turn over, and a voice. Kelly's voice.

"The car won't start! Amber!"

Amber looked up. Through the tears, she saw Kelly poking her head out of the Charger's window, and suddenly her head cleared and she was getting up. She staggered a little, but her balance returned even as she was stumbling for the car.

"Move over," she commanded, and Kelly slid to the other side. Amber got in behind the wheel.

"It won't start," said Kelly. "I know cars and this isn't gonna—"

Amber barely touched the key in the ignition and the Charger roared to life. Red headlights snapped on, catching Bill and Kirsty beating the crap out of Lucy. Amber put the car into gear, surged forward. Kelly knew what to do without Amber even saying it. She opened the door as they drew alongside Lucy, yelled, "Get in!"

Lucy kicked Kirsty away from her and spun, ran for the car, and jumped. Kelly caught her and pulled her inside and Amber slammed her foot on the gas and they peeled out of there. They scraped the gate as they passed, crashed on to the road, and in four seconds they were at the top of the street and turning right.

Amber took a series of corners, always staying away from other traffic. Lucy and Kelly swayed with each turn, until finally Amber started to slow down.

"Holy crap," Kelly whispered. She cleared her throat, and regained a little strength in her voice. "Okay then, before anything else, I would ask that everyone in this car go back to being more or less human. Can we do that?"

"Sure," said Lucy, and reverted. Amber followed suit.

"Thank you," Kelly said, and looked over at Amber, and grinned. "We're so cool."

Amber laughed, more from nerves than any sense of cheeriness. "Yeah," she said. "Yeah, we're cool, all right."

"Hush, you," Kelly said with a wave of her hand. "We so rock. Did we not escape the clutches of the damned? No offence meant to demon-kind, of course."

"None taken," said Amber.

"Likewise," muttered Lucy, rubbing her bruised jaw.

Kelly looked around the car. "This is a hell of a machine. I feel like we should be listening to Zeppelin or Skynyrd, y'know? Maybe some 'Carry On, My Wayward Son'. Let's see what we have here..."

Amber was focusing on the road, and didn't notice Kelly reaching for the radio until she flicked it on. Screams filled the Charger with more than just noise – they brought with them overwhelming anguish and fractured memories of pain and regret and loss that reached inside Amber's mind and wrenched it in on itself, and the Charger swerved into a parked car and jolted sideways on the empty street and Amber reached out, flailing, knocked the silver dial to the off position, and silence – warm, welcome, glorious silence – seeped through the car.

Amber blinked away tears. Beside her, Kelly was crying.

"What the hell was that?" Lucy asked, her voice small.

Amber shook her head.

With trembling hands, she restarted the car, and pulled into the side of the road. All three of them got out.

Kelly wiped her eyes. "I don't like that song," she said, before turning to Lucy. "We saved your ass."

"Your friends were trying to kill me," Lucy responded.

"They're not my friends," Amber said. "They're my parents. And... well, and their friends. But Kelly's right. We could have driven off and left you there."

"You were trespassing on state property."

Kelly nodded. "And we saved your ass on state property."

"You owe us," said Amber.

"I don't owe you jack shit," Lucy said. "If anything, you owe me. What, you thought those heads grew bullet holes by themselves?"

Amber frowned. "You were the one shooting at the Hounds?"

"No one else was gonna do it, and I figured you could use more than a running start."

"Thank you. Jesus, thank you. You saved our lives."

"Yeah, well, I didn't think you'd come straight back into town. If Novak finds you, he'll shoot you on sight. Probably me as well. Why couldn't you have just kept running?"

"Desolation Hill is the only place we're safe," said Amber, hugging herself to keep warm. "If you could convince Jesper to let us stay..."

"Not gonna happen," said Lucy.

Her radio squawked and they froze. They listened to a garbled message that abruptly cut off.

"What was that?" Kelly asked.

"Reports of shots fired," said Lucy. "You're gonna have to get going. I'll let you go this once, but, if I see you again, I've got to do my job."

"Your job is to protect and serve," said Kelly.

"Yeah," Lucy said, "protect and serve my community, which is a pretty messed-up place, morally speaking."

"We'll go," said Amber. "If Novak catches us, we won't mention you. But what deal did you make? I know about Naberius, I know about Hell Night, I know what happens, but this isn't that, is it? It's something else."

"We didn't make a deal."

"Then how did you get your power?"

"You really don't have time for this."

"Talk quickly."

Lucy sighed. "After Naberius was imprisoned, and Mayor Jesper started thinking about what lay in store for him, he decided the best thing to do was to try and kill Astaroth. But he didn't know how. He needed to experiment."

Amber frowned. "He summoned another Demon, didn't he?"

Lucy nodded. "A smaller one. A weaker one. He told you about the markings that keep Naberius in that cell? Those are the same markings he used to keep Ardat-Ko in a circle, down in his cellar, for over a year."

"Ardat-Ko?"

"Also known as the Smiling Demon. Every day for the first eight months, Jesper would go down into that cellar and try to kill her. Every day he'd fail. He started sending us down, with strict instructions on what to do. We didn't fare any better."

"Wait," said Amber, "how long ago was this?"

"Sixty years or so. I'm the first woman they had on the force. The only one, actually."

"Wow," said Kelly. "Sixty years. You look amazing."

"Thanks."

"There's no sagging at all."

"I can't take all the credit," Lucy said with a shrug. "A good fitted bra is essential. Anyway, Ardat-Ko. She didn't get hungry.

She didn't get tired. She didn't get angry. She just stood in that circle and smiled while we tried to kill her, over and over again."

"So what happened?" asked Amber.

"She started talking to us," said Lucy. "We had orders – do not engage her in conversation. But she knew things. She either read our minds or she read us... and one by one we began to talk back. She offered us great rewards if we released her. She wasn't as powerful as Astaroth or any of the big guys, but she told us that if we let her out, she could make us strong, let us live for many lifetimes..."

"Did you let her out?"

"I was tempted. I was. So were the others. But Novak was unshakeable. So Ardat-Ko offered *instant* power, right there from within the circle. She persuaded us to trust her with a small knife, and she cut off the fingers on her left hand. Her thumb too. She told us to eat.

"I didn't believe her. I thought she was trying to poison us. I knew that people who'd made deals could eat other demons to gain their strength, I'd heard about that – but we were ordinary. For all we knew, her blood alone would be like acid to us. But Ardat-Ko promised us that even ordinary people could absorb power by eating the flesh of a being like her. She was right. We felt stronger. Healthier."

"So you released her?"

"No," said Lucy, "we didn't. Novak said he didn't believe her. He said she'd just vanish the moment she was free. He wanted more power before he let her out. I don't think she minded. I don't think it hurt, what she did to herself. And anyway, once she was released, she'd just grow those limbs back."

"How much did you eat?"

"Her arm," said Lucy. "Her right leg. Half of her left. Every day she'd have a new portion ready for us. Every bite we took, we got stronger. We started to show signs of... well, of becoming demons ourselves, but we didn't stop. We couldn't. We got to her right thigh before she realised she wasn't getting out of there."

"And then you ate the rest of her."

"We did. The most unsettling part was that she kept smiling the whole way through."

"And Jesper knew about this?"

"Of course. The Chief tells him everything. Jesper loved the idea of having his own demon police force. We wouldn't be able to keep the town safe otherwise."

"You get a lot of demons through here, huh?" said Kelly.

"We do. And serial killers and psychos of all descriptions. Desolation Hill draws them in, but these last few days we've seen the numbers grow. Because of her." Lucy was looking at Amber.

"And you take care of them," said Kelly. "Demon cops, protecting their community. And what about the child murders? What do you do about them?"

Lucy's face turned stony. "What child murders?"

"For the sacrifice," said Amber. "To keep Naberius going, to keep him supplying the town with power."

"One a year," said Kelly. "Or hadn't you noticed that?"

"Lot of people go missing," Lucy said. "Not just in this town. In every town. Kids, too. It doesn't mean they've—"

"Do you know where the Narrow Man keeps the kids he takes?"

The words dried up in Lucy's mouth. Then she shook her head. "The Narrow Man is an urban legend. He's not real."

"He's taken another one," Kelly said. "Austin Cooke. Snatched him right out of his bedroom because the town voted for it."

"No," said Lucy, "Austin Cooke ran away. He was being bullied and he... he ran away. The voting thing is a scare tactic to keep little kids from misbehaving."

Kelly stepped right up to her. "I'm sure Austin was suitably terrified when the Narrow Man came for him."

"I don't know anything about that," Lucy said, shoving Kelly backwards.

"Where does he keep them?"

"He's not real!" she shouted.

"Where does he keep them?"

"He doesn't exist!"

"Where does he keep them?"

"I don't know!"

They looked at her.

She snarled. "You don't think we want to stop him? Me, the others... But Novak won't hear of it, and he's our Chief. He gives the orders, we carry them out."

"You're not carrying out his orders right now," said Amber.

"And I'm regretting that," said Lucy. "Just like I'm regretting helping you out against the Hounds. But hey, shit happens. You're gonna get in that car of yours, that goddamn *evil* car, and you're gonna pick up your friend and get the hell out of town. And you," Lucy said to Kelly, "you're gonna do the same. You think Novak or any of my fellow officers are gonna let you off with a caution if they catch you? You're dead. Understand that? They're gonna put you down, all of you. Go. Get out of here. And if I see you again? I'll shoot you on sight."

29

AMBER WOKE ON A couch with a blanket over her head.

For a moment, she didn't know where she was. Then she remembered the Hounds, and her parents, and Kelly directing her to the old man's house. Virgil someone. The van had already been there when they'd arrived, and Amber herself had taken Milo and laid him on to the back seat of the Charger. His pulse had been slow and his breathing shallow, but he was in the Charger and the Charger would heal him. It would. It had to.

Because tonight was Hell Night.

She pulled down the blanket, expecting it to snag on her horns, but it passed easily over her face. She checked her hands in the early morning light. Pale. Flesh-coloured. She hadn't shifted while she slept. The urge was there, she could still feel it, but it was lessened. Weakened.

She wasn't surprised. She'd been expecting it, actually. More or less depending on it.

She laid the blanket aside and sat up quietly. The others were still wrapped up in their sleeping bags on the floor of Virgil's living room. She'd only met him briefly the previous night. Kelly had introduced them and he'd gone off to bed. She wasn't sure if the other old man — Javier, she thought his name was — was Virgil's housemate or his lover. The thought of two old gay men living up here in Alaska would have made her heart warm were it not for the town they'd chosen to move to.

She put her shoes on and stood. The clothes she'd been wearing last night, or at least the rags they'd turned into, were now stuffed in a garbage bag. The ones she had on were wrinkled and let the chill in, so she hugged herself as she crept out of the room. Two raised his head, looked at her, yawned and went back to sleep. Amber walked over to the door that led to the garage, but hesitated before opening it. She uttered a silent prayer to someone, somewhere, and slipped inside. The Charger was parked on the other side of the van.

"Please be okay," she whispered. "Please be okay. Please be okay."

She rounded the van, approached the Charger, and leaned down to peer through the window. The blanket she'd used to cover Milo was lying on the back seat.

Milo was gone.

Coldness swept through her and she reeled away from the car, that parasitic car that healed and sustained him, but also fed off him. It hadn't occurred to her to wonder what it would do if he was too badly injured, if he died during the night. Would it leave his body be, or would it absorb it, consume it completely and leave nothing, not even bloodstains on the upholstery?

Milo walked up beside her. "What's wrong with you?"

She leaped away from him in shock, then grabbed him and hugged him. "You're alive!"

"Uh, yeah," he said, enduring the hug with his arms by his sides.

"I thought the car had eaten you!"

"Nope."

His clothes were fresh. He smelled of soap. She released him and covered her heart with her hands, feeling it beat. "You're okay?"

"I'm sore," he said, "but yeah. Feeling fine. I couldn't find my boots."

"They're gone."

"Damn," said Milo. "Those were my favourites."

He went to the trunk, which sprang open at his touch, and grabbed a pair of walking boots from his bag.

Amber watched him put them on. "You're sure you're feeling okay? You were pretty messed up."

"The car takes care of me," he said. "So do you, for that matter."

"I look after my employees."

Milo gave her one of those smiles. "Oh, that's right – I'm being paid for all this, aren't I? Bodyguard and chauffeur. How much do you owe me by now?"

"Forty or fifty grand?" said Amber. "No big deal. It's not like you're doing this for the money, after all."

"It's for the love of the work," he said, and straightened up. "So you want to fill me in on what's been happening? I noticed those two from the jail in the living room, and that's an old man's shower. There's a seat."

"His name's Virgil," said Amber. "He's not from here, and he's on our side. He might be gay."

"Good to know."

"The other two in the living room are Linda and Warrick. There's also a dog. My parents are here, too."

"In the living room?"

235

"In town. Astaroth sent them, but now they want Dacre Shanks's key so that they can make a deal with Naberius instead."

"Devious bastards, aren't they?"

"I know what the town festival is. They call it Hell Night. Jesper's freelancer, someone called the Narrow Man, he makes the sacrifice, Naberius gets juiced up, and the town gets juiced up right along with him. The town changes, and everyone over the age of eighteen shifts."

Milo frowned. "Into demons?"

"Yep. Oh, also? The cops are demons, too."

"I figured as much. Anything else?"

"A kid has gone missing. Austin Cooke. The Narrow Man has him. But we know who the Narrow Man is. He disguises himself as a guy called Moreno, and he owns a hardware store. Kelly and the others, they said he's a shapeshifter."

"Is that so?"

"You ever meet one of those before?"

"Not that I'm aware," Milo said, and opened the car door, reaching into the back seat. He came out with Phil Daggett's silenced handgun.

"But I still don't get it," said Amber. "Okay, Jesper killed kids because he was old and weak and they were easy prey, but the Narrow Man is, like, this big supernatural bad guy. So why doesn't Jesper tell him to go after some of the grown-ups?"

"Maybe because he wants the adults to share the blame," Milo said. He ejected the magazine and checked it. "If they all agree that this is how it should be done, if this is the price they're willing to pay for their precious Hell Night, then they shoulder the responsibility." Satisfied, he slid the magazine back in, then flicked the safety on.

Amber waited until he was done before saying, "We haven't had a chance to talk about what Jesper said."

"That old bastard said a lot of things."

"But he mentioned a Demon – Demoriel. You recognise the name?"

Milo shook his head. "I don't, but Jesper sounds like he knows what he's talking about, doesn't he? Add in the car thing, and it's a pretty safe bet that it's this Demoriel who turned me into what I am today. Not that it changes anything. Now that I know his name, I'm not about to go knocking on his door to ask him some questions."

"Okay," she said. "Just checking."

He smiled. "You really thought I was going to abandon you?"

"No," she admitted. "But I thought I'd give you the opportunity."

"Mighty kind of you, but you're stuck with me, I'm afraid."

"In that case, I have a plan."

"I'm sorry?"

"A plan," she said. "I have one."

He frowned at her. "Is it any good?"

"I'm not sure."

He leaned against the car and folded his arms. "Let's hear it."

"Well, I was thinking, what do we need to do? We need to get rid of the Hounds, right? We can't do that alone."

"Are you proposing teaming up with your parents?"

"What? God, no. No way in hell."

"Good," said Milo. "I don't think that'd be a smart move."

"Can I tell you my plan, please? Thank you. Here's what I understand about Hell Night. It's a blast of power, right? Or it's a, it's a needle full of adrenaline, and when it's plunged into Naberius's heart – like, metaphorically – his power explodes, and when it explodes it's siphoned off to recharge the barrier. But it also bubbles up here in town and changes ordinary people into violent, murderous demons. That's the side effect. That's what Jesper didn't expect. But he's adapted, because that's what he does. But the barrier is the main purpose. It gets recharged because it *needs* to get recharged. I woke up just now like this. Normal. No horns. You feel it, too, right? My skin isn't itching anymore."

"You think Naberius's influence is weakening?"

"I do," Amber replied. "I think each sacrifice releases a blast of power that recharges everything for exactly one year. We're in the last few hours of last year's sacrifice, and I think that if we can stop tonight's sacrifice from going ahead, the barrier will get so weak that the Hounds can break through. Maybe. Hopefully."

Milo looked at her. "Letting the Hounds in? That's your plan?"

"The first part of it, yes."

"The second part has a lot to make up for, just to warn you."

"We want the Hounds to ride in, because, once they're through, we give Naberius his sacrifice."

"Are... are you proposing *we* kill the kid?"

"It doesn't have to be Austin, does it? It doesn't have to be a kid. It can be anyone. In fact... I think it should be Jesper himself."

"And how does that help us?"

"Once Naberius gets his sacrifice, Hell Night begins, and everyone over the age of eighteen in this town will turn into a bloodthirsty monster. The Hounds come rolling in, and suddenly we won't be outnumbered. We'll have a whole army around us."

"Who would want to kill us as much as they'd want to kill the Hounds."

"Sure. But if we can – and I mean all of us – if we can find a safe place to wait it out, the Hounds – and my parents – will be the only targets available."

Milo scratched the stubble on his chin. "That's... that's a pretty good plan."

"Are you being sarcastic?"

"No, Amber."

She beamed.

"But that means that not only do we have to find the kid, but we're also going to have to snatch Jesper before tonight. Any bright ideas on how we do either of those things?"

"Snatching Jesper is easy. We still have Dacre Shanks's key, right? We're just going to stroll into Jesper's office, take him by the spindly arm, and stroll right back out again. As for finding Austin, Kelly and the others think that he's being hidden in the hardware store. Everything closes early today, at lunchtime, so that's when they're going to break in, and I think we should help them."

"They're going to break into a hardware store? In broad daylight?"

Amber faltered. "Well, I think... I think they're planning on going in the back door."

"They'd want to."

"So what do you think? Should we help them?"

Milo hesitated. He reached into the car, opened the glove box, put in Daggett's gun and took out his own holstered weapon, then straightened and clipped it on to his belt. "It might be dangerous," he said, "but it's not like I almost died last night. So why the hell not?"

30

Virgil drove them in the Sienna, his eight-seater minivan. Javier sat up in the passenger seat and they talked the whole way, hurling insults at each other. It seemed half-hearted, though. They were nervous.

Amber lay with a blanket on top of her, jammed in tight with Milo and Kelly. Kelly passed the time by tapping her fingertips on Amber's arm. It was a nice sensation. In the row in front, Two was licking Linda's face, much to her quiet disgust.

The Sienna pulled up. Nobody moved.

"Looks clear," said Javier.

"No one around," said Virgil.

The others sat up. They were parked in the alley behind the hardware store, separated only by a wall that even Amber herself could scale. Like Virgil and Javier had said, there was no one around.

"We'll wait here for you," said Virgil. "If we see anyone coming, we'll honk the horn and look nonchalant. Better hurry, though. Anyone comes through the front door and you're on your own."

Ronnie was the first out, then Warrick and Linda and the dog. Before he left the car, Milo leaned towards the driver.

"Mr Abernathy," he said, "I'm a big fan. I used to watch your show all the time. I think."

"You think?"

"I don't remember much about my life up until twelve years ago. But I remember your show."

"Well, hell, I guess it's something to be remembered by an amnesiac."

"Do you recognise me?" Javier said, smiling.

Milo frowned. "Should I?"

Javier's face soured. Amber nudged Milo and he climbed out. She followed, and Kelly closed the door after them.

They climbed the wall, congregated round the store's heavy rear door. Kelly gave the place a quick scan. "No alarm," she said. "I love small towns." She took a black pouch from her pocket and knelt by the door.

"Locks are her specialty," said Linda.

Kelly looked back at Amber and grinned. "I break into a lot of places."

Ronnie was looking at Milo. "I've been thinking about your plan," he said.

"Not my plan," Milo replied. "Her plan."

"Well then, Amber, I've been thinking about it," Ronnie said, "and I have a question. What happens if it works and the barrier does come down?"

"Uh, then the Hounds come in and the people tear them apart."

"That might solve your problem, but so what? We drive off, but next year it happens all over again."

"Not with Jesper dead."

"But there'll still be the Narrow Man. What's to stop him from sacrificing more kids?"

"I don't... I don't know."

"You're doing this for yourself," Ronnie said. "I get that, I do. But we're not leaving here until Austin is safe and this whole Hell Night thing is dismantled. Having you two around would give us a much better chance of doing that and getting out of here alive."

"We're not the heroes, kid," Milo said. "You are."

"So you'd be willing to just drive away and let this continue?"

"No," said Amber quickly. "We wouldn't."

"Yes, we would," Milo said.

"We wouldn't. We're... we're not going to."

Milo shot her a disapproving look, but didn't argue further. Amber looked at Ronnie.

"I mean... I guess we could try to kill the Narrow Man as well. Along the way. If we get the chance."

"That's what I like to hear," said Kelly, straightening up. She turned the handle, and pushed the door open. "We have entry."

Warrick took out the T-shirt he'd stolen from the Cookes' laundry basket and hunkered down, letting Two catch the scent. "Okay, boy," he said, "you got that? Yes, you do. Yes, you do. That's Austin, okay? He's why we're here. Good doggy. Now go find him."

He released his hold on Two's collar and the dog hurried into the store. They followed.

The store had a big front window, but it was filled with displays and decals that blocked much of the morning light. It was a small place, with four rows of shelves packed close together, each shelf laden with tools and equipment and thousands of small parts that Amber would never know the names of. It smelled of sawdust and oil.

"He's found something," Warrick said.

Amber joined the others over by the hose display. Two snuffled madly at the floor, then started scratching at the wall.

"You sure, boy?" Warrick asked. "You sure Austin's behind there?"

Amber half expected Two to give a bark in response, but apparently that wasn't necessary. Warrick attached a leash to Two's collar and led him away, and Ronnie and Linda stepped up, knocking on the wall.

"There's something behind this," Ronnie said. He took down the hoses as Linda ran her hands along the surface, searching for a join.

"It's a door," she said. "But the mechanism to open it could be anywhere."

"I found it," said Milo, stepping forward with an axe in his hands. He shifted into his demon form, and Linda and Ronnie took an involuntary step away. Even Amber, who had seen him like this a half-dozen times, found her eyes threatening to once again sink into that impossible black.

Two growled, then barked, and when he saw that no one was freaking out he bounded forward, sniffed Milo's leg happily before Warrick tugged him back. Milo swung the axe into the wall.

Amber found an identical axe in the next aisle, and shifted as she came back. She hacked at the door alongside Milo, building a tireless rhythm between them. The plaster fell away and the wood behind splintered. Cool air wafted through the gaps. Amber's muscles were strong. Her aim was true. She was so much better as a demon.

Now they could hear someone shouting, and it all went faster, each of them taking a side and chopping it down until the stairs were revealed.

Milo reverted. Amber, reluctantly, did the same. Milo went first and she followed, still gripping the axe. The others came after.

"Austin?" Milo called.

"Here! Down here!"

They descended into a deep, soundproofed basement. In one corner, there was a narrow mattress and blanket and a chain that ran from the floor to Austin Cooke's ankle.

Linda and Ronnie rushed forward.

"You okay?" said Ronnie. "Did he hurt you?"

"I'm okay," Austin said. "Please get me out of here. He put the key on the nail there."

Linda hurried to the wall, grabbed the key, and took it back to the boy. The padlock opened easily and tears came to Austin's eyes.

"Thank you," he said. "I thought he was gonna kill me. Thank you."

Ronnie straightened up and patted his shoulder. "We're going to take you somewhere safe, okay? You're not in danger anymore, Austin. You're with us now."

Then Two started barking like the Devil himself had arrived, and they turned to see the Narrow Man coming down the stairs.

31

THE NARROW MAN DIDN'T move with any sense of urgency. A tall man, with quiet eyes set too far apart in his pale face. A wide, thin mouth.

Austin whimpered, and Ronnie shielded him as they all backed away. Two's barks turned to growls, low in his throat, and Warrick kept a tight grip on the leash.

Milo didn't have to draw fast. He just took his gun from its holster, held it level with his waist. "We're taking the boy with us," he said.

The Narrow Man didn't answer, so Milo made a show of aiming for his leg.

"Give us the key – the one that takes you to Naberius. Hand it over and we won't need to hurt you."

When the Narrow Man didn't speak, Milo shrugged, and pulled the trigger. Amber flinched at the gunshot, saw the bullet pass through the Narrow Man's leg and burrow into the floor behind him. But there was no blood, no reaction, and definitely no screaming.

"Huh," said Milo, and fired again and again, emptying the gun into the Narrow Man's chest and head.

The bullet holes gaped. There was no red inside. No flesh. Just more of that same colourless skin, the texture of putty.

Milo holstered his gun, shifted, and swung the axe at the Narrow Man's head. The Narrow Man ducked, almost lazily, moving fast without seeming to hurry. Milo spun, swung again, but the Narrow Man grabbed the axe and pulled Milo into him. Milo snarled, red spilling from between his clenched teeth, and got a hand to the Narrow Man's throat and powered him backwards.

"Go," Amber said to the others as she shifted.

"We're staying," said Ronnie.

"Take Austin and run," she snarled. She knew they would. Their priority was protecting Austin, not fighting this shape-changing thing. Let the monsters fight the monster.

Warrick picked up Two and ran, with Ronnie and Linda dragging a terrified Austin behind them and Kelly following them all up the stairs. The Narrow Man shoved Milo away from him and Amber lunged, her axe blurring. She missed the Narrow Man's neck by a mere hair's breadth. He turned and she slammed her shoulder into his chest. He went stumbling and Milo kicked his legs from under him.

The Narrow Man fell and Amber and Milo brought their axes down. Their adversary twisted his body impossibly, like he didn't have any bones, and the axes bit into the ground. Then he snapped back into shape and lashed a foot into Amber's knee. Even as she was crying out, she was falling, and then she was on the floor, struggling with the Narrow Man.

Though it wasn't much of a struggle. Her strength meant nothing compared to his, and while her claws left deep furrows in his bloodless arms they brought him no pain that she could recognise. He got an arm around her throat from behind. Her black scales rose in defence, but he was squeezing against them, too, and all of a sudden she couldn't breathe.

Milo stopped trying to get a clear shot to the Narrow Man's head. Instead, he stomped on a leg, and brought the axe down. Amber glimpsed the Narrow Man's foot tumble away from them.

The Narrow Man didn't seem to notice.

Desperate for air, Amber put all of her strength into turning on to her side and then heaving herself on to her belly. With the Narrow Man still on her back, Milo now had all the targets he could ever want. She heard the axe fall again and again, could only imagine what damage it was doing. But the choke stayed on. She was close to unconsciousness.

And then all of a sudden she was gasping, sucking in air and rolling over, her eyes blurred with tears. Milo and the Narrow Man were locked together, fighting for control of the axe as they stumbled away from her. The Narrow Man's shirt was in shreds. So was his skin. Milo's red eyes were mere slits. He was snarling.

The Narrow Man stepped back without warning and Milo lost his balance, lost his hold, and the axe was torn from his hands as he fell to his knees.

Amber grabbed her own axe, launched herself at the Narrow Man. He spun, deflected her axe with his own. She swung again, and again he deflected, and a thought swept in from nowhere, that they were sword-fighting with axes. Before she could register how insane this was, his axe blade cracked against the scales on her shoulder and suddenly he was twisting her axe from her grip.

Holding an axe in each hand, the Narrow Man limped over to his severed foot and shoved his stump on to it, and it reattached.

Milo grabbed Amber, pushed her towards the stairs, and they ran.

Amber led the way into the store. The front door was open. She ignored it, went for the door out back, Milo right behind her. She crashed through. She jumped the wall, clearing it easily, landed beside the Sienna. Milo jumped down with her. Kelly had the door open, but her eyes flicked upwards.

"Look out!" she cried.

The Narrow Man landed between Amber and Milo. Amber dodged under the swipe of the axe, but Milo lunged at him. The Narrow Man dropped one axe and slammed Milo's head against the wall, then caught him as he stumbled and threw him on to the hood of the Sienna. The windshield cracked under the impact.

Amber glimpsed Austin's terrified face through the car window. The Narrow Man hadn't seen him yet.

"Hey!" she shouted, scrambling up. "Hey, asshole! Come get me!"

The Narrow Man didn't need much in the way of encouragement. Hefting the remaining axe in his right hand, he broke into a run so sudden that it took her by surprise. Amber cursed as she whirled, sure that at any moment that axe would cleave her head in two. Then she was running, fuelled by instinct and fear, the Narrow Man right behind her and gaining all the time.

She jumped another wall, found herself stumbling through someone's unkempt backyard. The Narrow Man landed cleanly.

She threw a lawn chair at him and ran round the side of the house. She tripped on a loose brick, got a hand to a windowsill, and rebounded off, leaving a bloody handprint behind. She was hurt. Jesus, she was hurt and bleeding and she didn't even know where the wound was.

A car passed on the street ahead. People walked. Kids laughed. She checked behind her, made sure the Narrow Man wasn't about to pounce, and reverted. Instantly, the pain swarmed in and she gasped. Her shoulder. Her scales hadn't stopped the axe from biting into her shoulder. Now she could feel the blood rushing from her wound, soaking her chest and belly and back, running into her jeans and underwear. She left a trail of blood as she stumbled from the sidewalk on to the street, clutching herself tightly. She looked back. The Narrow Man changed, too, became shorter, more filled out. His face rearranged itself into a younger version of Javier. Oscar Moreno walked after her with a friendly smile on his face, despite the axe held down by his side and his tattered clothing. Beneath his shirt, his wounds had closed up. No blood pumped.

But he was limping. The foot he'd reattached – it was tender. The Narrow Man felt nothing, but Oscar could experience pain.

Amber got to the other side of the road while he stopped to allow a car to pass, then she clambered awkwardly over a low fence, got out of sight behind the house there, and shifted. The pain was manageable once again and she started running, her mind alight with possibilities. She hurdled a low wall and carried on. She could hear him behind her, the Narrow Man, running. Catching up.

Good. Let him.

She jumped another wall, landed in another backyard. She

ran for the patio door, her scales prickling against her skin as she put her head down and crashed through the glass. She stumbled against the dining table. No alarm went off. No one cried out in shock. Beyond the tinkling of the glass, the house was quiet. She looked back as the Narrow Man dropped into the yard. He saw her, hefted the axe.

Grimacing against the pain in her shoulder, Amber ran for the hallway, grabbing a poker from beside the fireplace as she did so. She experienced a moment of blind panic when she couldn't figure out how to unlock the front door, but then stumbled out, pulling the door shut behind her.

A car passed on the quiet street, but she didn't revert and she didn't run. Instead, she stepped sideways, pressed herself against the wall, and crouched.

A moment later, the front door opened again. The Narrow Man was Oscar Moreno once again, and he stepped out, still smiling, still holding the axe, his gaze directed at the street, expecting to see her running.

But Amber wasn't running. Not anymore.

She straightened and swung the poker with all of her demon strength. It caught Moreno across the back of the head and he went down, went straight down to his knees, the axe clattering to the ground.

She hit him again, heard the poker crunch against his skull, and Moreno slumped face down. Blood began to mat his hair.

In this form, he bleeds.

Amber screamed at him, a scream of triumph fuelled by fear and hate, and brought the poker down a third time. She would have stood there and split his head wide open if a police cruiser hadn't swung round the corner. Before the snarl had even escaped her lips, the cruiser had braked and Novak was jumping out.

Amber dropped the poker and ran back inside the house, into the dining room towards the broken patio door. Two other cops, Woodbury and Duncan, were closing in. She stumbled backwards, turned left, ran down a short corridor into a bathroom, backed out and ran into a bedroom. She slammed the door, looked around. Novak passed the only window, his gun drawn.

Amber whirled, searching for a weapon. A shotgun, baseball bat, anything. She tapped her pockets. Found a key.

She pulled it out. Dacre Shanks's key. They'd tried it and it hadn't worked, but that had been out there, on the other side of the boundary. She was in Desolation Hill now, where the key had been made. If there was anywhere it'd work for someone who didn't have a damn clue how to use it, it was here.

She jammed it into the lock of the bedroom door and the image of another door, a door of dull metal, flashed into her mind with such startling clarity that it momentarily filled her vision. She turned the key, only dimly aware of what she was doing, then turned it again, and pulled it from the lock as she opened the door. She stepped out, not into the corridor of the house she was in, but into a concrete cell about the size of a modest living room. The door slammed shut behind her. It wasn't the wooden door she'd opened. It was metal. The one she'd seen in her head.

And in the centre of this room was a Shining Demon.

32

ASTAROTH HAD BURNED FROM within, turning all but a few jigsaw patches of his skin translucent. His brother was not so hellishly ethereal.

Naberius was on his knees in a circle, his wrists bound by short chains set into the floor, the manacles scratched with a hundred tiny symbols. Like his brother, he was hairless. Like his brother, his eyes were black. That was where the similarity ended. His dry, cracked skin was the colour of ash, and a paleness seeped from those cracks to bathe the cell in a weak, restrained light.

He looked up at Amber without surprise. It was as if he had only been trapped down here 20 minutes, not 200 years, such was the placidity of his features.

She opened her mouth to speak, but could think of nothing to say.

Instead, he spoke. "Release me." His voice was soft. "Release me from these chains."

Amber was strong. She was confident. In demon form, she was nothing like her old self. And yet here she felt all those familiar doubts and insecurities rising to the surface. Down here she was weak, despite her horns. Down here she was pathetic. "I... I can't," she said.

"You shall be rewarded. The chains bind me. Release me and I shall grant you your deepest desires."

Amber stepped backwards to the door. "I'm sorry," she whispered, and that's all she could think of to say. She turned, slid the key into the dull metal door, and screwed her eyes shut. She focused on a door she knew well, she pictured it in her head, and she turned the key twice and took it from the lock and she opened the door and stepped through—

—into her bedroom. In Florida.

The a/c wasn't on. It was hot and stuffy. Across the room, Balthazar and Tempest from *In The Dark Places* gazed mournfully out from their poster. Her laptop sat upon her desk. Her bed was made. She'd grown up here. It was her bedroom, filled with her things, yet it wasn't. Not anymore. The act of leaving, of running, had sealed this house away from her. It looked like her home and smelled like her home – that hot, cloyingly sweet smell – but it no longer *felt* like her home.

She stepped into the hall, moving quietly despite the fact that her parents and their friends were still in Alaska.

She didn't sweat. Of course she didn't. She could feel the heat, but it didn't bother her, not as a demon. She walked into the kitchen. Grabbed an apple. Took a bite and munched. Went to the refrigerator and found a carton of milk, poured herself a tall glass. She lobbed the apple into the sink, took the milk into the living room, leaving bloodstains wherever she went.

On the piano in the corner (her mother was a wonderful pianist) there was a framed photograph. A family photograph. Amber and her parents. Bill and Betty standing side by side and in front, smiling and oblivious to what was to come, was little girl Amber.

She dropped the photo, crushed it with her heel.

Taking another swig of milk, she dumped the rest of it over the couch and went back to her bedroom, dragging her hand along the corridor wall and smearing it with blood. She grabbed a bag, stuffed it full of clothes. She took her laptop, too, and a teddy bear she'd had since she was a kid. She put the bag on her back, closed the door, slid the key in and tried to remember what the doors looked like in Virgil's house.

"Goddammit," she said to no one.

The motel then. She pictured the room she'd stayed in, pictured the door. She wasn't in Desolation Hill anymore, but maybe the fact that she wanted to return there might spur the key on to cutting her a little slack. She focused, turned the key, and turned it again, then pulled it out as she opened the door...

...and stepped on to the landing in the Dowall Motel, and the first thing she heard was her mother's voice.

"He doesn't know anything," Betty said. Amber crouched, her fingers turning to claws once again. It took her a moment to calm down. She hadn't been detected. Her mother's voice was coming from below, in the lobby. They didn't know she was here.

Her mother spoke again. "Will you please stop him from crying?"

Amber got to her hands and knees and crawled to the banisters and looked down as Grant tossed Kenneth Dowall over the desk, where he had the good sense to stifle his moans and shut the hell up.

Grant, Betty and Bill stood around in all their red-skinned glory.

"Now what do we do?" Grant asked. "Go door to door? *Have you seen this girl?* It's done. It's over. Let's admit to this failure and go back to the job we were given."

"By Astaroth," said Bill.

"Yes," said Grant, "by Astaroth. Before he realises what we've been trying to do."

"You're scared," said Betty.

"Of course I am," Grant said. "And if you're not scared then you're a fool. Listen to me – we took the risk. We did. It was a worthwhile risk, but it just didn't work out for us. These things happen."

"It's not over yet," said Bill.

"The hell it isn't," Grant said. "We have to cut our losses."

"I've always hated that phrase," said Bill. "I don't lose, Grant. *We* don't lose. We find Amber – we find the key. None of this will matter when we release Naberius. Then we'll have all the power we'd ever want."

"There's no such thing," said Grant, "not for you two. Your ambition is going to get us killed."

A door was kicked open, somewhere Amber couldn't see, and two men came sprawling into view. They ended up on their knees.

"Found these two fighting outside," Kirsty said, walking in behind them. "More wannabe demons."

Serial killers. Amber's concern over their fate faded dramatically.

"I believe our luck is about to change," said Bill, smiling. "Gentlemen, so good to meet you. I have a feeling you're going to bring us some good news. We need some good news. My friends are beginning to doubt the course we are currently on. But you... you have been sent here to reaffirm the wisdom of our decision. What's in it for you, you ask? If you help us, you can live. That's a reward that just keeps on giving, now, isn't it? We're looking for a black Charger, gentlemen. Tell me at least one of you has seen it."

"We're looking for it, too," said the first killer. "I... I thought we were on the same side."

Bill smiled. "You're not on our side, little man. You're merely one of Astaroth's pawns. But you may be of use to us if you've seen the black Charger."

"I... I haven't."

Bill's smile faded. "Unfortunate," he said, and kicked the killer's face through the back of his skull. He turned to the other one. "What about you, my friend? Have you seen the black Charger?"

"Or the girl?" said Betty. "Overweight, with brown hair?"

The second killer licked his lips nervously. "I... I haven't seen her yet. Her name's Amber, right? The, uh, the demon girl? I haven't technically laid eyes on her yet, but if you want, if you think it could help, I can go outside right now and keep looking for her."

"No, that's all right," sighed Betty, and reached down and snapped his neck.

"What do we do if we can't find her?" Kirsty asked.

"We will," said Betty.

"How? She's going to be extra careful now that she knows we're here. We're not going to stumble across her again."

Bill sighed. "Are you still with us?"

"What?" Kirsty said. "What does that mean?"

"Are you with us?" he repeated. "We've gone over a hundred years working together, and haven't we reaped the rewards?"

"Sure," said Kirsty. "But now Alastair and Imelda are dead, *after* Imelda betrayed us, and the only reason the Shining Demon isn't trying to kill us right now is because he thinks we're bringing him your daughter. We're on dangerously thin goddamn ice."

"We just have to remain calm," said Bill.

Kirsty's eyebrows rose. "That's our plan? Remain calm? If the Hounds get Amber before we do, not only will we not have the key, but we'll have proven ourselves useless to Astaroth, and then we'll be right back where we were. I don't like being on the run, Bill. It doesn't suit me."

"This is ridiculous," Betty said. "We'll find Amber, all right? We're her parents. We know her better than anyone. We've been right on her heels every step of the way so far, haven't we? And she's not running anymore, so now is our chance to catch up with her. After everything we've done for you, Kirsty, I would think that a little good faith wouldn't be too much to ask for."

"Everything you've done for us?" Kirsty said, letting her anger cloud her perfect features. "It's your fault we're in this mess in the first place! At least *our* kids died when they were supposed to die!"

"Oh," Betty said, squaring up to her, "I'm sorry for raising a child who can actually *think on her feet*."

"You're proud of her?" Kirsty said, frowning. "You're actually proud of that little *toad*?"

Betty struck Kirsty — hard — across the face, and the slap stunned the room into silence.

"Now, ladies..." Bill said, stepping forward.

Kirsty held up her hand. "Don't say a goddamn word, Bill. Betty, you ever touch me again and I will rip your arm off."

"Fair enough," Betty said. "I'm sorry, Kirsty. I didn't mean to do that. We just need your trust for another few hours. Give us until midnight. I swear to you, we will find Amber, we'll get the key, and we will help Naberius tear Astaroth to shreds."

"Midnight," Kirsty said.

"So where do we start?" asked Grant.

"We start by having a backup plan," said Bill. "You're absolutely right, the both of you. We need to protect ourselves. Astaroth wants us to bring him either Amber or Jesper. We don't know where Amber is, but everyone knows where the mayor resides."

"He'll have guards," said Kirsty. "Maybe even more of those cops."

"We can handle it," Bill said. "We can handle anything. After you, ladies."

Betty walked out first. Kirsty followed, with Grant trailing after her. Bill took a look around and Amber ducked back.

When she looked again, he was gone.

33

SHE CALLED MILO, and Virgil came out to pick her up. Amber didn't say much on the ride back, just sat and bled all over his seat. Virgil assured her he didn't mind.

When she got back to the house, Linda did her best to patch her up. Amber took a few painkillers. She was crashing hard after all that adrenaline, so she went to lie down and feel sorry for herself while Milo headed back out with Virgil to visit the town's nuclear bunker. Two came with her, and she snuggled him and fell asleep, shivering despite the heavy blankets.

When she woke, the shivers had stopped and the painkillers had worn off and Two was kicking out in his sleep. Groaning, and moving slowly, she tipped herself out of bed and shuffled from the room. She smelled food. Javier was cooking for the house, and there was a plate set aside for her. Ronnie and the others had been over the morning's events again and again, she could see it in their faces – the triumph after finding Austin, and the wariness after their encounter with the Narrow Man. By the time she sat beside Warrick and involved herself in the conversation, they'd moved on to cheerier fare. They told her and Austin stories about their previous last-minute escapes. The way they told it, it was all chases and scares and running down mineshafts and through old hotels. They left out the murder and horror and death. Amber appreciated that. It was nice, this, being part of a group. She'd never experienced it before. It was comforting.

Milo and Virgil got back a little before four.

"The bunker will do us just fine," Milo said once they were all gathered in the living room. "It's basically a fallout shelter left over from the sixties, obviously never used. It's safe, secure, and far enough out of the way that no one will stumble across it. It's opened by a keypad, though, so we'll need the code."

"And where do we find that?" Ronnie asked.

"About five or six years ago there was this town-wide scandal," said Virgil. "Couple of high-school kids were using the bunker to party and drink and do whatever it is young people do nowadays. They were found out, grounded, and the mayor said the code would be changed — but I don't think he ever got around to it. You just have to find one of those kids, get them to tell you the code they used."

"Any idea who they were?" Linda asked.

"Don't remember their actual names," Virgil said, "but I remember a nickname. Ridiculous thing, it was."

"The Party-Monster?" Kelly guessed.

Virgil looked surprised. "You know him?"

"We've met."

"I know him," said Austin. "Well, not know him, but I know where he lives. I can show you if you want. There's a house at the end of Barn Owl Road with a purple truck in the drive. It belongs to his dad."

"So that's your job," Milo said to Ronnie. "Talk to this Party-Monster individual. We're going to need the bunker tonight."

"Still going ahead with your plan, are we?" Javier asked.

Milo looked at him. "You sound like you don't approve."

"Just playing Devil's advocate," Javier said. "You've gone to all this trouble to get Austin here back safely and stop the sacrifice... and now you want to sacrifice someone, anyway?"

"We want to sacrifice Jesper," said Amber, a little irritably. She immediately felt bad, but the pain from her shoulder was sending spikes into her mind. "He started all this. He's responsible for all the evil done in this town."

"I'm not saying he doesn't deserve it," said Javier, "I'm just questioning the wisdom. You've managed to get a check in the win column – shouldn't you just count your blessings and hightail it while you can?"

"Finding Austin does nothing to save Amber from the Hounds," said Kelly. "She helped us, now we're helping her."

"By turning this town evil," said Javier. "That's what'll happen, yes? When you do sacrifice Mayor Jesper, all that craziness you said will happen will actually happen, right?"

Amber looked away. "Right."

"And, while the town goes crazy, we're all sitting in the bunker? That doesn't sound very heroic."

"Then it's a good thing we're not heroes," said Milo. "The curfew's at eight, that's when all the kids have to get off the streets, and sunset tonight is, what, ten-thirty? Then it's an hour's wait until it's actually dark. So ten o'clock is when we meet at the bunker. It's tight, but I think we can do it. By then, Amber and I will have Jesper in tow and hopefully you guys will have the code to let us all in."

"You need any help?" Kelly asked.

"We'll be okay on our own," said Milo.

Kelly frowned. "Is it because I haven't showered today? Warrick takes forever in there."

"I really do," said Warrick.

"I'm gonna shower the moment we finish talking."

"It's not your hygiene," said Milo. "Amber and I, using Shanks's key, should be more than enough to snatch Jesper. The fewer the better. We bring him to the bunker, which you will have opened, we wait for the barrier to drop, and, when it does, we take Jesper to Naberius."

"Where you'll kill him," said Javier.

"Where we'll do whatever we have to do," said Milo. "Then we'll rejoin the rest of you while the town takes care of the Hounds, and wait till morning. Anyone have any questions?"

"Just ethical ones," Javier said. "But I don't suppose anyone's interested in those."

"What about the Narrow Man?" asked Linda. "We've taken his sacrifice away. We had hoped he wouldn't notice until it was too late, but obviously that chance has passed."

"Hey, yeah," Warrick said. "What's to stop him from just snatching some other kid?"

"We'll need to keep an eye on him," Ronnie said. "On Oscar Moreno, rather. I'll do it. The rest of you get the code and I'll tail Moreno, if I can find him."

"He knows your face," said Amber. "He knows all our faces."

"Oh, for God's sake," said Virgil, "we'll follow Moreno, all right? We're not completely goddamn useless, and he hasn't seen our faces."

"Uh, he's wearing Javier's, though," said Warrick.

"I'm an old man," said Javier. "He's not going to recognise me."

There were some uneasy glances passed around.

"We're not imbeciles!" Javier snapped. "We can find someone and follow him and make sure he's not off kidnapping any more children. It's not rocket science."

"But it might be dangerous," Ronnie said.

"Son, at our age going to sleep is dangerous," Virgil told him. "This is nothing."

"Well, okay," Linda said. "That sounds like a... like a good idea? Maybe? I think it does. We'll take Austin with us, then. Cool."

Virgil nodded. "That's settled."

"Amber's parents," Kelly asked. "Are they likely to cause us trouble?"

"If this were a complicated plan, maybe," Amber said. "But it's pretty simple. Simple plans have fewer things to go wrong."

"You hope."

Amber shrugged, the movement sending fresh waves of pain coursing through her. She clenched her teeth to stop from crying out.

"I got one more question," said Virgil, not noticing her discomfort, "just because nobody else seems to be asking it. What then?"

Milo glanced at Amber, then looked back at Virgil. "What do you mean?"

"I mean, what then? Supposing all this works out. The Narrow Man doesn't snatch another kid, you get the code for the bunker, you grab Jesper, the Hounds come in, you kill Jesper, the town tears the Hounds apart... then what? You're all going to ride off into the sunset? What's going to happen to Desolation Hill? What's going to happen to the people? Is the Narrow Man going to keep bringing those kids to that Demon they've got locked away?"

"We'll deal with the Narrow Man," said Ronnie.

"How?" Virgil asked. "I just got treated to a fifteen-minute, blow-by-blow account of how disastrously that went for you all this morning."

"He wobbled, though," Amber said tightly. "As the Narrow Man, yes, I don't think we hurt him one little bit. But, when he changed back to plain old Oscar Moreno, he limped. And he bled. I think when he's disguising himself as, well, as you, Javier, he can be hurt. Maybe even killed."

"So then we go after him when he's Moreno," said Virgil.

"I'm afraid it's not as simple as that," Milo said. "He changes form in a matter of seconds. We'd have to take him by complete surprise and I don't see that happening."

"Well, take me along with you," said Virgil. "I'll distract him, you hit him from behind. Whatever he is, he's a kid-killer, and kid-killers need to be got rid of."

"I'd agree with you there, sir, but things are moving pretty fast right now."

Virgil scowled. "I can still hustle when I need to."

"We're not hustling, sir, we're sprinting. I'm sorry, it's just too dangerous."

"Don't treat me like a goddamn child."

"I wouldn't dare, Mr Abernathy, but the reality of the situation is that you are old, and going after the Narrow Man is no job for you."

"You need me," Virgil said angrily. "If it wasn't for me, you'd have no idea who this Narrow Man was. I figured it out. This started with me."

"And it'll end with us," Milo said. "I mean no disrespect, but you'll have to view this from the sidelines. You can keep an eye on Moreno because you'll be out of harm's way, but that's as close to the action as you're going to get."

"Goddamn you, boy."

"Yes, sir."

"I don't mind staying away from the action," said Javier. "I was never much one for swinging punches, anyway. Used to get the stuntman to do all my fight scenes. Fat slob he was, a full head taller than me, but I'd still be able to sell it in the close-ups. I don't think anyone noticed."

"Everyone noticed," said Virgil.

"I noticed," said Warrick.

"Me, too," said Milo.

"Yep," said Javier, "nobody noticed."

34

AMBER SAT ON THE BED in the spare room, ignoring the pain in her shoulder and tracing her fingers over the contours of the brass key. Her eyes were closed and her mind was filled with a single image – the doors they'd passed through when they'd been taken to see Jesper. At first, she'd tried to picture the ornately carved entryway into the mayor's mansion, but the carvings were too intricate for her memory, and she felt that anything less than absolute certainty would bring her back to Naberius's cell underground. She didn't want to go back there again.

So she focused on the double doors leading into the drawing room. She could see these much more clearly, could still see Jesper's butler, whatever his name was, the guy with the burn mask, reaching for the handles, opening them. She felt confident that the picture was clear enough in her head. Fairly confident, at least.

Mildly confident, then.

The door to the spare room opened and Kelly came in, her hair still wet from the shower. "All set?" she asked.

Amber nodded, and stood. "I'm ready."

"Milo says you're leaving in five. We'll be going shortly after. I swear, this is military precision compared to our usual way of working."

"More casual, is it?"

"We have a Warrick and a dog. It pretty much has to be. How's your shoulder?"

Amber gave a big smile. "Really, really painful, thanks."

"I bet," Kelly responded. "Take your shirt off."

Amber blinked. "Uh... Sorry?"

"Your shoulder," Kelly said, opening the medical bag on the side table. "I have to change the dressing."

"Oh right. Yeah."

Kelly stood there, waiting, while Amber stood there, not moving. "So you gonna take it off, or are you waiting for me to take mine off first?"

Amber's laugh was forced, even to her ears. "No, no, you don't have to do that."

"Pity," said Kelly.

Amber didn't know how to respond to that. She grabbed the ends of both her sweatshirt and T-shirt, and hesitated. "I don't know how I'm going to do this gracefully one-handed," she admitted.

"Here," Kelly said, stepping forward, "I'll help."

Amber allowed her hand to be moved aside, and felt Kelly's fingertips brush against the skin of her waist. Gently, Kelly pulled the clothes up, over the belly that Amber was now sucking in, over her bra, and now over her head. They caught briefly on her ears, and then they were gone, and Amber's hair settled back into place as Kelly manoeuvred the clothing off the injured shoulder.

When she was done, Kelly put the clothes to one side and stepped back. "You're blushing," she said.

"Well, yeah," Amber said, laughing a little desperately. "But, y'know, it's only because I'm standing here without a shirt."

"Oh," said Kelly, and without a single hesitation she pulled her own shirt off and dropped it on top of Amber's. "There," she said. "That better?"

Amber did her best to look away. "Sure," she said, her voice strained. "I, uh, I love your tattoos."

"Thank you," Kelly said. She turned slightly, tapping her fingers on the image on her left shoulder. "See that? That's the guy who killed my parents and my sisters."

"Oh God... I'm so sorry."

Kelly tapped her bicep. "This one here? A killer clown, man. A frikkin' killer clown. I hate those bastards. That was my first time as an official member of the gang, though, so I guess he holds a special place in my heart."

Amber's eyes drank in the detail of her arms. "And these others? You've encountered all of them?"

"My tattoos are my diaries."

"But... there are so many."

"I guess there are. Linda and Ronnie would have more, if they had tattoos. And, although he doesn't talk about it, I have a feeling that Warrick would be covered from head to foot."

"Why?" Amber asked. "Why do you do it?"

"You know why."

"I really don't."

"Once you're on the Demon Road, Amber, you can never get off. So you're either a bad guy, or a good guy. We're the good guys. Same as you."

268

Amber didn't say anything to that, and Kelly started to work on the dressing. Her fingers were warm. Amber was finding it difficult to know where to look. As she removed the dressing, Kelly pressed against her for a moment.

"You're healing really fast," she said. "Like, a fraction of the time it'd take a normal person. Being a lowercase-d demon sure has its perks, doesn't it?"

Amber nodded. "Definitely perky," she mumbled.

Kelly wrapped up the used dressing and dumped it, then walked over to the medical bag on the side table. Amber watched the muscles move beneath the skin of her slender back.

"You're in such great shape," she said before she realised what she was doing.

Kelly shrugged. "I guess. We do a lot of running. Mostly from horrible people wanting to kill us. Tends to keep you trim, you know?"

She came back. "You're still blushing," she said.

"Am I?" Amber laughed. "Sorry. Just... y'know. I'm not used to having my shirt off in front of someone."

"Ah. I could take my pants off if it'd make you more comfortable?"

Amber burned hotter, tried to disguise it with another laugh. "No, that's all right."

"Pity," said Kelly again.

"You, uh, you just run, then?" Amber asked, to change the subject. "You don't work out or anything, or do yoga or Pilates or... boxercise?"

Kelly raised an eyebrow. "No one boxercises anymore. When was the last time you were in a gym?"

Now Amber's laugh was genuine. "Me? Never. Look at me, for God's sake."

"What do you mean?"

"I'm fat," Amber laughed.

Kelly glared. "Hey. None of that talk."

"Oh no, no, I'm not being mean to myself. I'm just being, y'know, honest. I'm overweight."

"So?"

"So I don't look good without my shirt on."

Kelly looked her square in the eye for the longest time, then stepped back and looked her up and down.

"Uh," said Amber, "what are you—?"

Kelly held up a hand for silence, and Amber complied.

Seconds dragged by. Eventually Kelly completed her examination. "Okay, Amber," she said, "you're overweight."

"Uh, I know."

"So what?"

"I just... I don't look good, that's all."

"I beg to differ."

"You look great, though," Amber said, her words speeding up. "You look amazing. I love your hair. It's gorgeous. And you're so pretty. So slim and so pretty. You've got such a great figure."

Kelly started to smile. "Why, Amber, are you coming on to me?"

Amber blinked. "What? No. What? I'm just—"

"Because as the person currently fixing your bandage, Amber, I am bound by a strict code of professional conduct. I can't kiss you."

"What? I didn't say anything about—"

"I can't grab you and kiss you," said Kelly, wrapping the

bandage around Amber's shoulder. "I can't pull you into me and press my lips against yours. It wouldn't be right."

"I... I know that, I'm just—"

"I can't pull your hair, either," Kelly continued. "I can't grab a fistful of your hair to pull your head back to kiss your throat. It's against all the rules, Amber."

Amber nodded.

"I can't nuzzle your neck," said Kelly. Her voice was a little softer now, her mouth right at Amber's ear. "I can't kiss your collarbone. I can't kiss the length of your jawline. I can't do it, Amber. It wouldn't be right."

Amber swallowed.

"While I'm tending to your wound," said Kelly, "I can't do any of those things. Not even if you begged me. Not even if you begged me to kiss you, Amber. Do you understand?"

"Yes," Amber whispered.

Kelly checked the dressing one more time, and stepped back. "There," she said. "All finished. Professional conduct no longer applies."

Amber stared at her.

Kelly moved in slowly. Her lips, when they brushed Amber's, were soft.

Amber kissed her back.

Kelly moved closer, pressing her body against Amber's. Amber didn't know what to do with her hands so she kept them by her sides. Kelly seemed to be okay with that. When the kiss broke off, Kelly was smiling.

"Hey, beautiful," she whispered, and they kissed again.

But of course Amber wasn't beautiful. They both knew it. Kelly was this gorgeous, tattooed redhead and Amber was a lump beside her. Amber visualised them, saw in her head how their kiss would look to someone watching. She didn't like that image. It threatened to dampen the fire she was feeling inside her. Amber didn't want that fire to go out. She liked it. She needed it.

So she used it. The fire flared and she shifted, and she pulled Kelly closer to her, kissed her harder, and she imagined how it'd look now and she liked what she saw. Two beautiful women, one tattooed and red-haired and the other horned and red-skinned, wrapped around each other, stumbling against the bed. Suddenly Amber wanted to see all of Kelly, wanted to kiss every last part of her, and her hands went to Kelly's pants, started dragging them down, and then she felt a hand on her chest and she realised Kelly was pushing her away.

"What the hell are you *doing*?" Kelly cried, backing off and wiping her mouth. "What the *hell*?"

"What?" said Amber. "What's wrong?"

"What's wrong? Look at yourself, for Christ's sake! You turned! You turned halfway through the goddamn kiss! What the hell's wrong with you?"

Embarrassment or shame or humiliation or something awful, something nasty, curled up from Amber's throat and filled her cheeks and burned her eyes and turned to anger, turned to snarling and sneering. "You're the one who kissed *me*."

"I kissed you without all *this*," said Kelly, motioning to the horns.

Amber barked out a laugh. "You can't handle me, that's your problem."

"What, did you think I'd like it?"

Amber grabbed her clothes and pulled them on. "I couldn't give a shit what you like or don't like."

Kelly shook her head. "Oh, come on, don't be like this."

"I'm not like anything. Obviously, I'm just not your type."

"It isn't that, Amber. Come on, I was taken by surprise, that's all. I didn't mean to hurt your feelings."

Amber laughed again. "You think you've hurt my feelings? My parents are trying to eat me, Kelly. You're just going to have to get in line."

She walked out, and Austin saw her and screamed. She ignored him.

35

IT WAS GOOD BEING back in the Charger. It felt right. The great black beast growled and roared at Milo's touch and swallowed up the blacktop as they skirted the inside of the town boundary. They stuck to back roads, trying to stay out of sight of the cops. Every now and then, Amber would catch a glimpse of a motorcycle through the trees, the weak rays of evening sunlight glinting off chrome. The Hounds could sense the weakening barrier, it seemed. Another few hours and it would dissolve entirely.

"You're upset," said Milo.

Amber looked at him. She hadn't bothered to revert. She didn't see the point of keeping up the pretence this close to Hell Night breaking out. "I'm fine," she said.

Milo nodded. She thought that was the end of it until he said, "You're clearly not, though. Are you sure you're okay to do this?"

"Yes," said Amber, growing irritated. "I told you, I'm fine."

Milo looked at her, but didn't respond. After a moment, she sighed.

"Let's not do this, okay? This sharing thing. For a start, you don't know how. And out of everyone – out of *everyone* – you should be the one person I know who respects the fact that when I don't want to talk about something, I don't want to talk about it. It's not a ploy to get you to ask me questions I secretly want to be asked. I don't want to be asked and I don't want to answer and I don't want to talk about this. Is that okay with you?"

Milo nodded again.

"Thank you."

He pointed out of the window, to the door of a small house they were passing. "What about that one? Is that interesting enough?"

Amber looked. "It's brown."

"Brown isn't interesting?"

"Not in a door, no. Look for something with a design to it. Something that stands out."

"Are you sure we can't do this with one of Virgil's doors?"

"No, I'm not. Maybe I could keep a normal, boring old door in my head, even when this black metal door is doing its best to sneak in there, but I don't want to risk it. It's easier, it's safer if I have a door I can easily visualise to come back to."

They passed another house. "What about that one?"

"What's special about it?"

"It's not brown."

"It's still just a door."

"I don't know what you're hoping to find," said Milo. "Most doors are just doors."

"Look for a memorable one."

"The longer we're out here looking, the greater the chances are of the cops finding us."

"I know that."

"And this doesn't have anything at all to do with Kelly?"

She shot him a look. "You prying?"

"I'm not prying. I'm asking a strategic question. If we're out here because of something that was done or said—"

"I wouldn't risk your life like that," Amber said. "I certainly wouldn't risk mine. We need to find a door like the one in the motel – something that stands out, that I can latch on to, but that doesn't mean we have to go into town."

"You've seen many doors like that around here?"

"That's what I'm trying to—" It came to her then. "Got it!" she said, whacking her hand off his arm. "I know where we can go!"

Milo frowned at her. "You know, you're pretty violent when you're a demon."

"You noticed that too, huh?"

A chain-link fence surrounded the summer carnival site, so they parked and went walking. Amber's shoulder was feeling a whole lot better by the time they found a gap and squeezed through. Whether this was down to her higher pain threshold as a demon or her rapid healing, or maybe just Kelly's newly applied bandage, she didn't know and she didn't care. She was feeling better and that's all that mattered.

They walked through long grass at the edge of the site to the slightly shorter grass on the site itself, where it grew up round the covered rides and shuttered booths. Milo touched her arm lightly and she saw the cautious look on his face a moment before she heard the voices.

They ducked low and crept forward. Three boys sat on the

carousel – two on the railing surrounding it and the third on one of the wooden horses. They looked Amber's age, maybe slightly older, and they were drinking beers and the one on the horse, the one with long hair and ripped jeans, had a cigarette dangling from his lips. The smoke wafted on the breeze.

"I thought he hated my guts," the long-haired guy said. "Remember all those times he said he was gonna beat the crap outta me?"

"I remember all the times you shat yourself about it," the bigger of his friends said, grinning.

"Whatever," said the long-haired guy, stubbing out his cigarette, "I always thought Cunningham hated me, that's my point. That's the point I'm making."

"But if he hated you then why would he want us to spend tonight with him and his friends?"

"Jesus Christ, Marco, would you please pay attention? That's what I'm saying! I'm saying he must not hate me because he wants to party with us tonight. I swear, you better not be this dumb later on. I don't want you embarrassing me."

"I'm not gonna embarrass you," Marco said, frowning. "Why would I embarrass you?"

"Well, I mean, let's face it, okay? You're not exactly scholarship material, now, are you?"

"What?"

"You're not smart."

Marco's face darkened. "Don't call me stupid."

"I'm not calling you anything. I'm just saying you're not smart. That's not the same as saying you're stupid."

"Yes, it is, Jamie."

"No, it's not. It just means you have a tendency to say and

do stupid things. Doesn't mean you *are* stupid. So long as you don't say or do anything stupid around Zak Cunningham and his buddies, we should be fine. This is a big night for us. We can't let anything go wrong."

The third boy, a dark-haired kid with a birthmark peeking up from the collar of his shirt, raised his head for the first time. "Jesus, can't the pair of you shut the hell up for five seconds? All week, tonight is the only thing you've talked about. You know how boring you've been? It's a party, okay? Get over it."

Marco and Jamie exchanged glances, and then the grins broke out.

"I think someone is feeling upset that he's too young for Hell Night," said Jamie.

"I guess you'd better get home," Marco jeered. "You don't wanna be caught out after curfew."

"Yeah, you wanna make sure you're tucked in with all the other little kiddies."

"Ha, look, poor baby is sulking. Don't make fun of him."

"Aw, I'm sorry, baby – please don't cry."

The boy with the birthmark smiled tightly, and got down off his perch, dusted off his jeans like he was getting ready to leave. Then he flew at his friends, shoving Marco backwards off the railing while he grabbed Jamie and dragged him to the ground.

"What's that?" he snarled. "What's that you're saying?"

He jammed his knee on to Jamie's throat and picked up a rock, held it over his head, ready to smash it down. "What's that you were saying about crying? Huh?"

"Jesus!"

"Speak up now."

"Let go of me, you psycho..."

The kid with the birthmark put a little more weight on his knee, then stood, allowing his victim to roll over and cough.

He threw down the stone. "You dickheads really think I give a shit about Hell Night? You really think I care that I have to wait another year? It's a town party. Big frikkin' deal."

Marco helped Jamie to his feet.

"Go on," said the boy with the birthmark. "Run off to play with Cunningham and his pals. Enjoy Hell Night while you can, assholes. Next year, it belongs to me."

Jamie and Marco hesitated, then turned, started walking away. The kid with the birthmark watched them, then let out a derisive laugh and set off in the opposite direction. Amber and Milo ducked down until they were all gone, then straightened up.

"Lovely kids in this town," Milo said.

Amber led the way through the carnival until they came to the Hall of Mirrors. She stared at the door, the very memorable door with its shiny silver surface. When she was satisfied, she nodded.

"You sure about this?" Milo asked.

"Now is not the time for doubt," she answered.

He shrugged.

Planting Jesper's double doors firmly in her head, Amber took the brass key from her pocket and slid it into the lock. The dull metal door did its best to squirm into her thoughts, but she kept it out, and turned the key once, then twice, and with Milo's hand on her shoulder she opened the mirrored door and stepped through.

The mayor's drawing room. Colder than when they'd been there last. The lights were on, dimming the sky outside. The doors had shut behind them. Milo went to open them, but stopped. Footsteps and voices approached.

"Here they are," they heard Jesper say. He sounded tired. "The troublemakers. When did they arrive?"

"Early this morning." Novak. "Caught the big guy over on Broken Branch Road. The other one my officers nabbed as he was walking along Main Street without a care in the world."

Milo opened the door a crack, and they peered through. Two men, one tall, the other tall and hulking, were on their knees with their hands cuffed behind them. The bigger guy was deformed – his head a misshapen lump, while the other was masked. Both were silent.

Chief Novak was standing at their backs while Jesper stood in front, gazing down at them.

"How many of you will we have to execute before the Shining Demon stops sending you into our quiet little town? Eh?" He looked up at Novak. "What's the matter with them? Can't they talk?"

"Neither of them do much more than grunt," said Novak.

Jesper sighed. "The silent types, huh? We've seen plenty of their kind over the years."

"Yes, we have," said Novak. "But I wouldn't get too close, sir. They heal fast."

"Well, of course they do," said Jesper. "They wouldn't be any use to Astaroth otherwise. Weapons of choice?"

"Machete," said Novak, then nodded to the smaller guy. "Butcher knife."

"Always popular," said Jesper. "Gentlemen, we have a zero-tolerance policy here in Desolation Hill for serial killers of both the living and undead variety. But you knew that. Everyone

280

knows that your kind is just not welcome here. Chief Novak, please tell our guests what lies in store for them."

"I'm going to shoot you both in the head," Novak said, hunkering down between them so he could talk right into their ears. "Again. Then, while your brains are busy unscrambling, we're going to cut up your bodies into little tiny pieces, and bury each part in concrete. We may not be able to kill you – not really – but we can certainly ensure that you never pose a threat to our town – or any other town – ever again."

Novak stood up and Jesper gave the nod, and Novak shot the bigger guy in the temple. Despite herself, Amber flinched at the gunshot.

As the killer slumped sideways, the other one tried to get up, but Novak shot him in the back of the skull before he'd straightened his legs. He fell face down, dark blood leaking from the smoking hole in his mask.

"I'll get this cleaned up," said Novak.

"See that you do," Jesper responded. "What about the boy?"

Novak hesitated. "Still on the run."

Jesper didn't say anything.

"Mr Mayor," said Novak, "I accept full responsibility for the mistakes that have been made over the last few days. My officers were just carrying out my orders."

"How hard is it to hand over two people in handcuffs?"

"I'm sorry, sir. If there's anything I can do to make up for my errors of judgement—"

"*Errors of judgement?*" Jesper echoed. "This goes a little beyond *errors of judgement*, Chief Novak. I gave you an order."

"Yes, sir."

"That you disobeyed."

"I... well, sir, I wouldn't say I—"

"Did you hand them over to the Hounds or did you let them run?"

"I let them run, sir."

"Then you disobeyed my orders."

"Yes, Mr Mayor."

"And you failed to ensure that those kids in the van left town. What is happening to you, Chief? You never used to make mistakes like this."

"Sir, if there is anything I can do..."

"There is, actually," said Jesper. "We need a substitute sacrifice in the next few hours."

"Sir?"

"Go out and get one."

Novak paled.

"You have a problem with that, Chief?"

"I... sir, what you're asking me to do is..."

"Is what it takes," finished Jesper. "You're willing to do what it takes, aren't you?"

Novak was quiet for a moment. "Yes, Mr Mayor."

Jesper let the seconds drag by, then he turned and walked out of Amber's line of sight. "Never mind. The Narrow Man has assured me that he will take care of it." Novak's shoulders slumped with relief. "Get this cleaned up and then get back on the streets. Hell Night starts on schedule."

"Yes, Mr Mayor. Thank you."

Jesper walked away, and Novak took hold of the masked killer's ankles and started dragging him backwards.

Milo closed the door, and Amber checked her phone. "No word from Javier," she whispered. "Whoever the Narrow Man is planning to take to replace Austin, he hasn't made his move yet."

"Or he has," Milo whispered back, "but he's killed Javier and Virgil before they could tell us."

Amber glared. "Jesus Christ... Why would you say something like that?"

"Because I'm a bad man," said Milo.

They went to one of the windows and waited for Novak to leave. They watched until they could no longer see the cruiser's tail lights, and then they left the drawing room, moving quietly. Milo held his gun in both hands.

They found Jesper in his office, a large room of floor-to-ceiling bookcases and big windows. His desk was wide and sturdy and looked old, and Amber figured that it had probably been owned by some president or other, once upon a time. That was the kind of thing Jesper would appreciate.

He stood up as they approached, his hands empty save for the pen he'd been holding when they walked in. No weapons.

"I thought I'd be seeing you two again," he said, worryingly calm. "No common sense, that's your problem."

"Lot of books," said Amber. "Read 'em all?"

"Every one of them," Jesper replied proudly. "You'd be surprised what you can get through if you have a few hundred years of reading time."

Amber traced her claws along the spines of some leather-bound editions, leaving deep scratches. "Anything by Annalith Symmes?"

"I'm afraid I've not had the pleasure."

"She writes the In The Dark Places series? It's very good. They made it into a TV show."

Jesper smiled. "Perhaps I'll give it a try."

"You do that. Probably better than most of the stuff you've got here. Do you have *The Bell Jar*? I had to read it for school. *Dark Places* is better. Less depressing. You're very calm, by the way, for someone who's about to be taken against his will."

"Me?" said Jesper. "Oh no, you're mistaken. I'm not going anywhere. You think now that the police are gone I am unguarded? Chief Novak and his officers are this town's line of defence – not mine."

"Talk while you walk," Milo said, motioning with his gun.

"I'm not going with you," Jesper replied. "Whatever you have in store for me, I have no interest in seeing. You really should have kept running, you know. Coming back here was a mistake."

The door on the other side of the room opened and the burned man walked in without urgency, carrying a silver case. Beneath his mask, his scarred face betrayed no alarm.

"You're going to want to stop walking," said Milo, "or I shoot your boss."

The burned man kept walking.

"Wesley has been in my employ for over thirty years," said Jesper. "I offered him refuge when nobody else would. I forgave him his sins and provided him with a home, a job... a purpose."

"Yeah?" said Milo, turning his gun on the burned man. "How about a casket?"

The burned man stopped.

"Wesley has been a loyal associate ever since," Jesper continued. "But, every so often, he is afforded the chance to return to his old ways, and he takes these opportunities with some relish, let me tell you. Perhaps you've heard of him? Wesley Sterling?"

"My memory ain't what it used to be," said Milo.

"No matter," Jesper said. "You've probably heard of his other name, the name he's known by in certain – darker – circles. Wesley Sterling, the Nightmare Man."

36

RONNIE DROVE, AND LINDA sat up beside him. Austin was seated behind them and he was telling them about the town and what a messed-up town it was. Kelly sat on the cushions and scratched Two's belly. She raised her eyes, saw Warrick looking at her.

He crawled over to sit beside her. "You okay, Kel?" he asked in a quiet voice.

She smiled. "I'm fine."

"Amber's a nice chick."

Kelly nodded. "I guess she is."

"She's really hot when she's a demon."

Kelly gave a non-committal shrug.

"Of course, it could be argued that she's hot, anyway, you know, because of who she is as a person." Warrick nodded. "It's what's inside that counts, really. That's what I've always said."

"When have you ever said that?"

"I say it all the time, but you're never around when I do," said Warrick.

"No? Where am I?"

"I think you're on the toilet."

"Every time?"

"Every single time I've said it."

"Well, ain't that something?"

"You know," said Warrick, "you can talk to me about all this stuff if you want. And it doesn't just have to be the fun stuff. Like the lesbian stuff. It can be about feelings, as well."

"The feelings are lesbian, too, Warrick."

"My point is, if you like someone and she doesn't like you... well, first of all, she's an idiot, because you're awesome. But, second of all, maybe she needs to figure out some stuff of her own first before she can let herself realise how amazing you are."

Kelly let her head rest on Warrick's shoulder. "You're a good guy, you know that?"

"I'm just super-sensitive about lesbian issues," he said, and she laughed.

"We're here," said Ronnie as they pulled over. Kelly knelt and peered out at a row of houses surrounded by trees. She zeroed in on the house with the purple truck out front, where a middle-aged man was boarding up the windows.

"Austin, you stay here with Warrick and Two," said Ronnie. "We're not going to be long."

Austin nodded, and Kelly opened the side door and got out. Ronnie and Linda joined her, and they walked up to the man hammering nails.

"Hi there," said Ronnie.

The man turned, frowned at them. "Who are you?"

"We're friends of, uh, of your son," said Linda. "He in?"

The man kept frowning. "You really shouldn't be here. Today's the day of the festival. You... you can't be here. We have a curfew in place."

"We're actually just leaving," Kelly said, smiling broadly.

"We're all packed up and ready to go, and we figured we'd stop by to see your son on our way out. We're not gonna be long, I swear. Two minutes."

"If he isn't here, we can wait," Ronnie said happily.

"No, no, he's here," said the man. "Go on there and knock. My wife'll take you to him."

"Thank you," said Linda, and she led the way to the front door and rapped her knuckles against it. A few moments later, a woman answered, her eyes widening in alarm when she saw them.

"They're here to see Kevin," the man called. "Let them in. They'll be two minutes, they said."

"You really can't be here," the woman said.

"That's what I told them. They're on their way out of town."

"But... but the curfew—"

"Let them talk to the boy!" her husband shouted.

"Fine, okay," the woman said, flustered. "In, in, in you come." She stepped back and they walked into a house that smelled of freshly baked cookies. "Third door on the left, there. Better hurry."

She hurried off, and Ronnie turned the handle of Party-Monster's door and pushed it open. "Hi, Kevin," he said.

The Party-Monster, wearing only a pair of boxers, leaped out of bed, dropping a video-game controller on to a floor that was littered with dirty clothes and food-encrusted plates.

Kelly was the last one into his room, and as she closed the door she put one hand over her nose and mouth. "Oh my God, it *stinks* in here."

"Jesus," said Ronnie.

"Is there a dead raccoon under the bed?" Linda asked, appalled. "I want to breathe through my mouth, but I don't want to swallow the smell."

"This is the most disgusting thing I've ever experienced," Kelly said. "And I was once thrown into a tub of bile."

"You hear that, Kevin?" said Ronnie. "Your room is worse than a tub of bile."

The Party-Monster just stared at them. He had a relatively hairless chest, with only a few curious wisps around his strangely large nipples. "What are you doing here?"

"We won't be long," Ronnie said. "We're after the code to the bunker. The nuclear bunker? We were told you know it." He looked around. "Have you ever cleaned this room?"

"Who let you in?" asked the Party-Monster.

"Your mom," said Linda. "You still live with your mom, by the way? There's nothing wrong with still living with your folks, of course there's not, but you still live with them like this? You're not a teenager anymore, Kevin."

"Party-Monster," said the Party-Monster somewhat feebly.

"You're a grown-up," Linda continued. "Do you have a job? Or is Party-Monstering a full-time occupation?"

The Party-Monster didn't answer.

"So you don't have a job, then. You live with your folks, you don't clean your room, you probably never even open a window in here, and you don't pay your own way."

Kelly shook her head sadly. "Oh, Party-Monster..."

"I don't have to explain myself to you," said the Party-Monster. "I don't have to explain myself to anyone. I do what I do. I am who I am. I party."

"Playing video games in your underwear is not partying."

"You just wait," the Party-Monster sneered. "You hang around a few hours, and then you'll see exactly what kind of Party-Monster I can—"

"We know that you change into a demon," Ronnie said.

The Party-Monster's sneer dropped. "Oh."

"We know it all. We don't care. The only reason we're here is to get the code to the bunker. You know it, don't you?"

"Why should I tell you?"

"Because if you don't I'll beat you up again," said Linda.

The Party-Monster puffed out his chest, which only served to accentuate how big his nipples were. "You caught me by surprise in the bar. Try that again and see what happens."

"I would step towards you right now, but I'm terrified of what I might step on," said Linda. "Have you ever washed these clothes?"

"You can wash 'em if you want," the Party-Monster said. He was getting braver. "You can start with these shorts I'm wearing. Come over here and get 'em. You or the redhead, I don't mind."

"I'm not really into naked men," said Kelly, "but if I were I'd probably still not be into you."

The Party-Monster laughed. "What are you, a lesbian?"

"Yes."

His eyes widened. "Really?"

He was definitely getting braver. This would not do. Kelly reached for the wires connecting his TV to his games console.

"Hey," he said, "don't touch that."

"Tell us what the code is or I'll pull out all of these wires and you'll lose your progress. I bet you didn't have a chance to press save when we walked in, did you?"

The Party-Monster licked his lips nervously. "You can't... you can't threaten me like that. That's not even a threat. I'll just replay the section."

"What Kelly is doing," Ronnie explained, "is firing the first salvo. This is our opening threat. Will it work? Probably not."

"But when it doesn't," Linda said, "we'll move on to another threat. And another one after that. You'll tell us the code eventually."

"But it's up to you how much it'll have to hurt, or how much you'll have lost, by the time you do," finished Kelly. "So, one more time... tell us the code or I'll pull these wires."

"Okay!" the Party-Monster said, hands up. "Jesus, okay! It's 4-0-1-5. It'll beep and a green light will come on."

Kelly released the wires. "Thank you."

"So you're... you're really a lesbian? And are you a lesbian, too?"

"Afraid not," said Linda.

The Party-Monster seemed disappointed, then looked at Ronnie. "You ever get involved?"

"I'm not sure you understand what a lesbian is," Ronnie said, "so we'll go while you google it."

The Party-Monster frowned, but Ronnie was already leaving the room, followed by Linda. Kelly desperately wanted to say something clever on the way out, but her desire to leave the smell behind proved somewhat overwhelming. She joined the others in the hall outside, shut the door, and breathed deeply again.

The Party-Monster's parents stood side by side, waiting for them.

"Are you leaving now?" asked the Party-Monster's mom.

"Yes, thank you," said Ronnie, smiling.

The relief that washed over their faces was palpable, and the mother took a plate from the table behind her and held it out. "Cookie?"

Kelly grinned. "Don't mind if I do."

37

OSCAR MORENO'S CAR WAS in his driveway. Virgil and Javier sat across the road in the Sienna.

"What's wrong with you?" Javier asked.

Virgil frowned at him. "What do you mean?"

"I mean you're all surly and bad-tempered."

"Don't I have a right to be? This town is infested with evil."

"Yeah?" said Javier. "So's Hollywood. You should be used to it."

"In that house, right now, is a... a *monster*, who may or may not have already abducted another child in the few hours since this morning. There could be a terrified kid in there *right now*, and what are we doing?"

"Well, one of us is getting very angry about something."

"We're *watching*," said Virgil. "We sit in this car, not knowing what's going on in there, while the other young people are risking their lives to battle the forces of darkness."

"And?"

"And that's what I want to do, goddammit. I was investigating all of this fine on my own. I figured out who the Narrow Man was and I was putting it all together, piece by piece. Sure, I was doing it slowly, and I didn't have all the pieces, but it was building to something. And now here I am – sidelined."

"Hmm," said Javier. "I notice at no time during that little monologue did you mention me."

"Well, forgive me, but as of yet you haven't done anything of particular note."

"I was *there*," said Javier, leaning in and jabbing the air, "every step of the way."

"Except the beginning."

"It's my face that sonofabitch is using!"

"He probably figured you were done with it."

Javier sat back, really pissed. "If you're so determined to get yourself killed, why don't you go get yourself killed? Why don't you march in there and search the place for any abducted children?"

"Because they're right," Virgil said miserably. "I'm old."

"And you don't know what the hell you're doing?"

"What do you mean by that?"

"I mean you're an actor, Virgil. You act. You pretend. You *do* remember that the show wasn't real, right? You've never battled the forces of darkness in your life. You wouldn't know where to start."

"Maybe not, but back in the old days—"

"If this had happened back in the old days, you still wouldn't have known where to start," Javier said. "These kids are young, yeah, but this is what they do. Let them take care of it."

"It just... it goes against the grain, you know?"

"Yeah, well, get over it. They've got their plans."

"So you're not even curious?"

"About what?"

"About why he chose your face."

Javier hesitated, then shrugged. "He must appreciate fine faces. Probably opened a lot of doors for him."

"Yeah," said Virgil. "Maybe. But wouldn't you like to find out?"

"Of course I would. But I'd like a lot of things."

"Do you know why you weren't a bigger star, Javier?"

Javier sighed. "If you mention goats one more time..."

"It's because you had all these things you wanted, whether it was this relationship or that job or that role... but you were never bold enough to reach forward and take them. You've played it safe your entire life, and that's what's kept you back all this time."

"I didn't realise you knew me so well."

"I'm a quick study. But it's never too late to learn to seize the moment, Javier. Seize the moment and take the chance."

"Cliché, cliché, cliché... This is why you've always needed a writer to put words in your mouth."

"You might fail," Virgil continued, "you might get rejected or scorned or, hell, even laughed at... but at least you took the chance."

"I've lost track of what you're trying to talk me into."

"We have to go in there, make sure the Narrow Man hasn't snatched another child."

"That's insane."

"How will you feel if we find out there is a kid in there that we could have helped? A kid that we could have saved, if only we weren't too cowardly?"

Javier sighed. "And will that shut you up?"

"Temporarily."

"Then I'm all for it, you crazy bastard."

They got out, zipping their coats up against the cold.

"Do we have weapons?" Javier asked.

"Only our wits."

"So no, then."

They crossed the street.

"Let's sneak around back," said Virgil.

"Good idea," said Javier. "Put off our horrible deaths by another few minutes."

"We're not going to die," Virgil said, lowering his voice now that they were passing round the side of the house. "If we're discovered, we'll just make something up. We'll improvise."

"You're terrible at improvising."

"Then you'll improvise."

"I'll ask him if he's found God."

"Yes," said Virgil. "Good."

"Unless you think the mention of God would set him off? Considering who he works for."

"Okay, we'll avoid mentioning God. How about if we're selling something? Like life insurance?"

"Who's going to buy life insurance from two old bastards like us?"

"We're not actually selling it, for crying out loud."

"Still, though... How about if we're selling encyclopaedias?"

"Fine, whatever."

"No one buys encyclopaedias anymore," said a voice right behind them.

Javier yelled and Virgil's heart almost burst in his chest, and they spun awkwardly as Oscar Moreno walked towards them.

Moreno was all smiles. "People use the internet to find things out these days. Encyclopaedia salesmen would have been a bad cover, gentlemen, even if I didn't know who you were. Now, you probably hear this all the time, but... but I am such a fan."

"We know who you are, too," said Javier. "And if anything happens to us your secret won't be a secret any longer. There are people who know where we are."

"I assure you, I don't know what you're talking about."

"You're a child-killer," said Virgil.

Moreno's smile dropped a little. "I would ask you to lower your voice, Mr Abernathy. I wouldn't go to your house and start flinging insults around, willy-nilly. Yes, I've killed children. But not exclusively. I've killed all sorts of people over the years."

"Why me?" Javier asked. "Why'd you take my face?"

Moreno smiled again. "I've always loved television. TV trained me, in a way. It showed me how to interact with people, how to form relationships... I studied it. My kind, we're not a social species, but there was always a part of me that wanted... a connection, I suppose. And now I have it. I have a family, because of you and your wonderful show and all the wonderful shows like it."

"But why me?"

"I came to Desolation Hill a long time ago," said Moreno. "I was nobody. I was this thing they called the Narrow Man. I had a simple purpose that I fulfilled. And I fulfilled it for many years. But I was missing something. I was missing an identity.

"Then you moved in, Mr Abernathy. I recognised you immediately, even if others did not. We've spoken, actually. Twice. I wore different faces each time, so you probably don't remember me."

"I meet a lot of people," Virgil said carefully.

"Of course," said Moreno, "of course you do. I knew you wouldn't remember me. I didn't have a personality back then. I do now. I realised I needed a face to build it around, a face to keep, as my own. Desolation Hill already had its Shroud – so now it needed Ernesto Insidio. It was with this face that I married, that I bought the hardware store, that I assimilated into this town. Mayor Jesper helped, of course, but it was this face that made it all possible."

"That's it?" Javier said, frowning. "That's all?"

Moreno looked concerned. "You were hoping for something else, weren't you? Something... more meaningful. Oh, I'm sorry. Now I feel bad."

"That's okay," said Virgil. "We got what we came for. Now we know. We better get back."

Moreno stepped into their path, wearing a look of deep, deep regret. "I can't allow you to do that, I'm afraid."

Virgil's knees began to actually tremble. "So what are you going to do? Kill us? Kill the Shroud and Insidio? Do you really want to do that? Could you live with yourself?"

"You flatter me," said Moreno.

"I'm sorry?"

"My performance must really be convincing if you believe I am capable of either remorse or empathy."

Virgil swallowed. "Then... then take us instead."

"I'm sorry?"

"They took Austin from you. Do you have another kid? If you do, for God's sake, release him. Let him live. We're old. If you're going to kill us, please, give our deaths meaning. Let the kid go."

"You would do that?" Moreno asked. "You, too, Mr Santorum? You would replace the child as a sacrifice?"

"Well, I... If you only need one of us, I suggest taking him. But if you need both... yeah, I guess."

Moreno made a surprised sound, deep in his throat. "Very well. And maybe the fact that there are two of you will make up for your advanced age. Quantity over quality, as it were. I accept your proposal. Mr Abernathy, the cellar door is unlocked."

"Here?" said Virgil. "This cellar?"

"I always move the sacrifice into my own house a few hours before they're due to die, just in case anything goes wrong. They can scream all they want – no one will hear. If you please..."

Virgil hesitated, but he could see no alternative than to just do what he was told. He gripped both handles and pulled, revealing the steps leading down. He went first and Javier followed, and lights flickered on. Moreno came last, closing the doors behind him.

The cellar was large and wide and clean. Also soundproofed. To their left, there was another set of stairs leading up to a door, presumably to the house itself. On the wall to their right, an array of shackles hung. There was no child down here.

Virgil gritted his teeth. "You don't have another kid, do you?"

"I have misled you," Moreno admitted. "I have my rules, you see. It is the town that decides which child shall be sacrificed. If I were to arbitrarily choose another, why would they bother to vote in the future? The process is important to them. The process is everything."

Virgil and Javier stood shoulder to shoulder. Javier made a whimpering noise, but stayed standing. His right leg was shaking so badly that Virgil worried it might pop off his hip – a not unlikely scenario, it had to be said.

"So now you're... you're just going to kill us?" Virgil asked.

"Now I'm going to chain you up," said Moreno. "And at precisely eleven twenty-four I will come back down and take you to Naberius."

"Okay..."

"And then *he* will kill you."

38

BENEATH A BLOOD-RED SKY, Amber stepped from the trees into a clearing, the golden leaves crackling under her feet. Balthazar turned to her, his shock of black hair falling over his ice-blue eyes, the sun catching his cheekbones, sharp as blades. Tempest, the woman beside him, was pale, her bronze hair long and tousled, her lips full and her green eyes wide. They clung to each other like the lovers they were, their features perfect, their passion barely contained, and they stood there while the trees stopped swaying and it all went quiet and Amber blinked, saw that she was not in a forest in Montana at all, but merely looking at one, and she stepped back, a peculiar kind of fuzziness working its way between her thoughts. It was a picture – no, a poster, an In The Dark Places poster – on a wall. On her wall, in her parents' house in Florida.

Amber looked round. Wesley Sterling, the Nightmare Man, stood by her old bed, holding a speargun. It was hot. Bright outside. She was already sweating. That was odd. She looked at her hand, at her small pale hand. Ah, that explained it. No longer a demon. She smelled something cooking. Did she smell it, though, or did she just think she smelled it? Did it matter?

Not really. She left her bedroom and walked down the long, long corridor to the kitchen. Much longer than she remembered. Her parents were here, in the kitchen, as was her demon-self. They parted and she walked between them, climbed on to the table and lay with her head beside the salad bowl, waiting to be eaten.

Her dad put his arm round her demon-self. "I much prefer you when you're like this," he said. "You're the daughter we always wanted."

"Oh, Dad," her demon-self giggled, and rolled her eyes.

Amber's mother stepped up, carving knife in hand. "Leg or breast?" she asked.

"Leg," said her dad, and her demon-self said, "She doesn't have much of the other." They laughed the way a family was supposed to laugh, with good humour and warmth. Behind them, Wesley Sterling loaded a spear into the speargun, which was roughly the length of Amber's forearm.

"This was my father's," Sterling said. "Only good thing he ever did, teaching me to use it."

Nobody else heard him, and Amber ignored him. Her mother carved a slice off Amber's leg and laid it on a plate. It was white meat, and steam rose off it.

"I don't want to be eaten," said Amber.

Her parents turned into demons.

"So?" said her demon dad.

"We don't care," said her demon mom.

"We're going to eat you, anyway," said her demon-self.

Amber shook her head, started to get up, but a dozen corpse hands emerged from the table and grabbed her, pulled her back down. She kicked and struggled and her mom carved off another slice. The kitchen was gone. They were in the Firebird Diner now.

"Please don't eat me," Amber sobbed. "I don't want you to eat me."

Her parents had full plates, and they ate with their fingers. When their fangs pierced the white meat, blood ran down their chins, dripped on to their clothes. So overwhelmed were they by the taste of Amber's flesh that they didn't hear her sobbing.

Her demon-self leaned over. "I hate you," she said.

"Please let me go."

"You're weak," said her demon-self. She was wearing Amber's Firebird uniform. It looked so much better on her. "You're ugly. You're pathetic. I hate you so much."

"I don't want to die."

"You deserve it, though. For all your stupidity. Think of the life I could have had if you'd been better. You think I'd have let them fool me? You think I'd have had to run?"

"Help me."

"Why couldn't you have been stronger? Why couldn't you have been better?"

Amber's demon-self picked up a plate of Amber's flesh and Wesley Sterling moved aside, allowing her to take it to the booth opposite. Two boys sat waiting. Amber knew them. She knew their names. Brandon. Brandon and Dan.

Her demon-self dropped the plate on the floor.

"You stupid fat pig," said Brandon.

Dan howled with laughter.

"You clumsy, ugly little troll," Brandon continued. "You did that on purpose."

Amber's demon-self looked back at her, and smiled.

302

"Oink, oink, little piggy," said Brandon.

Amber's demon-self took Brandon's head off with one swipe of her claws. Dan kept laughing until she pulled his throat out. Blood gushed like a fountain and Amber turned her head away so suddenly that she tore free of the hands holding her. She tumbled from the table, landed on a sidewalk, and it was dark, it was night, and she was alone apart from Wesley Sterling, standing over there with his speargun.

She heard a voice – Kelly's voice – raised in alarm. Amber got up. She didn't know this street. Didn't know the buildings. Didn't know this alley she was now running into, tripping on unseen things in the shadows. Kelly was ahead of her, but blocking her way out was Amber's demon-self.

"There's a toll to get by," said her demon-self. "One kiss. Just one little kiss."

Kelly shook her head. "Let me go."

"I'm paying you a compliment!" Amber's demon-self roared. "Can't you take a compliment? Stop playing the victim!"

She slammed Kelly against the wall and pinned her there. "I know you want me," she whispered. "Not her. Never her." The whisper was loud in Amber's ears, as Wesley Sterling walked up behind her. "I can see it on your face." Amber's demon-self glanced towards Amber. "Look at her. She's nothing. You want me. You've always wanted me. She's weak and pathetic and fat and ugly. Admit it. Admit it. You want me."

"I want you," Kelly said softly.

They kissed, and Amber's demon-self plunged her hand into Kelly's chest and pulled out her heart and Kelly kept kissing her. "You can have this," Amber's demon-self said, tossing the heart to Amber. "I'll have the rest."

Tears came to Amber's eyes, but thankfully Wesley Sterling stepped into her line of vision and blocked out the kiss.

"I like your dreams," he said.

The tears were turning the world into a blurry mix of light and dark.

"Most people have surprisingly dull dreams," said Sterling. "I like yours. I'd have liked to play in them, if only we had more time."

"Wake up!" Kelly shouted from somewhere behind him.

"But as good as they are," Sterling continued, "they're just the appetiser. The Ghost of the Highway... now he has some nightmares worth devouring." Sterling's blurred outline moved a little as he pointed the speargun into her face.

Amber's demon-self walked up beside them, in shocking clarity amid all the blurred details of the alley. "A speargun is a shit weapon," she said, and stepped into Amber and Amber gasped, like she was reabsorbing every violent thought she'd ever had, and the fuzziness vanished and she blinked. She wasn't in the alley anymore. She was in Jesper's office, with the floor-to-ceiling bookcases and the big windows and the desk that was probably once owned by a president. She was still in demon form, and Jesper was there, and Milo stood beside her with his head down and his eyes closed, and right in front of her with his finger tightening on the trigger of his speargun was the Nightmare Man.

Amber jerked her head to the side as she batted the speargun away. The gun hissed with compressed gas and the spear shot past her ear and thudded into the bookshelf behind. Beneath his plastic mask, Sterling looked surprised, and angry, but before he had a chance to recast whatever spell he'd put on her, she shoved him. He lost the speargun when he hit the ground and went sprawling. Jesper staggered back against his desk, actual fear on his face now, but Amber ignored him as Sterling scrambled to his feet. His features contorting with hatred, he slid a spear from his jacket, then dived for his fallen weapon. When he was in mid-air, Milo drew his gun and fired three times.

Sterling collapsed mere inches away from his weapon. Blood leaked from the bullet holes in his chest.

Amber raised her eyes to Jesper. He wasn't looking so confident now.

"We don't have to be enemies," the old man said.

Milo grunted, grabbed Jesper's arm, and dragged him after Amber as she headed for the door they'd come through. She shook away the last remnants of the dream and took the brass key from her pocket. Ignoring Jesper's attempts at bargaining, she did her best to visualise the mirrored door back at the carnival, but images of her parents eating her flesh kept sneaking back into her thoughts.

"I remember him now," said Milo.

She looked at him. "What?"

"I'll pay you," said Jesper. "Ten million. Ten million *each*."

"Shut up," said Milo, and turned back to Amber. "The Nightmare Man. I remember him. Or the stories, at least. Only two other people are known to have managed to break out of that... whatever that was. Trance, or whatever. Only two. And now you."

"I didn't much like the dream he had me in."

"Didn't like mine, either," said Milo, "but I was trapped in it. Not like you."

Amber shrugged. "I got lucky."

"Stop selling yourself short, kid," Milo said. "Own your awesomeness."

She grinned. "Awesomeness?"

"And you can shut up now, too, and concentrate on getting us the hell out of here."

Still grinning, she focused once more on the door in her mind. The memory of the other door, the dull metal door to the cell, nagged and niggled at the edges of her consciousness, but she kept it there, on the outskirts, where it couldn't interfere. She turned the key, and turned it again, and they stepped through and out, into the carnival site.

"What are you going to do?" Jesper asked as they shepherded him back towards the gap in the chain-link fence. He was breathing fast, his breath crystallising in small puffs of vapour. "Are you going to hand me over to the Hounds? I know you think I deserve it, and I probably do, especially after what I tried to do to you, but think about this, I want you to think about it..." He got in front of them and turned, hands out, trying to smile. "We join forces. Eh? We join forces and together we keep Astaroth out."

"Not interested," said Milo, taking Jesper's arm again and spinning him round.

Amber walked ahead, and reached the Charger first. She took the handcuffs from the glove compartment, putting the brass key in their place, and shut it. She got back out as Jesper stumbled against the car.

"You can stay," Jesper said, "for as long as you want. You'll be one of us. Part of the town. You'll be safe."

"Desolation Hill is the last place I'd ever want to stay," Amber told him, tossing Milo the cuffs. "The people here are no better than the killers Astaroth sent after us."

"No," said Jesper. "You're wrong. They're good folk."

"And what about the child sacrifices?"

"Necessary," Jesper said. "An acceptable necessity."

Amber shook her head. "There's something wrong with you. There's something wrong with everyone here. You're keeping a Demon trapped in a cell and you think you've got all the power? He's been infecting this whole town from the moment you trapped him."

Milo opened the trunk and motioned to Jesper. "In."

"Please," Jesper said, "whatever you want, I'll give you."

"We don't need your help," Amber said.

"I don't understand this!" Jesper cried. "What are you trying to do? If the Narrow Man doesn't bring a sacrifice to Naberius, the barrier will fall and the Hounds will get you!"

"Naberius will get his sacrifice," Milo said.

Jesper paled. "Me? You're going to give him me? You can't. You can't!"

He twisted from Milo's grip and started running.

"Oh, for God's sake," Milo muttered.

Amber ran after Jesper, catching up with him easily. A hand on his shoulder brought him to a panting, gasping stop.

"You can't do this," he said. "It won't even work! I've already traded my soul to Astaroth!"

"Astaroth and his brother can argue about that later," said Milo, walking up.

Jesper fell to his knees. Probably the first time those pants had ever come into contact with anything resembling dirt. "Please! I've hidden from him for all this time – he will torture me for eternity!"

"You kinda deserve it, though," said Amber.

"But how will that help you? How will any of this help you?

He'll still be after you when the barrier comes down. He'll still be after you once I'm dead."

"You won't have to worry about any of that," Milo said.

"I can help!"

"You're a child-killer," said Amber. "We don't want your help."

She hauled him up off the ground and they turned back towards the Charger. There was somebody leaning through the passenger window.

"Hey!" Amber shouted.

The boy with the birthmark, the one they'd seen with his friends on the carousel, jerked up out of the car, something in his hand. Phil Daggett's gun, still with its silencer attached. He bolted, disappearing through the gap in the fence.

Milo tore after him, leaving Amber alone with Jesper.

"You and me," Jesper whispered, "we can make a deal, can't we?"

"Shut the hell up," Amber said, dragging him to the trunk and throwing him in.

"Please!" he shouted as she slammed it shut.

"I'd keep quiet if I were you," she warned. "Last person we threw in there, the car started to eat him. You don't want to draw attention to yourself, you really don't."

Jesper quieted.

A few minutes later, she saw Milo walking back. His hands were empty and he looked pissed.

Well, this day was just getting better and better.

39

IT HAD JUST PASSED 9pm, and they took a road that skimmed the town boundary for a short way. At Amber's request, Milo stopped, and they got out. A minute later, they heard a motorcycle. The Hound drew up before them. Calmly, he dismounted, and took the few steps to the barrier. He pressed his hand against empty space and pushed, and empty space resisted.

But not without showing signs of weakness. That hand, that hairy-knuckled hand with the oil stains deep in the grooves of the palm, pressed upon the invisible barrier and for a moment Amber thought it would yield, break, and the Hound would be on her before she even knew what was happening.

But the barrier stayed intact. Barely.

"Won't be long now," said Milo.

Amber bared her fangs at the Hound, who didn't change his expression, and followed Milo back to the Charger. They got in. Jesper was quiet in the trunk.

They pulled back on to the road and drove on, leaving the boundary behind them. No other cars on the road. Everyone in town was preparing for Hell Night.

They left the road they were on, joined another, turned off that on to the narrowest road so far and took it until there were trees on either side and they were headed uphill. The narrow road met another narrow road, became a slightly bigger road, and continued on past a large concrete building set back a little, surrounded on three sides by trees. It was wide but low, squat and ugly and functional. There were three small sheds on the opposite side of the road, each with rusted padlocks hanging from rusted loops.

Milo swung round, parked outside the bunker. The heavy door was open, the lights on inside. Kelly came out and Amber watched her approach in the side mirror. She hesitated, then reverted. Milo said nothing as she got out.

"Hey," said Kelly.

"Hey," said Amber, not quite meeting her eye. "You got the code, then."

Kelly nodded. "How did you do?"

Milo got out and the trunk sprang open, and Jesper raised his head and blinked.

"Cool," said Kelly. "Any word from Virgil and Javier?"

"We were hoping you'd spoken to them."

"Linda tried calling, but got no response," said Kelly. "That doesn't mean anything. I saw Virgil try to answer a call earlier. He doesn't have a clue what he's doing."

Milo hauled Jesper out of the trunk. "Who's the Narrow Man going after now?"

"I don't know," said Jesper. "I swear! He didn't tell me! He just said he'd take care of it."

Milo glanced at Amber. "We'll give them another few minutes. It isn't even ten yet. If they're still not here by then, we'll go looking."

"I can help," said Jesper. "If you let me, I can speak with the Narrow Man."

"You're going to want to shut up now," said Milo.

"Can I talk to you?" Kelly asked, lightly touching Amber's arm. They walked over to the sheds. "Now's probably not the best time for this, I get that, but I just wanted to apologise for how I acted earlier."

Amber shook her head. "I'm the one who should be saying sorry. I panicked, I think. I didn't know what to do or how to act or—"

"No, Amber, seriously, I should have been more understanding. You probably didn't even mean to change. I'm the one who overreacted."

"Well, like, you couldn't have known, could you?"

"I'm really sorry," said Kelly. "Forgive me?"

Amber hesitated. "Ah, balls."

"What?"

"It wasn't an accident. I did mean to change."

Kelly smiled. "Were you trying to lie to me just there?"

"Slightly. You kissed me and I panicked, and I'm sorry. That's never happened to me before."

"What part?"

"You know, the... the whole..."

Kelly raised her eyebrows. "Was that your first kiss?"

"No," Amber said, laughing. "Of course not. Well, sort of. I kissed a boy in my class when I was nine."

"Who is he? I'll kill him."

They laughed, and Kelly raised Amber's chin to look into her eyes. "That was your first kiss," she said.

"Pretty much," Amber said. "I didn't want to disappoint you or do something wrong... I didn't know what I was doing, as you could probably tell."

"I couldn't tell anything of the kind," said Kelly. "That was a good kiss. It was a wonderful kiss. It made my insides all fluttery."

"Mine, too."

"But we could probably do better with a little practice."

"We should practise more."

"We should practise a lot more."

It was a moment, a cute moment, and Amber wondered if she should make a move, lean in and kiss Kelly, maybe, but she wasn't sure if there was a sign she should give first, something to warn Kelly what was about to happen. On TV, whenever Balthazar and Tempest kissed, it happened so flawlessly, so smoothly, that it made Amber think there might be some system in place for these things to happen, and now she was overthinking it, goddammit, and the moment was passing and she jerked her head forward and then back again, gave an awkward laugh and nearly fell over.

"You are so odd," said Kelly, apparently amused by the whole thing.

"You're going to kill me!" Jesper shrieked.

Kelly turned and Amber scowled and did the same, as Jesper staggered away from Milo, into the middle of the road. Ronnie and Linda came out of the bunker, followed by Austin and the dog.

"All of you!" said Jesper. "It might be him handing me over to Naberius, but you're all responsible. Are you okay with that? Are you? It's murder. You're going to murder me."

"Just like you were going to murder this boy," said Ronnie.

"That doesn't excuse it!" Jesper roared. "That doesn't justify it! That won't wipe the black stain from your souls! Believe me, I know!"

"You want to be gagged?" Milo asked.

Jesper ignored him. "Look at you. You're proud of yourselves, aren't you? You saved the boy. You're heroes. Only you're not. Because, in order to win, you'll have to murder me in cold blood."

"You kinda deserve it," said Kelly, leading Amber over by the hand.

Jesper whipped his head round to her. "That is not for you to judge."

"I'm not the one responsible for the deaths of, what, two hundred kids?" Kelly said, still holding Amber's hand. "I think I'm in a pretty good position to judge you."

"If you kill me, you'll be giving the Shining Demon what he wants."

"So?"

Tears filled Jesper's eyes. "Please. Please, when I die I'm going to hell. Please don't send me there now."

"You should've thought about that before you made your deal with the Devil," said Ronnie.

"I was young and naïve and greedy. I've regretted it ever since. I dedicated my life to making the people of this town as happy as I could. I've done good things."

"And along the way you've been responsible for two hundred kids being killed."

Ronnie's phone rang.

"I'm sorry," Jesper sobbed. "I'm so sorry."

"Shush," Ronnie said, putting the phone on speaker. "Warrick. What's the situation? How's the barrier?"

"The eagle has landed," Warrick said on the other end. "Repeat, the eagle has landed."

Linda frowned. "Has the barrier dropped or not?"

"What'd I just say?" Warrick answered. "'The eagle has landed' is code for 'the barrier has dropped'. I'm watching the Hounds roll in right now. That's the good news. Even better news is that they're not headed this way, so it looks like Milo was right about their radar being screwed up in here. Three of them are going straight into town. The other two are splitting up."

Ronnie nodded. "Good job, Warrick."

"I can see a lot of people standing in little groups, looking pretty excited. Won't be long now before they're running around killing each other like the murderous psycho demons they're dying to be. Don't tell Amber or Milo I said that."

"You're on speaker," said Ronnie.

There was a hesitation. "Did they hear?"

"They're standing right beside me."

"Dude..."

"Sorry."

"Why didn't you tell me?"

"I didn't know you were going to say that."

"Do they look mad?"

"They look fine."

"They don't look like they're going to kill me?"

"No, they really don't. Not at all."

"Okay, good," said Warrick. "I won't mention it when I see them. If I mention it, I'll only draw attention to it, and then it'll be this whole big deal and they'll feel embarrassed and I'll feel embarrassed and it'll turn into this huge awkward thing where no one will know what to say and we'll all be super-nice and super-polite to each other and... Am I still on speaker?"

"Yes."

"Oh, come on! Dude! A little warning, you know?"

"Get back here, Warrick, before you're seen. And before you say anything else stupid."

"Yeah," Warrick said, and sighed. "I'm really sorry, Amber and Milo. I didn't mean anything bad. Please don't hate me."

"We don't hate you," said Amber.

"When I said psycho demons, I didn't mean you. You're nice demons."

"We know. It's fine."

"Thanks for being cool, Amber. Milo, I notice that you didn't say anything just there, which might mean that you're mad, or it might mean you're just being your usual quiet self. I hope you're not mad, man. I'll see you in a minute. We can hug it out." He hung up.

Ronnie pocketed the phone, and turned to Amber and Milo. "Looks like Hell Night can begin."

"Yes, it does," Amber said quietly.

"I'm not hugging him," said Milo.

"So that's it?" Jesper asked. "One phone call and now you can bring me to Naberius? That's the signal? You're killing me! Don't you understand? You're killing me!"

"I said the same thing to you when we first met," said Amber.

"Is that what this is?" Jesper asked, eyes narrowed. "Payback for how I treated you? Is this some kind of petty revenge? Then maybe you'd want to beat me, before you hand me over? Well? Want to beat the old man, to make him regret ever messing with you? Hmm? Maybe crack some ribs, break my nose, blacken my eyes. Eh? Would that make you feel better? Would that make you feel like heroes?"

"Why does everyone keep calling us heroes?" Milo muttered.

"Then beat me!" Jesper roared. "Cripple me! Kick my head in! Kill me! If I'm going to die, then at least have the fortitude to do it yourselves!"

"Like you were going to?" Austin asked quietly.

Amber enjoyed seeing the look on Jesper's face, caught between anger and guilt and shame. It was a beautiful sight.

"We don't know how long the Hounds' radar will take to right itself," said Milo, eyes on the sky as the sun dipped to the horizon, "so we better do this now. Amber, you should probably get the key."

Amber nodded. It was her idea, after all. Her plan. It had sounded so easy when she'd first uttered the words. So simple. Kill Jesper. He deserved it. He more than deserved it. And yet here they were, about to deliver an evil old man to his death, and she couldn't even look him in the eye. She took a breath, a deep one, and Kelly squeezed her hand before letting go. Amber slipped into the Charger, opened the glove box, and reached in for the key.

A cold feeling blossomed in her chest and spread quickly outwards. It drained the blood from her face.

She hunched down, dug both hands in, pulling out maps and booklets and spare ammunition for Milo's gun.

"The key's gone," she said. No one heard. She got out of the car. "The key's gone," she said again.

They looked at her. Milo frowned. "What?"

She stepped away while he searched. No one spoke.

Milo stood. His hands were empty. "That kid," he said. "The kid with the birthmark who stole the gun."

"He took the key," Amber said.

Jesper barked a laugh. "Mice and men!" he said. "Mice and men and murderous demons!"

"Shut the hell up," said Ronnie.

Jesper ignored him. He was practically dancing. "What are you going to do now? Eh? You've let the Hounds in, but without Hell Night there's no one to take them on. They're going to find you. They're going to kill you!"

"Astaroth probably instructed them to kill you, *too*, dumbass," said Linda.

"You were going to hand me over to be killed, anyway," Jesper shot back. "Killing me to save yourselves, and now there's no point in even doing that. What's the plan now? Are you going to start running again? You'd better. The Hounds are coming for you."

The van came up the hill. Two demonstrated his happiness by running in small circles excitedly.

"The Narrow Man's key," said Amber. "We'll use that."

Jesper sneered. "You'll never get it."

"He can be hurt," said Amber. "Did you know that? I bet you didn't even know that. When he's Oscar Moreno, he can be hurt. I hurt him. I did it once and I can do it again."

"Then you'd better do it fast," said Jesper.

The van parked behind her, and the door opened and she knew something was wrong when Two started barking. Then there were was an arm around her throat and she was yanked backwards as Grant jammed a gun into her jaw.

40

AMBER SHIFTED, BUT GRANT just increased his hold on her. Kirsty shoved Linda, who went flying into Milo, and yanked Kelly towards her. Her parents were there, too, leaping from the van. Ronnie lunged at Betty, but she hit him, a strike that sent him spinning, and pounced on Austin as he tried to run. Two came hurtling at Bill, but he kicked him away, and the dog yelped and rolled in the dirt.

Milo had his gun out now, and held it in a two-handed grip, but he was outnumbered. Four guns against one.

"I'll rip your head off if you try anything," Grant said in Amber's ear.

"Drop it, Mr Sebastian," said Bill. "You shoot any one of us, and the other three will kill your friends. And my daughter, of course."

"Let them go," Milo said, not lowering the weapon.

"We plan to," said Bill. "As soon as we get what we came for."

"Hey, man," Warrick said, coming round from the driver's side with his hands open, "what the hell is going on? What the hell, man? I gave you a lift. What the hell are you doing?"

"They're Amber's parents," Ronnie said, teeth gritted.

Kirsty sneered at Warrick, revealing her fangs. "You are some kind of stupid, you know that?"

Warrick stared at her, then at the others, trying to comprehend the damage he'd done. "Shit," he said.

"Don't blame the idiot," said Bill. "We can be very convincing when we want to. He just gave a ride to some folk from out of town who've been caught up in all this madness... He was rescuing us, weren't you, Warrick?"

"You don't talk to me," Warrick said, hunkering down and wrapping his arms around Two protectively.

Bill laughed, then looked back at Milo and the others. "Give us the key. That's all we want. We don't even want Amber anymore. You're nothing to us now, sweetheart. Just hand over the key and we'll let you get back to whatever it is you're doing."

"We don't have it anymore," Amber said.

"I feel I have to warn you," said Kirsty, twisting Kelly's arm so much that Kelly cried out, "our patience is not to be tested here."

Betty smiled. "Things are, as you can probably tell, somewhat fraught between us right now. And the Hounds have breached that handy invisible wall that had been keeping them out, did you know that? You did? Oh, that's interesting. Have we... have we stumbled into the middle of some kind of plan? Bill, darling, I fear we may have inadvertently become a monkey wrench in the works."

"That is regrettable," said Bill.

"Very," said Betty. "But taking all that into account, I'm sure you can understand when we ask if we could just skip the part where you deny you have the key, and get right to where you give it to us. If we could do that, that would be peachy. Otherwise, we're going to start killing your friends. You seem to have a lot of them, for once."

"If you hurt anyone, you get nothing."

"We'll start with the ones you'd hardly miss," said Bill. "This old-timer only has a few years left in him, anyway."

"I'm not with them," Jesper said quickly. "I can help you, I can—"

Bill shot Jesper between the eyes.

Linda cried out and Ronnie cursed and Jesper's corpse toppled over backwards and hit the ground.

And Amber, staring at the body as the blood leaked out on to the dirt, felt a curious sense of regret, that she hadn't been the one to kill him.

Bill pointed the gun into Ronnie's face. "This one now? You don't seem too upset about that guy. Would I get more of a reaction if I were to shoot this one?"

"Or maybe we're taking the wrong approach," Betty said. "Maybe we should start with the youngest." She pressed her gun against Austin's head. "Now," she said happily, "will you please give us the key?"

"We don't have it," said Ronnie. "It was stolen."

Amber nodded. "Stolen from the car, Betty, I swear to Christ."

"We're not lying to you," Linda said.

"So who has it now?" asked Kirsty.

"We don't know," Amber said. "Just some kid. He didn't know what he was stealing, he just stole it."

Betty shook her head. "That's unfortunate. It really is." She held Austin at arm's length and her finger started to tighten on the trigger.

"I know!" Austin said. "I know who it is!"

Betty raised an eyebrow. "You do?"

"Yes! The kid with the birthmark! I know his name! I know where he lives!"

Betty lowered the gun, and hunkered down, smiling at him. "And can you take us there, young man?"

Austin nodded.

"What's your name?"

"Austin."

"Hello, Austin. I'm Betty. That's my husband Bill, and these are our friends. Would you like to help us get this key? If you do, I promise I won't kill you. Cross my heart."

Austin nodded again.

"How about that?" said Bill. "We have a peaceful resolution for once, if you discount the dead old man. We're going to take Austin here, and we're going to take the van, and we're going to retrieve this wonderful key we've been hearing so much about. And none of you are going to follow us, because if we've timed it correctly and the police in this town are even half as efficient as we've heard..."

The sound of cars, approaching fast. Headlights.

"Someone must have tipped them off," said Betty, smiling. "We'll take our leave of you now."

They all started moving backwards towards the van. Grant adjusted his hold on Amber, using her as a shield in case Milo started shooting, but there was space between them now, space to move. His overconfidence had left him open. Vulnerable. If Amber didn't make a move now, all would be lost, so she turned her fingers to claws and she swiped.

He didn't see her arm move, his black scales had no time

to form, and she ripped his throat out as easily as slapping him.

He let go of her and let go of his gun and stumbled, hands at his throat, his eyes wide and his blood pumping. Kirsty screamed and Amber threw Grant's gun to Milo, who caught it in his left hand as he fired his own gun with his right.

Betty pulled Austin into the van and Bill jumped in behind the wheel and suddenly there were cruisers speeding towards them and the air was filled with screaming and gunshots and sirens, and the cruisers skidded and the van lurched, wheels spinning, and Austin was crying for help, but the world was a jumble and Amber tripped over Grant's leg, almost fell.

She caught glimpses. Saw Milo exchange fire with Novak and his officers. Saw Betty, leaning out of the van, firing at the cops as the van fishtailed. Saw Kelly leap into the Charger. Warrick scooped up Two and ran for the trees. Officer Ortmann dived at Ronnie and Ronnie hit him and Ortmann went down, got back up again as a grinning demon. She saw Linda grab Ronnie's arm and they ran for the trees as well. Saw Milo dive into the dirt behind the Charger. Saw Kirsty coming straight for her.

Amber jerked back. Kirsty's claws missed, but she kept coming. She took Amber off her feet, screaming into her face the whole time. Amber twisted, threw her off, scrambled up as Novak started firing at her. She ran. Warrick and the others had gone into the trees heading down, towards town. She ran into the trees headed up, into the hills. Bullets struck branches close to her ear. She glanced back, saw Milo behind the wheel of the Charger as it sped away, saw the cops jump in their cruisers to give chase.

And she saw Kirsty, coming up the hill after her.

Amber ran on, reaching out for trees to grab on to, to pull herself up. She was almost at the top of the hill when Kirsty's claws swiped at the back of her right leg, slicing into the unprotected meat, and she cried out, fell, turned over as Kirsty descended on her. She managed to bring her good leg in between them, managed to settle her foot right between Kirsty's breasts while she grabbed Kirsty's wrists.

Kirsty's face was a mask of hatred. "I'll kill you, you bitch, I'll rip your—"

Amber straightened her leg with a snap, and she had time to register Kirsty's shocked expression before she was launched backwards. Kirsty fell for what seemed an eternity, the hillside dipping beneath her, refusing to halt her plummet. Finally, it was a tree that put an end to her free fall. She struck it and flipped round it, hit the ground and went tumbling down out of sight.

Amber tore her jacket off, twisted it, and tied it tight around her leg. She got up, grabbed a tree, and kept climbing.

She reached a road, a familiar road, and now she could move faster. She ran as fast as her injured leg would allow her, reached the bend, and then plunged into the trees once more, started climbing again.

"You bitch!"

Amber spun round, ducked low, hid behind a tree. She could see Kirsty on the road where Amber herself had emerged.

"I'll find you!" Kirsty screeched. "I'll find you and I'll kill you, you bitch! I'll rip your throat out! I'll destroy you!"

Kirsty screamed, then, a howl of pure anguish, and she dropped to her knees, holding her head and wailing. If Amber reverted right at that moment, she knew she'd actually feel sorry for her. Her childhood memories of the woman were good, for the most part. She had always seemed so glamorous, so happy. And Grant, the man whose blood was still on Amber's right hand, had almost been an uncle to her when she was growing up. He had been the only one, out of all of them, with whom she could share a joke. And she'd killed him, she'd torn out his throat the moment he'd given her an opening.

If Amber reverted, all of this would stab at her heart.

Amber didn't revert.

Kirsty got to her feet. She was unsteady, and wiping madly at the tears in her eyes. She turned then, walked back the way she'd come, and disappeared into the trees.

Amber searched her pockets for her phone, but couldn't find it. It was down there somewhere, lost in the trees and the darkness. Typical. She started climbing again. She took it slow. The pain in her leg was lessening. By the time she reached the top of the incline, she wasn't even limping anymore. She untied her jacket, wiped some of the blood off, and put it on. It was cold up here. She remembered the heat of Florida, the ever-present closeness of it, and she smiled. She liked the cold.

She reached the edge of Benjamin's property and paused a moment to gather herself. She gritted her teeth and waited for the pain to come, and then she reverted.

Sure enough, a truckload of pain slammed into her and Amber moaned. It wasn't just the fresh wound on her leg, either. It was her shoulder, too, and her ribs, and a dozen other bumps and bruises her demon-self had failed to register. She was limping again, too, as she walked up to Benjamin's door.

41

KELLY LEANED OUT OF the window, Grant's gun held in a two-handed grip. She didn't bother trying to shoot out the tyres of the cruisers giving chase down this narrow, winding road. Smaller targets were harder to hit – and she knew all too well the possibility of bullets just bouncing off that spinning rubber. Instead, she waited for her moment.

Novak was at the wheel of the car behind, of course he was, the demonic Chief of Police leading the pursuit, but his car was just a car, whereas the Charger was something else. It took the bends tighter, hugged the road closer, and when the cruiser veered a little too wide behind them Kelly pulled the trigger. She saw Novak's demonically grinning face contort as he twisted, and the cruiser hit the shoulder and left the road.

The next cruiser came up fast to their left. It slammed into them, nearly sent them into a tree, but Milo got the Charger back under control and returned the favour. Officer Ortmann juddered in his seat, but kept his nerve. Behind him, the third cruiser was giving them space. Kelly buckled her seat belt.

The road narrowed and the Charger surged ahead and they were driving single file again. Kelly didn't know where the hell they were headed and she doubted Milo did, either. The cops were firing, though, and their aim was improving.

They took the next bend and a barn loomed in front of them, dark against the twilit sky, and the back window exploded and Kelly cursed, ducked her head, felt the Charger hit something or get hit by something and she opened her eyes only for a moment in time to see the barn hurtling towards them.

They hit it and Kelly jerked hard into the seat belt and rammed her knee and hit her head and lost her gun and sank back into her seat when all the movement had stopped. Dazed, she blinked her vision clear, looked round as a cruiser screeched to a halt behind them.

"Aw man," she muttered.

Ortmann leaped out of the cruiser, ran at them from the driver's side, firing all the while, grinning that hideous demon grin. Kelly ducked, as low as she could get with Milo on top of her, shielding her from the glass. She reached for her gun, her fingertips brushing against it as Ortmann appeared at Milo's ruined window, sliding a fresh magazine into his automatic. In the stark silence that followed the gunfire, Kelly could hear only her breathing, the slide being pulled back on Ortmann's gun, and the Charger's door popping open. Milo kicked out and the door slammed into Ortmann and he staggered sideways.

Kelly reached under the seat, grabbed the gun, looked up in time to see Milo outside the car, catching Ortmann with a right hook that spun him on the spot. Milo's skin was black. Not just dark, but black, like shadow. His eyes glowed red.

Then it was all gone, and he was Milo again, and he reached in and she grabbed his arm and he pulled her out as the other cruiser came to a skidding, sliding stop.

Milo dragged her into the barn as the cops opened fire, their bullets splintering the wood. Once they were inside, Milo let go, ducked to the left while Kelly dived to the right. She kept her head down, started crawling. The barn was full of stacks of old machinery and piles of pallets. She got behind a tractor engine, stayed low.

She heard gunshots from inside the barn now – Milo was exchanging fire. She rose up, just in time to see Woodbury coming through the door after them, a shotgun raised to his shoulder. He was a big, ugly demon and Kelly charged him without thinking. Before he could swing the gun her way, she pressed it against his chest and jumped. He watched her come, his eyes widening almost in slow motion, too slow to do anything but accept the inevitable. Her headbutt shattered his nose and turned his body to putty that collapsed beneath her even as she landed. She swayed slightly, seeing stars. Woodbury wasn't unconscious, not fully, but he wasn't getting up on his own any time soon.

Kelly had just taken down a demon. All right then.

She fell to her knees, her head feeling like it was about to split open.

Milo rushed over, kicked Woodbury on to his belly, then used his own cuffs to secure the cop's hands behind his back. He shoved Woodbury's pistol into Kelly's hands, followed up with the extra ammunition, then picked up the shotgun in one hand and hauled Woodbury to his feet with the other.

"Stop firing!" Milo yelled, moving Woodbury to the door. "We've got one of yours! You make any move against us and he's the first one to catch a bullet!"

The firing stopped.

Milo pulled Woodbury back and let him fall. He collapsed, his grin still on, but his eyes closed. Kelly closed her own eyes and covered her head, waiting for the gunfire to resume and really take this headache to the next level.

Ten seconds passed. Twenty.

She crawled to a bullet hole in the wall, peeked through. The headlights of the two cruisers were on, making it difficult to see, but she could just about make out the figures of the cops. They were talking to each other, discussing their next move.

"How long do you think we have?" she whispered to Milo.

He didn't answer. He just reloaded his gun.

42

AT LEAST THEY WERE SITTING.

The ground was hard on his bony ass, but at least Virgil's back was propped up against the cellar wall. The shackles around his wrists were on long chains, too, which meant his hands could rest on his lap while he waited to be killed.

"Could be worse," he said.

"You're insane," said Javier. He was hunched over with his back to Virgil, like he was four years old and sulking.

"Comfort-wise, I mean," said Virgil. "We could be somewhere cold or damp, or we could be chained to the wall upside down."

"Why would we be chained upside down?"

"I'm just saying, we could be."

Javier swivelled his head, eyes narrowed. "Are you enjoying this?"

"What? Don't be ridiculous."

"Unbelievable... you're enjoying this. You think you're the Shroud and the evil villain has you trapped in his secret lair."

"Well, isn't that exactly what happened?"

"I hate you," said Javier, turning away again. "So much."

Virgil sighed. "I'm not delusional, you know. I don't think I'm the Shroud. But on some level... this is nice. Nostalgic."

"We're about to die," said Javier, "and I'm chained up in a basement with the lunatic who ruined my life."

Virgil blinked. "You really think I ruined your life?"

"Goat-molesters don't get the girl."

"I said I was sorry. I didn't know it'd have such a... Anyway. I'm sorry. Again. But we're not going to die, Javier. I'll get us out of this."

"You?" Javier said, almost laughed.

"I have a plan, okay? When he comes back and takes the chains off, you fake a heart attack. Then I'll grab him from behind. Amber said he's vulnerable when he's Oscar Moreno, right?"

"He'll still be strong enough to throw the two of us around the place."

"I'm not going to let him kill you, Javier. It's because of me that you're here. You should be... you should be back in the retirement home. You should be safe."

"I should be."

"I know. I'm sorry."

"At the retirement home, I'm on a schedule. Things are predictable there. I've come to crave predictability as I've gotten older. It's nice and reassuring. I eat and I sleep and I talk to people and I take my pills and I... and I wait for the inevitable..."

Virgil frowned. "Enemas?"

"Death."

"Oh."

Javier didn't turn – he just sat there with his back to Virgil.

"I think about death a lot. Especially lately. Especially since I met you again."

"Sorry about that."

"All this has made me wonder. Deals with the Devil. The Devil is real? So is God real? Do I have to start believing in God now?"

Virgil raised an eyebrow. "You don't believe in God?"

"What, just because I'm Latino I should believe in God? I should be a good Catholic? But that's another thing! Which branch of Christianity is the right one? Please don't tell me I have to be a Mormon. What are Baptists like? Or Presbyterians? And is this God the only God? What about other religions? Are they real, too? Do I have to start worshipping an elephant now?"

Virgil frowned. "Who worships elephants?"

"Don't the Hindus? Isn't their god an elephant?"

"You're thinking of Ganesha."

"Yeah, that's the one. The elephant-head one with all the arms. The point is, the goddamn point of it all is... if there is a Devil, there must be a God, and if there is a God, there must be an afterlife. Christ. I don't want to go to hell, Virgil."

"Why would you go to hell?"

"I've sinned," said Javier. "I'm a sinner."

"We're all sinners."

"Then we're all going to hell."

"You may be a sinner, but are you a good man?"

"How the hell should I know? How do you figure out something like that?"

"Do you try to do good in your everyday life?" Virgil asked.

"I... I guess... I mean, I don't try to do evil, so that counts for something, wouldn't you say?"

"I would. I think you're a good man, Javier. I think you've got nothing to worry about."

Javier still didn't turn round. Virgil didn't blame him. If there was a God, and there was an afterlife, it wouldn't be Javier descending into the fiery pits, it'd be Virgil. And, what's more, he'd deserve it, too.

"It's not your fault, you know," said Javier.

"What isn't?" Virgil asked, looking at Javier's back.

"What happened between me and Darleen Hickman. Now, it didn't help, of course it didn't help... but it wasn't your fault. She didn't love me, and I... I guess I didn't really love her, either."

"But being called a goat-molester was—"

"It was the final nail in the coffin, yeah."

"Right. Sorry."

"And... and you know I didn't *actually* molest that goat, don't you?"

"Yeah, I know," Virgil said. "It was brought on to set and it just didn't like you. It happens. I shouldn't have speculated as to the reasons."

"Do goats need reasons to dislike anyone?"

"Probably not – though I should say I haven't known a lot of goats."

"I have," Javier said wistfully, and he looked round and they both burst out laughing.

"I guess I owe you an apology," said Javier.

"Me?" said Virgil, wiping his eyes. "Why, for God's sake?"

"Cos I hated you," said Javier. "I blamed you for things not working out with Darleen, and none of that was your fault. I was bitter, I suppose. I saw you with beautiful women hanging

off your every word and there was I, standing in the background...
Never got married. Never had kids."

"Yeah," said Virgil, "because I did such a great job with all
that."

Javier hesitated. "I was... I was real sorry to hear about your
wife."

Virgil nodded. "She was a good woman."

"Yes, she was."

"And a good person. Much better than me. Those beautiful
women who hung off my every word... they were where it all
went wrong. I had a loving wife and a kid on the way and for
so long, for *so long* I resisted temptation. I felt so good about
that. So righteous. It didn't last. That strength didn't last."

"What did Oscar Wilde say? *I can resist everything except temptation.*"

"A smart man, that Mr Wilde."

"He was known for it," said Javier. "So you floundered. You
made a mistake. You're only human."

Virgil laughed again, this time without humour. "That's what
I said. That's how I justified it to myself. I'm only human. As
if being human meant being weak, or unfaithful, or cruel. She
wasn't like that. She never hurt me like that. I wasn't only
human, Javier, I was only me."

"But she took you back."

Virgil shifted a little on the floor. "She was a fool to. I made
her a truckload of promises I couldn't keep. By then my star
was fading, of course, and I didn't have all those beautiful young
women hanging off my every word anymore... So when it
happened again, years later, when there was a beautiful young
woman who was enraptured with me, I was... flattered. And
stupid. And weak."

"That's why your daughter doesn't want to see you?"

"I wasn't a good husband. I thought I was a good father, but obviously not. After her mother died, Tabitha got married, moved out to Alaska of all places... and eventually I followed. Been here ten years. Every day I'm ready to jump in that ridiculous car of mine and drive the forty miles to her house, to fall to my knees and beg her forgiveness and tell her how much I love her despite all my weakness and all my cruelty, and to tell her hey, look at my ridiculous car, big enough to take you and my grandkids away on a picnic or a... or a whatever. And all I need is the invitation."

They went quiet.

Javier turned away again. "You're an asshole," he said.

"Yeah."

"No reason in the world why that daughter of yours should forgive you. No reason why she should answer any of your calls."

"None at all."

"But I hope she does."

Virgil nodded, used his sleeve to wipe his eyes.

"Knew it," Javier muttered.

"You knew what?"

"I knew I still had it," Javier said, and got to his feet slowly. When he was standing, the shackles fell from his wrists.

Virgil stared. "How did you do that?"

"Did you forget?" Javier asked, then spread his arms wide, and bowed with an extravagant flourish. "Javier Santorum, Circus Magician and Escape Artist."

"You picked the lock?"

Javier grinned, holding up a thin pair of nose-hair tweezers.

"You beautiful man," said Virgil.

Javier chuckled, came over, and started working on Virgil's shackles. "Let's get these off," he said, "then open those doors and get to that bunker. I've had quite enough of my life being in danger for one day, thank you very much."

43

IT WAS SNOWING.

It was May, and it was snowing.

Amber limped to the window and looked out as the first flurries covered Benjamin's pickup truck in a dusting of white. "I can't stay here," she said.

"You're not going out there," Benjamin said from the table. The kitchen was warm. "What good can you do? You said it yourself, there's a woman looking to kill you and she's in those woods."

"I don't know that," Amber said. "She could be anywhere."

"She could be right outside," Benjamin said, getting up. "And what about those men from before? The bikers? You said they're in town now?"

Amber nodded. "It was part of the plan, but... But now it's all gone wrong."

Milo was out there, in the snow and the cold and the dark, with demons and Hounds, but Milo was Milo. He could take care of himself, so long as he had the Charger. But Kelly...

"Can I ask you something?" said Benjamin, and Amber turned. He cleared his throat. "Did you... are you responsible for nothing happening tonight?"

She narrowed her eyes. "You mean for you not turning into a demon? Yeah, we are."

"Oh."

"Do me a favour, Benjamin, okay? Try not to look so disappointed that you're not out there murdering your neighbours."

"What? I – I'm not, I don't know what—"

"I can see it on your face, for God's sake."

Benjamin looked away.

Amber pulled a chair towards her and sat. Her leg was bleeding badly. Her body ached. "All this started for me a few weeks ago," she said. "That's all. Weeks. I went from being an ordinary girl to being a demon with fangs and claws and horns..."

"I just want that for a night," Benjamin said quietly.

"You don't get it. It's been with me every moment since then. It's been a part of me. I've had time to get used to it. To acclimatise. But you? You don't get that chance, do you? None of you do. You get a blast of this and you go insane for a few hours. But you *want* to go insane, don't you? You're sitting up here, looking forward to it. You're waiting to go nuts."

"Amber, please..."

"It has to stop. It just has to."

"What... what are you going to do? What can you do? Your parents might even have that key by now."

"The Narrow Man has another one just like it," she said. "I'll... I'll pay him a visit, take the key, and get to Naberius before my parents do."

"And then what?"

Seconds went by. "I'll kill him," she said.

"How does that help anyone?" Benjamin asked. "Unless I misheard, your plan revolves around Hell Night actually going ahead, doesn't it? Then the folks down there will take care of the bikers."

"There is something else I could try."

"What? For heaven's sake, you're running out of time."

"I could eat him," she said.

Benjamin paled. "What?"

"We eat, we absorb power," Amber said. "That's our whole thing. Naberius is in chains. By now he's probably powerless... But I might get enough from him to be able to take on the Hounds myself."

"You can't... you can't be serious."

"It might be the only way."

"Amber... that's crazy."

She smiled, and forced herself to stand. "Welcome to my life. I'm going to need to borrow your truck."

"The keys are on the shelf over there."

She nodded. "Thanks, Benjamin. You stay up here now, okay? You really don't want to go venturing out on to the streets. Not tonight."

She limped over to the shelf, moved aside an old flashlight and a book. "The keys aren't here," she said, and turned just as Benjamin levelled his rifle at her from across the room.

"I'm sorry," Benjamin said, tears in his eyes.

The kitchen was warm, but Amber was ice-cold. "What are you doing?"

"You seem like such a nice girl," said Benjamin, "and I am really sorry about this, but I can't let you take away Hell Night."

"But that's what you want," said Amber. "You don't like what you turn into. You said it yourself, the things you do—"

"Are awful," Benjamin said, nodding. "They are. They're

terrible. But I need them. You won't understand, you couldn't possibly understand, but when I become that... that thing, I am freed of this old man's body. My joints don't ache... my bones don't creak... I stop being old. For one night a year, I feel young and strong and alive and... and I'm sorry, but I need that."

"Put the gun down," Amber said, limping forward.

"Not another step," said Benjamin. "Don't make me shoot you, Amber."

Amber kept moving slowly. "You're not going to hurt me," she said. "You're a good guy. I know you are."

Benjamin raised the rifle to his shoulder. "Please, stop."

She stopped. Her voice wavered. "You're not going to pull that trigger."

"I don't want to kill you," said Benjamin. "But I need you to stay put, and stay as you are."

"Why?" she asked. "What good will that do?"

Tears rolled down Benjamin's cheeks. "You have to be stopped," he said, "but I can't do it. I couldn't live with myself if I had your death on my conscience. So we're going to wait."

Amber frowned. "For what?"

"Hell Night."

"Hell Night's not going to happen."

"I have faith," said Benjamin. "Chief Novak's a good man. He'll make sure it continues, now that the mayor's dead."

"So we're going to wait until you shift, and then what? Then you'll kill me?"

Benjamin shook his head. "It won't be me. It'll be him. The demon."

"It'll be you," Amber said angrily. "It'll still be you, Benjamin."

"No, you're wrong. I can't control him when he takes over."

"You'll kill me," she said. "If you change, you'll kill me."

"*He'll* kill you."

"You're the one who'll be pulling that trigger, just like *you're* the one keeping me here right now. This is murder, Benjamin. You will be murdering me."

"No. It's not like that."

"Don't do this. Let me go."

"I can't."

Every fibre of her being wanted to shift, but she stayed as she was. "Then shoot me," said Amber. "If you're going to do it, do it. I'd rather be murdered by a human being than a demon."

"I'm not a killer."

"That's exactly what you'll be, Benjamin. Why waste time? You have the gun, so do it."

"No," said Benjamin. "No, we'll just wait. We'll wait here."

"I'm not waiting," she told him, her lip curling into a snarl. "If you're going to kill me, be a man and kill me. Otherwise, I'm walking out that door."

"Don't move, Amber, please."

"I'm walking out that goddamn door."

"Please don't make me do this."

"You don't have to do anything, Benjamin. You can put down the gun and let me walk out of here. You can let me take my chances outside. This doesn't have to end with you and me. We're not enemies."

"I'm warning you..."

"You're not going to shoot me, Benjamin," Amber said, and stepped forward.

The blast filled the room and Amber felt a tug in her belly, and all at once her legs didn't work and she was on her back, gasping.

Numb fingers scrabbled at her jacket, pulling it open. Blood was already pouring from the wound above her navel, soaking through her shirt. She tried pressing her hands against it. The blood kept coming.

"Just wait here," she heard Benjamin mumble. "We'll just wait here and it'll all be over soon."

The bullet must have gone straight through because there was more blood leaking from her back. She was lying in an ever-growing pool of her own blood and now the pain was coming. It flared suddenly and Amber cried out.

"Hush," said Benjamin. "Just hush now. It'll be all right. You shouldn't have done that. I told you not to move and you moved. Why did you do that? Why did you make me shoot you?"

There were a dozen responses to that question and every one of them was blown apart by the rising tide of pain that brought stinging sweat to Amber's eyes.

"Help me," she said, her words distorted. It hurt to breathe.

Benjamin hurried over, looked down at her. "The pain won't last long," he said. "The change'll happen any minute now. Then he'll be here to put you out of your misery."

He ducked out of Amber's line of sight, and she was left alone again, with just the ceiling and her pain for company. Another few seconds and she'd no longer be able to form coherent thoughts.

She couldn't prevent it any longer. Amber shifted, the sudden transformation making her cry out once more.

"I told you!" Benjamin said loudly. "I told you not to do that!"

Either the pain dimmed to a manageable level or else she was suddenly just able to handle it better – either way she could now raise herself up on to an elbow to look at Benjamin, who had the rifle aimed and ready to fire.

"Change back!" he commanded. "I know you can change back! You're not like us! Change back right this second!"

"You shot me," she said. "I'm dying. Please, you have to help me."

"I said change back!" he roared, advancing on her.

Instinctively, her black scales rose on her skin, locking into place to form armour in the time it took Benjamin's finger to tighten on the trigger. The bullet struck her chest, just below her left shoulder, smashing through her scales and she twisted, screaming.

Benjamin was standing over her now. "That wasn't my fault! That was your own fault! I told you not to change and you changed!"

She lashed out, caught him below the knee and sent him to the blood-splattered floor. He didn't drop the rifle, though, and he was swinging it towards her when she scrambled up. She ran for the window, leaped through, shards of glass scraping her scales. She landed in the snow, the pain almost making her black out, but she was up again a few seconds later, woozy, dizzy, almost running straight into a tree.

She pushed herself away from it and her scales retracted. With her arms crossed over her body, she started down the slope. She slipped and slid, bounced off one tree to the next in the darkness, but managed to keep upright. She found a trail and took it, grateful for the level ground. She glanced back at the bloody footprints she was leaving, and her foot struck something and she stumbled to her knees. She stayed like this for a moment, fighting to get the pain under control. When she was sure she wasn't going to puke or pass out, she looked back up the slope, and saw Benjamin.

He was coming for her.

44

THEY PULLED UP OUTSIDE Cole Blancard's house, the wipers clearing the snow from the windshield, and the woman peered out.

"This is it?" she asked. "You're sure?"

Austin nodded quickly.

She looked at him, dead in the eye. "If you're lying to us, we're going to be very upset with you."

"I'm not lying," said Austin. "They said a kid with a birthmark stole the key. Cole Blancard is the only kid in town with a birthmark on his face. And he steals things. He's always stealing."

"He a friend of yours?" the man asked from the front seat.

"No, sir. He hates me."

"Why's that?"

"I don't know. He always picks on me."

"A bully," the woman said. "We've never liked bullies, have we, Bill?"

"Not unless we're doing the bullying."

The woman chuckled. "This is true. This is very true. So, Austin, how about this for a deal? We all go up there, we knock on the door, you get us inside, and then we'll kill this bully for you. What do you say?"

Austin stared at her. "I don't... I don't want him killed..."

"Why the hell not?" asked Bill. "He's making your life a misery, isn't he? The little shit deserves it."

"Language," said the woman.

Bill shrugged, and got out of the van, treating Austin to a blast of cold air.

The woman – what did she say her name was? Betty? – gave Austin another smile. "I understand. You're reluctant to agree to someone being killed. That's natural. But it's also weak. Don't take this the wrong way, Austin, I don't mean to insult you – it's just that over the years my husband and I have realised how a little killing now and then makes life easier. This boy, what's his name?"

"Cole Blancard."

"This boy Cole, he's an obstacle in your way. He's stopping you from having a happy life – or at the very least he's *one* of the obstacles. There's nothing wrong in wanting to remove an obstacle, Austin."

Bill opened the side door. "The little voice that's saying no right now, that's your conscience. A conscience is very important for a lot of things, but equally important is to know when not to listen to it. Because your own conscience can work against you."

"It really can," Betty said, sounding terribly sad about it. Austin got out of the van, and she came after. The snow was coming down heavier now. "When you think about it, your conscience is really about other people. It cares what they think and how they feel and all sorts of stuff that isn't about you."

They started walking up to Cole's house, Bill and Betty on either side of Austin.

"Betty and I don't live like that anymore," said Bill. "We learned the hard way, believe me. But then we realised how much better off we'd be if we actually concentrated the most on ourselves."

"How selfish does that sound?" Betty laughed.

Bill joined in. "It does sound selfish, I admit. And hey, it is selfish! But there's nothing wrong with being selfish, Austin. It's the American way."

They got to the door, and Betty knocked.

"Ask to speak to Cole," she said softly, smiling.

"He'll be in his panic room," said Austin. "It's past eight. We have a curfew. His parents won't let him out."

"You'll have to be persuasive, then. When you see him, ask him where he put the key. Maybe even ask him if he'd give it to you. After that, I promise, we'll remove him from your life."

Bill put a fatherly hand on Austin's shoulder, as Cole himself answered the door.

Austin blinked. He hadn't been expecting this. The curfew.

Cole's eyes went to Bill first, then Betty, and lingered there for a moment, then he glanced downwards at Austin and frowned.

Bill gave Austin's shoulder a reassuring squeeze.

"Hi, Cole," said Austin.

Cole adopted that slow-blinking expression of his. "What?" he said gruffly.

"You, uh, you have a key," said Austin. "I think you took it from a car earlier today."

"Probably entirely innocently!" said Betty, and laughed. "We're certainly not accusing you of anything, Cole. Dear Lord, no."

Bill joined in, smiling. "But we do kind of need it, I'm afraid."

"Didn't take no key," Cole said.

"You see that?" said Betty. "It's so insignificant you didn't even notice you'd taken it! I knew you didn't do it on purpose!"

"Don't know what you're talking about," Cole said. He went to shut the door, but Bill stopped it with his foot.

"Are your parents home, by any chance?" he asked. "I know you have a festival tonight, and everyone's looking forward to it, but if we could have a word with your dad, I'm sure we'll sort everything out."

"He's my stepdad," said Cole.

"Is he in? Or your mom herself, maybe?"

Cole looked at them all, thinking slow thoughts. Then his eyes settled on Austin. "I remember a key now. Didn't think anyone owned it. Austin, you wanna come get it with me?"

"He sure would!" said Bill, and lightly pushed Austin into the house.

"Come on," said Cole, and walked off. Austin hesitated, but with Bill and Betty crowding him from behind, he figured anywhere was better than staying where he was.

He didn't like the smell of Cole's house. It smelled of boiled food and musk. Cole led him into his bedroom, which smelled a whole lot worse. Socks, sweat and dirty underwear. Cole closed the door behind them. It had a poster of a naked woman in chains pinned to it.

"Thought you were abducted," Cole said. "Thought you were dead in a ditch." When Austin didn't respond, Cole went over to his nightstand. When he turned, he was holding a brass key. "This the one you're looking for?"

Austin didn't know. "Yes," he said.

Cole examined it. "What's it open?"

Austin gave a clueless shrug.

Cole peered at it some more. "You tell your parents on me?"

"No."

"You brought them to my house."

"They're not my parents."

"Who are they, then?"

"Just... just some people I know."

Cole didn't say anything to that. He held out the key. "Go on then. Take it."

It was a trap. Austin knew it was. He'd seen Cole Blancard do this a hundred times, mostly with bags and books. Sometimes lunches. Once a phone – an expensive one – and when the kid had hurried forward Cole had dropped it. It landed on the screen, cracked the whole thing. Each one of those times, Cole had worn an expression of pure contempt, just like the one he was wearing now.

Except right now something was different. Cole had a new trick up his sleeve.

Austin crossed the room, careful not to step on the clothes that littered the floor. "Thank you," he said, even before he reached for the key.

To his surprise, Cole let him take it. Then he jammed the cold muzzle of a handgun into the underside of Austin's chin and slammed him back against the wall.

Austin couldn't move. He couldn't even breathe. Only his eyelids worked. He blinked quickly, like he was trying to rid himself of the eerie blankness on Cole's face.

"Want me to shoot you?" Cole asked quietly. "Want me to kill you?"

Tears came to Austin's eyes.

Cole didn't comment on them. He didn't care about tears. He held death in his hand.

"I could blow your head off," Cole said. "Boom. Blow it off. Your skull would be all over the place. Your brains would be my new wallpaper. This gun has a silencer. No one would even hear."

"P-please..."

"Would they care, even if they did hear? Everyone thinks you're still missing. Who are the people you're with? They the ones kidnapped you? The guy's a dick, but the woman's okay-looking. I might do her after I kill you."

"Please don't."

"No one would care. My mom wouldn't care. She's freaking out because Hell Night hasn't started. She didn't even notice that I'm not in the panic room. I could kill you right now and no one would give a shit."

Cole sniffed, then stepped back. After a moment, he lifted his shirt and tucked the gun into his waistband.

Austin took a shallow breath, and licked his lips. His mouth was so dry. He started to lean away from the wall and Cole tugged the gun free and leaped on him, jammed the gun into his cheek.

"Did I say you could move? Did I give you permission?"

"Please don't kill me," Austin sobbed, his knees buckling.

"I'll do whatever the hell I want, shit-for-brains. You bring those people to my house? You told on me?"

Austin slid down the wall. "I didn't, I swear."

"I know you did, you asshole. It's obvious. Why are you lying?"

Austin was kneeling on the ground now, his face pressed

against the wall with the gun still jammed into his cheek. Beyond the bedroom door, Bill and Betty were talking with Cole's mom.

"Please don't kill me, Cole."

"I'll kill you if I wanna kill you, dipshit. I'm the one in charge. You think anyone else is in charge right now? I could kill you, go out there, shoot those people you're with. If my mom says anything, I'll tell her to mind her own goddamn business. And if my stepdad comes out I'll blow his head off, too. He's been asking for it for years. I never liked that guy. Never. And now I can deal with all you assholes. Who's gonna stop me? Huh? Who?"

"I don't know..."

"No one. No one, that's who. You think Chief Novak's gonna take me down? Not a chance. They'll have to send a SWAT team after me."

"Cole, please don't kill me. Please let me go."

"Say my name one more time and I'll pull the trigger, you little toad."

"Sorry!" Austin said, squeezing his eyes shut. "Sorry!"

Cole cracked the gun against the side of Austin's head. Austin cried out and Cole's knee caught him right on the ear and that hurt even more than the gun had.

Knuckles rapped on the door. "Cole!"

His mom's voice. High and brittle. "Cole, hurry up now!"

Cole took hold of the back of Austin's shirt and pulled him to his feet, shoving him to the door as it opened.

"You should really go," Cole's mom was saying. "The festival is due to start any minute now. I really think you should go."

"We'll be out of your hair in but a moment!" Bill laughed.

Austin and Cole stepped out into the corridor. Everyone saw the tears, but no one cared.

"Why aren't you in the panic room?" Cole's mom said to Cole, her eyes glittering way too brightly, but Cole ignored her.

"Boys," said Betty, smiling, "there you are! Cole, did you find that key?"

The gun dug into the small of his back, and Austin held up the key. "He found it," he said.

The way Betty's eyes fell on it, it was like she'd been waiting her whole life for this moment. "Oh good," she said softly.

Cole's breathing hitched, and he took the gun from Austin's back, but before he could make his move another door opened and a man came out.

Cole's mom wrung her hands. "These people were just leaving. I told them the festival is about to start. Why hasn't it started? It should have started by now."

Cole muttered something and shoved the gun back into his waistband.

"Actually, it might be delayed a little longer," Cole's stepdad said. "I'm going out to see what I can do to..." His eyes fell upon Austin, and he smiled. "Who do we have here?"

"Bill and Betty," said Bill.

"Bill and Betty," Cole's mom said, nodding quickly. "Yes. Bill and Betty, this is my husband—"

"Oscar," said Cole's stepdad, stepping forward. "Oscar Moreno. How do you do?"

45

THE BARN WAS OLD and cold. It had a hayloft without any hay, and snow drifted down through the hole in the roof.

Kelly ran her fingers across her forehead, wincing at the pain. It was already swelling. She wondered how Amber's shoulder was holding up, then wondered about Amber. She glanced at Woodbury as he lay there, unconscious, and looked up at Milo.

"Why are we here?" she asked.

Milo kept looking out. "What?"

"There's no point to this," she said. "What does this achieve?"

"What are you talking about?"

"I mean it's done. It's over. They've got no reason to..."

She got to her feet, waited until she was steady, and walked to a hole that had been blasted in the wood by the shotgun that Milo now held.

"Hey," she called through the jagged wood. "You out there. Why are we doing this? We saved the boy and we stopped Hell Night. That's what you didn't want us to do, right?"

There was no response.

"But we've done it. It's done. So what are we doing here? We're standing in the cold, freezing our butts off, shooting at each other, and for what? For nothing. So I have an idea. We all walk away from this. What do you say?"

She could hear voices now, the cops talking among themselves. Then Lucy's voice. "Kelly. That you?"

"Hey, Lucy. What's up?"

"Kelly, I'm going to need you to let Woodbury go."

"We can't do that," Kelly replied. "He's the only reason you guys aren't storming this barn right now."

"That's not true," Lucy said. "You're right. Hell Night hasn't happened. Whatever you've done, you definitely seem to have stopped it. We might be willing to walk away, like you want, but we need our colleague released to us before we can make that decision."

"Nonsense," Kelly called back cheerily. "You can decide that right now. You get in your car and drive away. We get in our car and do the same. We let Woodbury go when we have all our friends back. We drop him right at the town boundary."

"We can't negotiate like that, Kelly. It's not how we do things."

"Oh, Lucy, have you ever really tried?"

There were footsteps now. Lucy stepped into the full beams of the cruisers and walked forward with her hands up. The snow danced crazily in those lights.

"That's far enough," Milo said.

Lucy nodded, and took a few more steps before stopping. She wasn't wearing her demon face anymore. "I just want to talk," she said. "I just want to sort this out, the same as you. I don't want either of you getting hurt. I don't want Woodbury to get hurt, or Ortmann. And I certainly don't want me to get hurt. That's my number-one priority, right there. But you've got to understand my position. I can't make any kind of deal with you, no matter how informal, when you have a gun to my friend's head."

"We do understand that," said Kelly, "honest we do. But you have to understand that we can't exactly trust you."

"I've never lied to you."

"Your honesty is admirable, Lucy, but let's not forget that the Desolation Hill Police Department has been facilitating child murder since long before you were born. You've looked the other way your entire life. Everyone in that uniform has. Everyone in this town has."

"We did what needed to be done."

"That's a terrible excuse."

"I know," said Lucy. "I know it is. But you've changed all that. Naberius didn't get his sacrifice. We don't know what that means. Do you?"

"We do not."

"It might mean it's over," Lucy said. "If that's the case, you've helped this town break free. No one's going to want to thank you for that – no one except the kids. And me. Kelly, I give you my word that no harm will come to you if you release Woodbury. I don't give you my word as a police officer – I know that doesn't mean anything to you. I give you my word as a human being."

"You're a demon, Lucy."

"Only sometimes."

"I'd love to believe you. I really, really would. But I'm afraid I'm going to have to ask you to back away now. We'll release Woodbury when we see your tail lights."

Lucy shook her head, and started forward. "I can't do that, Kelly."

"Stop walking."

"Please understand my position."

"Stop walking!" Milo shouted.

Lucy stopped. "We don't have a lot of time," she said. "If the Chief arrives, he takes over. You don't want to be on the end of that. Ortmann and me, we are willing to let you walk away. Guys, please, this is our chance for everyone to get out of this in one piece."

Kelly looked at Milo.

"New proposal," he said. "You back off. We get to my car. When the car is turned around and ready to drive, we let your friend go."

"You drove your car into the side of a barn," Ortmann called.

"She's sturdy," said Milo. "She'll be fine."

There was a moment of low talking outside, then Lucy raised her voice. "We're cool with that," she said. "We're putting our guns away." One set of headlights cut off. A moment later, the second set died, and Kelly's eyes began to adjust.

Milo passed the shotgun to her and picked up Woodbury, grunting at the man's weight.

"Ready?" he whispered.

Kelly nodded.

They walked out. Lucy and Ortmann stood together, hands at their sides.

Kelly smiled at them. "This weather, eh?"

"It always snows on Hell Night," said Ortmann.

"Is that so?" said Kelly.

"Well... not always. But mostly."

Kelly laughed. "Look at us, talking about the weather. This is all very civilised."

Lucy shrugged, but her eyes stayed wary. "Goes to show what can be accomplished with a little common sense. How's our guy?"

"I headbutted him."

"You must have a hard head."

"That's what my teachers always told me."

She would have carried on, would have light-heartedly asked for some Tylenol, but at the sound of a motorcycle her heart dive-bombed in her chest.

A single Hound came roaring through the broken fence. Milo dropped Woodbury, started firing the shotgun. The cops spun, shifting into their grinning selves even as they drew their weapons, adding their firepower to Milo's.

"Forget about the bike!" Milo commanded. "Aim for the rider!"

Bullets hit the Hound, jerking his torso, but not stopping him, not making him fall.

"Back!" Lucy cried. "To the barn!"

Kelly went first, and when the last of them were through she pulled the door shut. The bike roared so close and so loud she was sure the Hound was going to burst through, but he veered at the last minute, forced off by shotgun blasts.

There was a sudden ceasefire. Kelly joined Milo at a window, just in time to see the Hound ride round the side of the barn. Everyone turned, keeping track of the noise, reloading as they did so.

"Woodbury is still out there," said Ortmann.

"The Hound's not interested in him," Kelly said, sliding in her last magazine. She racked the slide just as the bike's engine cut off.

"Spread out," Milo whispered.

While the others moved to cover as many entrances as possible, Kelly crept to the ladder, climbing it as quietly as she could. She got to the hayloft and crawled for a while before rising into a low crouch. The wood creaked beneath her weight.

The hole in the roof was more than big enough for her to pass through. It opened up on to a dark sky laden with clouds. She jumped for a broken beam, pulled herself up, and balanced on one knee while she reached for the hole.

And the Hound's face appeared right in front of her.

She cried out, fell back, fired blindly and hit nothing, and the Hound landed before her as she fell on her ass. She shot him in the shoulder, then switched targets, aiming for his leg. He wobbled, almost fell. She fired again, and again, keeping him off balance, making him totter, and then she went for the final shot, the shot that'd force him out of the hayloft, that'd send him crashing to the ground, and the gun clicked on empty.

"Aw hell," she said.

The Hound straightened up, that calm expression never leaving his face. Christ, she hated that calmness. What she wouldn't give to see some anger, or hatred, or even some goddamn annoyance flicker across those features. But no. All she got was calmness.

"Kelly!" Milo yelled, and threw his shotgun to her. She grabbed it and fired and the Hound flew backwards and was gone.

Her ears ringing, she crawled to the edge, as more gunfire erupted. The Hound was back on his feet, but being peppered by bullets. He stumbled against the wall, and then Milo was there, plunging a pitchfork through the Hound's arm, pinning it to the wood.

Lucy grabbed the second pitchfork while Ortmann took hold of the Hound's other arm. Once it was flattened against the wall, the middle prong skewered it.

Kelly climbed down the ladder as the others paused a moment to catch their breath. The Hound didn't struggle. He just stood there, arms splayed, looking at them.

"So how do we kill him?" Ortmann asked. He, like Lucy, had reverted once the immediate danger had passed.

They all looked to Milo, who looked at Kelly. "Could I borrow your phone?"

She handed it over and he paused, trying to remember a number. He punched it in, held the phone to his ear.

"Gregory," he said, "it's me." He paused. "Who else would be calling? Yeah. Anyway, you have any idea how to kill a Hound of Hell? We've got..." He paused, listening for a moment. "I'm sorry, are you going to continue this conversation on your own, or would you like me to contribute? You're the closest thing we've got to an expert, so I'm consulting you. We've got one of them. Yes. Don't worry about that, he's not going anywhere. He's... No, I... All I want is... Jesus, do you know how to kill one or not?" Milo listened. "Yeah," he said. "That seems like a good enough place to start as any. I'll let you know how it goes."

He hung up, tossed Kelly's phone back to her.

"So?" Lucy asked. "What is the expert opinion?"

"The expert opinion is that the Hound is unlikely to survive without a head."

Kelly frowned. "That's it?"

"It would seem to be."

"I could have told you that."

"Any one of us could have told you that," said Ortmann.

"But yours would not have been an informed opinion," Milo said. He walked up to the Hound. "You hear that? We're going to take your head off. How's that make you feel?"

The Hound's expression didn't change.

"Christ, you're annoying," Milo muttered. He held out his hand. "Someone give me a shotgun."

Kelly gave him hers, and walked outside. Woodbury was moaning in the dirt. A shotgun blast filled the night, and then another. And then another. Three shotgun blasts to obliterate a skull. Another hard head.

Milo and the officers walked out of the barn.

"So?" Kelly asked.

"Turns out Hounds really can't survive without their heads," Milo said.

Lucy looked at them both. "So what happens now?"

"Now you go one way and we go another," said Milo, "and if we see each other in town, we pretend we don't. Can you live with that?"

Lucy and Ortmann exchanged glances, and Lucy nodded. "Yeah," she said. "We can."

46

AUSTIN HAD NEVER MET Cole Blancard's stepdad, and now he was glad of that fact. Oscar Moreno was looking at him like they shared a secret, and totally ignoring Bill, Betty and his own wife.

"What's that you're holding?" Oscar Moreno asked. "A key, is it? What a nice key that is."

"It's ours, actually," Betty said. "We just came to retrieve it from your son."

"Stepson," said Cole.

Oscar's eyes flicked from Austin to Cole. "You had it? Really? What are the chances?"

The atmosphere in the house changed. All at once it went from staged politeness to all cards on the table.

Oscar took a step forward, but Bill put a hand to his chest, held him off.

"You know what the key is, don't you?" Bill asked.

"Of course," Oscar said, smiling. "I own its twin. I never thought I'd see it again, though, not after it was given to that dreadful man who never stopped talking. But here it is, in my very own house. It's come home."

He tried moving past Bill, but got shoved back for his efforts. The smile never left his face.

"In that case," said Betty, "we'll take yours, too. May as well have the full set, wouldn't you agree?"

Oscar shook his head. "Oh no, I'm sorry, I can't give it to you. I need it for my work."

Bill and Betty turned into demons so quickly that Austin never even saw the change. But all at once there they were, red-skinned and horned, and Cole cried out and Cole's mom stumbled backwards. She had a strange look on her face, though. It wasn't shock — it was merely surprise, like they weren't supposed to be able to do that.

And then Oscar Moreno changed. His transformation wasn't as smooth as the demons, but it was no less effective. He grew taller, his arms and legs lengthening, his body getting thinner as it stretched. His face changed, too, his hair receding to a wiry mass, his skin getting paler. His eyes sank to each side, widening the space between them. His nose got smaller. His mouth widened.

The Narrow Man.

Violence erupted and Austin fell backwards, twisted, and ran into the kitchen. The back door was locked. Cole's mom was shouting, and there were grunts and crashes and Cole came running in after him, his eyes wide with madness. He tugged the gun, but it was caught in his waistband.

The key. Austin had heard Linda and Kelly talking about what it could do. It had sounded ridiculous, like magic, but what was going on in that hallway right now was magic, so Austin jammed the key into the locked door and twisted. An image of another door, a dull metal door, filled his mind as he twisted again, then he turned the handle and yanked the key out and suddenly Cole was barging into him and they both fell through.

The door slammed shut behind them and they were in darkness.

It wasn't the darkness that night brought. There were no stars above. No street lights. This was the dark of an enclosed space. At first, Austin thought the dark was absolute, but that wasn't true. The darkness lifted to gloom just ahead of him. While he waited for his eyes to adjust, he listened to the only sound he could hear over his own beating heart and shallow breathing. A sucking noise.

"Cole?" he whispered. Cole didn't answer.

Austin suddenly had the awful feeling that Cole had somehow circled round behind him, that he was standing there with that gun out, that he could see Austin perfectly in the dark and he was smiling as he watched his prey begin to panic.

But then the gloom lightened even more, and Austin could make out someone kneeling ahead of him.

He started forward on his hands and knees. His fingers brushed over something metal. The gun. He seized it, feeling its weight, feeling a rush of reassurance and excitement that passed as quickly as it had come. He sat back on his haunches, raising the gun. He didn't need to see it to know it was shaking badly in his grip.

He could see the figure better now. It wasn't Cole. The dim light (dim, but getting brighter) seemed to be coming from within him. It was a man, definitely a man, and he was on his knees and holding Cole Blancard in his arms.

Austin stood, turned, ran straight into the door and jammed

the key into the lock. At the last moment, he remembered the twisting rule, and he turned the key and turned it again, all the while picturing the last door he'd come through, the door to Cole's bedroom, the one with the naked woman in chains on it, and he opened the cell door and stumbled through, into the hallway.

He turned, glimpsed the glowing figure as it sucked the life out of poor Cole Blancard, the psychopathic thug who had bullied Austin since he was eight years old, and right before the door slammed shut the figure erupted with a startling orange light. Then the door was closed and the house was normal again.

Austin stuffed the key in his pocket. He still had the gun, and even though he had no intention of using it he gripped it tighter as he hurried to the front door.

Bill and Betty fought the Narrow Man in the snow outside.

Their claws tore through the Narrow Man's clothes and raked his flesh, but while his clothes remained torn his flesh closed up over the wounds, like putty. The demons, on the other hand, weren't nearly so quick to heal. They had black scales growing on their skin, like armour, and while the scales were enough to deflect swipes, when the Narrow Man jabbed straight at them, those long, thin fingers of his actually slipped between the scales, and drew blood. From the looks on their faces, Austin could tell that Bill and Betty hadn't expected this. They circled him warily, snarling their hatred. The Narrow Man stood ready between them.

Cole's mom stayed on the lawn. She wasn't shouting anymore. She just stood there, not even looking at the fight. Her head was raised slightly, and cocked to one side like a dog listening to a sound in the distance. She turned, then, and Austin could see her smiling face. Her eyes were closed. Her arms were out to either side. She looked like she was waiting for God to reach down from heaven and pick her up. Austin realised the hair on the back of his neck was standing up. There was something in the air, a charge, and it was building. Intensifying.

Then something rippled.

Austin couldn't tell what it was. It wasn't the ground, not really, and it wasn't the buildings, it was the space around him, around them all. The space rippled, just for a moment, just for an eye-blink, and the whole town rippled with it, and Austin recognised the sensation. He felt it every year when he was down in the panic room. This was the feeling that preceded every Hell Night.

It was beginning.

Cole's mom laughed. It was a short, sharp laugh, cut off by a cry of pain. Her spine arched and her hands splayed and her legs snapped rigid. Her skin deepened to a rich yellow in the street light, and she grew taller while her hair lengthened and knotted. Her T-shirt tore as a ridge of white bone jutted sharply from her shoulders and along her arms. The angles of her face were sharper now, her brow more pronounced, her jaw wider. She laughed again, a laugh of pure joy, and Austin saw her teeth, packed into her gums like a shark's.

Austin watched this transformation and almost missed what was happening to the street. The road cracked and the grass grew, turned coarse and wild, briars sprouting like weeds. The houses creaked and groaned – the creaks of Cole's house sounding like screams to Austin's ears – as they lengthened and narrowed and twisted. Street lights and house lights alike turned orange and red and flickered like flames.

There were real screams now, screams and shouts and laughter, and demons were emerging from houses up and down this street.

47

AMBER WAS DYING.

The pain had simultaneously faded into the background and regrouped to jab at her with every beat of her heart. A whole lot of blood that she needed to stay inside her body was now on the outside. It was drenching her clothes and dripping to the snow-covered ground. It was smearing on branches and splashing on leaves. She was cold. She was so cold that she would never complain about the heat again. Her fingers were numb. Her head was light. She was dizzy. And even though she was dying she was aware of one thing: Hell Night had begun.

She felt it. The energy flowed through the ground, the air. It flowed through her battered body, through her trickling blood – it would have forced her to shift if she wasn't already in demon form. Through the trees, from where she was hiding, she saw what it did to Benjamin. In the moonlight, she could see how tall he had gotten. His skin looked red, a dirtier red than her own, and he was standing straight. He looked bigger, healthier. Stronger. He held the rifle with the butt resting on his hip. His laugh drifted up to her.

"*Amberrrr...*" he called, like they were playing a game.

Gritting her teeth, she started moving again, no longer going up the hill, but circling him, doing her best to get back to the farmhouse. She needed his truck. She needed to get away.

She lost sight of him, but every few seconds he'd call her name, allowing her to track his position. So far, it was working. She was moving sideways and he was moving up. Hopefully, he'd keep going. Hopefully.

She almost fainted. The blackness came on so suddenly that it rocked her. But she kept her eyes open, fought against it, and the feeling passed and when she looked up she could see the farmhouse. Along the side was a tall stack of chopped wood, held in place by an old gate Benjamin had rigged up. Beside the gate was a large wooden block with an axe buried in it. The last time she'd swung an axe, the Narrow Man had taken it away from her. This time would have to be different.

Amber was thirsty. God, she was so thirsty.

She started down, finding it hard to keep her weight on her injured leg. The uneven ground made things a whole lot worse. She slipped, nearly went tumbling, but lunged sideways, managed to slam her shoulder against a tree to stop her fall, managed to keep from howling in agony. She clung on, biting her lip against the pain, and once she was steady she listened.

Benjamin wasn't calling her name anymore.

She couldn't wait. Time was against her. Every moment that passed was another precious drop of blood. Holding on to the tree, Amber moved round it, let go, allowed her lead leg to slip through the dirt. Controlling her descent, she reached out, snagged a branch, snagged another one. Down here the ground was firmer and she was walking again – well, *limping* – and she got to the next tree and took a moment, scanning her surroundings, listening for Benjamin.

All she heard was the wind and her own heartbeat and, in the distance, gunshots. And screams.

The axe was maybe ten steps across open ground. Ten limping steps across open ground. Amber didn't have a choice. She stepped out of cover, started for the farmhouse.

"Boo," Benjamin said from behind her.

She swung round and he swung the rifle and she raised her arms and the scales did their best, but the rifle smashed and her left arm broke, she could feel it, and she went down, and Benjamin laughed as she screamed and tossed aside the remains of the weapon as he stalked after her.

"You're right, you know," he said, smiling and showing her his fangs. "Of course you're right. I've been waiting for this all year. We all have. We love it. It's what keeps us going."

The pain was blinding. Amber rolled on to her right side, somehow finding the strength to push herself away from him with her legs. He kept up easily.

"And you wanted to take that away from us? Away from me? That was never going to happen."

She hit the gate that contained the log pile, brought her feet in, got them under her.

Benjamin watched her stand on legs made of Jell-o. "You know what I'm going to do? And I'm amazed this hasn't occurred to me before. I'm going to take your advice."

The axe. It was right next to her. She could just reach out now, wrap her fingers around the handle, maybe pull it free with one tug, swing it into his neck before he had a chance to react. Maybe. Maybe she could do it if she hadn't just been shot twice. If her arm wasn't broken. If her strength wasn't leaving her.

"I'm going to eat you," said Benjamin. "Maybe I'll absorb your strength. What do you think? Maybe I'll even be able to stay like this all year round. It's worth a shot, isn't it? What? You're inching towards the axe, huh? Go ahead. Go for it. Let's see who's faster."

She hesitated. Benjamin grinned. She moved.

Benjamin dived for the axe, but Amber just swung the log she was holding, felt it crack into Benjamin's face, felt it snap him round, and as he staggered she took hold of the axe and yanked it free and roared as she swung. Benjamin turned away from her, caught the blade in the back, and he jerked straight and toppled, face down into the snow.

Amber dropped to one knee and then fell sideways, clutching her broken arm, crying with the pain.

She lay there for a long while, and the night was quiet again – quiet except for the gunshots and the screams from down in Desolation Hill.

"A-Amber?"

She kept her eyes closed. "What?"

Benjamin's voice was muffled. Strained. "I think… I think I'm hurt. I think… oh Jesus, I think you've done something to my back…"

She didn't answer. She was too busy dying.

"Are you still there? Amber? Do you think I'll be okay? This town, it heals us after every Hell Night, in the hour after sunrise. Those who aren't dead, I mean. Heals us right up. But I… I don't know. I think you've hurt me too bad. I can't feel anything."

She cracked one eye open. "So?" she asked. "You shot me. Tried to kill me."

"I'm sorry about that," Benjamin said. "But during the day I'm a different person. You know that. I'm a good person. I'm already old, for Christ's sake. I can't be old and crippled, too. You can't do that to me."

She couldn't just lie here. Milo was out there. And Kelly. Amber started crawling.

"Are you still there? Amber?"

"I'm here," she said.

"I'll help you," said Benjamin. "I'll fight with you against the people who have come to hurt you. The whole town will fight by your side."

"Hush now," Amber said as she reached him. She prodded his leg. "Can you feel that?"

"I... I'm not sure. Are you touching me? I can't feel anything. I'm numb. I can't even wiggle my fingers or toes."

"That's probably a good thing," Amber said. She tugged his pants leg up, revealing a red, surprisingly hairless calf. She opened her mouth wide, and tore out a chunk with her fangs.

"What are you doing?" Benjamin asked. "What was that sound?"

Amber chewed, blood running down her chin, and swallowed. It was so good. It was so frikkin' good. She tore out another mouthful of meat.

"Are you... what are you doing? Amber? Are you... are you eating? What are you eating? What is there to...?"

He faltered, went quiet, and as she was on her third mouthful he started screaming.

*

Amber stood up. She took off her jacket, let it fall. She lifted her sodden top, ran a finger over the bullet hole in her belly. It was closing up nicely. The same with the wounds in her chest and leg. Her arm, too, was mending. No pain anymore – just that pleasant feeling of warmth. The blood was sticky, though. Her hands and face were caked in it, and it drenched her clothes.

She opened the door into Benjamin's farmhouse, went to the sink and splashed herself with water. She didn't mind the cold. She washed her hands and face and her happy little smile stayed where it was. When she looked up, she saw the keys to Benjamin's truck, right there on the windowsill.

Well, all right then.

48

WHAT FIRST TIPPED VIRGIL off to the possibility that something bad had happened at the bunker were the two dead bodies lying in the middle of the road.

He swung the Sienna round, parked it on the hill heading down. In case they needed to make a fast getaway.

He looked at Javier and Javier looked at him, and they got out of the car and approached the corpses. Slowly. The first was an old man. The mayor. Virgil had never met him, but he knew his face well enough. Jesper. The cause of all this hardship and pain, now lying there, covered in a sprinkling of snow with a hole in his head.

The second corpse was a demon, a red one, like Amber. His throat had been torn open. Javier made a sound, like he was going to be sick, but he managed to keep his lunch down and they walked to the bunker. The door was open and the lights were on inside.

Virgil led the way in. At the bottom of the steps there was another door, bigger and heavier than the first. Through it, a cheerless concrete hall with harsh lighting and dozens of bunk beds along each wall. There was a kitchen unit and a dartboard and a card table and rooms at the back, probably filled with canned goods.

"Hello?" Javier called, even though it was pretty obvious the place was empty. "What do we do now?"

Virgil looked around. "I have no idea."

"We could stay," said Javier. "Close the door and wait out the night. In the morning, we get in your car and we drive."

"Drive where?"

Javier shrugged. "Your daughter's place."

"She doesn't want to see me."

"I don't care," said Javier. "We have a hell of a story to tell her and even if she doesn't believe us, which she won't, at least it'll get you talking."

"I don't know," said Virgil. "It'd be awkward."

"You almost got me killed," said Javier. "You owe me, so we do what I say, and I say we drive straight to your daughter's place first thing in the morning."

Virgil hesitated, then nodded. "I guess I do owe you."

"Damn straight." A few seconds ticked by. "Do you think the others are okay?"

"I really hope so."

"The guy out there, he's a demon like Amber's a demon. You think that's her dad?"

"I don't know," said Virgil. "Maybe. The other guy's the mayor."

"I figured."

Virgil took out his phone, searched for the numbers that Linda had put into it. He eventually found them, called Kelly and then Amber without the call being picked up. Then he called Linda herself.

"Virgil!" Linda said when she answered. Her voice was hushed, like she was hiding. "You're okay!"

"I am," said Virgil. "I'm at the bunker with Javier. What happened?"

"Amber's parents came. They took Austin."

Virgil went cold. "No. No, no, no."

"What?" said Javier. "What's wrong?"

Virgil held up a hand to silence him as Linda continued. "Then the cops came. I'm with Ronnie and Warrick. We're heading back to your place."

"We'll meet you there."

"Virgil, wait, it's not safe here. Hell Night has started. We're... Jesus, there are demons everywhere."

"Are you in danger?"

"Yes," she whispered. A rustling followed, the sound of running, and then she spoke again, breathlessly. "We're doing our best to stay away from it all. I have to go. Virgil, if you can, leave. Just drive out of town. Drive and keep going. Good luck."

She hung up without waiting for an answer.

"Austin's been taken," Virgil told Javier. "Hell Night has started. They're trying to get back to my house to lie low."

"Did she say what we should do?"

"She said we should run."

Javier nodded. "And what are we *actually* going to do?"

"Go back to my house. See what we can do to help."

"Right then. Let's get going."

They climbed the steps out of the bunker just as another demon emerged from the treeline. Her hair was as red as her skin and she was quite breathtakingly beautiful, despite the tears running down her face.

She saw them and they froze.

"You," she said. "Who are you?"

"Uh," said Virgil.

"Do you know Amber? Are you helping her? Does she like you?"

Virgil didn't say anything more. Javier kept his mouth shut.

"Screw it," the demon snarled, stalking forward. "I'm going to kill you, anyway."

"Back, back, back," Virgil whispered, and they stumbled inside the bunker and slammed the door after them, turning a wheeled handle that locked it.

The demon began pounding on it from the other side.

"I'll kill you!" she screamed. "I'll kill you!"

They hurried down the steps, stood at the bottom beside the second door, the heavier door, ready to close it if the first seemed in danger of giving way.

The demon pounded and screamed and pounded and threatened, and after two or three minutes they began to hear sobbing, and then the barrage stopped and the sobbing went away.

Javier glanced at Virgil. "Think it's a trick?"

Virgil didn't answer. He climbed the steps, put his ear to the door, and heard nothing.

Javier went off to find the toilet, and by the time he'd returned Virgil had made up his mind. "I'm going to take a look outside."

Javier nodded. "That's stupid."

"I can't just stand here."

"Stand over there, then."

"I'm opening the door, Javier. Turn out the lights."

Grumpily, Javier found the light switch and plunged them into darkness. "Fine," he said. "But if she kills us..."

He didn't really have anything to say after that.

Virgil turned the wheeled handle slowly. It creaked and he winced. He kept turning, expecting the demon to kick it open at any moment and send him hurtling down the steps. But she didn't kick it, and he opened the door without smashing any bones.

He peered out, and signalled to Javier to come join him. Together they watched as the demon hunched over the other demon's corpse in the middle of the road. They watched her crying, watched her throw back her head and scream at the moon. Then she dipped forward again.

"Jesus," Virgil whispered.

Javier frowned. "What is she doing?"

"I think she's... eating him."

"Christ!"

She was talking, too, talking to the corpse. They could hear her sobs. Her words were distressed and muffled by a full mouth, but it appeared that she was apologising. Quite right too.

"If this is what she does to her friends," Javier whispered, "what do you think she's going to do to us?"

"She's not going to get to us," said Virgil. "We're going to make a break for it. We get to the car, I take the brake off and put it in neutral, we roll downhill. She won't even know we're gone."

Javier nodded. "You go first."

"You're sure? You don't want to volunteer?"

"It's your stupid plan."

Virgil glowered, but there was no time to argue. She was eating pretty damn fast.

Moving as quietly as he could, he crept forward. As he crossed the road, he did his best to keep low, but his back was playing up again. Thankfully, she didn't look round.

He got to the Sienna, took the keys from his pocket carefully, without jangling them, and turned, gave the signal. Javier nodded and closed the door to the bunker behind him. But instead of creeping, or sneaking, or even moving remotely stealthily, Javier took a slow, slow step. Then another.

And eventually another.

Virgil waved him on, cursing him silently, but Javier didn't change his tactic. He was maybe six steps away from the car and the demon lady still hadn't noticed him, but as she tore off another chunk she fell back and turned away from the corpse, weeping. All she had to do was raise her head and she'd be looking straight at Javier.

Virgil felt his heart hammer painfully in his chest. Javier stared at him, ashen-faced and frozen in place.

Virgil waited until his heart stopped trying to leap out through his ribcage, then peeked at the lady demon as she wiped her eyes. She looked over at the bunker, and snarled.

Virgil motioned for Javier to lie down. Javier nodded, and began to sink slowly to the ground.

The lady demon stood and wobbled slightly, like she'd had too much to drink. But if she was drunk then she was an angry drunk. She roared and Javier flinched, but by some miracle her eyes still hadn't flicked in their direction.

Lying flat on his belly, Javier held out his hands. Virgil reached for them, took a good grip, and, ever so slowly, he pulled Javier behind the car.

Together they watched the demon lady march to the bunker,

and begin to pound once more on the door. Incredibly, it was even louder than before. She was stronger. Angrier. The door began to rattle.

Virgil opened the driver's side door. The dome light came on. The demon didn't notice. He got in as quickly as he could, turned out the light, and took off the brake. Javier got in the other side, just as the Sienna started to roll downhill.

They heard a shout behind them. She'd seen them. They slammed the doors shut and the Sienna picked up speed, and in the rear-view Virgil watched the demon lady sprinting after them. She was fast. She was extraordinarily fast. He jammed the key in the ignition and turned it and the engine came to life and the dashboard lit up and he slammed his foot on the gas.

49

THE DOWALL MOTEL BURNED.

The flames that consumed it licked the air and sent the snow flurries swirling. It stood atop its perch, up on that hill, and it burned like a beacon of madness. In its windows, a figure danced. Whether it was Kenneth or Belinda Dowall, Kelly couldn't say, and the Charger wasn't moving slow enough for her to gauge.

A demon landed in the street ahead of them and roared, and the Charger ran right over him.

Hell Night had begun, which meant that Naberius had had his sacrifice. Which meant another child had died.

"Amber's parents are real pieces of work, huh?" Kelly said.

Milo didn't answer.

The last time Kelly had been down this street, the way had been smooth. Now the road was jagged and cracked, with chunks rising over the sidewalk like a swollen river bursting its banks. Her phone buzzed. She swiped the screen.

"Linda!" she said. "Where are you? You okay? I've been trying to call!"

"We're good," Linda said. "For now. Listen, we made it back into town, but—"

"We're in town, too," Kelly said. "Me and Milo. Where are you?"

There was a moment of whispered exchange, and then, "Just coming up to the corner where Briar Lane meets Briar Road."

"Briar Road," Kelly said to Milo. "You know it?"

He nodded, pointed right. "Two blocks that way."

"We can be there in thirty seconds," Kelly said.

"Kelly, no," said Linda. "We think we're being followed. We're gonna try to lead them somewhere. If you and Milo can... hold on... shit."

"Linda? Linda? What's wrong? Linda?"

The call cut off.

"They're in trouble," Kelly said.

Milo nodded, started to turn the wheel, then braked, his eyes on the road ahead, to where Austin Cooke sprinted into an alley, pursued by a pair of hollering demons.

"Catch up with your friends," Milo said as her door opened all on its own. "Stick to the shadows. I'll get Austin. Meet up at Virgil's place."

Kelly didn't even have time to respond. She stepped out and the Charger leaped forward, the door slamming shut, and for the briefest of moments she was bathed in its tail lights. And then it was gone.

"Right," Kelly muttered, slipping the handgun into her waistband. Shielding her eyes from the swirling snow, she jogged on to the sidewalk, started moving towards Briar Road. It took about thirty seconds for her to realise that sticking to the shadows was a problem when the streets were so well lit. Granted, it was a hellish light, of an almost greasy quality that made her stomach swim uneasily, but it was still light, and it threw the shadows far away from each other. But, whenever she could, she stuck to the shadows, because all the monsters were dancing in the light.

She passed carnage, and brutality, and depravity. At regular intervals the town became alive with screams. How Virgil could ever have stayed indoors and fooled himself into thinking these were shouts of celebration, she did not know.

Denial, she supposed. An awful lot of it could be laid at the feet of wilful denial.

She passed a girl who had spikes growing from her body, feasting on a small pile of junk food. The girl snarled at her, and Kelly speeded up.

She approached the turn on to Briar Road and slowed down, took a peek round the corner. It was clear. She hurried up the slight hill, nearly tripping over loose slabs of sidewalk that Hell Night had thrown up.

"I do declare," said a voice behind her, "if it isn't our favourite redhead, come back to pay us a visit."

Kelly's heart went cold, and she turned. Ricky and Dave from Sally's bar grinned at her through grotesquely misshapen faces. They were each a different kind of demon, sharing only the same look in their eyes.

Kelly ran.

Ricky and Dave laughed and gave chase. Kelly ran until the street evened out. They were right behind her. When it became clear she wasn't about to outrun them, she went for the gun, prepared to whip it out as she spun round. And then something slammed into her and she hit the ground, went sprawling.

"Oooh," said the Party-Monster, looking like a real monster this time, "look what I caught."

Kelly got up and backed away as the three demons advanced, clearly relishing the moment.

"You run pretty fast," said Ricky. "For a girl."

"Ignore him and his blatant sexism," Dave said, moving closer. "He doesn't know how to woo a lady."

"You're making fools of yourselves, the both of you," said the Party-Monster. "The redhead's a dyke, remember? She's not interested in the noodles you're packing."

Kelly's mouth was dry. "I don't want any trouble, fellas."

They laughed at that.

"You really *must* be new here," Ricky said, "because Hell Night is all *about* trouble. You don't have to ask for it. You don't even have to want it. We deliver it to you."

"On the house," said the Party-Monster.

"Besides," said Ricky, "we owe you. You whupped our asses first time we met, didn't you? We had no idea you and your friends could fight like that. Guess you showed us, huh?"

"I'm sorry," Kelly said. "I'm sorry, all right?"

"Little late for apologies. When it got out that I'd had the shit kicked out of me by a dyke, you know what happened? Ridicule. Public ridicule."

"So what is this?" Kelly asked. "This is all because I'm gay, is that it?"

"Gay or straight's got nothing to do with it," said Ricky. "Hell, I was screwing the Party-Monster not half an hour ago in the middle of Main Street."

"That's right, he was," said the Party-Monster.

"Walking around in the daytime, we got all these little fears and insecurities and prejudices and they all mean so very much there, in the sunlight... but y'know what? When Hell Night rolls around, no one gives a good goddamn about any of that stuff. When we're like this, we do what we wanna do. We do *who* we wanna do."

"It's a very liberating experience," said the Party-Monster.

"So ask," said Ricky.

Kelly could feel the cold metal of the gun against her hip. "I don't understand. Ask what?"

"You know."

"I don't. I swear."

Ricky chuckled. "Ask us what we're gonna do with you. Go on. Ask. You know you want to."

Kelly blinked. "What... what are you going to do with me?"

The Party-Monster howled with laughter.

"We're gonna kill you," said Dave, delighted.

"Every year," said Ricky, "we try to kill someone in a new way. You know what we've never tried? Guess."

"I... I don't..."

"Go on, guess. Guess how we're gonna kill you. Hey, we're not totally unreasonable. We're actually pretty nice guys once you get to know us. So we'll give you a chance to get out of this in one piece, how's that? If you guess correctly how we're gonna kill you, we'll let you go."

Dave slapped Ricky on the back. "Nice one! Genius! How about it, Red?"

"No," said Kelly. "No, I can't play that. But, if you let me go, you'll—"

"We're not letting you go," said Ricky. "You're playing the game or you forfeit. If you forfeit, we kill you. So... now do you wanna play? You can have three guesses."

"Play!" the Party-Monster chanted. "Play! Play! Play!"

No way out. Kelly swallowed. "If I get it right, you'll let me go?"

"Yes," said Ricky. "Guys, you good with that?"

"Gambling's no fun unless you risk losing something," the Party-Monster said, grinning.

"How many people have you killed?" Kelly asked.

"Lots," said Dave.

"And you killed them in new ways each time?"

"Each and every time," said Ricky. "That's enough. This isn't Twenty Questions. Three guesses as to how you're gonna die. First guess?"

Her thoughts jumbled together even as she tried to separate the possibilities into categories. Beating, stabbing, shooting, all probably used up. "Drowning?" she asked.

"Ooh, drowning," said Dave. "We should keep that for next year."

"Not drowning, Red," said Ricky. "Second guess."

"I don't know, I... it could be anything."

"Yeah, it could."

"Burning then."

Ricky's grin widened. "I like the way your mind works. But no. We've already burned someone to death. Did that on our second Hell Night. Third and final guess, Red."

"Give me a clue."

"No clues."

"Please, anything. Give me anything. A hint. Anything."

"I think we should give her a clue," said Dave.

"You're just sweet on her," Ricky told him.

"I'll do it," the Party-Monster said. "Okay then, you red-headed rug-muncher, you want a clue? Get ready for some history.

We're gonna kill you in the same way that Henry the Eighth killed two of his wives."

"Beheading!" Kelly shouted triumphantly. "Beheading! He had their goddamn heads chopped off!"

She went to run between them, but Dave blocked her way.

She backed off. "You said! You said if I guessed it right you'd let me go!"

"You didn't guess it right," said Ricky.

"Bullshit! Henry the Eighth had Anne Boleyn and Catherine Howard beheaded! I know my goddamn history!"

"You do," said Ricky, "but the Party-Monster doesn't."

The Party-Monster looked confused. "I thought he had his wives hanged."

Kelly paled. "That's not fair. He's the one who got it wrong, not me."

"But what you failed to take into account is how dumb the Party-Monster is. And for that alone you deserve to hang. Come on. We've already got it all set up."

She went for the gun, but the Party-Monster grabbed her arm, started dragging her after Ricky and Dave.

"You shouldn't have called me Kevin," he said. "Maybe I'd have let you go if you hadn't called me Kevin."

"I didn't call you Kevin," Kelly managed. "That was Linda."

"Still, though."

She got a hand to the gun as they turned on to Main Street, but when she saw the huge crowd of demons congregating around the square she left it in her waistband. Firing a gun now would only get her killed faster. Ricky and Dave shoved other demons out of their way, and the Party-Monster dragged her right into the throng. Curiously, though, none of the other demons were looking at her.

"They got one," the Party-Monster said. He turned back to Kelly, grinning at her excitedly. Like they were friends. "They got one!"

He let go of her, and vanished into the crowd.

Kelly tried to follow. She didn't want to imagine what this mob would do to Amber if they grabbed her. She didn't know what the hell she'd do if it was *Amber* they'd grabbed – she only knew she'd do something. She'd have to.

The crowd was a living, breathing thing, and it moved and jostled and every now and then Kelly would catch an elbow that would send her crashing into someone else's hardened skin. In this snarling sea of fangs and claws and horns and wings, she couldn't even see Ricky or Dave anymore.

She tried moving sideways, but the crowd surged and she cried out as she was squeezed to the front like toothpaste from a tube. Suddenly she could see what they were all gathered here for: they'd captured a Hound.

Laughing and jeering, the demons pinned the Hound to the square itself, right where the ballot box used to be. This Hound had a tighter beard and tattoos on his bare, muscled arms. If the Hound had tried to struggle before this, he had ceased by this point and lay on the ground, calmly awaiting his fate.

His fate arrived in the form of the Party-Monster, yanking the cord of a brand-new, just-looted chainsaw from Oscar Moreno's rival hardware store. It roared to life and the demons laughed louder. There was some shoving as they reorganised themselves so that the Party-Monster could stand over the Hound's left arm. Grinning, he lowered the chainsaw, and the chain bit into the Hound's bicep.

Blood sprayed. The demons howled. The Hound made no sound as his arm was severed. Kelly could barely watch.

The Party-Monster held the chainsaw over his head, his face splattered with blood, and welcomed the cheering. He spun in circles, whooping and hollering like Leatherface at the end of *The Texas Chainsaw Massacre*, nicking whichever demons were dumb enough to be standing too close. Then he stepped over to the Hound's other arm, and the crowd leaned in, and Kelly got to her hands and knees and started crawling through the forest of legs. She got kicked a few times, kneed a few times – once hard enough to cause her vision to cloud – but then the forest broke all of a sudden and she was out.

She got up on shaky legs, felt for her gun, and realised she had lost it somewhere in the melee. She could go back for it – but seriously, screw that. She hurried away from the crowd, back the way she had come, only turning again at the sound of Ricky's voice.

"Ladies and gentlemen!"

She peered up. Ricky had climbed to the very top of the snow-covered scaffolding outside the Municipal Building, and he was now holding his arms out while he waited for the chatter to die down, like a dictator about to address the masses.

Once it was quiet enough, he began his speech.

"You wanna see something cool?" he shouted. The demons shrieked their approval. *"I said, you wanna see something cool?"*

So far, Kelly was unimpressed by Ricky's speech-making skills.

"Check this shit out!" Ricky hollered, and there was a pause as the Party-Monster appeared behind him, dragging the Hound. Blood still flowed from the stumps that were once his arms, but the Hound didn't seem to be bothered by it. Another few seconds

passed while Ricky placed a noose over the Hound's head and tightened it, and the demons began to chant impatiently. Finally, it was ready, and Ricky stepped to one side, making a grand gesture for the Hound to throw himself over the edge. Instead, the Hound merely stepped into Ricky, nudging him off balance, and Ricky toppled backwards and screamed all the way down to the street. His sticky end was hidden from Kelly by the crowd, who took a moment before erupting into laughter.

Once they were finished laughing, they started chanting again, and the Party-Monster grinned down at them, grabbed the Hound, and shoved.

The Hound plummeted. Halfway down, the rope went taut and his body snapped straight and his head popped clean off. It all happened so quickly, with so little fuss, it was almost ridiculous. The Hound's body slipped from the noose and crumpled to the ground and the head followed it down, bouncing twice and then rolling. One of the demons ran up, kicked the head like he was trying for a field goal.

The crowd went wild, and Kelly left Main Street in her wake.

She headed back towards Briar Road, and froze when she heard a dog barking. Two? Keeping low and doing her best to move quietly, she ran from shadow to shadow, closing in on the sound.

She lost it and stopped, trying to ignore the laughter and the screams from the streets around her, doing her best to focus. The dog didn't bark again. Whether it was Two or not, she took off once more, heading in that general direction, and she rounded a corner and ran straight into a psychopath with a gun.

50

He knew it was useless, trying to outrun them. Even in human form, Marco Mabb and Jamie Hillock were bigger and stronger and faster than Austin was.

In demon form, it wasn't even a competition.

They played with him, toyed with him, offered him glimmers of hope and then, finally, they overtook him, shoving him and laughing as Austin fell in the snow.

"Out past curfew!" Mabb howled.

"Naughty, naughty!" crowed Hillock. His hair was even longer as a demon, and threatened to cover the startlingly ugly face that had resulted from his transformation. "I swear, Blancard's gonna wish he was here for this one. He really doesn't like you, kid."

"Really," said Mabb. Unlike Hillock, Mabb had gotten better-looking as a demon. His skin was a dark gold.

"We should take him to Cole," Hillock said. "Kill him in front of him."

"Cole's in his panic room," Mabb reminded him. "We could video it. What do you think?"

"No, asshole," Hillock said. "Remember the rules. No videos. No pictures. We can't tell anyone about tonight."

"Shit, yeah. Okay then, we'll just kill the little turd here and go back for Cunningham and his friends. Give them what's coming to them."

They closed in and Austin stood, breathing hard, and raised the gun.

Hillock laughed. "Holy crap! Check it out!"

"Is that a silencer?" said Mabb. "He's got a silencer on it! That's so cool!"

"Now we're definitely going back to Cunningham. Take that with us, walk right up to him, shoot him between the horns. Nobody, and I mean *nobody*, does to us what they did. Nobody."

Mabb nodded. "We'll give them something to laugh about. We'll see who the big man is when we're done with them. Vengeance is sweet. Give us the gun, shit-for-brains."

"Stop," said Austin. "Stop or I'll... just stop..."

"Bet you can't even fire that thing," Hillock said. "Bet you can't even pull the trigger."

"I will," Austin said, gritting his teeth. "I'll shoot you."

"Then go ahead," said Hillock. "Shoot us. I dare you."

The gun was heavy, and trembled in Austin's hands. Still, he didn't let it drop.

Mabb and Hillock laughed again, and stepped forward, and Austin yanked hard on the trigger. He expected a *pffft*, like in the video games, but the silenced pistol snapped loudly and bucked in his hands.

"Jesus!" Mabb yelled, his eyes wide while his hands clutched at his belly. "He shot me!"

Mabb staggered back and Hillock followed, pulling Mabb's

hands away so he could see the wound for himself. Austin didn't know what to say. He fought hard against an overwhelming urge to apologise.

"Well, holy crap," said Hillock. "You did it. You actually did it."

"I'm gonna kill you!" Mabb howled, but was too busy being in pain to attempt it.

"I didn't think you'd do it," said Hillock. "Didn't think you had the balls. Cole always says you're a chickenshit little runt, but wait till he hears about this."

"He won't," Austin said. "He's dead."

Mabb stopped howling, and Hillock raised his eyebrows. "What's that?"

"Cole's dead," said Austin, speaking louder this time. "And, if you're not careful, you'll be dead, too. You better leave me alone."

"You killed Cole?" Mabb asked in a small voice.

Austin swallowed, and nodded.

"You?" Hillock said, stepping forward. "You killed Cole Blancard?"

"Stop walking," said Austin. "Stop walking or I'll shoot you."

Hillock didn't seem to even move, and yet suddenly he was close enough to smack the gun from Austin's hands.

"You killed Cole Blancard?" Hillock said again, lifting Austin off his feet by his shirt. "You murdered our friend?"

"Jamie," Mabb whimpered, "I think I'm dying."

"Shut up," Hillock snapped.

"He shot me in the belly, man."

"Shut the hell up, dickhead! The little man here just confessed to the murder of our friend, didn't you hear him?"

"I think he killed me, too, Jamie."

Hillock threw Austin down and stalked back to Mabb, who was bent over and moaning. "What?" he demanded. "What the hell is wrong with you, Marco?"

Mabb pointed at Austin. "He shot me. You saw him."

"So?"

"So I think I'm gonna die, man."

"What do you expect me to do about it?"

Mabb dropped to his knees. "I don't know, Jamie, I'm scared."

"Don't be a pussy."

"It's not being a pussy to be scared of dying."

"Yeah, it is, and you're being one right now. Man up, for Christ's sake."

"I'm so cold..."

"Of course you're cold," Hillock said. "It's Alaska. Stop exaggerating."

"I really am dying, though."

"Then die! Jesus, Marco, just die already and get it over with!"

Mabb's demonic face told Austin all he needed to know – that Hillock's indifference to his fate hurt him more than any bullet ever could.

"You dick," said Mabb, and reared up, grabbing Hillock and slugging him right across the jaw. Hillock wobbled but didn't fall, and slammed his fist into Mabb's wound. Mabb screamed and stumbled and fell to his knees, and Hillock's shadow danced as red headlights lit him up.

Milo's black car hit Jamie Hillock so fast he was thrown ten feet into the air. He landed as a jumble of broken bones wrapped in demon skin, howling in pain.

The car swerved round and came rolling to a stop beside Austin.

"Climb in," Milo said. "Let's get you to something approaching safety."

Marco Mabb looked up. "Excuse me, sir," he said. "Could you take us to a hospital? I've been shot. And you ran into my friend."

Milo ignored him, so Austin did, too. He got in the car.

51

THE TOWN WAS TWISTED.

It was a nightmare version of its daytime self, the streets narrowed and crooked and the buildings long and bent. Nothing fit. To Amber, it was as if each selfish piece of Desolation Hill had shouldered the others out of its way. The Municipal Building hunched jealously over the square, the stores on Main Street jabbed and strangled their neighbours, and the church reared away from it all, tall and spiked and vicious.

But, if the town was twisted, its inhabitants were merely showing their true selves.

She drove by demons carousing on the streets. They fought and screwed and danced and destroyed. They were bloodthirsty and insatiable and quick to anger. Three demons having sex in a store window suddenly started arguing, and the window smashed as they fell through, tearing at each other's throats. Other demons laughed at them as they passed.

They were giddy, Amber saw. Giddy with malevolent delight, and high on the rush of adrenaline and endorphins that came with giving themselves over to their baser instincts. Not one of them was trying to fight it. And why would they? They'd been looking forward to this night for the last year. Twelve months' worth of lust had built up. Twelve months' worth of grievances could now explode into full-blown fury. Old debts were looking to be settled. No slight would go unanswered.

Amber thought for a moment of all those kids and all those teenagers down in their soundproofed panic rooms, their parents unable to get at them, unable to tear them apart or feast on their flesh. She imagined games being played or movies being watched. She imagined them sleeping, safe and warm in their peaceful, pleasant soundproofed cocoons, while outside hell had come, raging and vengeful, to stalk the jangled streets of their town.

Two demons were up ahead, beating the crap out of each other in the snow. She recognised the smaller one as the old man from Fast Danny's, the fisherman who had the crusts cut off his sandwiches. He had horns now, and fangs, but he went down and the bigger one laughed, started kicking him. He lost his balance and stumbled out on to the street, and Amber clipped him as she passed. In the side mirror, she watched him twirl and fall, and then the demon fisherman got up and started kicking him, howling with laughter the whole time.

She left them in the distance and returned her attention to the road, and braked.

A Hound sat astride his bike in the middle of the junction ahead. Waiting for her.

Amber sat very still, feeling the pickup tremble beneath her, barely aware of the smile creeping across her face.

She threw the pickup into gear and slammed her foot on the gas. The pickup lurched, gained speed quickly, hurtled straight for the biker. The Hound rode to meet her, a bullet fired from a gun. But Amber's pickup was a tank shell, and tank shells beat bullets.

Usually.

The pickup hit the bike and the hood crumpled and Amber was lifted from her seat and crashed through the windshield and flew, but flew badly, and landed worse, the road scraping at her chest and face and knees and belly.

She lay in the middle of the street, making little sounds, but not moving.

The Hound got off his bike. She heard this, didn't see it. All she could see was the road and the sidewalk and the bus stop with its bench and a poster for a movie that had already left theatres by the time she'd fled Orlando. She listened to the Hound walk up. He stood over her. She wanted to turn her head, look at him, but her body was slow to obey. She wriggled her fingers and toes. They were still working. That was good. She wasn't paralysed. Her horns had saved her, maybe. Or her scales. Or her strength. Or the power she'd absorbed when she'd eaten Benjamin – maybe that had done the trick.

She couldn't feel it anymore. The buzz. That electricity. It was gone. She'd used up most of it healing from the gunshot wounds, and now the rest of it was gone. Stupid. Why hadn't she worn her goddamn seat belt? Stupid.

She managed to turn her head in time to see the Hound draw back his foot and kick.

The boot connected with her side and lifted her off the ground like she was a football. She smashed through the bus stop in a storm of glass beads and torn movie poster. She landed and rolled, hit the wall on her hands and knees and stayed there, wheezing. Boots crunched on glass behind her and then he was pulling her off the ground by her horns. She went to slash at his throat, but couldn't raise her arm high enough, and felt her ribs slide against each other when she tried.

He hit her, his fist slamming into her belly. Fresh pain sliced through her. She dropped to one knee and the Hound brought his own knee in. It struck her in the side of the head and the world rocked. She felt his hands on her horns again, felt the sidewalk moving beneath her. He was dragging her backwards after him as he walked to his bike. Amber's struggles were feeble. Pathetic. She would have been ashamed if she'd had the luxury.

He dumped her beside the bike, then searched through his saddlebags. She heard the rattle of a chain and tried to crawl away, but he stomped on her ankle. She turned over, clutching her ribs and moaning. The Hound was looking down at her, a heavy chain in his hands, but Amber's gaze flickered over his shoulder, to where the demons perched on the wreckage of the pickup.

Seven of them. Maybe eight. Different colours, different types. Some slim, some bulky. Some with horns, some without. One with wings. One with sharp, bony protrusions at every major joint. They perched there like gargoyles, silent. The Hound sensed them, and turned slowly. They observed him through narrowed eyes.

One of the demons, the smallest of them, screeched, and they descended on the Hound. He grabbed the nearest, his hand lighting up and the demon howled in pain, but another one hit him and he stumbled. There were too many, and they were drawing blood now.

The Hound bled, just like anyone. Just like Amber.

She got up, holding her ribs, trying not to cry out. Not that she could distract the demons from the fight even if she'd wanted to. They shrieked with unbridled joy, a stark contrast to the Hound's grim silence.

She hurried away before any of them remembered she was there.

She turned the first corner she came to, started down it. Two demons slammed against a parked car on the other side of the road. At first, Amber thought they were having sex, but then she changed her mind, decided they were trying to kill each other.

She carried on, emerging on to Main Street. Back to Virgil's. All plans were now scrapped. It was too dangerous out here. She had to reach Virgil's place, hide with the others. If there were any others. If they weren't all dead by now. If Milo wasn't dead by now.

Or Kelly.

A naked demon stepped out through a broken window on to the sidewalk. It took a few moments for Amber to recognise her as Brenda, the waitress from Fast Danny's.

"And who might you be, beautiful?" Brenda said, walking closer. "Don't think I recognise the face."

"I'm just passing through," said Amber.

"Ohhh," said Brenda. She jabbed at the air with her finger. "You're the tubby girl, aren't you? Heard you were more trouble than you were worth. Certainly got prettier, though."

Amber held up a hand. "You're going to want to back off there, Brenda."

"Are you the reason for the delay?" Brenda asked as she neared. "Usually, Hell Night starts just as the sun goes down. I was standing in my backyard, waiting for the change... When it got dark and nothing happened, I started to cry, I'm not gonna lie to you. I've been waiting for this. Hell Night is the reason I never take a vacation. I never have to."

"If you take one more step, I'm going to kill you, Brenda."

Brenda stopped walking, but kept smiling. "We can't let you leave. See, we're all nuts when we're like this, yeah, but we're not *too* nuts. We've got our rules. We try our very best not to kill each other or set fire to anything. Those are tricky ones. No one blames you too much if you break those. One of the more concrete rules is not to go after the kids. That's an important one. Of course, every so often, someone will crack. Last year it was Joy Sinclair, the grade-school teacher. She went after one of the little shits who'd been making her life a misery. We all understood, of course, but rules are rules. She's spending tonight in one of Chief Novak's cells, as punishment. We need our rules or else we won't have a town to wake up to.

"One of those concrete rules, steadfast, we call it, has to do with visitors. Anyone who isn't from here must leave before the festival begins. And anyone who's caught here once the festival has begun? They don't get to leave. Ever."

"You don't want to do this, Brenda."

"Yeah, I do," said Brenda. "Yeah, we all do. You're a visitor and you have to die. It's how we've kept Hell Night a secret for all these generations." Her smile widened. "Death to outsiders."

Brenda came at her and Amber raked at her with her claws. She expected Brenda's protective scales to form, but none did, and Brenda shrieked and staggered, holding her injured arm, blood running through her fingers.

A sudden wave of anger hit Amber, and she stomped on Brenda's knee, snapping it sideways. This ridiculous woman who thought she could be a threat. To her? To Amber? After everything she'd been through? She hit her then, a backhanded blow, and Brenda twisted and crumpled and rolled over and started screaming for real now, like she'd finally realised just who she had gone up against.

"You're not like me," Amber snarled. "This happens to you once a year. But I can do it anytime I *want*."

Brenda was in no condition to reply. She just kept screaming – wailing, really, a high-pitched wail of pain and self-pity that hurt Amber's ears and stoked the anger already burning inside.

Amber batted Brenda's hands away and crouched over her, started hitting. "Stop it," she ordered. "Stop. Stop making that noise." Brenda's blood smeared against the scales that had formed around Amber's knuckles. The wail stopped after ten seconds or so, but Amber kept punching, just to make sure she had shut up.

When she was done, Amber stood, ignoring the pain from her broken ribs and curling her lip in disgust at the pathetic mess that lay silent and still at her feet.

"Look at our little pride and joy," said her father from behind her. "Did we or did we not raise her right, wife-of-mine?"

Amber turned without haste, glaring at her parents as they came over.

"We certainly did, husband," said Betty, smiling. "I like to think this suddenly merciless behaviour comes from my side of the family."

"Nonsense," said Bill. "That look in her eyes is all me."

52

Bunch of goddamn serial killers.

Not even undead serial killers, either. They'd made no deals, they'd been given no powers... they were ordinary, garden-variety psychos, and yet they'd managed to capture Kelly's whole entire goddamn gang.

It was embarrassing is what it was.

"Isn't this great?" said the one called Sam, looking out of the window of the *Chronicle* office, across the snow-covered streets of Desolation Hill. "Isn't it just awesome?"

The cords were digging into Kelly's wrists and her jaw was hurting from where Sam had hit her, so she wasn't sharing his enthusiasm. Sam's fellow serial killers were there to pick up the slack, though.

"Look at them out there," said Goulder. "See their teeth? Their claws? Demons, man. That's gonna be us. As soon as this night is over, that's gonna be us."

Sure, they had guns, and sure, Kelly and the others had each stumbled across them purely by chance instead of being lured into some kind of ingenious trap... but that was hardly the point. The point was Kelly's arms were decorated with enemies endowed with supernatural talents, and now it looked like she was going to be killed by four complete amateurs.

"I cannot wait," said Demer. At least Kelly thought his name was Demer. He was the tallest of the men, and the skinniest. Sam had the worst haircut and Goulder was the heaviest. "I'm so frickin' pumped for this. Am I ready? I was born ready!"

He laughed – a strange, high-pitched giggle that appeared genuine yet sounded false.

Beside her, Linda had her eyes closed and her breathing was slow and steady. Having her hands bound kicked up her claustrophobia, but she was dealing with it. So far.

"Y'all are celebrating before the job is done," said Bowsher, scowling. Bowsher was the oldest, and the most serious, and definitely the one with the ugliest scowl.

"But now we have demon-girl's friends!" said Sam. "The Shining Demon will bestow upon us everything we've ever wanted! We've got this, man!"

"We ain't got spit," said Bowsher. "Before you start making plans for what happens after, how about we figure out if she'd even be willing to exchange herself for the well-being of these good folk? What does everyone think of that little plan?"

The others glanced at each other, chastised.

"I guess that'd be okay," said Demer.

"You guess?" Bowsher said, marching up to him. "Is that what you said, you little pissant? You guess?"

Demer wilted. "I mean, you know, it's, it's a... It's what..."

Bowsher cupped his hand to his ear. "What's what? What's that? Speak up, asshole!"

"It's a good plan," Demer said quietly. "It's what we should do."

"You're damn right," Bowsher said abruptly, and turned to Kelly and the others. "I'm assuming one of you has her phone number?"

Kelly didn't say anything. Her friends remained quiet.

Bowsher sighed. "We're gonna start killing you. If you don't cooperate, we're gonna start killing you. We'll start easy, though. We'll kill the dog first."

Two, tied up next to Warrick, growled.

"You stay the hell away from him," Warrick said.

"And then we'll kill you," said Bowsher. "Then it'll be the chick with the boobs. Then Handsome here. Red, you're the last one we grabbed, so you're the last one to go. Let's see if you can hold out that long."

"We don't have her number," Ronnie said. "We barely know her."

"You're lying," said Sam. "What, you think we stumbled across you by accident? Ronnie? I been watching you. You're tight with the demon girl." His eyes flicked to Kelly. "This one, especially."

Bowsher nodded. "I heard about that, yes, indeed I did. Sam here is something of a Peeping Tom, see, and he reported back to us some hot and steamy lesbian action as seen through a window, oh *hell*, yeah. I am all for that, by the way. Live and let die, that's my motto. Sam, you okay with gay people?"

"Course," said Sam. "I'm from New York."

"I have no idea what that's got to do with anything, but fair enough. What about you, Demer? Demer? Oh, for Christ's sake, stop sulking and answer the goddamn question. Do you have a problem with the homosexual person?"

"No," Demer mumbled.

"Well, thanks for sharing. See that, Red? We are three progressive individuals. Goulder, however, is not nearly so culturally advanced as the rest of us. Goulder, what is your stance on homosexuality?"

"It's disgusting," said Goulder. "But lesbians aren't so bad."

"Hear that?" Bowsher said. "Even Goulder, who was raised by the most evil of Bible-bashing preachers in this great nation of ours, is onboard as far as lesbians are concerned. Y'all have his blessing, I daresay. But you gotta ask yourself a question here, Red. How do your dirty little fantasies stack up against the lives of you and your friends? Is she worth dying over? Is she worth watching your friends, and your dog, die painful deaths?"

"She doesn't have a phone," said Kelly.

"Bullshit."

"She doesn't. Phones are too easy to track."

"Every teenage girl in this goddamn country has a goddamn phone. From this point on, every lie you tell will be a bullet."

He nodded to Sam, who aimed his gun at Two.

"Do not harm my dog!" Warrick shouted.

Sam switched his aim, pressing the gun against Warrick's head. "You wanna go first? Fine with me."

"Warrick," said Ronnie.

"Do not threaten my dog," Warrick said through gritted teeth.

Bowsher waited a few seconds. Then, when nobody was shot, he nodded. "Well, okay then, back to what I was saying. The truth from this moment on, you get me?"

Kelly glared at him.

"Does demon girl have a phone?" Bowsher asked.

"Yes," said Kelly.

"And do you know her phone number?"

"Yes."

"Good," Bowsher said, smiling.

Demer walked up at that moment and put his gun to Bowsher's head and pulled the trigger, and Bowsher's head came apart in all sorts of stomach-churning ways.

"Holy crap!" Sam yelled.

Goulder stormed over. "What the hell did you do?"

"He shouldn't have said those things to me," Demer mumbled.

"So you shot him? *You shot him?*"

"He pissed me off," said Demer. "He disrespected me."

"He was yanking your chain, man! It's what he did!"

Demer shook his head. "There's no excuse for disrespect."

"Demer, you crazy bastard, you can't go around killing everyone that disrespects you, man!"

Demer narrowed his eyes, and Goulder held up his hands and backed off.

"Hey," said Goulder, "I am not disrespecting you right now. You have my utmost respect. I do not call you crazy bastard as an insult, or a slight. I use it as a term of endearment. That being said, you just shot and killed Bowsher for words that came out of his mouth in the heat of the goddamn moment."

"You gotta learn some impulse control," said Sam.

"That," Goulder said, nodding. "Impulse control. That's exactly it. I mean, I get it, man, I do. I'm a serial killer, just like you are. We've all got issues. But this is a very special night, one where all our dreams can come true. Now we made a deal, when we got here, that we would work together. The four of us. Four serial killers working towards a common goal. That is unheard of, my friend. We are breaking the mould. So you can't, and I say this with all due respect, you cannot go around shooting your partners in the goddamn head."

"He shouldn't have said those things," Demer muttered.

"I understand that."

"I was in a really good mood."

"I know, man. And he upset you. He ruined your good mood. But the three of us can only go forward if we trust each other. Do you trust us, Demer?"

"I guess."

"And we wanna trust you. We really do."

"You can."

"You just killed Bowsher, dude. Killed him. He was one of us."

"I just... I got confused," said Demer. "I got the red mist."

"Hey, brother, I know. When that red mist settles in, you're not in your right mind, are you? You can't be blamed for the things you do."

"He kept jabbing at me," said Demer. "Poking. You don't... you don't poke the bear."

"You do not," Goulder agreed. "You are the bear he should not have poked."

"I'm sorry I killed him."

"Hell, that's okay. Water under the bridge, you know? But, the thing is, we need your word that you're not gonna turn around and kill us over something stupid that we say."

"I promise."

"You do, huh? Sam, that okay with you?"

"Sure," said Sam. "Whatever."

"It's good with me, too. Demer, we're in this to the end, you get me? We're in this until all our dreams come true."

Demer nodded, an uncertain smile playing at the corners of his mouth.

"Good man," said Goulder. He took the gun from Demer's hand. "I'm just taking this as a precaution. We don't want you to get overexcited again, do we? You goddamn nutcase."

"Hey now," Demer said, and Goulder shot him in the heart.

Sam shrieked and hopped back on one leg as Demer fell, dead.

Goulder immediately turned. "You know why I had to do that."

"You killed him!"

"I had to."

"But what was all that you were saying about us having to trust each other? You made him trust you and you killed him!"

"Demer was unstable, Sam. Jesus, come on. How can we work with a guy who's liable to shoot us for saying the wrong thing at any moment? Did you trust him not to kill us?"

"No," said Sam, "but still... that was cold. He was one of us. Four serial killers working towards a common goal. Those were your words, man. Those were your words and then you lulled him into a false sense of security and—"

"I'm gonna need you to calm down, Sam."

"Or what? You gonna kill me, too?"

They stared at each other.

Goulder laughed. "No, I'm not gonna kill you. Course I'm not. You gonna kill me?"

"Hell, no."

"So we're okay? The two of us?"

"We're good."

"Bowsher and Demer... we didn't need them."

"Bowsher was all mouth," Sam agreed. "And Demer was nuttier than a squirrel's jockstrap. Better off without them."

"Truer words never spoken," said Goulder. "This is still our night."

"Yes, it is."

Goulder turned to Kelly. "Now then, the demon girl's number?"

Sam put his gun to the back of Goulder's head and pulled the trigger.

It went click.

Goulder turned to him slowly. "You. Dick."

The blood draining from his face, Sam spun and ran, and Goulder took careful aim. His finger tightened and the shot rang out and he caught Sam in the lower back and Sam grunted, staggered, reached behind himself like he was trying to scratch an itch, and then he fell over and lay still.

"Goddamn," Goulder whispered, then turned to Kelly and the others. "You try to build a community, you know? You try to form an alliance. This is what happens when you dream too big. I should've known. I should've known to keep my dreams manageable – like the Shining Demon granting me power. That I can do." He pointed the gun at Kelly's face. "Call your girlfriend."

He wasn't going to ask again, she could see it in his eyes. Awkwardly, because of her bound hands, Kelly took her phone from her pocket. "She might not answer."

"You better hope she does."

Kelly found Amber's number, pressed call. She put it on loudspeaker so Goulder could hear. The gun didn't waver. The phone rang. Each inquisitive dial tone was a countdown to that trigger being pulled. Kelly closed her eyes.

There was a crash and she jumped, thought for a millisecond that it was the gunshot that would end her life even while her brain was registering the sound of breaking glass. She looked up as a demon with wings – actual *wings* – landed through the east window. Goulder fired three times. Three times, the demon grunted, but his skin was too tough for the bullets to penetrate. He stalked forward with big teeth and a manic grin.

Goulder fell back against a desk and the demon lunged at him, mouth open to bite, and Goulder jammed his pistol into that mouth and pulled the trigger.

Maybe the bullet would have exited through the back of the demon's throat, leaving him injured but enraged, were it not for the skin that refused to break. As it was, the bullet must have ricocheted around in the skull and turned the demon's brain to grey-matter stew, because he collapsed immediately, one eye dripping from its socket.

Goulder straightened up, got his bearings, and chuckled. He turned and Kelly drove her elbow into his jaw. He staggered and Kelly dived for the gun, but he shoved her away. She fell back and heard him shriek and there was a crash and now she could hear Two, growling ferociously. She looked to see the dog's jaws clamped around the killer's wrist.

Ronnie grabbed the fallen gun and Warrick called off Two. Immediately, Goulder reared up and immediately Ronnie put him down again.

"You should really have tied our hands behind our backs," Ronnie told him.

Goulder looked up, his wrist mangled and blood pumping from his nose, and managed a helpless shrug. "You just... you just didn't look that dangerous."

"Yeah, well," Ronnie said, "appearances can be deceiving," and he clubbed Goulder into unconsciousness.

When he was done, and as he was paying the others the money he'd lost from a month-old bet, Two came over, sniffed Goulder's head, and then humped it to satisfaction.

53

SOMEWHERE IN DESOLATION HILL there was an explosion. It was followed by hollers and cheers and howls, lauding the destruction, revelling in it. Somewhere else a car crashed. Alarms went off. Gunshots rang out as cops fought to keep the murders to a minimum. Madness seeped through the night like a fog, wrapping its tendrils around everything and everyone. On one end of Main Street, beyond the square, there was a riot. On the other end, Amber stood facing her parents.

"This the part where you try to kill me again?" she asked.

Betty shared a sharp-toothed smile with her husband. "Are you liking this new attitude? I have to confess, I am."

"This kind of assertiveness would certainly have made for more dynamic family dinners," Bill said. "Instead, we had to sit there with a bored, uninterested lump who barely looked up from her phone."

"Always on those messageboards."

"Those forums."

"With her online friends."

"Well," said Amber, "at least I wasn't killing my own kids. What were their names, by the way? My brother and sister?"

"We called her Carolyn," said Betty. "We called him James."

"What were they like?"

"He was... unhappy," said Betty. "We didn't treat him particularly well. By the time Carolyn arrived, though, we had all agreed that the best way to approach what we were doing was to treat all of you children like real, actual people. We reasoned that you would be easier to handle if you were raised under the illusion of happiness."

"There were stumbling blocks," said Bill. "Carolyn proved to be just as difficult as James, in the end. But we learned. Then you came along, naïve and blinkered and so obsessed with your own self-imposed loneliness that you never for one moment questioned anything around you."

Betty smiled again. "The perfect daughter."

"Indeed she was."

"You can try to play on my insecurities and make me feel bad," said Amber, "but, once again, at least I'm not killing my own kids."

Betty laughed. "Feisty. I like it."

"And it actually makes me proud," Amber continued, "to know that my big sister and my big brother were problems for you. It helps me know them, just a little. I mean, really, are you so surprised that things have worked out the way they have? Alastair's dead. Grant's dead. Imelda betrayed you and helped me. When you look at it, and think about it, everything I've done to ruin you and your lives and everything you've worked for... well. I'm just carrying on the family tradition."

Her parents weren't smiling anymore.

Then something hit Amber right between the shoulder blades with the force of a wrecking ball, and she flew forward. Betty dodged out of the way as she went sprawling, and Amber didn't even have time to look back before someone was grabbing her hair.

"You little bitch!" Kirsty screamed, and slammed Amber's face on to the road. Through watering eyes, she glimpsed Kirsty stand, and then her boot came in. Scales formed, but even so the kick almost took her head off. Amber tried to roll away, tried to ward her off, tried to speak even, but her body was slow to respond and Kirsty wasn't giving her much of a chance. Another kick flipped her on to her back, maybe broke another rib, and now Kirsty was straddling her, her fists coming down like pistons.

Then those hands wrapped around her throat. Amber's scales formed, but it was no use, Kirsty was just too strong. At first, Amber thought this strength came from anger, but there were pieces of bloody meat in Kirsty's clenched teeth. Kirsty was sizzling after eating, but, unlike Amber, that strength hadn't been used up healing gunshot wounds.

Amber tried to slice through Kirsty's fingers, but her claws tapped uselessly against Kirsty's own scales. She blinked away tears, looking for help, holding her hand out to her parents who were standing there, looking at her. Laughing.

"He liked you," Kirsty snarled. "Grant actually liked you. And you kill him? *You kill him?*"

Darkness closed in on the edges of her vision. All Amber could see now was Kirsty, every muscle bunched and her eyes burning with hatred. Amber had no strength of her own left. Every moment that passed without oxygen sapped her reserves.

Bizarrely, her mind drifted to the second season finale of In The Dark Places. Balthazar was being drowned by his brother, submerged in the stream that ran behind his estate. Their eyes locked through the rushing water and Balthazar's final act of defiance was to flip Gideon the bird. It was a good final act. Iconic even. Back when Amber had a decent phone, that image was her wallpaper.

Weakly, Amber gave Kirsty the finger, stuck it right in front of her face, in honour of the greatest show ever put on TV.

But instead of ignoring it and continuing to choke her, as Gideon had – which had led to months of online speculation as to whether or not Balthazar was truly dead – Kirsty's face twisted and she grabbed Amber's finger and wrenched it, nearly broke it, but Amber could actually cry out in pain now that she was able to breathe again.

Amber's other hand found a spot on Kirsty's right side that wasn't protected by scales, and she grew claws and slid those in. Kirsty's eyes widened and she gasped and moved and Amber threw her off, then rolled over, sucking in air, stumbling and then getting to her feet as Kirsty rose to her knees, clutching her side.

"I'm going to kill you," Kirsty said. "I'm going to rip your throat out."

"Now, Kirsty, just wait a moment," said Bill. "I want you to think about this. Our plans are a tad up in the air right now, agreed?"

"Screw your plans!"

"We need to talk to Amber. That's all. We need her in order to find a solution to all this. We need her, for the moment, alive."

Kirsty stared, incredulity momentarily overtaking her rage. "She killed Grant," she said, like she was explaining it to four-year-olds.

"We realise that," said Betty. "And we know we're asking a lot."

"She dies now," Kirsty said, turning back to Amber. "She dies right now."

Kirsty started to lunge, but there was suddenly someone behind her, holding her in place with a grip she couldn't break. It was Glen, it was dreadfully pale Glen, and Amber only had time to glimpse his dreadfully pale face before he clamped his mouth down on Kirsty's neck.

She stiffened, tried to cry out, but nothing came, and blood started trickling to her collarbone as Glen drank. Bill and Betty stared, too shocked to move for a few seconds. Then Bill rushed forward, and Betty followed, and Glen wrapped his arms around Kirsty, turned his dead eyes on Amber for a moment, and then took Kirsty up with him, and they vanished into the night sky.

54

FOR A LONG MOMENT, nothing was said.

"There's something you don't see every day," Bill muttered.

Betty grabbed Amber, hurled her off her feet and she smashed through a sheet of plywood and the store window it was put up to protect. She hit the ground and rolled and lay in the dark for a moment, getting really sick of people throwing her all over the place.

Bill and Betty stepped into the travel agency office after her.

"You have a vampire friend, do you?" Betty asked. "Not smart, sweetheart. You can't trust them."

"You mean like I can trust you?" Amber said as she got up. Glass fell from her hair.

"We're not having this discussion right now," Betty said. She was a mere silhouette against the street lights outside. "There are two keys that will take us to Naberius. A shapeshifter has one of them – we'll leave it with him. Your little friend Austin vanished with the other. Where would he have gone?"

Amber frowned. "Did he use it? The key, did he use it?"

"He used it," said Bill. "Where did it take him?"

Amber sagged against a desk and shook her head.

"Amber, where did it take him?"

She looked up. "Naberius needed a sacrifice to set off Hell Night."

"So?" said Betty. "What does...? Oh."

"He's dead?" Bill asked. "The little brat got himself killed? What happens to the key?"

"It's probably still down there," said Amber. "Looks like your plan is screwed, *Dad*. You may as well start running again."

"Don't talk to your father in that tone," said Betty.

Amber couldn't help it. She laughed.

"Well, there appears to be only one way of salvaging the situation," Bill said. "We have to bring her to Astaroth."

Betty looked at him. "You don't think he'll find out we tried to betray him?"

"I think he already knows, but, if we present her to him on a silver platter, he may overlook our... eagerness."

"I always hated when you did that," said Amber. They looked at her, waiting for an explanation. "Talking about me like I wasn't there. It made me feel invisible."

"Childhood is a difficult time," Bill said dismissively.

Betty touched her husband's arm and he turned, and they all looked out through the broken window as a demon with skin the colour of moonlight staggered into view and dropped, gasping, to his knees.

And then a Hound appeared behind him.

Bill and Betty ducked down and Amber dived behind the desk. She waited a moment, then peeked out as the Hound, big and bearded with tattoos on his bare arms, laid a hand on the demon's shoulder. The demon screeched, his body locked in agony. The Hound's hand glowed and the demon started to sizzle. Steam rose from his skin, his eyes, his mouth...

He was being burned from the inside out.

The screech was cut off. The demon sighed and died, and fell forward, and the Hound turned his head, looked right through the window.

Suddenly Bill was grabbing Amber and hauling her to her feet. "We have her!" he called. "We have her for you! We did as Astaroth commanded!"

Amber tried to pull away, but Betty smacked her across the face, and when her thoughts managed to rearrange themselves into some form of coherence she was already being dragged out on to the street.

The Hound stood waiting, and when she was close enough he reached for her – and for Bill.

Amber jerked rigid at his touch, so fast that she almost snapped her own neck. She screamed, was only dimly aware of Bill's screams adding to hers. Her body burned. Every nerve ending was on fire. She could feel her insides starting to boil.

Then it all went away and Amber dropped to the ground, gasping, the pain a memory, the heat fading as fast as it had arrived. Bill was beside her, shaking his head, trying to stand, trying to help his wife, who was dragging the Hound away from them. The Hound twisted, grabbed Betty's throat, and slammed her to the road. Before his hand could start glowing, Bill charged into him and they went tumbling.

Grimacing, Amber got up. She watched her parents fight the Hound, watched them slash and strike and scramble up when they were knocked down. Then all of a sudden the Hound was coming for her and Amber's eyes widened and she ducked his grab and raked her claws across his face.

His sunglasses fell and the Hound snarled. She recognised him. It was the one who had broken his own neck to get at her in the forest.

He lunged at her and Bill grabbed him and Betty came in low, ripped the Hound's kneecap away with one bloody swipe. The Hound dropped to one knee and Betty seized his arm and Bill secured the other one, and Amber stepped forward and thrust her hand through his beard and dug her nails into the meat of his throat.

Then she tore it out.

The Hound made a gurgling sound and her parents released him. Both hands went to try to stem the flow of blood, but it was no use. He fell forward on to his hands and knees, then dropped to the ground and Bill stomped on his head until it splintered into mush.

The sound of a motorcycle made Amber turn, and a single headlight lit up all three of them. Another Hound. Jesus Christ, another one.

The bike stopped and the light cut off, and now Amber could see the Hound astride the machine, watching them.

Her parents ran. They didn't say anything, didn't even try to talk their way out of it. They just spun on their heels and ran.

Amber allowed herself a short moment of pleasure at the sight of them fleeing, then looked back at the Hound and felt her insides go cold. He got off the bike. Walked up to her.

She flew at him and then a gunshot rang out and she stumbled as the Hound keeled over backwards, a hole in his head. She turned, expecting to see Milo walking up.

Chief Novak approached, that demonic grin stretching across

his face as his gun drifted in her direction. "On your knees. Hands behind your head."

"Seriously?" she said. "I can't catch one break? I can't get a minute without someone new trying to kill me?"

"Apparently not," said Novak.

Amber looked down the barrel of his gun, and did as he'd instructed.

"This is your doing, I presume," he said. "Endangering a whole town to save yourself."

The Hound moved, the hole in his head already healed. He sat up, and Novak shot him in the temple and he flopped back down.

"The Shining Demon himself could just walk on in here and there would be nothing we could do to stop him," Novak said. "For what? So you could prolong your life for another few weeks? He was always going to find a way to kill you. It was inevitable. You wouldn't be able to run forever."

"I don't care about forever," Amber muttered. "Just about right now."

"Now? Now I kill you. With the mayor dead, and you dead, maybe the rest of the Hounds will back off, though I doubt it. Not after this." Novak holstered his gun, hunkered by the Hound, and gripped him under the chin. His nails grew long and cut into the meat, and with some difficulty he pulled the head off. He straightened up and tossed it away. "But I have to try, don't I? This is my town. I have a duty to protect it."

Then she heard it, the sound, and she looked to the junction, hope flaring in her chest. It built and built and then the Charger roared across the intersection.

And it was gone again.

Amber sagged, and looked back up at Novak.

"Unfortunate," he said. "I would've really liked to have seen who was fastest on the draw."

"It would've been Milo," Amber said. "He reads cowboy books."

And then, screeching round the corner, the beast of black metal, the Charger, with its red headlights and its engine fuelled by the souls of the dead. It braked, and the engine cut off, and the door creaked wonderfully as Milo climbed out.

He took off his jacket, threw it on the back seat, and started walking towards them.

It was almost odd to see someone not in their demon form, but here he was, tall and mean and looking like someone had just kicked his dog.

Novak reverted to normal, probably to keep things fair, but he kept that smile on his face. His hand hovered by his holstered gun. "Mr Sebastian," he called, widening his stance, "you are right on time. Amber tells me you read westerns. It might not be high noon, but I'm sure you can appreciate—"

Amber lunged, flattening her hand against Novak's holster. Immediately, he tried to draw, but the gun caught, and Milo had already fired two shots into his chest. Novak fell to one knee, gasping.

He coughed. Blood sprayed. His chin dipped to his chest, but he raised his eyes to Milo as he reached them. "You cheated..."

Milo ignored him and frowned at Amber. "You okay?"

"Barely."

Beside them, Novak fell forward, his eyes wide and unseeing.

"Barely okay will do for now," said Milo, and started walking back to the Charger. "Let's get going."

55

VIRGIL'S HOUSE WAS DARK, but he didn't need the lights on to see.

He undressed to just his socks and underpants, and opened his wardrobe. Sliding the shirts and slacks off to one side, he took the garment bag from the rail and laid it carefully on the bed. He moved slowly, methodically, the way he used to back in the old days, just before he went on set.

The costume, he'd once said to Johnny Carson, informed the character as much as any research. Buttoning those buttons, tying that tie, tilting that hat just right – they were all part of the mask of the character. Except, in the case of the Shroud, the costume also came with an *actual* mask.

He dressed. The shirt first. Then the tie. The trousers and shoes. Vest. Cufflinks.

He became aware of Javier standing in the doorway. "What the hell are you doing?"

"It's not over yet," said Virgil, not turning round.

"I know," said Javier. "And I repeat, what the hell are you doing?"

"Preparing."

"For what? A reunion show?"

"You feel it, too, don't you? The Narrow Man is coming."

"Are you professing to be psychic all of a sudden?"

"Warrick told me about the Demon Road."

"Yeah? Where's it go?"

"No, it's not an actual road. It links people, places..."

"Oh God, is this one of those 'road of the mind' things they used to talk about all the time in the sixties?"

"It's how the world works," said Virgil. "That's how I understand it, anyway. Whether it's coincidence or fate or destiny or divine intervention, we're all connected. Just being here, right now, will have connected you to forces beyond your comprehension for the rest of your life."

"Seeing as how, these days, telephones are beyond my comprehension, that's not too difficult. Why on earth are you wearing those clothes? If the Narrow Man does show up, you're going to be letting the others handle him, aren't you? Virgil?"

"They've got their hands full."

"You're not the Shroud, Virgil."

Virgil put on his jacket. "Someone has to be."

"There!" said Javier, jabbing a finger at him. "That is exactly the sort of line you'd utter right before an act break! For God's sake, you're an old man. You understand me? We can talk and talk about how we're still relevant, how we still matter – and you know what? We're one hundred per cent right about both those things. But we *are* old. Our bodies are slower and our minds are clogged with so much experience that they're starting to spring leaks. Your mind, Virgil, in particular has started to spring some pretty major ones."

"He killed a boy," Virgil said. "The Narrow Man."

Javier nodded. "Yes. He killed a bully. You heard what Austin told us. A thug. A psychopath in waiting."

"Still a boy, Javier. In many ways, still a child. Those others – Ronnie and Kelly and Linda and Warrick, Milo and Amber – yes, they're young and strong and they do this sort of thing a lot... but they didn't prevent that, did they? It slipped away from them, and the Narrow Man killed a child."

"It's not your responsibility."

"I saw Oscar Moreno kill my neighbour. I've known who the Narrow Man is for the past week. If it's not my responsibility, then whose is it?"

"I... I don't know, Virgil. But you can't do this. He'll kill you."

"If he does, I'll be sure to take him with me."

"No, you won't. He's a monster. He'll kill you without thinking about it. You won't get near him."

"But I'll try," said Virgil, folding the mask and putting it in his pocket. "I'll try, goddammit."

Javier shook his head and walked away, and Virgil picked up the hat, but didn't put it on. The clothes felt good. Maybe a little tighter in some places, maybe a little looser in others, but they felt good. Felt right.

He visited his collection of props and costumes from the show, and very carefully folded a coat and slipped it into an overnight bag. Then he did another check of the windows and doors, and Linda came looking for him.

"You're looking dapper," she said.

"One does one's best."

She smiled. "Milo's back."

He nodded. "I'll let him in."

He left the overnight bag in the kitchen and went into the

garage, waited for the Charger to pull all the way in, and then he shut the garage door. Amber got out first and he stepped back, quite involuntarily. This was the closest he'd got to her when she was in demon form, and she was quite intimidating. Still, he was glad to see her.

"That's everyone," he said when Milo got out of the car. "Ronnie and the others got back a few minutes after you headed off again."

"Is Kelly with them?" Amber asked.

"Yes, indeed, all present and accounted for, dog included."

Amber nodded, pleased with the answer, but looking conflicted nonetheless. After a moment's hesitation, she changed back into the normal girl with the bright smile Virgil had come to know. She went to walk past him and he hugged her.

"Oh," she said. "Um. Okay. I like your suit."

"Thank you." He gave her a squeeze, then stepped away. "We were worried about you," he said. "Kelly, especially."

Amber chewed her lip.

"Ah, and I have this for you," he said, taking the brass key from his pocket and handing it over. "Austin had the presence of mind to keep it on him. Clever young man."

"Yeah," said Amber, only half listening to him.

"Into the house, you two," Virgil said. "It's cold in here and I'm an old man."

He ushered them through the door, into the warmth.

"Stay away from the windows," he reminded them. "And no lights, please. If any neighbours are around, they'll come knocking, and they won't be gentle."

They headed for the dark living room, smelling hot chocolate and coffee before they'd even reached it. Austin sat in one of the armchairs. Linda and Javier shared the couch and Warrick sat on the floor, cuddling up with Two. Ronnie stood by the window, peeking through the curtains occasionally, and Kelly was on her feet the moment Amber walked in. Everyone had a steaming mug either in their hands or close by.

Kelly and Amber looked at each other like they had something important to say that neither of them could voice. Virgil shrugged to himself. Young people.

"All right then," he said, "here's how things stand at the moment. Mayor Jesper and Chief Novak are dead. Some of us may have reached an accord with the other police officers, but don't count on it lasting. The demon in chains—"

"Naberius," said Linda.

"—Naberius, thank you, he has had his sacrifice – a classmate of Austin's."

"He wasn't a classmate," Austin muttered.

"One of the demons after Amber is also dead," said Virgil.

"Two of them, actually," said Amber. "There's only my parents now, and I'm pretty sure they've already left town."

Virgil nodded. "Okay then. And how many Hounds do we know are dead? Kelly, there's the one Milo killed, and the one you saw hanged. That's two."

"Novak killed one," said Amber, "and I killed one with my parents. Family time, I guess. I saw a bunch of demons go after another one, but I don't know if they managed to kill him."

"So there might be one left," said Virgil. "Unless anyone saw anything else? No? You're sure?" He sighed. "Okay then, so we possibly have one more Hound at large."

"And the Narrow Man," said Javier.

"And him, yes. Plus the fact that it is barely midnight, and

426

Hell Night has just got started. I think we can all agree to stay here and keep our heads down, yes? Sunrise is a little before five. If we can hide here until then, we shall all see the morning."

"What if the Hound comes for me?" Amber asked.

"The Hounds can be stopped," said Milo. "We've seen that."

"They can be stopped by overwhelming force," Amber responded. "A gang of demons will stop one of them. A load of guns will stop one of them. We don't have either."

"But we have each other," said Warrick. When everyone frowned at him, he wilted. "Sorry. I wasn't listening. What are we talking about?"

"Goddammit," Ronnie said from the window. "He's found us."

There was a scramble as everyone went to look. Everyone except Virgil. And Javier.

Ignoring Javier for the moment, Virgil addressed the others. "The Narrow Man?"

"Walking up the middle of the road towards us," said Linda, being very careful not to move the curtain. "Like he's out for a midnight stroll."

"Can he see us?" Warrick asked. "I feel like he can see us."

"But Hell Night has already started," said Kelly. "Why is he coming after us?"

"We got his boss killed," said Amber. "Maybe he's loyal." Her voice brightened. "So maybe we don't have to fight him. Maybe, if we tell him who actually killed Jesper, he'll go after my parents."

"He's after me," Austin said softly. They looked at him. He swallowed. "When he took me, he said the town had decided. He said whoever gets the most votes has to die."

"But the vote doesn't mean anything anymore."

"It does to him," said Virgil.

Milo loaded his gun. "We'll stop him."

"I should run," Austin said.

"You're staying with us," said Ronnie.

"Hey, hey," said Linda, "we have another development."

Now Virgil could hear it – an approaching motorcycle.

"Oh great," said Warrick. "We get the Narrow Man and the last Hound? Seriously? At the same time? We're done. Game over, man. Game over."

Ronnie frowned. "Where'd the Narrow Man go?"

"He's hiding," said Kelly. "Jesus. The Hound scared him away."

"Everyone down," Milo said, and Virgil watched them all move smoothly away from the window. A single headlight washed by, and the sound of the bike slowly peaked and started to recede.

Amber frowned. "Is he slowing down?"

"He could be getting more attuned to the town," said Milo. "If that's the case, he might be closing in on your location."

"Could you just chill?" Warrick asked. "He's riding away, isn't he? He has no idea you're here, Amber. None."

Then the bike got louder again. The Hound had swung round.

"Oh, for God's sake," said Warrick.

Then the sound of the bike cut off.

In the distance, gunfire and car alarms.

Linda crawled to the window, peeked out.

"See anything?" Ronnie asked.

"The bike," she whispered. "Ah shit. He's on foot."

The tension in the house twisted up another few notches. Only Milo seemed unperturbed.

Virgil beckoned to Austin and Austin came over. Virgil clamped his hands on the boy's shoulders. "No matter what happens," he said, "you stay by my side, you understand? You do not run off. The only time you run off is when I either tell you to or I'm too dead to tell you. You got that?"

"Yes, sir," said Austin.

Two began to growl.

Milo put his finger to his lips, and walked slowly to the front door, his gun held in a two-handed grip. He stopped before it, stood there, then reached out to open it.

The door flew off its hinges and crashed into him, he went down, the gun went flying, and the Hound stepped over him as casually as a man steps over a dog sleeping on his porch.

Amber became a demon again and she let out a roar and ran at him, and the Hound caught her by the throat and took her off her feet, slamming her into the wall. He took a step back and swung her into the opposite wall. The others ran to help, but Virgil backed away, keeping Austin behind him. His heart beat a dangerous rhythm that sent darts of pain shooting along his left arm. His knees buckled and he would have fallen if it wasn't for Austin, keeping him upright.

He shook his head, unable to speak, and clutched Austin's shoulder. He could see through to the kitchen. Kelly crouched there, holding out her arm. Virgil nodded, pushed Austin in her direction. Austin hesitated, but the shouts and the crashes spurred him on.

While the heroes fought the Hound, Virgil struggled to draw breath. He saw Milo charging the Hound from behind. Saw Warrick go down and Linda getting back to her feet. Saw Javier in the corner, looking startled at all the violence.

It was clear that the Hound wasn't going to be beaten. Ronnie was already unconscious, or worse, and now Milo joined him.

"Hey!" Amber shouted.

The carnage paused.

"You're after me, aren't you?" Amber continued. She had claws for hands. Virgil didn't know how he hadn't noticed that before. "Then come on. One last chase, asshole."

And she turned and jumped straight through the window.

It was an impressive exit, and in response the Hound threw Milo down and strode to the door. For a wonderful moment, Virgil thought he was going to follow her – but he stopped, and turned back, and Virgil had the sneakiest suspicion that he wasn't as dumb as he looked. Why give chase, after all, when he could make his target come to him?

The Hound pressed a fingernail to his wrist and sliced. Blood flowed, dripping from his forearm in a steady stream, and he walked in a circle around Milo.

"Hey," said Javier, "what's he doing? Hey, you! Stop doing that!"

The Hound easily ignored the shouts of an old man, and when the circle was complete the blood began to steam, and then it caught fire—

—and in that instant both Milo and the Hound disappeared.

"Amber!" Linda screamed. "Get back here!"

Virgil forced himself to stand. It wasn't over yet.

Amber ran back in. "Where is he? Where the hell is he?"

"He disappeared," said Javier. "He took Milo with him. Just disappeared."

Amber stared at him for a long moment. "Shit," she said, and bolted. Virgil heard her kicking open the door to the garage.

Linda limped over to Ronnie and checked his pulse and Two ran over to Warrick, started licking his face.

"I'm okay, boy," Warrick mumbled. "I'm okay."

Amber ran back in, tugging the stopper out of a large leather pouch. She poured a circle of black powder around herself, then threw down the pouch and tapped her pockets. "A match!" she shouted. "Something!"

Warrick pushed himself up on to his elbow and dug a hand into his pocket. Coins and tissues and lint fell as he tossed her a cheap lighter. Amber caught it, flicked it, put the lighter to the powder and the powder went up, the fire looping in both directions, and she straightened as they met and then she disappeared.

Warrick blinked. "Everyone saw that, right?"

Linda folded her jacket, put it under Ronnie's head. "How's everyone else? Javier?"

"I'm good," said Javier. "But Virgil looks like he's having a heart attack."

"I'm fine," Virgil said gruffly.

"Kelly," said Linda, "how about you?"

From the far corner, Kelly groaned and Virgil's eyes widened.

His legs were numb, his feet dead weights, but he forced himself to walk, to hurry to the kitchen. The back door stood open. He plunged into the cold night air, managed to get to the gate in his fence without toppling over. The gate swung open and he stayed there for a moment, breathing, then plunged onwards.

On the trail behind his house, he saw Austin being led away by someone who looked just like Kelly. But of course she wasn't wearing Kelly's clothes. Virgil had missed that the first time.

"Austin!" he shouted. "Run!"

The Narrow Man, still wearing Kelly's face, whipped his head round and Austin took that moment to tear free of his grip and run into the woods.

The thing-that-wasn't-Kelly looked at Virgil, gave him a smile, and followed the boy.

56

Amber had been here before.

Astaroth's castle, with walls of stone that reached high beyond the wooden rafters, high into the darkness and the emptiness above. Here, the cold air danced to the distant symphony of screams and sobbing that rattled the stained-glass windows, in which each scene was another depiction of the depraved, the wanton, the butchered. Tapestries hung from those stone walls, different from those she had seen last time she had been here. Terrible splendours, new and fresh and eager to offend in their explicit extravagance.

No welcoming committee this time. No sign of the ungendered thing called Fool. Perhaps her arrival had gone unnoticed. She hoped so. This castle was one of many in the kingdom over which the Blood-dimmed King ruled, and as such it had its rules which could not be bent, bypassed or broken. It struck Amber that hell, no matter its faults and its cruelties, was at the very least honest. She wondered if heaven was half as trustworthy.

One of the rules for visitors, and this was the rule that had been repeated to her the most, was that she should never, under any circumstances, step outside the circle. Ever.

So Amber took a deep breath, and stepped out of the circle.

When the walls didn't come crashing down upon her and she wasn't immediately cast down into the fiery pits, she hurried through the first doorway, and found herself in a winding corridor with narrow windows on one side. Beneath a coal-black sky, and across a forest of twisting, clutching, grasping trees, a vast city rose from the horizon. There was a palace at the centre of that city — she could see it from here. She could even appreciate the beauty found in its sharp edges and sinister angles. The palace of the Blood-dimmed King, no doubt.

The corridor split into three directions, but only one was wide enough for her to comfortably fit. Even so, as she made her way through, her shoulders began tipping off the walls, again and again, until she was moving sideways, then grimacing and squeezing further.

There was an opening ahead. She just had to squeeze a little more. Just a little...

And then she was stuck.

The wall in front crushed against her belly and chest. The wall behind crushed against her ass. She could extend her left arm out into the opening, but she couldn't even turn her head without jamming her horns. It was hard to breathe. Amber tried to suck her belly in, but she had no purchase with which to move. She couldn't go forward or back. Panic began to claw at her mind.

"Hello," said a voice.

Her eyes widened. "Fool? Fool, is that you?"

A silhouette appeared in the gap ahead. "Caught," said Fool. "If the Master knew it'd be this easy, he wouldn't have sent the Hounds after you. All he needed was a tight space."

"Help me."

"Why?"

"I'm stuck."

"No – why would I help you?"

She did her best to smile. "Because... because I'll help you in return. I'll take you away from here."

"Away?"

"I'll bring you back with me."

"Away from here? But the castle is my home."

"Then what do you want?" she asked. "Tell me what you want and I'll do it. But first get me out of here."

"Hmmm," said Fool. "I don't know. You're a tricky one, Amber Lamont. You gave me Edgar Spurrier and told me it was Gregory Buxton."

"I'm sorry about that, I really am."

"The Master was not pleased with me. The Master punished me."

"I'm so sorry."

"The Master did not want Edgar Spurrier. He let me have him. I changed him. He wouldn't stop talking so I gave him a new name. He is Bigmouth now."

"Edgar *did* talk a lot."

"It's nice," said Fool. "Having a pet is nice."

"I'm glad you like him," Amber said. "It's always good when people enjoy their presents."

"Bigmouth was a present? For me?"

"Of course," said Amber. "And you like him, don't you?"

"Bigmouth is ever so much fun!"

"Good," said Amber. "I'm so glad. But you owe me now. You get that, right? I brought Bigmouth here for you, and now you have to repay the favour. That's how presents work. You understand?"

"Yes."

"Take my hand, Fool. Pull me out."

Fool's hands closed around Amber's and she was pulled and tugged and she didn't budge.

"Come closer," she said. "Closer."

When Fool was close enough, she grabbed what clothes she could and pulled. Fool made some strangled noises, but she was dragging herself through now, inch by inch, and then she pushed Fool back, reached over with her other arm, gripped the edge of the wall and kept going. Her head was out. She gasped and sucked in a breath and heaved again and stumbled out into the corridor beyond.

"Holy crap," she said, raking her claws through her hair. "Holy crap."

She got herself back under control as Fool stood. The patchwork robe it wore was torn where she'd grabbed it.

"Sorry about that," said Amber, and Fool turned to her. Its bald head was caked in ash-grey foundation and its thin lips were hidden somewhere in that smear of red lipstick. All of this Amber had seen before. Its teeth of broken glass that rose from bloody gums no longer shocked her. Instead, it was the thick shards of glass that had been plunged into each eye that now made her gasp.

"Fool," she whispered, "what happened to you?"

Fool tilted its head, then said, "Oh! The eyes! Yes, this was the Master's punishment for me being fooled by Amber Lamont." It giggled. "Fool being fooled."

"The Shining Demon did this to you? Did it hurt?"

"Obviously."

"Oh Jesus..."

"Don't worry. Bigmouth makes up for it. Having a pet is nice."

"Fool, a Hound arrived here a few minutes ago. He had someone with him. Where did they go?"

"It doesn't matter."

"Yes, it does, Fool. It matters to me. I have to find my friend."

"No, Amber Lamont," said Fool, "it doesn't matter which way they went. All ways lead to the same place."

So Amber started running.

The corridors here were wider. Much wider. She turned corners and ran on. In some corridors, the screams were so loud that she expected to burst into a torture chamber. In others, they were so faint it was like she was leaving them behind. But there were always new screams. That was the one constant in the land of the Blood-dimmed King.

She passed through junction after junction, chose a direction at random, and ran on. The geography of the castle was impossible. She was never in the same place twice and yet she should have been, she should have criss-crossed and doubled back, but every step she ran was a step on to fresh ground. She was running through another junction of corridors when movement caught her eye. She followed it, moving quickly but quietly now, catching up to her quarry.

Then she saw him.

In the land of the Blood-dimmed King, the Hound's true form was revealed. He was bigger, bulkier, his hair longer and thicker, his skin a deep mottled brown. His heavy jaw jutted awkwardly, like it had been repeatedly broken and badly reset.

Sharp teeth strained against his lips. The Hound's nose had melted back into his face, and his eyes were a simmering yellow. He dragged Milo by the ankle. Milo was too unconscious to care.

Amber spent too long trying to figure out a plan of attack. Before she'd even looked around for a weapon, the Hound was entering a grand hall of mirrored walls, at the centre of which was a throne, and, atop that throne, Astaroth, the Shining Demon.

Fierce orange light burned from within him and, reflected in the thousands of mirrors, lit up the whole hall. Upon his translucent skin were islands of black, like missing jigsaw pieces.

Amber's time was up. The moment for sneakiness had passed.

She sprinted after the Hound, intending to shove him aside, grab Milo, and run. But he saw her coming – of course he did, how could he not? – and he turned, catching her with a swinging arm. She had thought the Hounds had been strong on the streets of Desolation Hill – but here, this Hound's strength was something else entirely.

She flew across the room, hit the ground, and her broken ribs jangled and she screamed so much she thought she might pass out.

The Shining Demon gazed at her, and smiled.

"There you are," he said.

57

EDISON'S SHARD JUTTED OUT high over the old quarry like an accusatory finger, pointing to the mountains in the west. When Virgil had first moved into town, he had held the notion that the highest point in Desolation Hill had been named after Thomas Edison and his work with electricity. He'd been living there five years before someone, he couldn't remember who, told him that no, it was named after Edison Samuels, a young man who had hurled himself from its heights a hundred years earlier. As Virgil climbed, using the trees for purchase, he couldn't help but re-evaluate his assumptions about young Mr Samuels. Perhaps it hadn't been a maudlin disposition that had sent him plummeting to his doom – perhaps it had simply been an unwillingness to live with the things he had done during Hell Night – or the things he was about to do.

Virgil leaned his shoulder against a tree and angrily sucked in air. His body was failing him. His stupid old muscles weren't up to the task anymore. His lungs were capable of only the shallowest of breaths. His legs burned and his hands shook, and his heart...

He pushed himself upright. His heart could wait. His pain

and discomfort could wait. There was a boy up here and a monster chasing him. The ailments of an old man meant nothing compared to that.

He heard a shout. There. Beyond the trees. Movement.

He adjusted the overnight bag on his shoulder, and moved onwards. One foot in front of the other. Funny how difficult the simple things could get, like walking. And breathing.

He reached the last of the trees. Austin had backed himself on to Edison's Shard, where the wind alone might have been enough to pluck him away. Stalking him was the Narrow Man, his too-wide smile spreading across his face.

Virgil fumbled in his pocket with shaking hands, pulled out the mask and used it to wipe the sweat from his forehead. Then he looked at it, at the empty eyeholes, and, while a part of him felt ridiculous, another part, a larger part, felt right. Felt good.

He pulled on the mask, and it fitted just like it had forty years ago. Then he put on his hat, tilted it just right, like all the best crime-fighters did, and straightened himself the hell up.

"Hey," he shouted. His voice was lost to the wind, so he shouted louder. "Hey! Come and pick on someone your own size!"

Javier was right. Virgil's dialogue was pretty dreadful without a scriptwriter.

But at least he'd got the Narrow Man's attention away from the boy. Virgil walked forward towards the cliff edge, putting every ounce of strength he had into pretending his body wasn't about to fail at any moment.

"This was what you wanted, wasn't it?" Virgil asked. His words sounded wrong. Thick. His mouth was dry. "You wanted a showdown, didn't you? The Shroud versus Insidio, one last time? Well, here you go."

440

Virgil stood his ground while his adversary moved closer and loomed over him. Up close and personal, the Narrow Man's eyes were bottomless pits leading straight to hell. There was an emptiness in there, a void, that would have turned Virgil's skin cold were it not for the sharp wind that had already succeeded in that regard.

But those eyes also looked into Virgil, and, as much as he tried to fight it, Virgil knew what the Narrow Man saw in there. He saw a faded actor and an old man. He saw a bad heart and all the pills that were needed to keep that heart ticking. He saw a shrivelled presence, the stooped shadow of the man he had once been.

The smile faded on his adversary's face, and settled into a thin, wide line. The Narrow Man turned away, walked back towards Austin.

Virgil was failing.

He broke into a run, a desperate, old man's run that nonetheless took him past the Narrow Man and out on to the Shard, because he was such a non-threat that the Narrow Man didn't bother to stop him. Gasping, Virgil stood in front of Austin as a trembling, decrepit shield. They were close to the very point of the Shard now. There was mud beneath his feet. Virgil tried not to look to either side, tried not to look down. He must be 300 feet up. The wind plucked at his clothes. He focused on the task at hand.

Fine. So Javier was right. Virgil needed a scriptwriter. So what? His body might have been failing, but his mind was as sharp as ever.

"This is where it ends!" Virgil called out. "This is where I put a stop to your decades of evil!"

The Narrow Man froze, listening to words that had been written years earlier, that had been first spoken when the cameras rolled for the final episode of *When Strikes the Shroud*.

"For too long you have walked this earth," Virgil continued, "destroying the lives of those you meet. No more, you hear me? No more!"

The Narrow Man came closer, the smile on his face again, and Virgil gave him a smile back beneath his mask.

"Do an old actor a favour, why don't you? You say you're a fan? Here's your chance to be part of it all."

Virgil threw him the overnight bag. It was unzipped, and gaped open when it fell. The Narrow Man reached down slowly, pulled out the velvet frockcoat.

"That's the real thing," Virgil told him. "The actual coat worn by Javier Santorum when he played the part of Insidio. There were three. Javier has one, one was ruined during filming, and I snagged the last. You took the face of my arch-enemy. I think it's time you *became* my arch-enemy, what do you say?"

The Narrow Man smiled. He held the coat out in front of him, admiring it, and then with a flourish he twirled it as he shapeshifted. He slipped an arm into the sleeve and he got a little shorter, a little broader. He reached back and slipped in the other arm and his skin became awash with colour and black hair grew from his scalp. He shrugged the coat up on to his shoulders and his features rearranged themselves and became those of Oscar Moreno, otherwise known as Javier Santorum, otherwise known as Ernesto Insidio.

"It is an honour," said Insidio, actually talking in that rasp that Javier adopted for the part, "to face you in your final moments."

"Yeah, yeah," Virgil said, backing away a little more on the

442

muddy outcrop as Insidio neared. He reached behind, his fingers tapping Austin's sleeve, making sure he was in place. Insidio took another step.

Virgil met him with a jab. It rocked Insidio, made him slip in the mud, set him up perfectly for the haymaker, but now it was Virgil's turn to slip and his fist clipped Insidio's chin instead of putting him on his back.

Still, for something that would appear to be the second last punch he'd ever throw, it *had* been a decent jab. He'd have to be happy with that.

Insidio had an answer to it, of course. He caught Virgil in the side with a punch that, Virgil was pretty sure, broke his ribs. All the air rushed from his lungs and the right side of Virgil's body now seemed to be made entirely of sharp pieces. Virgil stumbled, gasping with the pain, and Insidio hit him again and Virgil's hat flew off, vanished over the edge into darkness.

He couldn't see. His mask had become dislodged. He'd forgotten that used to happen during the action sequences. Scowling, he ripped it off, threw it straight into Insidio's face and then dived at him, tried to wrap his arms around him. But he slipped again and dropped to his knees as Insidio staggered from his grip.

"Run!" Virgil shouted. "Run, Austin!"

Austin darted away from the tip of the Shard, passing Insidio while he was still regaining his balance. Virgil was suddenly acutely aware of the emptiness behind him. He took a glance, saw nothing but the darkness of the quarry. The freezing wind shot up the back of his shirt, making his jacket flutter like a cape.

Insidio turned away from Virgil, pointed at Austin as he stood there, on solid ground now and halfway to the trees, not wanting to abandon Virgil to his fate. He was a good kid.

"Don't go far," Insidio rasped. "I counted the votes. Tonight is your night to die."

Ignoring the pain in his side and the hammering in his chest and the ice that was travelling down his left arm, Virgil powered to his feet and grabbed his old enemy. He wrapped his arms around him and Insidio frowned and grunted, no longer enjoying the game, but Virgil didn't give him a chance to stop playing.

He turned, twirling them in a clumsy, mud-drenched dance until they teetered on the very tip of Edison's Shard, and Insidio's eyes widened as he realised what was about to happen.

Virgil threw himself over the edge, and took Insidio with him.

The fall was cold. Insidio shrieked and flailed, but didn't shapeshift. He didn't have time to become the Narrow Man again. He was stuck in this role he had assumed. Just like Virgil.

They plummeted, and Virgil smiled, and the darkness welcomed them.

58

IN THE MIRRORED HALL in the Shining Demon's castle, Amber curled into a ball, unable to breathe.

"I admit," Astaroth said, "you have surprised me. After all the promise you showed when you first started running, I never imagined you would simply return here of your own volition. For what? For the well-being of your friend? I was never going to harm him, Amber. He is not mine to harm."

Amber looked up to see Fool walking over to where Milo lay, a heavy chain in his hands.

"Let him go," Amber croaked.

Astaroth looked at her with his black eyes. "Your friend is being returned to Demoriel, the Demon that blessed him. He is no longer your concern."

Moving slowly, and feeling his way, Fool secured the chain around Milo's neck.

"You have me," Amber said, shaking her head. "Let him go."

"You can only bargain when you have something of equal value to offer," Astaroth said. "Your hands are empty, Amber."

Tears coming to her eyes, Amber pushed herself up on to

one elbow. She still wasn't breathing right. "Not his fault," she managed. "All mine."

"He helped you run."

"I asked him to. Please. I'll do anything."

Astaroth paused. "Interesting."

She seized on the interest in his voice. "Name it." She struggled to her feet. "Tell me what to do and I'll do it."

"You would agree to a bargain so readily?"

"I'll do anything."

He made a sound, an amused sound, like a laugh, but not quite. "You killed my representative," he said. "He had been most loyal. For a hundred years, he spoke with my voice on Earth. He was my eyes, my ears, my hands. He enacted my wrath, secured my vengeance, delivered my judgement. And you killed him."

She nodded. "What can I do? How do I make that up to you?"

"I am in need of a new representative."

Amber nodded again. "I can find him for you. Absolutely. Tell me where to start looking."

"You," said Astaroth, standing. "You will be my representative."

Amber blinked. "What?"

"You have cheated me. Evaded me. Insulted me. I sent the Hounds of Hell after you, and only one returned – and he could only manage to bring me your friend. You are proving yourself worthy of the position."

"But... but I can't be your representative," said Amber. "I don't... I'm not *bad*."

"Human morality is of little interest to me," Astaroth replied. "If you say no, your friend will be delivered to Demoriel, who most likely will devour his soul upon seeing him. And you I will torture, humiliate, and degrade. I will make you suffer for a hundred thousand years, or until I grow bored of your screams. Now what do you say to my offer?"

"What... what will it mean? What will I have to do?"

"Whatever I tell you. Your first act is a simple one – ensure that no harm befalls my brother. I want him in that cell for eternity."

"Do I have to... do I have to stay here?"

Astaroth smiled with cold amusement. "Your place is among the living. For now."

"And Milo goes free, right? You'll let him return with me?"

"Of course. But this is your final chance. Do you accept?"

"I... I accept," she said.

Astaroth smiled again. "Good. Unchain him, Fool."

Fool did as he was told.

"You may take him back with you when you are done," said Astaroth.

"When I'm done doing what?"

"Why, you eat of my flesh and drink of my blood, of course," said Astaroth, holding out his arm.

"Oh," said Amber.

Her legs wouldn't work right, but eventually she got them moving, and walked slowly to where the Shining Demon stood. He didn't say anything more, didn't offer further instructions, so she lightly took his arm and guided it towards her mouth.

She'd eaten Alastair. She'd eaten Benjamin. She'd eaten a dead man, and she'd eaten a man alive. She had crossed so far into the realms of unexpected behaviour that she'd thought there would be nothing she was not prepared to do. And yet taking this first bite...

She bit down slowly, her fangs sinking into Astaroth's surprisingly tender flesh. Golden blood spurted, filling her mouth with its sweetness, spilling down her throat. Her eyes fluttered closed and she held on to his arm with both hands now, her teeth cutting into the meat. Christ, his blood was amazing. Warmth spread from her throat, from her belly, outwards. It reached her ribs and the pain went away and she could feel them, she could actually *feel* them, begin to repair themselves. Cuts and bruises and breaks and fractures were all absorbed into the spreading warmth.

She pulled her mouth away slightly, chewed, swallowed, and it was dizzying. She'd never tasted anything like it. It was more than nourishing – it was more than intoxicating. It was pure pleasure. Her heart hammered in her chest. Her skin sizzled with electricity. She took another bite, ripped out a chunk of meat, swallowed, then clamped her mouth on his arm again. She moaned, down deep in her throat. Her left leg was shaking. She twisted a little, ploughing fresh furrows, drinking more blood. The pleasure was building. Rising. Jesus, it felt like...

She was going to explode. Wave after wave of sensation swept through her, stronger and stronger each time, and it built and built and finally there was nowhere left for it to go and the wave crested and she *did* explode, every single nerve ending singing out in rapturous harmony, every cell of her body dancing on fire and she cried out and her knees went and she lost her grip on his arm and she collapsed, gasping, to the stone floor.

Astaroth passed a hand over his mangled forearm, and his hand brought healing.

"You have eaten of my flesh," he said, "and you have drunk of my blood. You will be my voice on Earth. You will be my eyes, my ears, my hands. You will enact my wrath, secure my vengeance, and deliver my judgement. Stand now."

Slowly, Amber stood, watching her reflection in the mirrored walls as she did so.

She was taller. She was even taller and stronger than before. Her clothes strained to contain her. Her skin was still that glorious, glorious red, but now it positively shone. Her horns had grown, too. They were practically *antlers* now, majestic and proud. She was beyond magnificent. She was something else entirely.

"Kill the Hound," said Astaroth.

Amber dragged her gaze away from her reflection.

She was taller than the Hound now, even without her horns. His yellow eyes were wide. He growled, and stepped back. Astaroth ignored him, kept looking at her.

"What use have I for one Hound? His brothers failed me. He failed me. Kill him and I can start afresh."

Amber blinked, her mind slow to process the instruction. She noted the shock and fear on the Hound's strange face, saw the snarl of defiance that revealed the pointed, jagged teeth. She couldn't kill him, even if she'd wanted to. Her fingertips itched. He was too strong, too fierce. He'd knocked her to one side with a casual sweep of his arm. In this castle, in the domain of the Blood-dimmed King, he was too much. She was outmatched. And she wasn't a killer. She didn't just kill on command. A sharp pain jabbed at the space behind her eyes.

Not that he was innocent, of course. He was anything but. The Hound was a murderer, a monster who obeyed the order to kill without question. This Hound in particular had been the one who'd attacked her on the street, who'd dragged Milo behind his bike. If anyone deserved to be killed, it was him.

But she couldn't do it. He was bigger than her, stronger than...

No, wait. He wasn't. Not anymore.

Amber stepped towards the Hound and the headache went away and her fingertips stopped itching. The Hound reached for her and she flinched, surprised to see her left hand encircling his wrist. Without knowing what to do next, she yanked, pulled the Hound off balance. She shoved him as he stumbled by her and launched him suddenly backwards.

She was stronger than him. She was much, much stronger.

The Hound roared and came at her and Amber turned her hands to claws. One swipe took the fingers of his right hand. Another tore through his clothes and flesh. He spun, staggered, clutching his arm to his side. His throat was right there, ready to be slashed, ready to be cut open like Grant's throat had been cut open.

Amber stayed her hand and he reeled away from her.

The headache came back, driving needles into her brain. Her claws itched like crazy. She felt sick. She was going to puke. All that lovely warmth was now a distant memory. She was suddenly so cold. She started to shiver. There was a foul taste in her mouth. She wanted to spit, but she had no saliva. Her mouth was dry. Her belly roiled with acid.

She thrust her arm out and her claws glided into the Hound's back, lacerated his heart from behind and now Amber was warm again, and when her magnificent claws swiped his head from his body she relaxed, breathing out and smiling. She didn't see the

Hound fall. Her eyes were on her reflection. She hadn't thought it was possible, but she was now even more beautiful than ever.

The Shining Demon spoke to her, then, and she listened, and nodded, and said she understood. He walked away, and as he left the light in the hall faded. When he was gone, Amber looked round. Fool was gone, too. Only the Hound and Milo remained, and the Hound was dead.

She scooped Milo into her arms, and walked out the way she'd come. The castle laid itself open to her, and she took each turn with the conviction that she was going the right way.

But the warmth inside was fading. Each moment that passed took with it a little of her height, of her strength, of her horns. Their loss was an odd sensation. Even though she was returning to her normal demonic stature, she felt lessened, like this was the consolation trophy she'd been handed after letting the grand prize slip through her fingers.

She arrived back in the room she'd started in and her mood was already darkening. All of a sudden she was cold, and lost again, and unsure, and the doubts descended on her like spiders from the rafters.

She turned at a noise, and saw a creature in the darkness watching her. It made a sound, a two-syllable utterance that was almost like Amber's name.

She frowned as it shuffled out from the shadows. Naked, its skin was flayed in places, pulled back off glistening muscle by black wires that pierced its flesh. Its belly was bloated, its fingernails missing, and its lower jaw had been detached. Clumsy attempts had been made to fix it back into place with wire and thread and hooks, so that now it hung there, like a gaping, impossibly wide mouth.

"Hello, Edgar," she whispered.

At the mention of the name, tears sprang to the creature's eyes and its face — what there was left of it — crumpled. It turned away from her, as if it was ashamed, and Amber walked on to the circle of fire that was still burning. On the ground before it were six glass vials. She laid Milo within the circle, and examined the vials. Each contained golden liquid.

Astaroth's blood.

Despite Edgar Spurrier's racking sobs from behind her, warmth exploded in her heart and she smiled, she laughed, and she held the vials close to her chest and closed her eyes. "Thank you," she whispered. "Thank you."

She had six vials. Six more opportunities to get bigger and stronger and more beautiful. The thought made her happy — happier than she'd been in a long, long time.

She pocketed the vials, very carefully, and stepped into the circle of fire. At her feet, Milo moaned, and she took him back to Desolation Hill, and left Bigmouth to his hell.

59

IN THE MORNING, the town lay in ruins.

The snow had melted and the streets had returned to their normal sizes during the twilight that followed the sunrise. Buildings no longer loomed crazily. The cracks in the roads had healed over and now the only damage remaining had been done by the town's inhabitants.

When dawn had come, the people had reverted. Amber had been outside. She had watched them fall to their knees, weeping at their loss, each one of them feeling the same pain yet isolated in their own grief. One by one they dragged themselves home, still crying uncontrollably, and closed their front doors.

The cops had come, then. Lucy Thornton and the officers who had survived the night came in trucks, picking the dead and the injured up off the ground. They would have gathered up the remains of their very own Chief Novak, but Amber hadn't been around to see that. She wondered how they were coping with his loss.

Once the dead were taken away and the injured were carted off, the clean-up began. Glass was swept and sidewalks were washed of blood. Rubble was collected. Torched and trashed cars were towed.

At around nine, the people re-emerged from their houses, their tears dry. They replaced windows and fixed doors and hammered and drilled and worked, and they did all this silently. They didn't look at one another if they could help it. They didn't make eye contact.

The kids weren't allowed out yet. Amber didn't know if they were still in their panic rooms or if they were just confined to their houses. Either way, the town had to be made presentable for the lies to continue.

Amber walked back to Virgil's house. The Charger was parked on the road outside and the van sat on the driveway. Warrick was checking it when he saw Amber.

"She's been shot," he said. "Look. Three bullet holes."

She looked. "Did they hit anything important?"

"Just bodywork. Still, though... she's injured. My baby is injured."

"She'll live. And how are you?"

"Me? I'm fine. Everything's in working order. A few extra bumps and bruises, but those are to be expected, are they not? Hey, maybe if I sat in the Charger for a while..."

"The healing thing only works on Milo, I'm afraid."

"Yeah," Warrick said dejectedly, "that's what I figured. It's some car, all right. He was knocked around pretty rough last night and this morning it's like nothing happened. That's a handy vehicle to have in this line of work." He slapped a hand on the van. "You hear that, you lazy thing? Milo's car heals him when he's hurt. When was the last time you patched me up, huh?" He rolled his eyes, and they settled on the Charger. "How long has he had it?"

"Hmm? Oh... God, I don't know. You'd have to ask him."

"I've tried talking to him about it. Have you noticed how hard it is to get a straight answer out of that guy?"

"Milo has a complicated history."

"I'd imagine so."

In the morning light, at this angle, and with his hair swept back, Amber could see now the lines round Warrick's eyes and across his forehead. She realised he was older, much older, than she had originally thought. In his thirties, certainly. Maybe even early forties.

"Kelly's in the living room," he said. "In case you wanted to talk to her before you leave. You know." He shrugged, then went back to examining the van.

Amber walked into the house through the open doorway, passing Milo on his way out. They nodded to each other. Kelly wasn't in the living room, but Austin sat on the couch and Linda had her arm wrapped round his shoulders. Javier was in the armchair in the corner, eyes fixed on his phone. No, not his phone. Virgil's phone. Its screen had lit up.

"A text from his daughter," Javier said, his voice hollow. "She wants to meet him for coffee."

Amber didn't know what to say to that.

"What about you?" Linda asked Austin. "Do you want us to call your folks? We could let them know you're okay."

Austin took a long moment to answer. "No," he said. "They let me be taken. Why should I go back? Why should I stay?"

"Because it's over," said Linda gently. "The mayor and the Narrow Man are both dead. There's going to be no more sacrifices, which means no more Hell Nights."

"So?" Austin looked up. "You think that's gonna make folks here into better people? Really? Just because they won't be able to transform into demons doesn't mean anything. It doesn't change anything. It doesn't change *them*. They looked the other way while we lost one kid a year to that thing in the cell. My parents looked the other way when they lost *me*. And all of you are gonna get in your cars and vans and drive off and I don't know what I'm supposed to do."

Nobody said anything until Ronnie walked in. "You try to have a normal life," he said.

Austin's mouth twisted, but Ronnie kept talking.

"You do your best to be happy. You go to school and you make friends and you get educated. And then, when you're done with school and you're done with this town, you call us, and we'll come back for you."

Austin's eyes widened. "I can... I can come with you?"

"Always room for one more in the van," Warrick said, walking in. "If that's still what you want."

"It will be."

"What about you?" Kelly asked, and Amber turned. Kelly stood there, arms folded across a *Dark Places* T-shirt. "Don't know where we're headed next, but if you want to tag along..."

Amber hesitated. "I can't," she said at last. "I'd love to, really I would, but I can't. Not yet, anyway."

"We could help you," Kelly said. "I know we're not exactly a match for whoever the Shining Demon sends after you next, but there's safety in numbers, Amber. If you and Milo hook up with us, we'd be able to watch your backs."

Linda nodded. "It's what we do."

"And first order of business," said Warrick, "is using that fancy key of yours to go kill us an uppercase-d Demon. Let us cleanse this town of his stanky, *stanky* evil so Hell Night shall never happen again, what say you, fine warrior?"

"I... I appreciate that," Amber said. "I appreciate the offer. But things have... they've changed. My circumstances, I mean."

"Changed how?" Ronnie asked.

"I can't... I'm really sorry, but I can't allow you to kill Naberius."

Kelly frowned. "What are you talking about?"

"Astaroth wants him to suffer."

"So? Who gives a crap?"

"Astaroth was going to hand Milo over to be killed," Amber explained. "I couldn't just stand by and watch. I couldn't let it happen. It's my fault he got hurt in the first place. If I hadn't come here, Virgil would probably still be alive. All of this, all of it, is my fault."

"Amber, slow down. What are you talking about?"

"Astaroth," Amber said. "He's made me his new representative."

Kelly paled, and stepped back.

"Bullshit," said Ronnie. "That's just pure bullshit. Amber, come on, that's... You can't seriously have..."

Warrick shook his head. "But then that'd mean you're... you're working for him. You're working for the Shining Demon."

"He didn't give me a choice."

The slap came hard enough to bring tears to her eyes, and the stinging that followed burned her cheek. Kelly dropped her hand back to her side.

"You're the enemy now," she said. "You're his lackey. His

henchman. You're the one he sends to collect his offerings. You're the one who drags people back to him."

"No," said Amber. "Kelly, no, that's not what this is."

"Then what is it? Come on, explain to me, explain to us all, how this isn't you joining the other side."

"I... Kelly, I didn't have a choice."

"Jesus Christ..."

"I didn't. He was going to hand over Milo to be killed. He was going to torture me for a hundred thousand years. That's what he said – a hundred thousand years. What did you expect me to do?"

"I don't know," Kelly said angrily. "Not agree to it, maybe?"

"How would that have made any more sense than what I did?"

"At least you wouldn't have traded away your goddamn soul."

"No," said Amber. "No, I'd still have that, I guess. And I could have watched him flay it in front of me. I'm sorry, okay? I'm sorry for disappointing you, but really, what the hell did you expect? I don't travel the country to help people. I'm not like you. I don't get into trouble on purpose. I'm doing this, all this, to save my own life. Did you forget that part? I'm not a hero. I'm not going to throw my life away over a principle. Yeah, I'm Astaroth's representative, but so what? It's not like I'll be hurting any of the good people of the world. That's not who I'll be sent after. I'll be sent after the demons, the people who've already made their deals, who've already killed. I'll be punishing the guilty."

"You don't know who you'll be punishing."

Amber looked into Kelly's eyes, saw the anger in there, the defiance, and she shook her head. "This is exactly what I needed right now, Kelly. This is just perfect. Thank you so much for your patience and understanding."

"Hey, this was *your* decision," Kelly responded. "Don't you dare try to make out like I'm the one being unreasonable here. There's a right way to do things and a wrong way and you've obviously made your choice."

"I guess I have," Amber said, and she shifted. Kelly stepped back at the sight of the horns, and Amber moved past her. She walked out of the house, heading for the Charger. The others followed.

"You running away now, is that it?" Kelly asked. "Well, why the hell not? You've got your new job to start, after all, and a boss you wanna impress."

Milo watched Amber approach, and started the engine. The passenger door clicked, and swung open. He was with her. She knew that, just by the roar of the Charger. She got in, slammed the door.

Kelly walked up to the open window. "If you drive away now, the next time we meet we might be enemies. Have you thought about that? Does that even mean anything to you?"

"Sure," said Amber. "It means you better watch yourself."

She met Kelly's eyes, saw the hurt in them, and willed herself not to cry as Kelly leaned over.

"The more you do it, the more you'll be prepared to do," Kelly said, her voice soft. "You're a good person, Amber, I know you are. I knew it from the first moment we met. But, for all your good intentions, you can't say for certain who you'll end up hunting in the future."

"No, I can't," said Amber. "But I can tell you who I'm going to be hunting now."

Kelly took a moment. "Your parents," she whispered.

And, despite everything, Amber smiled.

DEREK LANDY

AMERICAN MONSTERS

THE DEMON ROAD TRILOGY

Bigger, meaner, stronger,
Amber closes in on her murderous parents
as they make one last **desperate** play for
power. Her own **last hopes of salvation,**
however, rest beyond vengeance, beyond the
abominable killers — **living _and_ dead** — that
she and Milo will have to face.

For Amber's future lies in her family's past,
in the **brother and sister** she never knew,
and the **horrors beyond imagining
that befell them.**

25.08.16

KEEP YOUR EYES ON THE ROAD

by following Derek @
po.st/demonroad
🐦/dereklandy